DRAGON'S BREATH

DENICALIS DRAGON CHRONICLES – BOOK FOUR

BY
MJ ALLAIRE

Bookateer Publishing
www.bookateerpublishing.com

Layout and design by Ryan Twomey

ISBN: 978-0-9819368-2-6
Library of Congress Control Number: 2010908684

Dedication

This book is extremely dear to my heart because without a very special place in New Hampshire, this story would not be what it is.

My primary dedication for Dragon's Breath goes to Susie, Bonnie, Erica, and the rest of the gang in Raymond, NH, and to the place where Kennard the dragon was born in my imagination, Kennard Hill Cabin. Kennard the muck dragon came to be all because of a little, unremarkable, rust-colored puddle next to a trail we were hiking on.

To Ryan – my editor, cover designer, and number one supporter – thank you for all your hard work, but more than that, thank you for believing in the world of Euqinom as much as I do. Your confidence is what keeps me going.

Each time I sit down and think about who I would like to dedicate my latest book to, I find it amazing how many people come to mind. I couldn't do it without my fans – know that when it comes to the Denicalis Dragon Chronicles series, I do it for you.

Thank you,

MJ Allaire

Connor + Liam ~
never stop reading!

MJ Allaire

V

PROLOGUE

A small cluster of dark, unidentifiable figures stands quietly in a crooked line a few feet away from a shadowy form, where it lies motionless on a narrow, desolate beach just before the arrival of twilight. The heights of the shapes vary, ranging in staggered sizes. Not far away, a larger group of odd-looking creatures stands like statues slightly behind the group of human shapes in respectful silence.

As the sun continues to set in the west, the unidentifiable group of friends stands in a mournful, wordless huddle around the horizontal object lying on the firmly packed sand. It remains where it fell, cold and motionless on the grainy expanse of earth not far from the place where the water meets the land. The shape is that of a once vibrant yet now lifeless corpse.

A colorful blanket of darkening clouds litters the sky above them as a soft, cool breeze caresses their bodies after a long, life-altering day. The rippling edge of the nearby lake licks the shore in a rhythmic, gentle cadence as it whispers liquid condolences to those who grieve.

Other than those surrounding the corpse and the repetitive back and forth motion of the waves brushing the shoreline, the rest of the beach is deserted. The eerie growls heard the previous night have fallen silent and the fog that covered the lake earlier that morning has since transitioned upwards with the rising of the sun, evaporating into the sky above them like a ghost. Even the previous day's spinning, fish-spewing funnels are nowhere to be seen across the horizon of what had been a dark, menacing body of water the night before.

The mourners watch in quiet disbelief as the surrounding shoreline suddenly comes to life, giving birth to dozens of sand crabs as they erupt from their hiding places like lava from sleeping volcanoes. The emerging hard-shelled creatures of varying shapes and sizes have oddly-shaped, spine-covered, spindly legs, and pay no attention to those huddled near the body where it waits like a stone. The well-armored platoon of crustaceans works quickly, as if driven by a single mind, each taking a place next to an empty location alongside a sling brought by a newcomer. After working in unison to spread the sling out like a flattened alia leaf, the crabs turn and make their way toward unmarked, yet unquestionable, locations next to the last body from the battle.

The group of mourners watches the scene in silence, somehow knowing what was happening – what MUST happen – to their former comrade, each of them struggling with their own flood of emotions – stifling cries that begged to be released…

Each one understanding that grief is both a powerful emotion and demon that everyone must face…

Each one hoping the demon from this particular day is one that can be overcome with vigilance, time, and a little bit of luck.

The only sounds heard as the sand crabs take their invisible stations alongside the corpse are the gentle lapping of the waves against the shore, restrained liquid cries for the loss of one so special, one so young, and the *click, click, clicking* of the sand creatures as they speak to each other in their foreign tongue.

Perhaps the crabs are sharing tales of other senseless deaths? Perhaps they are asking each other why something so unfortunate, so *wasteful*, had to happen to this particular human on this particular day? Perhaps they are offering sympathies in a strange language that, no matter how hard the humans try to understand, will remain forever misunderstood?

Once the sand creatures have completely surrounded the fallen hero, many of them move in harmony to raise his body off the sand. As they work together, countless other crustaceans rush beneath the body to help support the weight. Then, inch by slow inch, they move together, carrying it toward the laid out material like a group of peasants bringing offerings to a king. The clicking sounds intensify as the sand creatures transport the body to the sling, where they finally set it down on the thickly woven fabric with indescribable grace and gentleness.

The two largest of the non-human creatures watches the proceedings in silence.

Once the body has been moved, the crabs shuffle into a scattered, broken line at the border of the lake, just shy of the water's edge. As the tide rhythmically pulls away then returns, small waves lap at their armor-covered legs. Although the water is cool, the sand creatures seem to not notice.

The sound of a sniffle breaks the silence as a trail of tears cascades down one of the mourner's pale, thin cheeks.

Today they have lost a friend.

Dragon's Breath

One

After walking through what appeared to be a large, lifeless valley of tall grass that crinkled like small branches under their feet, the girls eventually found themselves on the edge of a thick blanket of evergreens. Looming not far beyond this line of trees was a wide, snow-capped mountain.

"Uh oh," Diam said with a shiver. "It looks like we don't have much choice than to head up and over *that*."

"I know," Tonia agreed, "and I don't know how we're going to manage it because we just happened to leave our winter clothes at home."

"Perhaps we can find what we need in the woods?" Kaileen suggested. As her brown eyes darted between those of her friends, it was obvious she didn't really believe in her own suggestion any more than they did.

The girls stood staring at the scene for a few moments when Diam finally asked the question they had all been thinking.

"Well, what do we do then?"

"I don't know," Tonia answered in an exasperated tone, "but I don't think we have much of a choice other than to keep going the way we're going."

Diam nodded.

"I feel it, too. The invisible rope is still pulling us in that direction, isn't it?"

1

"Yeah," Tonia said. "Oh, how I wish the boys were here."

"Me, too," Diam agreed with a frustrated sigh. Kaileen nodded her accord as well.

"Why don't I lead the way for a while," the kalevala suggested, anxious to get out of the rising sun and into a more familiar, darker environment.

Without saying a word, Tonia gestured both her understanding and concurrence with a wave of her arm, indicating her approval.

Kaileen sent an encouraging smile towards her new friends and began leading the way into the line of shade trees. Surprisingly, the kalevala seemed to sense the path of least resistance, and for quite a while the girls made decent progress as they became more enveloped by the surrounding forest. After an hour or so, they found themselves making their way past a large and oddly colored puddle next to the leaf strewn path.

"Ew," Diam said. "This puddle isn't anything like what we'd see back home."

They stopped for a moment as three pairs of eyes scoured the leaf-littered, motionless body of murky, uninviting water. A towering blanket of trees covered most of the area above the polluted puddle. It didn't appear to be fed by any fresh water, such as from a stream or waterfall, so it was no wonder the convoluted body of liquid looked the way it did. In rare places, narrow streams of sunlight filtered through the branches above, creating misplaced glittering diamonds on top of the copper and amber blanket of moisture. As Diam had pointed out, this stagnant body of liquid was nothing like those cool, blue ponds near their village. In fact, it was just the opposite, and was definitely not the kind of water any of the girls would ever consider drinking, no matter how thirsty they were.

Like many ponds near the village, lily pads and fallen leaves were scattered across the top of the sometimes sparkling slop, but the main difference here was this water very closely resembled a somewhat large, uninviting, rust-colored puddle of spoiled soup.

"That's just gross," Tonia said with a crinkle of her freckled nose, while Kaileen simply looked on in curious silence.

"I wonder if any animals in the woods really drink out of this disgusting place," Diam said absently.

Tonia began to shrug in answer when suddenly a large, round shape erupted from the center of the puddle with a splash. The trio of girls shrieked in a chorus of surprise while Diam and Tonia immediately drew their swords. Without thinking, Tonia's left arm shot out in front of Kaileen, who was standing beside her, protectively forcing the kalevala behind her.

"How dare you speak so offensively about something of which you know nothing?" the creature in the center of the puddle croaked angrily. "This is my home!"

Dark brown, faintly luminescent strings of slimy mud dripped like elongated slugs down the side of the angry creature's face, where they dangled like long forgotten saliva from its mouth and lower jaw. A few black, partially decayed leaves that had obviously been lying in the stagnant, brown liquid for quite some time were haphazardly plastered on the top and sides of the new arrival's head. As the girls watched in nervous disgust, one of the more rotten and slime-covered pieces began sliding down the side of the sticky creature's face.

At first, the creature appeared to be too wrapped up in these young girls standing just a few feet from the edge of his abode to notice the decayed fragment crawling down his face like a forgotten memory. The creature stared at the girls as the leaf slowly slid down its cheek, when suddenly, with the flick of a wide, black tongue, the decayed leaf disappeared in the blink of a firebug into the creature's mouth.

Although the unappealing puddle creature was silently chewing the leaf it had just consumed, its round, bulbous eyes glared like ancient orbs of coal at the girls from either side of its glistening, speckled head.

"What is it?" Kaileen whispered nervously as she leaned toward Diam.

"I'm not sure but I think it's some sort of amphibian," Diam answered, wishing they had a third weapon for the kalevala to use in situations such as this.

Her mind racing, Diam turned her attention back to the puddle creature and added, "I'm sorry if I offended you. I had no idea anyone… any*thing*… actually lived here."

"And sorry you should be," the gooey creature mumbled as

it began slowly lifting its upper torso higher, until it was halfway out of the puddle.

Tonia raised her sword in response to the creature's movements and her defensive gesture didn't go unnoticed. The puddle inhabitant turned and looked directly at her, glaring at her with a wordless, angry stare.

"We're just passing through," Tonia said in a defensive tone, uncomfortable under the creature's intense gaze and unwilling to put her sword away.

"Of cooourse, you are," the puddle creature answered sarcastically. "Just like the rest of them, I'm sure!"

As the creature's comment floated away on the cool breeze that suddenly filled the forest, Diam's full attention focused on its last sentence.

"Like the rest of whom?" she asked as her eyes narrowed in a stern, distrustful glare of her own.

Without answering, the creature's entire body suddenly began gyrating, creating ripples across the murky, liquid mirror it sat in. As its shaking movements became more intense, some of the leaves and muck hanging on it began sloughing off, falling into the puddle with a *plop*. Once most of the mucky material had returned to the puddle where it belonged, the creature stopped shaking.

"Much better," it answered with the hint of a smile while ignoring Diam's question.

It was easier to get a better look at the creature now that it was only partially submerged in the puddle, especially since most of the sticky, decaying material had fallen back into the swill.

"The rest of anyone who happens by here," the creature eventually answered as it eyed each of the girls in turn.

The eyes on either side of the frog-like creature's head were dark and round, oddly reminding Tonia of a few of the mud puppies back in the village. This oddity in front of them certainly looked different than anything they had seen before, but it no longer look very menacing, she thought. She allowed her sword to drop slightly at her side, but she wasn't ready to put it away just yet.

"Why, thank you," the creature said as it turned to look at

Tonia. "I'll take that as a compliment."

"Huh?" Diam asked in confusion. How much of the conversation had she missed?

"Your friend just paid me a compliment," the creature answered as it nodded in Tonia's direction.

They could see roughly half of the creature's body above the liquid, and indeed it did appear to be some sort of oddly formed frog. While its head and underside appeared similar to other frogs the girls had seen, this one looked like it had a large, misshapen hump on its back.

"A birth defect, possibly?" Diam questioned in her mind before turning her attention back to the frog.

"Oh, I beg to differ!" the puddle creature said argumentatively, but Diam shook her head back and forth with curt confusion.

"What are you talking about?" she asked with a frown. Apparently there was a conversation happening that only this strange creature in the center of the puddle understood. "Tonia didn't say anything," she added, referring to the frog's suggestion that Tonia had given it a compliment.

"Oh, but she did," the creature argued with a reassuring wink. As its face lit up with an innocent smile aimed at Diam, a small drop of slime fell from its eyelid and dripped into the puddle near its front right leg.

Plink!

"It's reading my mind," Tonia stated with sudden understanding as she scowled at the creature.

"This could open the doorway into some serious trouble," she thought worriedly.

When they were in the cave near the village, Tonia had been able hear Celio and Merlia talking when no one else could, which had been harmless to the turtles as well as helpful for the four friends. Now that the tables were turned, however, Tonia found she didn't think it was such a great idea anymore.

"I was thinking that this... thing... doesn't look very menacing," Tonia explained to her friends. She hesitated for a few seconds as she stared at the creature in the puddle. Just as its mouth began curving into an appreciative smile, she added wryly, "but we all know how looks can be deceiving."

"Touché," the creature said with a slow, measured nod.

"Explain what you were saying a minute ago," Diam prodded the creature. "The rest of whom?"

"The rest of anyone… everyone," the creature said.

Without any indication that it was about to do so, its black tongue shot between its still smiling, narrow lips and licked first one eyeball, then the other.

"Ah, much better. I can see you more clearly now."

"Well, have you seen some boys come through here recently?" Tonia asked in a hopeful tone. "They would look a lot like me – we're related."

The creature blinked once, then twice, yet remained silent. It closed its eyes and tilted its head slightly to the left in apparent concentration. Tonia waited patiently, allowing the creature time to consider her question. She couldn't help but hope it would remember that it had seen her brothers.

"One boy's name is Micah, the other is Nicho," Tonia prodded as the frog's head tilted back to its original position while its eyes remained closed. Tonia turned to glance at Diam, who shrugged her shoulders in response.

Instead of telling her what she wanted to hear, however, the creature's sticky tongue shot out of its mouth, snatching up an unsuspecting, large beetle as it flew by. The slimy creature did this with its eyes still closed. As soon as the beetle was deposited into its mouth, the girls couldn't help but hear an unnerving, crunching sound.

"Mmmmmmm," the creature mumbled as it slowly opened its eyes. Although it chewed its snack slowly and with obvious enjoyment, a partial smile played at the edges of its wide, sealed mouth. After another couple of chews, it licked its narrow, brown lips and turned its attention back to the girls, who were waiting with growing impatience along the edge of the puddle.

"I really must come out and play more often!"

It turned to them with a strange look of surprise as if suddenly remembering they were there.

"I'm sorry – you were saying?"

Tonia sighed in exasperation.

"Boys! I was asking if you'd seen two boys, either by

themselves or together! Have you?"

"My, my, my! No need to get your feathers all ruffled there, missy! And in answer to your question, no I haven't seen any boys, neither together nor apart," the creature answered curtly with what looked like an attempt at a pout.

"No Nicho – no Micah…" it added as an afterthought.

While the creature and Tonia were bantering back and forth, Diam took a moment to really look at the odd shaped thing standing in the middle of the rusty, slimy puddle.

It had many characteristics of a frog – round, beady eyes on either side of its head; a long sticky tongue used to catch flying bugs out of the air; and it lived in a wet, if not very appealing, environment. What was the saying her mother said sometimes? If it walks like a duck and quacks like a duck, it must be a duck?

Well, this thing must be a frog then, right?

"Pfffft," the creature hissed towards Diam. "Do not belittle me like that."

"Scratch that," Diam thought. "This wasn't just a plain old, ordinary frog – this was a mind-reading frog!"

"You really know very little about this world," the creature said with a narrow smile. "May I enlighten you just a little bit?"

Before any of the girls could answer, the liquid surrounding the creature began to vibrate and ripple again, but this time was different than the last. The girls watched in silence as the frog's head slowly dropped down, its almost nonexistent nose pointed sharply toward the water. It looked as though it was about to dive back into the same place it had emerged from just a few moments before, but it didn't. Instead, the slimy creature slowly turned away from the girls where it held this odd position in complete silence. The brown water surrounding the creature continued to ripple and after a few seconds the girls suddenly saw the long, misshapen hump on the puddle creature's back quiver as it began to change shape. They watched as it grew both larger and wider before it suddenly split in a surprisingly straight line right down the middle. With an unsettling, ripping sound, the upper layers of skin across the creature's back began to peel away from the lower layers before they ultimately extended out on either side of its wide, dark brown, mottled body.

Without saying a word, the girls nervously took a few steps away from the puddle.

"What are you?" Tonia whispered, and as all three girls watched in silent amazement, the appendages suddenly began unfurling with a wet, sticky sound.

Wings!

"I am a muck dragon," the creature said proudly as it raised its head and turned back toward the girls.

"A muck dragon?" Diam asked quietly. As soon as she heard the word dragon she glanced over at Tonia. She knew more than anyone else that Tonia's life-long dream had always been to see a dragon. Back in the village they'd all heard stories about "dragons of long ago" but none had been seen in a very long time. And right now, right here, in front of their very eyes, was a real, live dragon!

Or was it?

"I don't believe you," Tonia said matter-of-factly, unwilling to accept the fact that her first experience with a dragon would be with one that appeared to be nothing more than an overgrown, disfigured, slime-covered frog. She'd had many dreams about seeing a beautiful dragon sleeping peacefully in the valley, or a graceful dragon with rippling muscles flying through the sky as free as the wind – NOT some strange-looking oddity living in a slime-filled puddle feasting on large beetles and decayed, stinking leaves!

"You don't look anything like a dragon," the young girl replied in a sharp, argumentative tone. "In fact, you look more like a frog than anything else! Just because you have wings, or whatever those things are that are supposed to resemble wings, it doesn't make you a dragon!"

"Ah, I should have known," the muck dragon said snidely. "You who have wanted to see a dragon your entire life would naturally be the first to disbelieve."

"Well then, if you really are what you say you are, prove it," Tonia said firmly. "If you really are a dragon, let's see you breathe some fire!"

The muck dragon smiled and nodded in silent ascension. After pausing to look from Kaileen to Diam, its gaze finally settled on

Tonia where it lingered for a few seconds as if frozen in time. With a twitch of its head, the creature cleared its throat, closed its eyes, and took a slow, deep breath as it held its extended, glistening wings parallel to the ground. The girls all watched in quiet expectation as the creature's sides slowly expanded as they filled with air. They could hear the long intake of breath and as they watched, the liquid surrounding the dragon began to ripple again with fluid vibrations. After what seemed like minutes, but in reality was only seconds, the dragon reared its head backward until the girls thought the back of its head would touch the base of its wings. At the point where the head could not go back any further, it suddenly recoiled forward like a sling shot.

Tonia watched in amazement as the creature proceeded to fulfill her request. For a half a second, a small ray of hope began to replace the doubt in her heart about the strange creature standing in the middle of the brown puddle, but her hope quickly returned to doubt as the scene finished unfolding. Instead of shooting a stream of flames into the air, a short, wide stream of slimy muck was expelled from the creature's mouth with an almost choking sound. The slimy conglomeration landed in the puddle with a splash, halfway between it and the girls.

Plop!

Tonia shook her head in disgusted, bittersweet triumph.

"See! I told you! You're nothing but a phlegm-filled frog with a dragon-sized imagination who *wishes* it was a dragon!" Tonia said with a huff. "Come on girls, let's go! We don't have time for this garbage."

With an abrupt toss of her long, brown hair over her shoulder, Tonia turned and began walking around the puddle with the intention of leading her friends further into the forest.

"Wait, you don't understand!" the muck dragon cried out. It quickly folded its wings back into his body and took a fumbling, splashing hop towards the girls.

"Please wait – let me explain!"

Tonia ignored the puddle dragon's distressed cries, angry they had wasted so much of their precious time with this lying, disgusting creature. She had no intention of giving it any more.

"Tonia, hold up a minute," Diam said in sympathetic

exasperation.

With an aggravated stomp of a foot on the leaf covered ground, Tonia stopped and looked at her friend with obvious impatience. After a few seconds she finally turned to look back at the puddle creature with a glare of anger and disappointment.

"Thank you," the creature said in a trembling, uncertain whisper. It looked at each girl in turn, beginning with Diam then moving briefly to Kaileen. When its eyes finally found Tonia, however, they lingered there with a pleading look of hope.

"Let me first introduce myself to you. My name is Kennard," the creature said with a sigh before offering a slight nod toward each of the girls. Not surprisingly, although Diam briefly nodded back, the visitors remained silent.

Unbothered by their lack of a verbal response, the dragon continued.

"It *is* true – I *am* a dragon, but I am neither the kind of dragon you know nor the kind you would expect to find, in this lifetime or any other. This fact, however, does not make me any less of a dragon – no, not at all. I'm just a little different than that which you apparently expected."

"A little?" Tonia asked, unable and unwilling to hide the sarcasm in her voice.

The muck dragon continued as though it hadn't heard her snide remark.

"Should I be punished because I look different than other dragons? Or from what you *perceive* other dragons should, or *would*, look like?"

Tonia, suddenly overcome with guilt at her reaction to the oddity waiting patiently in the puddle, turned her gaze downward and began tapping the side of her shoe with her sword.

"No," she muttered with a frown.

Kennard smiled at the young girl but she didn't notice. She was still staring at the ground.

"Very good!" Kennard said cheerily. "Now that we have *that* out of the way, let's talk about a few other things."

Tonia raised her eyes to look first at her friends, then the dragon.

"Go on," Diam offered and the puddle creature nodded

appreciatively.

"I have not seen these boys you speak of, but I do know of them."

The girls exchanged hope filled glances as Kennard's next words surprised them all.

"I knew you were coming."

They stared at the muck dragon with bewilderment as they each tried to make sense of his words.

"You knew?" Diam asked. "How?"

"Word travels fast in this world, faster than you may ever understand or believe. Many of us have knowledge of the outsiders who have entered our world – and we are aware that they have been scattered to different locations. We also know *why* you're here," the dragon said with a reassuring smile.

"Well, please enlighten us, because that's something we definitely don't know, but we probably should, don't you think?" Tonia said. Her earlier guilt had dissipated and her voice again dripped with sarcasm.

Without waiting for the creature to answer, Tonia abruptly turned and made her way a few feet down the path to a dry log where she sat down with a sigh. Although the creature in the puddle now had a name, she remained doubtful about both it and its intentions. As a result, she stared at him with an edge of mistrust while she kept her weapon close by her side.

"We know we're here, wherever *here* is. We also know we're separated from the boys, but we don't know *why* we're here, nor do we have any idea about how to find my brothers," she added after she sat down. Following Tonia's lead, Kaileen and Diam made their way over to the long, round piece of tree trunk and sat down beside their friend.

"You are here to help save Gruffod," the dragon answered with both obvious pride and love in his voice.

"Gruffod?" Diam asked. "Who is Gruffod?"

"I've heard of him," Kaileen answered, surprising her friends as she broke her long silence. "Back when I was in the cave."

The kalevala nodded with the memory as she continued.

"I remember bits and pieces of a story about a special little dragon that was hatched from an egg some place very far away.

The story mentioned how this dragon was hunted for its scales and claws, but that's all I really know."

"Very good," the muck dragon said, believing he now had the full attention of his audience. "What you say is true.

"Gruffod certainly knows he is special. Unfortunately he also knows Lotor wants to kill him, when the time is right, so he can use the magical scales and claws to create some very powerful spells. Lotor wants to be the supreme ruler of Euqinom, and in order to do this he must wait for the dragon to grow. It is said that the larger the dragon, the larger the scales and claws are, and, as a result, the more powerful his spells will be.

"For many, many years, Gruffod was able to limit his growth, which angered Lotor beyond belief! It angered the evil sorcerer even more to know he had no special spells strong enough to stop Gruffod from controlling his size! What was worst of all to Lotor, however, was he has searched for this special little dragon for years and years and supposedly has never been able to find him."

The girls listened in silent curiosity, picturing an adorable little dragon and an angry, evil sorcerer who remained unable to get what he wanted.

"But alas, in recent months, Gruffod is nowhere to be found and many of this world believe Lotor has finally captured the dragon, which would be quite unfortunate indeed!" Kennard said.

"Why is that?" Kaileen asked as she struggled to contain her curiosity about this missing, magical creature she'd heard about when she was younger.

"He comes from two very special bloodlines," Kennard explained. "His mother's side of the family has beauty and love while his father's side has strength and agility."

"That doesn't sound like anything special," Tonia mumbled with obvious doubt.

The dragon looked at her in surprise for a few seconds then sat down in the center of the puddle and smiled.

"Well – it may not *sound* like anything special, but believe me when I say it is! It was said there was magic in both bloodlines, and when he was just a dragonlet, it became very obvious that

Gruffod got the best of both worlds. He has an incredible amount of magic flowing through his veins, which is why Lotor is so hungry to get his hands on Gruffod's scales and claws! And like many other things in life, the larger things grow, the stronger they become. In Gruffod's case, he does become stronger as he grows, but not stronger in just a strength sense. Everything about him – his love, his agility, and his magic – grows as he does."

Kennard stopped and looked at the girls, fixating on Tonia's deep, brown eyes.

"Do you now see?"

"No," Tonia said curtly as she shook her head with doubt. "If Gruffod is so special and strong, why would he need to worry about some sorcerer getting his scales and claws?"

The dragon chuckled before answering.

"It is *because* Lotor is such a powerful wizard," Kennard explained. "Although he cannot cast a spell to force Gruffod to grow, Lotor can use his magic in other ways. He could capture Gruffod right now and slay him in an instant, but it would do him no good since Gruffod hasn't grown enough for his scales and claws to be of much use to the sorcerer. It would be a waste of both his time and magic at this point."

"Hmm," Diam said, as she considered Kennard's words.

"Gruffod has remained a physical adolescent for quite some time," Kennard continued, "but word has it something changed and, unfortunately, he began growing... which was not by choice."

"So what happens now?" Tonia asked, a hint of curiosity creeping into her voice.

"Some say he went into hiding while others suspect he's been captured, which would be a very grave turn of events, indeed. In either situation, no matter what the reason may be, he *must* be found," Kennard said with a frown.

"Well," Tonia said in a somewhat sarcastic tone, "You say you're a dragon, right? So if you are what you say you are, why can't you just go out and find him yourself? If you can hear my thoughts, can't you hear those of your own kind?"

The dragon stared at her with sad eyes as it slouched slightly back into the mire.

"Therein lies my predicament," Kennard answered in a flat tone. "I know you still doubt I am a dragon, and for this I don't blame you, for I do not look like one, nor, unfortunately, do I breathe fire like I used to – like I wish I could again. Those days look like they are long gone for me…"

Tonia felt a pang of guilt stab her in the heart. She so wanted to see a dragon someday, more than ever before, and the only thing she wanted more than that right now was to see her brothers and the rest of her family again. But her brothers and family were nowhere around, and, as far as she could tell, this odd-looking creature in front of them meant them no harm.

With a sigh, she slid her sword into its sheath at her side.

"Tell us about it," she offered as she passed the slimy amphibian an apologetic smile.

"Long ago I was one of the many dragons flying from one end of Euqinom to the other, as free as could be. Life was very good for us until Nivri came along and changed things," Kennard began.

"Who's Nivri?" Diam interrupted as she absentmindedly rustled her feet in the leaves in front of the log.

Kennard hissed disrespectfully.

"He used to be one of Lotor's assistants, but now he is the *other* power-hungry sorcerer all creatures in this world must deal with."

"Great," Tonia muttered with the shake of her head. She leaned in towards Diam, sandwiching Kaileen between them. "It looks like we have two evil sorcerers to worry about instead of just one!"

"The Euqinom special of the month – two for the price of one!" Diam quipped. Tonia smiled in answer but Kaileen remained silent as she kept a cautious eye on the strange being in the puddle.

"Many creatures in this world talk just like they do in other worlds. After listening to bits and pieces of conversations it's easy to figure out Nivri is searching for the missing amulets so he can overtake Lotor. Unfortunately for him, it looks like that won't happen anytime soon…"

The muck dragon paused and glanced up at the girls.

14

"Why won't that hap...?" Diam began to ask as Tonia interrupted her friend.

"Wait a minute. You just said missing amulets... do you mean missing amulets as in more than one?"

"Ah, yes, the amulets," Kennard said with a nod. "You know of at least one, I presume?"

"Are you talking about the Dragon's Blood amulet?" Kaileen asked, surprising her friends with her sudden willingness to participate in the conversation again.

"Yes, that is one," Kennard said.

"But you said 'amulets', so there are more?" Tonia prodded as she leaned forward on the log.

"Yes, Dragon's Blood has already been returned to the dragons," Kennard said. "As a matter-of-fact, Micah returned it to Ronnoc yesterday."

"Huh?" Tonia asked. "You mean Micah, as in my brother Micah?"

"Yes," Kennard said.

"Wait!" Tonia said as she frowned at the puddle dragon. "I thought you said you hadn't seen any boys come through here!"

"That's exactly what I said," Kennard answered with a nod. "You asked if I had seen the boys, and I said no. That was the truth."

Tonia stared at the creature in disbelief.

"However, if you would have asked me if I knew about the boys, I would have said yes. It's all in the way you asked the question."

Tonia's eyes narrowed but she fell silent.

"But how do you know the amulet has been returned?" Diam asked.

"Nivri has cast a spell on the dragons so we cannot communicate with each other very well, but every once in a while one of us will pick up another dragon's thoughts. And in case you're wondering, Nivri also cast a spell on me which effectively changed me from a dragon into a charming puddle prince."

"Can you see him? Can you see Micah?" Tonia asked as butterflies began swarming in a tight cluster in the pit of her stomach.

Her brother was a pain in her neck sometimes – okay, maybe more than sometimes – but she couldn't imagine life without him. To be fair, she couldn't imagine life without either one of her brothers. She'd thought they'd lost Nicho forever in the cave, but somehow they had managed to outsmart the angry, evil Muscala only to become separated after going through the mysterious rainbow portal.

What had they gotten themselves into?

"No, I can't see him right now, but I do know he surrendered the amulet," Kennard said.

"He did?" Diam asked with a frown, "To whom?"

"To Ronnoc, the dragon guard," Kennard answered, "Which is just as it should be."

"The amulets belong to the dragons," Kaileen stated in a knowing, yet firm tone.

"Yes, they do," Kennard said with an agreeable nod. "Two more and we will be ready to give Lotor and Nivri a run for their money!"

"What do you mean *two* more?" Tonia asked as her mouth fell open in surprise.

"Your brothers are now on their way to find the Dragon's Tear," Kennard explained quietly.

"Right now?" Tonia asked. "Are they okay?"

"Yes – for now – which leaves the three of you."

Tonia looked at Kennard with a blank stare.

"What about us?" she asked as her eyes squinted with distrust.

"You must fulfill your destiny," Kennard explained. "The Dragon's Breath is waiting for you."

"Dragon's Breath?" Diam asked. "What is that?"

"It is the third and final amulet," Kennard explained. "Once we have recovered each of the three amulets we can begin the next phase in saving Euqinom."

Tonia looked at the frog creature with doubt-filled eyes as Kennard added one last thought.

"It is your destiny."

"Our destiny?" Diam questioned as her eyes narrowed into slits.

"Yes, your destiny," Kennard repeated. "This is why you

16

were brought here."

"We weren't *'brought here'*," Tonia stated matter-of-factly. "We came into this strange place through some sort of portal…"

"I know you did," Kennard interrupted patiently, "but once you came through the portal, couldn't you feel something… some strange, unseen force… drawing you toward the east?"

The girls looked at each other in silence. They had all felt the invisible force pulling them… that was for sure.

"You must find the Dragon's Breath amulet and return it to the dragons," Kennard said quietly, worried that this feisty young girl and her friends may not be convinced enough to help the creatures of Euqinom in their unfortunate predicament.

"Why us?" Tonia asked. "Why can't the dragons just go and get the amulets themselves?"

"A magical barrier around each of the missing amulets prevents the dragons from finding them. The barriers are waiting for those who hold the stones…"

Kennard's voice drifted off as he let the words sink in.

'Those who hold the stones…'

"But we didn't 'hold the stones'," Tonia said in a frustrated, argumentative tone. She found it hard to believe the mystical, not to mention strange, dragons in this odd world might really need their help.

"Micah was the one who held the stones – he was the one with the special ability to make them light up."

"This we know," Kennard said calmly, "but you and he are of the same bloodline. You have the same magic running through your veins, young one."

As Tonia stared at the glistening creature, she tried to determine if this was all just an evil, non-humorous hoax or a true request for help. They were just kids, for heaven's sake! One day they just happened to stumble upon an unexplored cave in a humdrum forest. Then, by a huge stroke of luck, they somehow managed to escape from a deranged, hungry snake after following an easily excitable bat that just happened to be able to talk to Tonia through her thoughts! Now, to top it all off, she and her two friends found themselves in front of a slime covered frog who believed he was a dragon, who was asking them for help to save a world where

17

dragons lived…

Was she losing her mind?

She turned and gave a puzzled look to Diam, and then Kaileen, as the dragon softly continued.

"You may not know it, and you may not believe it, but you and your brothers come from your own special blood line, young one. If you do not agree to help us, our once beautiful world where dragons used to fly freely through the blue skies above will become our absolute worst nightmare."

Tonia turned to look at Kennard. His head was lowered with sadness as he stared at a reflection of the trees above him in the puddle. She watched him in confused silence as a lone tear slipped slowly down his cheek, down his chin, and finally fell with a mournful *plink* into the puddle at his feet, turning his reflection into a blurry mess.

The girls stared at the puddle creature for a moment, thinking about everything he had said. It was their destiny to retrieve the Dragon's Breath amulet – their destiny to be in this world in the first place. What should they do now? Believe this creature and put their trust in him, or turn their back on him and trust their own instincts?

"Tonia…" Diam began.

"I know."

Without looking at either of her friends, Tonia stood up and made her way to the edge of the puddle.

"Come to me," she said to the frog with a new voice of authority.

The muck dragon immediately raised his head then turned and headed toward Tonia. He moved slowly as he made his way through the puddle, trying not to splash the girl with the straight, brown hair. When he was just a few feet away, she unsheathed her sword but held it at her side. She stood completely unmoving just inches from the puddle, waiting for him like a mother waits for her child when the child is in trouble, as her anger and frustration tottered like a rock at the top edge of an endless ravine. The dragon seemed not to notice the drawn weapon and took one more splashing hop towards her when she suddenly extended her sword. The frog stopped less than two inches away from the tip of the blade, staring not at the weapon but at the girls deep, brown eyes. Kennard, although obedient, showed not one ounce of fear on his brown, speckled face. He stood motionless, staring at the beautiful, pale-skinned girl before him, waiting like a well-trained mud puppy for its owner's next command.

Diam stood up and took a few slow, hesitant steps toward her best friend with Kaileen following close behind her. Diam wasn't sure what Tonia was doing, but to be safe she drew her sword as well, taking her place at Tonia's left. Kaileen had no weapon but stood fearlessly on Tonia's right.

"Look me in the eye," Tonia said in a harsh, partially contained whisper as she held her unwavering sword directly out in front of her. The sharp point of the weapon was less than a hair's length away from the muck dragon's throat, but he seemed not to notice. It was almost as if he was in a strange trance of obedience.

"Now tell me every word you've spoken here today is true," the young girl turned sudden warrior whispered harshly to the dragon. The coffee colored creature stood fearlessly in front of her while staring dutifully into her liquid brown eyes. Although her friends stood on either side of Tonia, Kennard did not see them. All he saw were the two pools of cool, brown cream staring at him above a feminine, freckled nose. Her friends could have been in another world and the dragon wouldn't have noticed they were missing. At this second in time, it was just Tonia and Kennard. Everything and everyone else in the world was gone.

Tonia was faintly aware that her friends had moved from the log to either side of her, but this wasn't really something she thought about or cared to think about. She didn't want to play any more games with this puddle creature. She was tired, hungry for real food, and scared to death that she would never see her brothers again. All she wanted was a straight answer. Was that too much to ask?

Without even realizing what she was doing, she took command of the situation, subconsciously determining once and for all to get the truth out of this slimy, odd-looking, so-called dragon. Either he was or he wasn't a dragon, and the story he told her was or wasn't true. She was steadfast in her desire to find out the truth once and for all!

19

If she found out he was lying to her, she would end his slimy, puddle-loving existence with one thrust of her sword... right here, right now.

Diam and Kaileen waited in nervous silence as Tonia and Kennard stared deeply into each other's eyes. There was so much tension in the air that Diam was certain she could cut through it with her sword, possibly opening up another portal into yet another world. It felt as though a thousand butterflies were fluttering around in her stomach, yet she took an unwavering stance by her friend's side, no matter what the outcome. She waited with baited breath for the dragon to answer Tonia's unmistakably serious question, and after what seemed like an achingly long hesitation, the dragon finally spoke in a quiet, confident whisper.

"'Tis true."

Time froze for all involved as Tonia continued to stare at the misshapen dragon, which now stood at silent attention before her. His wide, onyx colored eyes stared back at the young girl as if held by some magical trance, and neither girl nor dragon moved. After a few more nearly unbearable seconds, Tonia slowly lowered and re-sheathed her sword.

"Very good then," she answered curtly as she took a step backwards.

Although she still found it hard to believe the puddle creature was really a dragon, she was as certain as she could be that the creature at least *thought* it was telling them the truth. Next to her, Tonia heard Diam release a long sigh of relief.

"So what's our next step?" Kaileen asked, relieved the tension in the air was gone as quickly as it had arrived. For a few moments during that tense episode, her mind took her back to a place she was in no hurry to return to – in fact, she hoped to never return there. As if she was seeing it all again, she was carried back to the cave, where she and her family had lived for years in constant darkness and fear from the giant cave snake named Muscala.

"Well, if our next step is to head off to find this other amulet, why don't you join us?" Diam asked the dragon, but as soon as she'd said the words she suddenly worried that she'd made a mistake, because neither Tonia nor Kaileen had approved of her suggestion. Thankfully, she sensed that neither of her friends objected.

As Kennard considered her question, he slowly sat down in the slimy muck at the edge of the puddle, obviously comfortable with the strange environment.

"Herein lies another of my predicaments," he explained. "A spell was cast over me, turning me into a frog in this god-forsaken location, as you can plainly see. I've been surviving here, but not really living."

"That's an even better reason for you to join us then, isn't it?" Kaileen offered, somewhat puzzled.

The muck dragon smiled at her.

"And how I would love to! Unfortunately, if I leave here, I will be leaving my life behind."

"But it sounds as though you're not happy here," Tonia said as her brows lowered and her expression transformed into a frown. "Maybe we could find other muck dragons for you to live with?"

Kennard shook his head vehemently.

"You don't understand," he said as his eyes suddenly flashed with anger. "The spell that was cast on me limits me in many ways. The most obvious way was by turning me into a frog, but by far the worst way is by forcing me to stay in this location. The farther I stray from this glorious puddle of slime, the weaker my heart becomes."

The girls looked at Kennard in silence as they considered his plight.

"If I were to leave this place for an extended period of time," the muck dragon added, "my heart would eventually stop beating completely."

The girls stared at Kennard, unsure of what to say.

"Are you sure?" Tonia finally muttered. "How do you know this?"

Listening to the dragon's story, she could feel anger beginning to boil through her veins. She simply couldn't understand how or why anyone could be mean enough to cast such a life-altering, confining spell on any creature, dragon or otherwise. The more she heard of the twisted ways magic was used in this world, the more she began to despise those behind it...

"Yes, I am sure," Kennard answered as his eyes filled with sadness.

"Not long ago, I decided to explore the nearby woods, hoping to find some special, untraceable way to escape. I assumed that if I left at night, using the cover of darkness as my only ally, perhaps I would have a chance at freedom. Unfortunately, I couldn't deny the fact that the farther I strayed, the weaker I felt. With every step I took away from the puddle, my breathing became shallower and my heartbeat weakened, until I soon realized I had no choice but to turn back. When I finally did, the closer I got to my liquid home, the stronger I felt."

"How far away did you get?" Diam asked. She could just imagine how much this must upset Tonia, especially knowing how much her friend loved all creatures...

Except spiders, of course.

"I made it nearly to the other side of the mountain," Kennard said, "then I turned back. As I neared the puddle, a large, black bird flew overhead and landed in a nearby tree. It was laughing at me."

"A bird was laughing at you?" Tonia asked in disbelief.

"Yes, but it wasn't any plain, ordinary bird," Kennard explained. "I'm certain it was one of Lotor's minions. It sat on one of the upper branches of that tree right there," the muck dragon said as it lifted one of its front legs in an attempt to point at one of the nearby trees. "It was laughing at my obviously failed attempt at freedom. It carried on this way for a moment or two before it finally told me what I already knew but hadn't been willing to admit to myself..."

"That you couldn't break the spell?" Diam asked.

Kennard shook his head in denial.

"No, that I would die if I tried to leave."

A billowing cloud of silence filled the air around them as the girls considered the muck dragon's predicament. It seemed to envelope them, absorbing even the sounds of the dried leaves beneath their feet. They could sense the undeniable yearning for freedom, but they could also see how torn this creature was about the entire situation.

"What was worse than that," Kennard added, "is the bird spoke to me with Lotor's voice. It was quite unnerving, so it was."

"I'm sure it was," Tonia agreed with a nod. "So what do you think we need to do then? How do we get wherever it is we need to go?"

"Well, I'm glad you asked," Kennard replied with a smile. "I was hoping to see you, hoping that I could do my part in defeating the vile creatures that are ruining our beautiful world, all for greed and power."

Without another word, the muck dragon turned and hopped over to the far edge of the puddle. Once there, he stopped next to a very wide, tall tree which appeared to be growing out of the side of an impressively large hill. The tree was nearly as wide as the abyss Nicho had fallen into back in the cave, and appeared to have grown itself halfway in the rusty colored pond and halfway on what appeared to be dry land next to the murky water. It was undoubtedly both the widest and tallest tree Tonia had ever seen.

Kennard glanced back at the girls with a wink then turned back towards the tree. In seconds, they heard an odd whistling sound and suddenly the leaves covering the ground near the far end of the puddle came to life as if caught up by an underground gust of wind. They couldn't help but stare at the multitude of tiny, glowing red lights blinking beneath the leaves.

"What is *that?*" Kaileen asked in a harsh whisper but neither Tonia nor Diam answered.

They stared in awe as a large number of what appeared to be grayish-brown bundles of fur suddenly began moving in a raised area of leaves on the ground near the tree directly in front of the muck dragon. Unsure about what they were seeing, Tonia and Diam drew their swords in anticipation of a possible attack. As if they read each other's minds, they slowly took a few steps around the edge of the puddle, heading toward the tree, while Kaileen followed a cautious step behind. Uncertainty covered each of their young faces as they watched the flurry of activity near the dragon.

Dozens of furry creatures moved the plethora of leaves littering the ground near the gargantuan tree. After a moment of unleashed rustling and scurrying, the smaller creatures finally uncovered what appeared to be a large, wide piece of bark from one of the nearby trees.

"What's happening?" Tonia called out to the muck dragon in a loud whisper, afraid to draw attention to them yet unable to remain quiet.

"There's nothing to fear – come around and see for yourselves," the dragon replied in a reassuring tone.

Tonia glanced back at Diam, who nodded her approval before the younger of the two led the rest of the way around the outer edge of the brown puddle. As she got closer, Tonia finally got a better look at the odd colored, furry creatures moving through the leaves. They appeared to be some sort of large rodents.

"Are these rats?" she asked Kennard, feeling as though she needed clarification for what she thought she was looking at. She stopped a few feet away from the muck dragon and realized that the dozens of fur balls scurrying around in the leaves at their feet were indeed rats, as she suspected, but these were unlike any kind of rat she'd ever seen before. Every one of the scurrying creatures was roughly the size of a very small mud puppy, and they were similar in color to the puddle, not light gray like those she would occasionally find in the forest near Uncava. Their most strange characteristic, however, was not the color of their fur – it was the color of their eyes.

Every rat, as far as she could tell, had an eerily narrowed pair of glowing, ruby red eyes.

"What's that for?" Diam asked as she pointed at the large piece of tree bark the scurrying ground creatures had managed to completely uncovered.

The hollowed out piece of bark looked as though it had been torn right off the side of a very tall tree, but after quickly glancing around them, Tonia decided it was either from an unseen side of one of the nearby trees or from another piece of the forest from an altogether different location. The bark was lying with the external side facing the ground and was at least eight feet long. Each end had another piece of thick, light brown bark wedged securely into it and upon closer inspection, appeared to be somehow strapped in place with some type of bark or tree vine like nothing she'd ever seen before. On the upper, internal side of the bark, Tonia noticed three pairs of thick, crude-shaped handles set roughly two feet apart on each side of the inner wall.

Was this some sort of boat? If it had a couple of oars in it, it would be. The ends of it were round and non-pointed, so if it really was a boat, it was a strange looking one for sure.

"Wow," was all she could say.

"Yes, it is surprising to see such a contraption in the middle of nowhere on the side of a mountain, isn't it?" Kennard asked, misunderstanding the reason for Tonia's comment.

"Well, yes it is, but that's not why I said that," Tonia retorted. "These rats are... quite a bit different from those we have at home."

"You can say that again," Diam whispered, but both Tonia and Kennard seemed to not notice she had spoken.

"These are my friends," Kennard said with a reassuring smile as he waved one of his front legs in a wide arc, referencing the rodents still scurrying in the leaf litter around the giant tree. "They are going to help us get you where you need to be."

"They are?" Tonia asked as she slightly raised one eyebrow. Next to her, Kaileen watched the odd-looking furry creatures with a curious twinkle in her eyes.

"She's probably thinking how great it would have been in the cave to have just a few of these rodents for playmates," Diam thought.

"And to answer your question," Kennard continued as he turned his attention to Diam with another smile, "yes, this contraption will be your method of transportation."

All three girls looked at Kennard with dramatic scowls.

"Is it a boat?" Tonia asked, voicing her earlier question to herself.

"In a crude sense, I suppose you could say it is," Kennard said with a wink. In response, Diam chuckled out loud as a funny thought crossed her mind.

Tonia threw a questioning glance at her friend, but before she could ask for the reason behind the oddly timed chuckle, Diam continued.

"Are we going to slide down the mountain in this thing?"

While they waited for the puddle creature to answer, both

girls simultaneously thought back to the countless times they had enjoyed sliding down one of the larger hills near the village on old, tattered, animal hide sacks.

"This could be fun!" Diam whispered in Tonia's direction, but her friend appeared to be deep in thought and didn't answer her.

"How will this work?" Tonia asked after a few seconds. Diam could sense the nervousness exuding through her friend's pores.

While Diam watched her, Tonia found herself struggling with her conscience. Although she'd made a promise to herself that she would try her very best to trust this creature, a silent, nagging doubt remained in the back of her mind, stubbornly refusing to leave.

A rustling of the nearby leaves interrupted her thoughts when a dozen or so rats suddenly appeared from the shadows behind another of the nearby trees, dragging a cluster of woven vines behind them.

"Ah, thank you, my little assistants!" Kennard said with a smile to the approaching rodents before turning back to the girls. "Our friends remembered the rest of the hardware we'll need to begin our journey!"

"*Our* journey?" Kaileen asked, suddenly participating in the conversation after a long stretch of silence. "I thought you said you couldn't go with us."

"No, no, my friend, I didn't say I *couldn't* go with you – I said if I *did* go with you I would be leaving my life behind," Kennard corrected the kalevala.

"Please, please, please stop talking in riddles," Tonia said with an exasperated sigh.

"Forgive me," Kennard said as he hung his head with obvious regret. After taking a deep breath, he added, "Please understand, it has been a long time since I've had decent conversation, with creatures of any kind."

He paused for a few seconds.

"And for you, my friend the kalevala, to answer your question, the answer is yes, I will be accompanying you on your journey."

Kaileen stared at the muck dragon in shocked silence, totally surprised to hear him referring to creatures of her kind.

"How do you know what I am?" she whispered as her wide,

almond-shaped eyes suddenly flashed a mixture of anger and confusion. Raw emotion swiftly covered her face as memories of the slaughter she'd survived in the cave pushed themselves to the front of her mind like despised, uninvited guests.

Her mother, her father, her siblings, her friends... all gone.

"Some of your kind used to wander through the forest of Euqinom in our not-so-distant past," Kennard said, "but I haven't seen any kalevalas around here for quite some time now."

The faint glimmer of hope that had been creeping like a snail into Kaileen's heart suddenly died out like a flame in a rain storm. Without a word, Diam reached back and rubbed the kalevala's back empathetically.

After waiting patiently for further questions from Kaileen, but hearing none, Kennard turned to Tonia.

"As for your method of transportation, we will use it to get you to the other side of the mountain."

"We will, huh?" Tonia asked with a slight hint of sarcasm. "And how do you propose we do that? This contraption surely won't move easily over the bumps through the forest, especially going uphill!"

"Ahh, and therein lies the difference, young one, for we will not be traveling uphill," the muck dragon said before quickly adding, "I apologize. That sounded like another riddle, didn't it?"

Without waiting for Tonia's response to his apology Kennard turned back toward the large tree.

"Borsha!"

The girls all jumped at the booming voice emanating from the large amphibian, but it didn't take long before their attention was drawn to a flurry of activity in the mixture of yellow, brown, and orange leaves near the mammoth tree.

"Let's enlighten our guests then, shall we?" Kennard said with a nod and accompanying mischievous smile.

As the girls watched, dozens of rodents suddenly began climbing the face of the enormous tree next to Kennard. Some entered the mucky liquid and latched onto the tree, eagerly waiting for the muck dragon's next command, while others formed into the shape of a crude, uneven square above the water line. Once all the participating rodents were in place, Kennard whispered a single word.

"Begin."

Each of the rats above the waterline remained motionless, while those in the water suddenly descended beneath the surface of the murky, slimy fluid. Without the least sign of hesitation, the remaining rodents above the waterline turned and stared at an area of the tree immediately in front of their narrow, sharply clawed feet.

The girls watched in amazed silence as another magical, albeit irrational, miracle began to place.

Earlier, as the rats scurried here and there, their eyes had glowed like soft, almost welcoming, scarlet colored, miniature candle flames. Now, an unmistakable change began happening in their brightly glowing orbs. The rose colored aura that earlier filled each of their small, almost hairless eye sockets had changed from a soothing scarlet to a bright crimson. In the blink of a firebug, the shade of light suddenly transitioned from one that had been almost calming to one that burned as brilliantly as the sun.

Without a sound, each of the rodents glared in deep concentration directly at the lower trunk area of the large tree.

The girls didn't move. They could only watch in silent awe as these strange creatures worked their own special magic on the seemingly ordinary tree they had surrounded. After a few more seconds of intense silence, the squared off area of the tree trunk suddenly disappeared, leaving a gaping black hole in center of it.

With their mission accomplished, the rats quickly jumped to the ground and landed in the leaf litter around the tree. At the same time, those rodents that had disappeared in the brown puddle at the base of the tree suddenly surfaced with a muffled splash, clinging to either side of the tree, precariously close to the newly created gaping hole. They shook in an effort to rid themselves of excess moisture and slime, then climbed around the edge of the tree until they, too, settled on the ground just a few feet away.

"Wow," Diam said, afraid to believe what she'd just witnessed.

"Yeah," Tonia agreed. "I'm not sure if I like the implications of this."

"Neither do I," Kaileen quietly agreed.

The muck dragon passed the visitors a reassuring smile.

"Magic is a beautiful thing when it is not abused," he said.

The girls continued to stare in amazed disbelief at the hole in the tree when the expression on Tonia's face suddenly changed.

"Um, wait a minute."

"Yes?" the dragon asked as he waited patiently for the rest of the question he knew was coming.

Tonia stood on her tippy toes as she peered curiously into the depths of the dark, uninviting hole.

"Is the water actually going *in* there?" she asked in amazement.

"That it is," Kennard answered.

"But it doesn't look like the water level in the, umm, puddle, is going down at all," Tonia said.

"It's not," Kennard replied with a smile. He loved seeing how the visitors reacted to some of the simplest things.

"But how can that be?" Tonia asked, mystified.

"That's just another part of the wonderful magic of this world," Kennard said in a thoughtful, melancholy tone. "'Tis the magic that will no longer be shared or experienced if we don't find the final amulet and stop Lotor and Nivri from wreaking havoc everywhere in their quest for power and domination of this once beautiful world."

Tonia sighed, looked at Diam and Kaileen, and shrugged her shoulders, then immediately looked back at Kennard with furrowed brows.

"We need to talk this out," she said to the muck dragon as she gestured to herself and her friends.

He smiled and sat down in the brown muck with a squishy *plop*.

"As you wish."

Without further hesitation, Tonia, Diam, and Kaileen took a few steps away from the puddle and huddled together, creating an oddly shaped circle as they wrapped each of their arms over the shoulder of the respective girl standing next to them. Completely forgetting that the muck dragon could read their minds, they lowered their heads into the center of the circle and stared down at their feet.

"Well?" Tonia began as she repeatedly scrunched her fingers on Diam's and Kaileen's shoulders without realizing she was doing so. "I hate to say this, but I really don't think we have much of a choice here."

Diam sighed and nodded her head, agreeing with her friend.

"Yeah, I feel it, too. It's almost as if this is where we were meant to be."

"It looks like the frog – I mean dragon – whatever it is, was expecting us," Kaileen added as her friends nodded. They stood together silently for a few seconds before the kalevala continued.

"Tonia," she said as she raised her raven colored eyes to look at her friend, "I know you have your doubts about this strange creature in the puddle, but I have to say I believe him. He looks like a frog, but I have this – sense – that he truly is a dragon and knew, somehow, that we would be here."

The girls each turned to glance at the mucky creature who sat contently in the middle of the puddle. His previously wet, slimy skin was no longer glistening as it dried in the warm morning air. He was successfully snacking on unsuspecting insects as they flew by while waiting for the girls to finish their discussion, seemingly unaware that he was being watched. After a few seconds, the girls refocused their attention on their feet again.

Tonia took a deep breath and slowly let it out, finally understanding how Nicho must have felt when they were in the cave and he was the one making the decisions for the small group of explorers. She found that she didn't much like having this new responsibility, but she understood she was stuck with it no matter how uncomfortable or unwanted it might be.

"I think you're right," Diam agreed. "I think we need to just go with it. There is definitely something pulling us eastward. I don't think any of us will deny that. He," she nodded her head toward the muck dragon, "knew what kind of creature Kaileen was, so obviously there's more going on than we know. We all saw the snow covering the top of the mountain, and I don't know about you, but I really don't think we're equipped well enough in any kind of way to try to make it over the mountain on our own. We don't have enough food or the proper clothes…"

"Okay, okay, you've convinced me," Tonia said as she squeezed her best friend's shoulder in a conscious, knowing gesture. She turned back briefly to look at the muck dragon. She caught him looking up at the trees for a few seconds before he turned his wide, dark eyes and met her curious stare. He smiled at her but she didn't see it – she had turned her attention back to the leaf litter on the ground within her circle of friends.

"Are we in agreement then?" Tonia asked Diam and Kaileen. "I really don't want to make this decision alone."

"Yes," Diam answered.

"Yes," Kaileen agreed. "And always remember you are definitely not alone."

Tonia broke away from the circle and hugged the kalevala.

"Thank you," she whispered.

Diam stood waiting patiently for her turn, and when it finally came, she wrapped her friend up in a bear hug.

"No, thank you," Diam said as she fought to control her emotions. Although she didn't envy her friend for taking control of the situation, she did love and admire her.

"I'm proud to be your friend, Tonia."

Tonia squeezed Diam back and said, "Me, too. Now let's get this adventure on the road!"

The girls broke away from their circle and stepped back to their previous places next to the puddle. Once there, Tonia looked directly at Kennard and met his dark eyes with her own brown ones.

"Let's do it."

"Wonderful!" Kennard said. As he stood up, his lower torso created a wet, sticky sound as it was released from the muck. Surprisingly, no one seemed to notice.

"Wait," Diam said. "What about food?"

"Food?" Tonia asked with a chuckle. "Diam, are you sure you're not related to me? Do you get that from Micah? He's *always* thinking about food!"

Thinking of her brother brought a crooked smile to Tonia's lips. Ah, yes, Micah and his food.

"Well, I was just thinking we're almost out," Diam explained, "and since we don't know where we are going…"

"That certainly is good thinking," Kennard replied, "but rest assured there will be food for you on the other side of the mountain."

"Definitely?" Tonia questioned as she offered Diam a nod of approval for her question. "You mean as in, we really don't need to worry about trying to find anything now?"

"Absolutely," Kennard answered.

"What about some frog's legs?" Diam asked with a chuckle as her eyes darted toward the dragon.

Up to this point, it seemed as though the dragon hadn't heard their whispers, but the look in Kennard's eyes right now made Diam regret her humorous comment.

"I'm sorry," she said, "I was just kidding."

Kennard nodded at her.

"Apology accepted."

Turning to look at Tonia he asked, "Are we ready then? We really must be going."

Tonia glanced back at Diam and Kaileen, who each nodded their approval.

"Yes, we're ready," Tonia said. "What do we need to do?"

Kennard's eyes were filled with excited anticipation for their impending journey.

"First, we must drag our previously hidden boat over to the water. Next, we'll have you three climb inside. Finally, after hooking me up to it, we'll be on our way."

The girls nodded as he added, "First we need the boat. Can you push it into the water? It's really not as heavy as it looks."

As requested, the girls moved behind the wooden boat and carefully pushed it into the murky, rust colored puddle.

"Won't it get stuck?" Tonia asked, worried that they may all have to first walk through the puddle in order to position the boat wherever Kennard wanted it. Once they accomplished that, they would still have to climb inside of it. Wouldn't that be fun, to be sitting in the boat trying to avoid sticky, mucky foot prints? She could think of better things to do...

"You'll be quite surprised, I'm sure," the muck dragon said with a smile. "My home is not very pleasing to the eye, but the environment does have its advantages... trust me."

As the boat entered the outer edge of the reddish-brown puddle, it suddenly became much easier to push – so easy, in fact, that Diam had to grab Tonia's arm when her friend began falling forward.

"Whoa, there, missy!" Diam said with a smile. "I don't think you want to dive head first into *this* body of water!"

Tonia regained her balance and looked at her friend with an appreciative smile.

"Thanks!"

The boat slid across the puddle of muck as easily as a bunny rabbit would slide across a frozen pond. It came to rest just inches from the muck dragon's front legs.

"Perfect!" he said before adding, "except for one minor detail…"

Without waiting for his new friends to guess at what was missed, Kennard added, "You forgot to get in it first!"

Tonia sighed again in exasperation. She really didn't want to have to walk through the puddle to get to the boat.

"No worries," the dragon said as if reading her mind. "Come on over next to the tree – there are some stones over here you can walk across."

As he motioned towards the tree the girls suddenly noticed a half a dozen large rocks forming a make-shift path directly to the boat.

Tonia shook her head in amazed silence as she led her friends over to the rocks.

"Do we need to be in any particular order?" she asked before they began stepping across.

"Not at all," Kennard answered as he watched her gaze shift from the rock nearest the bank before eventually lingering on the one closest to the boat.

"Do you need my assistance?" he asked.

"No, I don't think so," Tonia answered as she began making her way independently across the rocks. Thankfully, the stepping stones weren't spaced very far apart so she was able to easily balance herself on them, one at a time, until she finally reached her destination. Kennard stood up and held the opposite side of the boat stable as Tonia stepped into it. Once she was settled,

Diam followed suit, and eventually Kaileen did as well. As soon as they were all settled in the boat, holding onto the makeshift handles, Kennard spoke again.

"Thank you, my leatherback friends!"

With that, the rocks the girls had just walked across began rising up out of the water enough to allow their heads to surface.

"Turtles!" Diam said, surprised. "I *thought* those were some funny looking rocks!"

Tonia frowned.

"We didn't hurt them, did we?" she asked.

"Oh, not at all," Kennard said. "We've been expecting you! They are just a small number of creatures in this world who will be happy to help you in your quest."

Tonia considered this as the turtles wound their way slowly through the puddle.

"Thank you," she called out to them, but they gave no indication that they heard her. They were already focused on their next adventure.

"Why didn't they acknowledge me?" Tonia whispered.

"They know you are appreciative of them," the dragon said with a small smile. "Now, are we ready to go?"

"We think so," Tonia nodded.

"Very well then," Kennard said. As an afterthought he added, "Oh, my! I almost forgot!"

Without explaining his comment, the muck dragon turned and hopped out of the puddle before making his way around the tree with obvious excitement. Amazingly, he did this without hopping on any of the rats that were still moving around in the nearby leaf litter. The rodents quickly divided themselves from one large cluster into two smaller ones, creating a narrow, misshapen path leading toward some hidden location behind the tree.

"Pardon me," the girls heard the dragon mumble.

When Kennard got part way around the tree, he stopped. None of the girls could make out what he was doing when suddenly they saw a flurry of leaves flying through the air around him. They all leaned back in the makeshift boat as they tried to see what was happening. After a few seconds, they saw

34

not only leaves flying through the air behind the dragon – they soon began to see dark clumps of earth as well.

Tonia frowned. Since she was in the very back of the boat she had the best view of the dragon. She watched him curiously for a few seconds before she found herself unable to contain a chuckle of her own.

"What's he doing?" Diam whispered.

"Believe it or not, it looks like he's digging!" Tonia answered.

Diam turned back to glance at Tonia in disbelief but said nothing. How much stranger could things in this already strange enough world get?

After digging for a few more seconds, the newly disguised, dirt and leaf covered frog peeked around the tree at them.

"Almost done!" he said sheepishly.

"Wait! What are you doing?" Diam called out. "Do you need our help with anything?"

The dragon smiled at her and ignored her question. When he shook his head, a small clump of dirt tottered on top of his head for a second or two before falling to the ground at his feet.

"I have something for you – a gift for each of you – before we leave!"

Without another word, the front half of his body disappeared behind the tree again, where he resumed digging.

The girls waited patiently for the dragon to find whatever 'gift' he was searching for that was buried somewhere behind the tree. After seeing a continuous stream of unwanted dirt and leaves being relocated for a few more seconds, the frog finally stopped digging and sat up. The girls heard a strange clinking sound as unidentified objects were knocked together but they were unable to tell by the sound what the objects might be.

Satisfied with its find, the frog finally settled back on his hind legs and turned to look at his friends, a sense of accomplishment pouring over him. The entire front of his body was covered with dirt and leaves, but the girls managed to make out a cluster of pale colored items in Kennard's arms, which were held securely against his chest area. Kennard smiled at the girls briefly before he began the task of ambling awkwardly back toward them, obviously not completely comfortable with the effort required trying to walk on two legs instead of hopping on four.

"You know, if my body was in the shape of a dragon, instead of a frog, this would be so much easier!" he said with unbridled sarcasm. It took a bit of time for the frog to successfully make his way to the edge of the puddle, but he didn't stop there. Instead, he ambled a few more steps away until he had made it to an area just beyond the boat. Tonia frowned as she wondered what he was doing, but before she had a chance to ask, the frog lowered himself down to the ground and jumped into the far end of the puddle with a *splash!*

A split second before he jumped, Tonia realized what he was about to do and did her best to shift forward, pushing the other girls towards the front end of the boat. If there was one thing she was certain of, she did *not* want to find herself covered with puddle slime! At first, she couldn't understand why the frog made such a scene out of jumping into the puddle from the place he had chosen, especially since it appeared as though the entire puddle was roughly the same depth. After a half a second, however, she found herself quite surprised when the frog hit the liquid rust and disappeared completely beneath the surface.

"Hey!" she called out, unable to believe they had all just seen the frog disappear into the surprising depths of the water with whatever items he'd been carrying.

"Kennard?"

The liquid sludge in the puddle rippled violently for a few seconds and the boat rocked in chaotic response. The girls held onto their respective handles as they waited for the dragon to resurface, but after a minute or so, there was no sign of him. They stared silently into the puddle as the waves finally began to die down.

"Wow, what was that about?" Diam whispered as she gripped the handles on the inner walls of the boat. "Surely he didn't need us all here for *that*, did he?"

"I don't know," Tonia began. She shook her head in angry denial.

"Let's wait a little bit," Kaileen said as she shifted on her seat and released the handles she had been holding. All three girls stared at the place in the puddle where the frog dove beneath the surface for a few seconds, but there was no sign of him at all.

He had disappeared.

"I don't think he's gone," the kalevala added quietly.

When the ripples across the top of the murky puddle of swill had dissipated to almost nothing, the silence around the pond was broken by a sudden, upward explosion of muck, slime, and leaves, as the frog emerged from some unseen location below the surface. In a blur of movement, Kennard landed with a muffled splash close to the place where the girls had first seen him, which thankfully was far enough away from them that they didn't get wet. Although he was thoroughly soaked and still covered with a small amount of slime, he was infinitely cleaner than he had been just a few moments before. In fact, there was not a single trace of dirt anywhere on either him or the items he continued to hold against his upper body.

"Ah, sweet victory," he said with a proud smile as he slowly made his unsteady way back to the place between the girls and the tree.

Tonia stared at the odd, protective way Kennard carried the unidentified prized possessions in his arms. It reminded her of young mothers in the village in that the way he carried the items was very similar to the way they held their small children to their chest. Upon closer inspection, she suddenly realized the items Kennard held appeared to be a couple of two-foot long, carved, decorative bones.

"What are they?" Kaileen asked curiously, but as soon as the words left her mouth, her breath caught in her throat with both surprise and recognition.

The puddle dragon extended one of his short, yet muscular, front legs away from his body in slow motion, almost as if he was struggling to relinquish the items he held so protectively against his chest. When he finally extended his arm, the girls saw he held three intricately carved short swords in his wide, webbed hand.

"These, my young friends, are for you," Kennard said in a low whisper.

"Wait a minute," Tonia said as she threw a questioning look at Diam. "Don't those look similar to the spear we found in the cave?"

37

"Yes, I think they do," her friend agreed.

"Where in the cave?" Kaileen asked with a soft, shaking voice.

"We found a skeleton," Diam began, but before she could continue the muck dragon interrupted her.

"These aren't just any old, plain kind of weapons, you know," Kennard interjected as he shook his head and frowned. "These, my friends, are some very, very, special swords."

"How is that?" Tonia asked in response. She was curious to find out all she could about these beautiful weapons that looked so similar to the one Nicho had been carrying in his backpack the last time she had seen him.

"Rumor has it they once belonged to some, shall we say, quite privileged castle inhabitants," Kennard explained. "As you can plainly see, they are hand-carved, which makes them special regardless of who their previous owner may have been. It was also said, however, that only those with… certain special abilities… could use these weapons as they were meant to be used. Unfortunately, I'm not privy to any other details than that."

Tonia sighed in frustration but said nothing.

"I am certain, however, that you and your group of friends, including your brothers, possess some very special abilities," Kennard said as his eyes roved from one girl to the other before they finally rested on the one with the chestnut colored eyes.

"Tonia, the real question to ask is this: Will any of that magic show up now, when I hand these over to you; will it be later, when and if we find the next amulet; or perhaps, will there be no signs of magic at all?"

The girls considered the muck dragon's questions for a moment before Diam spoke up.

"Wait. Why *not at all?*"

Kennard squinted his eyes as he became lost in his own thoughts for a few seconds before answering the older, darker-skinned girl.

"Perhaps the magic is gone."

"But how will we know?" Kaileen asked as she frowned at the dragon.

"I'm not completely certain that we will. Unfortunately, we may not know one way or the other unless the magic decides to show itself to us," the muck dragon answered.

"Why don't we find out right now?" he suggested as both his expression and tone brightened.

Without waiting for an answer, Kennard carefully handed one of the beautifully carved bone swords to each of the girls, beginning with Kaileen. As he handed the third and final sword to Tonia, the rest of the group watched with anticipation for any signs of magic.

Would the beautiful weapon begin to shine like the sun or a beacon in the night as soon as Tonia touched it? Could it possibly light up with a low, soft, welcoming glow like one of the stones as it was placed in the palm of her hand? Or, perhaps, might Tonia even light up with a mystical, magical glow of her own?

No one spoke as the young girl extended her opened palm toward the muck dragon. Just before she was about to take the weapon, she paused and pulled her hand back nervously. She looked up at Kennard, who offered a silent, encouraging nod to the brown haired girl.

Tonia took a quick breath and held her hand out again, then slowly wrapped her fingers around the handle of the sword. Diam and Kaileen watched with bated breath as their friend took the weapon from the dragon.

Nothing spectacular happened at all. No glow, no blazing brightness, no mystical aura appeared around their friend. In fact, it seemed almost as though Kennard had handed Tonia nothing more than a simple stick he'd found lying on the ground.

"I guess that answers that question," Tonia said as she exhaled in relief. Without further hesitation, she brought the weapon up toward her eyes so she could examine it more closely.

The entire handle of the sword was littered with various wildlife carvings – bears, raccoons, birds, and fish, among others. There were also odd symbols peppering the handle in no discernible pattern. The sword, itself, was surprisingly light, and although the bone handle was hollow and looked very fragile, it felt strangely sturdy and comfortable against the skin of her palm.

"It's beautiful," the young girl said quietly as she turned it over and over in her hand. "I'm almost afraid I might break it or damage its beauty if I hold it too much."

"Ha!" the muck dragon scoffed with a partial chuckle. "Trust me – you won't break it. It is made from some of the strongest material in this world."

"What's it made from?" Diam asked curiously as she examined her sword in much the same fashion as her friend had done.

"Dragon bones."

All three girls stopped examining at their newly acquired weapons and stared at the dragon in surprise. Although he'd caught them off guard with his last words, he remained relaxed while a small smile played at the corners of his wide mouth.

"'Tis true," he said as he nodded in answer to their unspoken questions.

"Wow," Diam said in amazement. "Are you sure you want us to have them? I mean, umm, are they part of your family?"

Kennard laughed lightly at Diam's obvious discomfort at her own question. She stared at him in silence, unsure about how to take his reaction.

"I'm sorry," Kennard apologized. "I suppose, in an odd sort of way, they are a part of my family, but it is fine, really. Please believe me when I say if I wasn't comfortable with giving them to you, or didn't want to give them to you at all, I never would have."

Diam nodded once before looking at her friends. As she glanced at Tonia's weapon, she noticed the carvings on it were different than those of her own. Curious now, she turned and examined Kaileen's sword as well, and wasn't surprised to find that the kalevala's weapon was also unique.

Each sword was special in its own way.

"What are we supposed to do with these?" Tonia asked as she turned to glance down at her sword from the village, which was resting in its sheath at her side.

"I can't fit two swords in my sheath."

"I would suggest that you replace the sword at your side with the one I gave to you, and put the existing one in your bag," the muck dragon suggested in a questioning tone.

"But what about Kaileen?" Diam asked. "She never had a sword, so she doesn't have a sheath. She doesn't have a bag,

40

either."

"Ah, yes, thank you for reminding me! I knew I was forgetting something else!" the muck dragon said with an impatient sigh.

Kennard quickly turned to look back toward the tree, but there was no indication he was about to return there. Instead, after hearing a curt, high pitched whistling sound, the girls saw the leaves around the base of the tree rustling once again. After a few seconds they realized the movement was coming from the rats, which had turned and were heading toward the puddle as they dragged an unidentified object behind them.

Kennard shifted carefully towards the shore and retrieved the item from the rats. He quickly thanked his small, furry friends before he turned and headed back to the waiting girls. When he reached them, he held the item out to Kaileen.

It was a belt made from thick strands of woven, dark green tree vines. Hanging from one side of the belt was a sheath that had been mysteriously created from numerous thick, pungent smelling leaves.

"And this is for you," Kennard said to Kaileen as she took the belt from his webbed, outstretched hand.

The kalevala handed Diam her sword then worked with the belt for a few seconds before finally figuring out how to secure it around her waist. Once she had it situated where she felt most comfortable, Diam handed Kaileen her weapon. The kalevala inserted the sword into the sheath – it slid into place like a hand into a glove.

"Thank you," the kalevala said.

"Absolutely," the muck dragon said with a smile. "We must make sure everything is just so before we can begin our journey. Once we leave, there will be no turning back."

The muck dragon turned to look toward the tree and addressed no one in particular.

"My forest friends, are we ready?"

The girls said nothing as they watched hundreds of glowing red lights shine towards them from the leaves and underbrush near the tree. An accompanying orchestra of rodent squeaks answered the dragon's question.

"Very good – they are ready," Kennard interpreted with a

nod as he turned to the kalevala.

"Since you are sitting up front, would you be so kind as to hook me up?"

"Hook you up? You mean, as in hooking you up to the boat?" Diam asked with a frown of confusion.

They had seen some strange things over the past two days, but seeing a large, slime covered frog harnessed up to a make-shift boat would definitely take the chickleberry pie.

"Why, yes! Silly girl! Did you not realize what the harness is for?" Kennard asked teasingly.

Without waiting for an answer, he turned back toward the tree. The girls heard another whistling sound, this time softer than the previous one. Before the girls understood what was happening, some of the rats quickly reappeared with a small cluster of vines. They scurried up onto the dragon and, with surprising ease, untangled the disorganized cluster of woven tree life and began looping the confining contraption this way and that across and under the frog. Once he was properly fitted with the harness, the rats jumped back into the leaves next to the puddle and quickly disappeared. The muck dragon nodded in wordless acknowledgment as he made his way in between the boat and the tree.

"There is an eyelet there, which you should be able to hook my harness through," he said to the kalevala with a wink. Kaileen nodded and leaned forward, carefully securing the harness to the front of the boat.

"Won't we be too heavy for you to pull?" she asked as her fingers worked nimbly to thread the ropes through the harness.

"Not at all," Kennard said. "I'm sure you couldn't really tell if I showed you, but after living in this slimy environment for quite some time, I now have special pads on my feet. The liquid from my home has had plenty of time to coat the inside of the tree while we've been talking, which will make it much easier for me to pull you through the tunnel."

As he said this, a handful of rats on the ground suddenly jumped onto the tree before swiftly making their way a few feet into the tunnel entrance. Once there, they stopped and waited expectantly for their next command. Seeing this, nearly all the remaining rodents from just outside the entrance climbed into the tunnel as well and waited behind the smaller group.

"As you can plainly see our rodent friends are anxious to begin the journey. They will be accompanying us as well," the muck dragon said.

"They will?" Tonia asked, "But why?"

"To light our way as we travel, of course," Kennard explained. "In addition to many of the nearby trees blocking much of the sunlight from the area around the puddle, it's understandably quite a bit darker in the tunnel. We'll need their assistance as we make our way through the dark underpass. It has been a long time since I've journeyed along this particular route and we don't want to assume everything now is as it used to be."

Diam leaned forward and said to Kaileen, "You'll probably feel right at home in the tunnel, I bet."

The kalevala nodded as she stared into the dark hole in the tree.

"Are we ready then?" Kennard asked his hairy friends.

As the girls peered into the opening of the tree, they found themselves quite surprised at how the rodents reacted to the dragon's question. The oversized rats immediately began squeaking and dancing in place just inside the tunnel, some splashing in the slime to express their excitement. They were quite obviously ready and willing to be off on their expedition.

The muck dragon turned back to his new friends in the boat. "Girls?"

Kaileen looked back at Diam, then Tonia, who nodded and answered, "Yes, I suppose we're ready."

"Should we expect anything in particular?" Diam asked.

Kennard chuckled at the lack of clarity in her question.

"Like?" he asked as he gently prodded for more information.

"You know… things like other dragons, scary spiders, crazy bats, or hungry snakes?" Diam said as she stared at the harnessed frog in front of the boat.

"Yes, I supposed you could," Kennard said with a smile and one final wink.

"You can expect an adventure!"

Before the girls could comment, the muck dragon turned and

faced forward as he called out the command his smaller, furry friends had been waiting for.

"Let our journey begin!"

Before Tonia could change her mind, the rats led the way deeper into the tunnel while the girls grabbed their respective boat handles and held on for the ride of their lives.

TWO

Dozens of glowing, fiery-eyed rodents led the group of travelers deeper into the cool tunnel of blackness, providing miniature lamps into an otherwise completely lightless world. Quite a few of the rats clamored along the high walls and jagged ceiling of the tunnel, while others splashed delicately through the wide, moving stream of slime that coated the floor. Roughly one third of the rodents followed the makeshift boat from behind.

As the glowing-eyed creatures pushed onward, leading the group deeper and deeper into the tunnel in search of the exit on the other side, the girls nervously held the inner handles of the boat. They rode in silence for quite some time as they listened to the rhythmic, sloshing footfalls of the muck dragon as he pulled them steadily through the slime-covered tunnel. It took Tonia and Diam quite a bit longer for their eyes to adjust to the darker environment, but as the friends suspected, Kaileen's adjusted fairly quickly to the darkness after having lived in a similar environment for her entire life.

Diam leaned toward the kalevala.

"What do you see? Is there anything in here worth telling us about?"

"Not really," Kaileen answered as she turned to speak to her friend over her shoulder. "It's pretty much just a bumpy, slimy tunnel, as far as I can tell."

45

"Well, that's good I guess," Diam said.

"How far do we have to go?" Tonia called out to the muck dragon.

"It depends on how clear the tunnel is," Kennard answered in between splashy footsteps.

Although the frog wasn't pulling them incredibly fast, it did seem as though they were making good time. Tonia couldn't imagine it would take them very long to make it through the tunnel at the speed they were going. So far, the tunnel appeared to be fairly straight. Besides, how wide could the base of the mountain really be?

As soon as this thought passed through her mind, she discovered she'd thought it too soon when Kennard suddenly called out a warning.

"Hold on!"

As the muck dragon's voice echoed through the tunnel, the girls followed his warning and grasped their respective handles tightly. Just as they did, the tunnel took a sharp turn to the left.

As soon as he realized there was an unsafe curve in the tunnel ahead, Kennard tried to slow down, but it wasn't enough. As he led them into the curve, the front right corner of the wooden boat caught the right wall of the tunnel. In response to the impact, the sled then bounced off of the left wall of the tunnel as it began rounding the curve. Kennard did his best to slow the boat as fearful squeals echoed through the tunnel around them. The boat immediately bumped into the back of the frog and he carefully slowed down until they all finally came to a stop. A large number of rats that had been leading the excursion suddenly reappeared behind the dragon, flooding the area around them in a soft, rose-colored light.

"Are you okay?" the muck dragon asked the girls worriedly as he looked quickly from one to the next. Each of them was wide-eyed with fear, but thankfully no one was hurt.

"I'm so very sorry," Kennard apologized. "I had no idea the tunnel was going to curve like that."

"I thought the rats were lighting the way," Tonia said as her feelings of fear were replaced by those of anger.

"They were... they are," the frog answered defensively. "But when the majority of them disappeared around the curve, I couldn't see the path as clearly as before. I will be more careful from now on."

"I would hope so," Tonia said as her eyes flashed.

Diam threw Tonia a worried, disagreeable stare. When Tonia saw the look in her friend's eyes, she mentally chided herself.

"You can't really expect us to help you save your world if we're dead, you know."

A hint of a smile played at the corners of Tonia's lips as the frog nodded apologetically.

"You are very right."

"Wait, I have an idea," Diam said.

She reached down between her feet and opened her bag. After rustling around inside it for a few seconds, she happily removed her torch and rock sparkers.

"Why don't we use a torch to help light the way?" she asked with a smile.

"You have a torch?" Kennard asked curiously.

Diam glanced back at Tonia before she answered the dragon.

"Yeah, I think we kind of forgot we had them."

Tonia nodded

The dragon looked from Tonia to Diam then chuckled. It was a short, croaky sounding laugh.

"Well, let's see if we can get it fired up!"

Diam handed the torch out to Tonia, who held it over the edge of the boat. Without a word, Diam began striking her two rock sparkers together as she tried to light the torch.

One strike…

Two strikes…

Three strikes…

Nothing.

She sighed in frustration and glanced at Tonia. Her friend simply nodded her head and continued to hold the torch in place, confident Diam would successfully light it.

"You can do it," Kaileen said encouragingly as she smiled at the older girl.

Diam returned the kalevala's smile but said nothing. All she could do was try again.

One strike…

And the torch suddenly jumped to life in a small pyre of flames.

Kaileen clapped her hands together as Tonia patted her friend's leg.

"I knew you could do it!"

Diam smiled and returned the rock sparkers to her bag.

"Now we can really see where we're going!"

When the girls turned to look at the muck dragon, the focus of their attention changed as each of them suddenly noticed a hundred thousand glittering, miniature lights which completely covered the walls and ceiling of the tunnel.

"What in the world…?" Tonia began as her voice drifted off. She moved the torch from one side of the boat to the other as they all stared in awe at their enchanted, sparkling environment. She was suddenly entranced by the thought of how something as simple as an underground, or under *mountain*, tunnel could look so different in both light and dark and still be the same place. It was stunningly beautiful.

The girls surveyed the area with gaping mouths and wide eyes as Kennard watched them in silence. The frog smiled when he realized they were too busy gawking to notice. He turned his attention to his furry friends waiting patiently around them – some were quietly clinging to the walls and ceiling around the boat while the rest waited in front of him. Now that they had the torch to light their way, the glowing eyes of their rodent friends were no longer quite as bright as they had been just moments before.

"Wow."

It's the only word Diam could muster. She was completely taken aback by the transformed appearance of the passageway.

"This is quite interesting to see," Kennard said in response to their reaction. "Although the entrance into the tunnel is through a tree, the interior of the tunnel appears to be made from something quite different than ordinary tree bark, wouldn't you say?"

Tonia nodded as Diam struggled to find her voice to ask a question.

"What are they?"

"They look like diamonds," Tonia said as she answered her friend's question with another. "Don't they?"

"Yeah, they do," Diam agreed.

"It's beautiful," Kaileen whispered, mesmerized by the glittering stones that reminded her of the first night they found themselves on the outside of the cave. The onyx blanket above them looked something like this, but the twinkling lights in the tunnel were so much closer than the stars in the sky had been.

Their eyes slowly roved along the walls and ceiling around them for a few seconds before Kennard found himself regretfully interrupting them.

"I'm sorry, but we really must be going."

The nearby rodents squeaked in response, but remained in their positions as they patiently waited for the command from the dragon.

"Okay," Tonia said as she handed Diam the torch. "Kaileen, would you mind holding this, since you're in the front? But if you're not comfortable with it, we can trade places."

"I'm fine," Kaileen said as she took the flickering stick of fire from Diam. "As long as we don't run into any tunnel walls."

Kennard snorted at her obvious attempt at humor and threw her a hint of a smile.

"Very well, then," the muck dragon said to the nearby rodents. "Carry on!"

As soon as the words were out of his mouth, the rats began leading the way into the tunnel. Without further hesitation, Kennard gently pulled the boat as he followed the rodents, moving faster and faster until he was pulling the girls at a comfortable speed behind him. Diam leaned into Kaileen's back in an attempt to provide some stability to her since the kalevala now only had one hand to hold on with. Once they reached a somewhat steady, and thankfully slower, gait, Kaileen no longer needed Diam's help.

"Thank you," the kalevala said with a turn of her head in an attempt at looking over her shoulder at her friend.

They traveled in silence for a while, each girl trying to peer ahead of them to see what might lie around the next corner of the tunnel. Now that they had the extra light from the torch illuminating their path, the passageway appeared to be completely empty of any signs of life or obstructions.

After a short time, Tonia and Diam began talk about how exciting it would be to find the boys when suddenly they heard an almost shrieking chorus of squeaks ahead. Not surprisingly, the forward motion of the boat immediately began to wane as the frog slowed down. Each of the girls peered forward nervously to see what was going on.

Directly ahead of them, in the center of the tunnel, they quickly detected a short, yet wide, lump of rock that was completely blocking their path.

"Well it's a good thing we were able to see *that*," Tonia said as she patted Diam on the back with praise. "Very good thinking, my friend."

The muck dragon slowed to a stop just a few feet from the wide, gray stone.

"Oh great," Tonia said as she frowned. "Does this mean we're going to have to step out and carry the boat over?"

Kennard curiously peered over the rock that blocked their path. Kaileen, quiet as always, held the torch higher into the air as she tried to provide the muck dragon additional lighting.

The wide stone in the tunnel ahead was roughly two feet long and a foot high. Thankfully, it didn't completely block the floor of the passageway – there was a narrow, two inch high gap beneath it, which allowed the thin stream of slime to continue flowing into the darkness beyond.

"It would appear so," the dragon finally said in response to Tonia's question.

As he turned back to look at her, Kaileen's gaze moved from the orange and yellow flame rising above the top of the torch to something beyond the fire, on the ceiling…

But there was only part of a ceiling.

If they hadn't stopped to avoid crashing into the rock blocking the tunnel, they would have never seen the wide, gaping, pitch-black opening in the passageway above them. Nestled around the opening of the hole were what appeared to be three very large, very round, charcoal colored balls.

"Umm, what's that?" Diam whispered in a quiet, nervous

tone as she pointed over the muck dragon's head.

He looked up and smiled.

"Ah, we're here already!" he said as he turned to look at the girls.

"What do you mean?" Tonia asked.

"This is where we needed to stop," he answered. He turned and glanced at the object blocking their path and mumbled, "Although I don't remember hearing about a large stone being in the way..."

"Why?" Kaileen asked. "Why did we need to stop here?"

"Why? Why? Because unless we find what we need while we're here, there will be no need to continue on. That's why!" the muck dragon said as his eyes squinted partially closed. His mind wandered as he thought about something he chose not to speak.

"You're doing it again!" Tonia scolded the muck dragon as she wagged an incriminating finger at him. Kennard stared at her with a look of total blankness for a few seconds before his face finally crumpled into a frown as he realized what she was talking about.

"I suppose I am," he admitted in a now familiar, apologetic tone.

"And...?" Tonia asked as she prodded him for more information.

Kennard sat down without answering her. Tonia was about to scold him again when she suddenly realized the reason he wasn't talking was because of the strange, rasping sounds he was making as he breathed.

"Are you okay?" Diam asked. The puddle dragon didn't look all that great.

"Yes, I'll be fine," he answered quietly as he tried to catch his breath. "I just need to rest for a moment."

Diam noticed the dragon avoided looking at them as he gazed, instead, into the darkness of the tunnel beyond the large stone. She chose not to say anything about it.

In the growing silence, she glanced at Tonia as she remembered the story the dragon had shared with them before they entered the tunnel. He spoke of a spell that had been cast upon him – a spell that was meant to prevent him from leaving the area around the puddle. None of them had any idea how far they would have to go, but she suddenly understood the distance they had traveled through the winding tunnel so far must have taken its toll on the puddle creature's heart.

Each of the girls stared at the dragon with expressions of worry and dismay, but with a carefree wave of an arm, and valiant attempt at an unconcerned smile, Kennard continued his story.

"This is where you must go to retrieve the amulet," the muck dragon said, "but we must discuss a few things before we go any further. Why don't you step out of the boat and stretch for a few minutes?"

"Oh, brother, why does there have to be a stipulation with everything?" Tonia asked quietly as Kaileen nodded and stood up before stepping carefully out of the boat. As soon as the kalevala was standing on solid ground, Diam and Tonia took turns and followed.

"Oh, yeah, it feels good to stretch," Tonia agreed as she held her arms out to her sides before lifting them over her head. "Sitting in one position for that long makes the body cramp up, doesn't it?"

"You don't have to tell me about it," Kaileen said. "At least you had room to stretch out your legs! There wasn't much leg room up in the front…"

While the girls stretched and walked around a bit Kennard enlisted the help of some rats who assisted him by removing the harness. The girls chatted with each other as they patiently waited for the muck dragon to continue his story.

When the harness was finally lying inside the boat, Diam couldn't remain quiet any longer.

"Okay, lay it on us. What is it we need to discuss?"

"Well, first of all, you must know your next step in the journey," Kennard began. Hearing no questions or comments from any of the girls, he added as he pointed above their heads, "You must go up there and find the amulet."

Each of the girls looked upward as Kaileen instinctively held the torch higher in the air in an attempt to brighten the area above them.

"Very funny," Diam said as she shook her head in denial. "Unless you plan on dragging the boat up there, I just don't see it happening."

The entrance to the hole above them brightened only slightly from the single source of light Kaileen held above their heads. Unfortunately, it wasn't enough to see very far into what looked like some sort of tunnel going vertically upward into the mountain. From what they could see, it appeared to be perfectly perpendicular to the path they had been traveling.

"Of course I wasn't planning on dragging the boat up there! That would be silly, as well as impossible. The pads on my feet are well equipped to run through the slimy path in the tunnel, but going up there... well, that would just take a miracle! Oh no, my feet are not designed to climb upward along tunnel walls, no they're not!" the muck dragon said.

Tonia cleared her throat and Kennard continued before she could scold him yet again.

"No, I will not be the one to accompany you on that journey, unfortunately, but before we get into that, let's talk about jewelry."

The older, darker skinned girl felt her stomach fill with butterflies as the muck dragon's gaze turned to and settled on her.

"You, young one... you have something very special in your possession, do you not?" Kennard asked Diam.

Her eyes darted to Tonia nervously and without realizing she was doing it, her hand brushed along the edge of her pants, feeling for the lump she knew would be there. She looked back at Kennard and answered him in a nervous, quiet whisper.

"I'm not sure I know what you are talking about..."

"Oh, come now," the muck dragon said with a smile. "I know all about the special piece of jewelry you carry, and I understand why you are so protective of it. Of course I do! That is not the real question though, is it?"

His eyes locked on hers for a few seconds before he asked another question.

"Do YOU understand why you are so protective of it?"

Tonia and Diam took a step away from the dragon and Kaileen quickly followed. Tonia's hand nervously found the handle of her bone sword in its sheath. She let it rest there, prepared to draw it in a split second if necessary. Did this creature draw them this far into the cave just to steal the ring? If not, what was really going on?

"It's special," Diam answered curtly, unwilling to say anything more about the strange, mystical ring she carried in her pocket.

"Let me tell you about it," the muck dragon said as he smiled. "Please, don't be afraid. This is all part of your destiny."

Kennard understood their apprehension and sat down near the large rock. The girls remained nervous and unsure. They stood their ground as they waited for him to continue.

"The ring belonged to Alyshana, the bride of a very special sorcerer who has since disappeared from this world," the muck dragon began. "That sorcerer was Scurio.

"The ring was made from the finest silver and held a stunning, swirling green stone in the center. Green was Alyshana's favorite color, and Scurio wanted nothing more than to dote on his beautiful, young, dark-haired bride, so he acquired a special green gem. After casting a spell of love onto the jewel, he gave it to her as a token of his undying devotion. From the day she received it, she never let it out of her sight."

"What happened to it?" Kaileen asked, drawn into the story.

"A few years after they were married, Alyshana disappeared. When she vanished, it was assumed the ring disappeared with her. As far as we in this world know, neither she nor her gift of love was ever found," Kennard said.

"But we didn't find the ring here," Tonia said, feeling a bit of vújade as she remembered how, less than twenty four hours ago, they had been saying the same kind of thing to the crazy monkey in the tree. She also knew full well the dragon would read their minds and understand what the item was in Diam's pocket even if they chose not to tell him about it.

"We found it back in the cave by our village," she added.

"'Tis true?" the dragon asked in a surprised tone.

"Yes," Diam answered, "and not long after we arrived in your world, we saw something happen because of the ring that none of us could explain, even if we tried."

Kaileen's eyes widened with the memory of the scene at the

54

apple tree as she nodded silently.

"I see," the dragon said as he picked up on their memories of the earlier theft of the ring. He smiled slightly as he captured the scene showing the monkey's unfortunate fate after placing the small piece of jewelry on its finger.

"I'm sure you were quite surprised with the outcome of the entire circumstance at the apple tree?" Kennard said in a questioning tone.

"Yeah, surprised is one way to put it," Tonia said as the other girls agreed by nodding their heads.

"There is one thing you must understand," the muck dragon said. "No matter what you surely think after what happened to the monkey, Alyshana's ring is not evil."

"Uh huh," Diam said as she nodded her head sarcastically, "and no matter how much you try to convince us otherwise, I just don't see us ever believing anything else."

Kennard considered the older girl's words for a moment. "Would you mind showing it to me?"

As Kaileen glanced at Tonia, the muck dragon added, "If I remember it right, the ring has a beautiful green stone in the center of it, but every so often the stone will swirl as if pale, white clouds are moving across the surface of it... is this correct?"

Tonia nodded at Diam who reluctantly removed the small, brown bag from her pocket.

"Yes, we've seen the cloudy look you're describing," Tonia admitted.

"Can you remove it from the bag?" Kennard asked quietly. "Please..."

"It's okay," Kaileen whispered, surprising the others.

Diam gave the kalevala a questioning glance. Kaileen nodded in silent reply and Diam pulled on the draw string that held the tiny bag shut. She looked up at Kennard then nervously dumped the ring into the palm of her hand and held it out for the dragon to see.

"Ah, yes, the Ring of Alyshana," the dragon whispered before dropping his chin to his chest. When he raised his head a few seconds later to look at Diam, the girls could see tears in his eyes.

"It has been a long time..." he began, then closed his eyes and

55

shook his head. The girls watched him take a deep breath and slowly let it out. Something about the ring obviously struck an emotional chord in him.

"I'm sorry," the frog apologized. "This is just another sign that you are the chosen ones – you are here to save our world."

Tonia glanced at Kaileen, then Diam, before turning back to the dragon.

"So what do we do now?" she asked as Diam protectively closed her fingers around the ring. She held the bag open with her other hand and dropped the piece of jewelry back into it, quickly returning it to her pocket.

Kennard smiled at them.

"Now that I know for sure you indeed *do* have possession of the Ring of Alyshana, I must tell you what you need to do with it. Then we can move on to the next step."

Kaileen linked an arm through Diam's as they waited in nervous silence for the muck dragon to continue. Diam smiled at her friend then turned her attention back to the dragon.

"I'm sure you already know you must go up there," Kennard said as he pointed at the tunnel above them. Just as Tonia was about to question him, he held up his hand and silenced her.

"Please, let me finish."

She nodded and remained silent.

"You will need to go up that tunnel until you reach the top of the mountain. Once you get there, you will find yourselves in quite a different environment, but we'll get to that in just a moment. You," he said, looking directly at Diam, "are the one who will need to lead now."

"Lead?" Diam asked, not wanting to take over Tonia's position for even a moment. "How am I supposed to lead when I don't even know where we're supposed to be going?"

"I will tell you," Kennard said patiently, as understanding filled his eyes. He knew how difficult this must be for this group of young girls, finding themselves in a strange world, with strange creatures, and even stranger magic, which they really didn't understand.

"You must wear the ring when you arrive at the place at the top of the vertical tunnel," the muck dragon said to Diam.

After seeing firsthand what the magic of the ring did to those who choose to wear it, Diam immediately replied, "Are you crazy?"

"Absolutely not," Tonia exclaimed in response to Kennard's suggestion. "We didn't come all this way for her to wear the ring and become a pile of ashes!"

"Wait, let me finish," Kennard said again as he tried to get their attention before things got too far out of hand.

"The ring is a very special piece of jewelry, which I know each of you understands now, more than anyone," the muck dragon began. "I do not doubt for a minute that a less than desirable outcome would fall on any creature with a tainted heart who decided to wear the ring. This was obviously the case with the situation you refer to…"

"Hold on there a minute, Mr. Croakster," Diam said in a tone that carried both fear and anger. "This is almost too much!"

She sighed in exasperation and looked up into the tunnel above them as she tried to gather her thoughts together. After a few seconds, she lowered her bright, shining eyes and stared in anger and confusion at the frog.

"First of all, are you telling us that we are going to have to somehow climb into and up a vertical tunnel when there's no obvious way to get up there to begin with…"

Her voice echoed off the tunnel walls as it rose in both pitch and volume near the end of her sentence. Just as Kennard opened his mouth to answer her, Diam's right arm shot up from her side and she pushed her opened palm towards him in a quite obvious and authoritative halting gesture.

"And second of all, are you telling ME that I have to wear the single, solitary, absolutely most dreaded piece of jewelry I've ever laid my eyes on once we DO go up there… IF we are able to somehow even make it to the top?!?!?!"

The tall, thin, dark-haired girl stared at the muck dragon as her eyes glared like a blazing campfire. She was on a roll and was nowhere near ready to stop. Kennard fully understood the mixed emotions that were so obviously flowing through the young girl standing like a warrior in front of him. He held his position in complete and respectful silence until she was through.

Diam began to tremble as the enormity of what she was feeling inside threatened to overwhelm her.

First, they had to deal with the snake in the cave and retrieve the amulet that helped them create the portal. Then, they were faced with the horde of thieving monkeys in the apple tree. Next, they found themselves dealing with a frog who believed with every grain of sand in the world that he was a dragon! Here they are, trapped in this strange world, with this crazy creature who was nothing more than a stranger to them, really, who remained completely straight faced and serious as he explained how they would need to do the impossible by going vertically up the tunnel above them! And now, to top it ALL off, miracle of miracles, he was trying to convince her that she would need to wear the ring that turned the monkey into nothing more than millions of floating ashes in the wind…

It was almost too much.

She sighed as she lowered her trembling arm and allowed her eyes to drop to the tunnel floor as she tried to regain control of her emotions. She took a deep breath, then another, as she struggled to compose herself. After a few seconds, she continued speaking in a harsh, angry whisper, which echoed quietly through the tunnel in an unquestionably serious tone.

"Listen to me, Kennard. You weren't with us back by the apple tree, so you can't possibly know, no matter how well you might be able to read our minds, just what it *looked* like when that crazy, thieving monkey realized he was in more trouble than he could handle; you can't know what it *smelled* like when his burning flesh and fur filled the air around us as the ring did… whatever it was that it did… to him; and you definitely can't know how it *sounded*, listening to his screams, his absolutely tortured cries of pain, as the ring slowly, mercilessly changed him from a breathing, conniving, living creature, into nothing more than a few thousand dust flakes falling from the tree. His remains eventually landed among the dirt and leaves all around us, destroyed and forgotten like those who came before us."

Diam saw Tonia nodding her head from the corner of her eye, but she remained focused on the creature that sat just inside the outer edge of the light ring from the torch a few feet away. The muck dragon nodded in thoughtful understanding, and when he was certain Diam was through, he spoke.

"'Tis true – I was not there with you. I did not see, smell, or hear all that you did, and I suppose part of me is thankful I didn't."

He sighed.

"I do, however, see the memories in your mind and, believe it or not, I can totally feel your confusion and pain. I understand your mixed emotions – pity for the monkey for what happened to him, sorrow at his resulting demise, and at times a nearly unbearable anger caused by his taking something that did not belong to him.

"Above all else, he met his destiny…"

The girls considered the muck dragon's words as he gathered his own thoughts for a moment.

"But you must understand; this creature who took the ring – it was not for him. What's worse, I believe deep down that he knew this, yet refused to believe it. His greed turned out to be stronger than his desire to do the right thing, which turned into his undoing.

"The ring knows who it waits for…"

His voice drifted off as if fading away and Diam found herself glancing at Tonia. When she turned to look back at Kennard, he added something that made her breath catch in her throat.

"That person is you," the dragon said as his eyes focused intently on Diam.

"How do you know this?" she asked quietly, wanting to believe him but afraid to at the same time.

"How do you know that it waits for me? How do you know that it won't turn me into a pile of dust as soon as I slip it on? I want to believe you, but the thought of putting that one piece of jewelry over my finger terrifies me!

"Don't you get it? I don't want to die!" she said in a harsh tone as her eyes blazed with fear and confusion, and as she finished her sentence, a lone tear trickled down her cheek.

Tonia knew her friend was becoming more upset the more they discussed the ring, but for some reason she couldn't interrupt the conversation. She had a feeling that Diam and Kennard

59

had to work through this part of the journey on their own, and although she knew without a doubt the ring had some kind of special powers, she honestly didn't know if she should believe what the dragon was telling them or if they should just turn and walk away. A big part of her, that voice somewhere inside her head, was also telling her to just close her eyes and make their spider web full of problems disappear, but she knew better than that. She could almost hear Micah telling her to "suck it up and deal with it," which she'd heard from him more times than she'd like to remember.

"I know you're frightened," Kennard said to the young girl who stood shaking like a toddler before him, "but you must understand that each of you has a special role to play."

Kennard's own eyes glistened brightly in the flickering torch light.

"Diam, do you believe you are in our world for a reason?"

Diam hesitated for only a second before she answered.

"Yes."

"Good," said Kennard as he tried to give her a reassuring smile.

"No matter what you think about me – who I am or *what* I am – you must understand that we are in this together," he offered as his eyes passed over each of the girls in turn. "If you fail, we fail. You are in this world to help save us – us meaning not just the dragons, but all creatures – from certain fate. It is up to us to help you, in every way we can, to succeed in reaching your destiny."

His serious stare lingered intently on Diam again.

"If you die, we all die."

The girls stood quietly in a semi-circle, listening to the puddle dragon while considering what few options they had.

Fight or flight.

Either they trust this strange creature and decide to do what needed to be done to fight, or they turned their backs on all creatures in this world, including this odd-looking dragon, and return the way they came...

If that was even possible...

"Besides," Kennard said quietly, "what good would it do us to try to harm you? You obviously have more than luck on your side to have gotten this far."

The girls looked at each other as Kennard continued.

"I can do nothing more than ask you to please believe me…"

"Okay," Diam said with a resolute sigh, "If I were to believe you, what would I need to do?"

Kennard smiled with relief but tried halfheartedly, and unsuccessfully, not to show it.

"When you reach the top of this tunnel," he said as his eyes turned upward, "you must put the ring on your finger. When you do, if your heart truly believes everything you've seen and heard here, the ring will work its magic through you to do what needs to be done."

"Does it matter which finger she puts it on?" Kaileen asked as she held their main source of light firmly in her hand.

Like her friends, the kalevala was nervous about the path before them, but felt they didn't have much of a choice. The dragon convinced her he was believable when she realized he knew what kind of creature she was. After thinking her entire life that their kind only resided in the dark, damp cave they'd left just a few short days ago, Kaileen was both surprised and excited to know this muck dragon knew about kalevalas, especially because this familiarity was happening in a totally new and unfamiliar world.

Perhaps there were others of her kind here? Did she dare even think that she was not the only kalevala left in the world? In *all* worlds?

"Okay, so that solves the mystery of what we do with the ring once we get to the top of the tunnel, but what about the one that explains *how* we get up there?" Tonia interrupted Kaileen's thoughts. She heard, but couldn't help how her voice was dripping with sarcasm again.

"I'm glad you asked," Kennard said without noticing the tone of her voice. "Unfortunately, I'm fairly certain you won't care for my answer."

His wide, onyx colored eyes bored into Tonia's brown ones and held her gaze as if in a visual duel. When Diam spoke up, the dragon broke the stare with the young, brown-haired girl and turned to look at the speaker.

"You're not going to try to carry us up there, are you?"

The muck dragon laughed in an odd way. If his body had been that of a real dragon, it probably would have come out as a snort, but since he was more like that of a large amphibian, it came out sounding remarkably like a sneeze.

"Of course not," he continued, chuckling lightly as his eyes glanced upward again.

Although the muck dragon tried to play off Diam's question like it was no big deal, Tonia could hear in his voice how serious their situation was. Not only that, although the muck dragon was laughing as he looked at them, she noticed that his eyes were no longer smiling.

The dragon stared off into the distant tunnel for a few seconds before he finally spoke again.

"Do you trust me?" he asked quietly.

There it was – the question of the day. None of the young adults from the small village of Uncava had ever dreamed they would be where they were right now, and it all came down to one of the simplest questions in the world.

This was the question that kept nagging Tonia in the back of her mind. It was the question that was whispered by the smallest voice as it communicated in a language the young girl couldn't understand, but then again, understanding the language wasn't really necessary.

She knew the doubt was there. Even when she'd thought she'd conquered it, the nagging unease continued to haunt her – in both her heart and her mind. She suddenly realized that her doubt in this creature obviously still hadn't changed to trust when she'd thought it had.

As a result, it all came down to this one, single, simple question.

Did they really trust him?

The muck dragon had led them here, into this dark place filled with shadows, and who knew how many other unseen creatures. He'd given them more information about the amulets, about her brothers…

Again, her mind wondered how her brothers were doing, but she couldn't allow herself to dwell on that right now.

It all came down to trust.

Kennard had said her brothers were okay, 'for now'… she either had to believe or disbelieve him.

"Tonia," Kennard said quietly, interrupting her thoughts. He knew if he couldn't convince her right now, the chance of any of them believing was very slim.

He could see it in her eyes that the line had been drawn. It had been drawn from one side of the tunnel to the other, from one girl to the other, from one dream to the other. It was drawn and there would be no erasing it.

For the muck dragon, it all came down to a single, simple question, and he knew there was no turning back.

Which side of the line would she choose?

Whose side was she on?

Fight or flight?

Stay or go?

He hoped he'd given them enough. He hoped for his sake, for their sake, and for the sake of their entire world.

Which side of the line was she on?

Total silence filled the cave as the young girl and the frog stood fixated on each other for a moment while each of their minds raced with endless questions and no answers. They stared at each other, lost in their own thoughts, as Diam and Kaileen watched and held their breath.

Everyone knew this was major. They all understood that the next few moments would make or break the deal.

Tonia felt as though time stood still, almost as if she could sense what was about to happen next. In response to her premonition, butterflies began fluttering in magnificent, overwhelming swarms in the pit of her stomach and she felt helpless to do anything about it.

Kennard finally broke the silence.

"Do you trust me?"

His soft voice echoed through the tunnel and he took a slow, hesitant step toward the beautiful young girl with the freckled nose. He wanted her to look deeply into his eyes, to stare into and through the doorway to his soul, so she could see the true dragon within him. At this moment, he wanted nothing more than for this young girl before him to recognize the love and good intentions that completely filled him – his eyes, his heart, his very being.

Tonia's initial reaction was to take a step back as the frog moved slowly forward, but she fought against the impulse. Instead, she realized her right hand was close to the sheath of her sword. She touched it with the side of her thumb, but did move her hand to withdraw it.

"Trust me," Kennard whispered again, knowing if he didn't get through to them now – if he didn't get through to *her* now – he probably never would… and all would be lost.

"I give you my word, on all that I am, all that I have been, and all that I will ever be, I will not harm you. Look into my eyes and see the truth. See that I want nothing more than for all of us to live as we were meant to live."

He stared into her wide, brown eyes as they stared back at him. He saw fear and understanding in them, but he also thought he saw a flicker of something else as well. Before he could identify it, it was gone.

"Trust me."

THREE

In the lower levels of the Castle Defigo, a man stands quietly in the dim torchlight and stares with deep yearning through the bars of his prison cell. He's been a lone prisoner in this wretched place for most of the time he's been in this unfamiliar world, but since the previous day, he can no longer say he is alone.

In the cell to his left resides an odd-looking creature named Zacharu who, like the man, is being held prisoner against his will. He met this non-human being the previous day when he was taken to a separate holding cell as punishment for not giving Nivri, the evil sorcerer who lived here, the information he was looking for.

Zacharu was also being held prisoner in the castle, but his situation was a bit different than the man's. He had been one of Nivri's minions, a servant of sorts, for a short period of time, but due to recent events, he was now just another prisoner locked up in a dank, gloomy cell.

After spending many days and nights in his prison cell, the man had recently discovered yet another prisoner who was being held in the cell to his right. Although he had not yet seen this other creature of captivity, over the course of the past few minutes, he had been trying to communicate with it. He was now not only trying to accept the fact that there were two other prisoners down here with him, but he was also finding it difficult to understand how he could possibly be communicating with this creature without actual, spoken words!

As he silently watched shadows jumping helter-skelter across the wall farthest from the flickering torchlight, the voice in his head drew him out of his reverie.

"Have you heard of me, human?" the mysterious creature in the cell to his right asked, but of course the voice was only being heard in the man's head.

"No, I've never heard of you," the man answered back mentally, still thoroughly confused with idea that he was actually able to communicate this way.

As he wondered about the identity of this mysterious creature, he quickly reviewed people and events from his past. He'd heard many stories during his lifetime about many different things, but he could not recall ever hearing any story about or reference to a creature called 'Little Draco'.

"Who are you?" the man asked with his mind as he shook his head in answer to the creature's question without even realizing he was doing so.

He glanced around at the walls lining his cell before his eyes turned back to the large room outside of his cell. He still expected his quiet voice to echo through some of the nearby prison cells, but it didn't. Oddly, it felt almost as if he were trying to keep a secret. Although he could hear his voice in his mind, silence continued to fill the gloomy chamber around him.

"You may call me Draco, human. There are many things I would like to tell you, but our time together is precious so I will only explain those things I feel are most important.

"I need your absolute attention. Do I have it?" the mysterious creature asked curtly.

"Yes," the man projected back to him.

"Very good," the creature replied.

"First of all, you must do whatever you can to free yourself of this wretched castle. You are a smart man… that much I sensed as soon as I saw you. Next, find your way out of here and head straight west. Depending on how fast you travel, you should soon reach a small, very special village hidden in a cave system. Once there, find the leader of the group and explain to those living there that you've found me."

"But how will they know…" the man began to question, but he was interrupted by the creature's reassuring voice.

"You have my word that everyone living in the hidden village will be more than willing to help you as you continue working your way through your part of our valiant attempt to save this world.

"Be sure to take care as you travel, human. You are in unfamiliar territory and it will not take much for you to lose your way. In addition to this, there are creatures here in this world who will be… how can I put this… most eager to find a stranger in this land. Be wary, human, and as quickly as you can, bring as many members of the village that you can recruit, for it won't be long before we have an epic battle on our hands…"

"Wait a minute," the man said out loud, without realizing he'd done so. He was focusing on how confused he was – more now than ever before.

"Who are we going to fight?"

Zacharu heard the human's question but chose not to ask again what he was talking about. He'd heard stories of people losing their minds in captivity, but now, for the first time, he was seeing it for himself.

"That is not important right now," the mysterious voice answered in response to the human's question. "First, you must focus on finding your way out of your current predicament. Once you have acquired your freedom, you will find the answers you seek. Just remember the things I have said here…"

Draco stopped mid-sentence. In the distance, they clearly heard footsteps approaching in the lower level of the castle.

The man grew silent, deep in thought where he stood at the door of his cell, his large, white hands wrapped around vertical bars. As soon as he realized someone was coming, he quickly took a few steps back and leaned against the wall that separated his and Zacharu's cells. As he listened to the footsteps getting closer and closer to the dungeon, the man was thankful Draco had fallen silent.

Only a small amount of time had passed since the man and Zacharu had been brought down here, and he found himself wondering what could possibly be bringing their visitor or visitors back down into the chilly, gloomy depths of the castle. Could it be he was about to have another enlightening, or attempt at an enlightening, meeting with Nivri? Or were they about to be returned to the boxes of darkness located somewhere in the castle above, instead? He tried his best not to show his nervousness as the visitor walked into the light produced by the limited number of torches.

Not surprisingly, the face was a familiar one.

Orob was quietly walking straight towards the human's cell and in a few seconds, the man could see the guard was carrying something in his hands. Although he couldn't make out what it was, it appeared to be something long and cylindrical.

Zacharu broke the silence from his cell as he addressed their visitor.

"Let us out of here, Orob. We have done nothing wrong! I refuse to be kept locked up when I have done nothing to deserve it!"

Orob glanced briefly at Zacharu but did not change his course. Within a few seconds he stood directly in front of the door to the man's cell. As he stopped and peered through the bars at the human, the man had a better view of the item the guard carried with him. It appeared to be some kind of parchment or scroll.

"Human," Orob began as his eyes narrowed, "My Master asked me to bring this to you. He would like you to carefully read through it. When you are finished, he will welcome any questions you may have."

"What is it?" the man asked cautiously as he wondered what the psychotic sorcerer was up to now… he was almost willing to bet it was nothing good.

"You could say, perhaps, that he has had a change of heart and has decided to offer you a deal of sorts," Orob replied.

The expression on the guard's face was emotionless as he looked at the man through equally blank and distant eyes.

"A deal?" the man asked quietly. Had he misheard the guard's words? "What kind of deal?"

Without answering the question, Orob pushed the scroll through the bars at the man. When the man didn't move to take it, Orob released the rolled paper and it fell to the stone floor and bounced a few times before stopping a few feet away from the man's feet. With a satisfied nod, Orob turned and walked back the way he had come.

"Wait, Orob... what is this?" the man asked as he bent to pick up the tubular item. The guard, however, continued to walk away without even the trace of a glance over his shoulder.

"Orob?" he called out again, but it was useless. After a few seconds, the guard's rhythmic footfalls faded away into silence.

The man stared down the hallway after the guard for a moment before shaking his head in both confusion and exasperation. Were all the residents of this castle as unpredictable as those he had encountered so far? One minute he was being tortured for information he did not have and the next he was being offered a deal. He just didn't understand it... not one bit.

Leaning back against the rock wall, he allowed himself to slide down until he was sitting on the floor. For a brief moment, he entertained the thought of crunching the newly acquired scroll into a little, paper ball with his hands, then throwing it through the bars of his cell as hard as he could, watching it land somewhere out there on the cold prison floor. His curiosity, however, got the better of him. With a sigh of defeat, he began to methodically unroll the tube.

He unrolled it slowly, first one inch then another. It didn't take long for him to notice a strange picture at the top of the parchment. It was some sort of symbol, almost like an insignia or letterhead. As he continued carefully unraveling the scroll, he began to make out just what the symbol was – a round, glass ball mounted on an intricately carved dark stone base.

The sphere was filled with a hazy, blue coloring and appeared to be some sort of crystal ball – very similar, in fact, to those supposedly used by wizards and sorcerers from long ago. He smiled as he imagined the ancient ones using a finely rolled alia leaf, almost like a straw, to blow smoke through a small hole in the ball, filling it with magical tendrils of swirling vapor.

The base of the ball on the parchment stood out much more than the ball itself. While the ball was a hazy, light blue color, the base, in complete contrast, was much darker and almost black.

The tiny carvings around the base appeared to be some kind of metal, which accentuated the detail on the carvings quite a bit.

As he continued to study the symbols on the scroll, his eyes were eventually drawn to the carvings on the stand, which served as a foundation to the crystal ball. He gently turned the scroll this way and that and squinted his eyes in the dim light of the prison cell, eventually drawing the scroll closer in an attempt to make out some of the finer details. With a small smile, he thought he could barely discern what appeared to be a castle on the left side of the carved base, and there, on the other side, was a beautifully drawn dragon. Its wings were spread in full flight and its neck was extended as if it was about to spew forth a burst of fire on whatever lay in the unseen darkness below.

Something at the center of the blue orb, just above the dark base, suddenly captured his attention. With regret, he pulled his eyes away from the carvings and focused on the round, glass ball mounted on top of the stand.

For less than a second, the blue color in the ball swirled briefly and the man gasped for breath in surprise. He stared at the scroll in disbelief as he instantly wondered if his imagination was playing tricks on him again. Although many strange things had occurred over the past few days, the man still couldn't help but question his imagination before questioning anything else. It had always been very active, and he was an absolute believer in the saying 'old habits are hard to break'.

With a puzzled expression on his face, he began to unravel the scroll further when something about the crystal ball caught his attention yet again. His hands stopped their movement as he stared at the carefully drawn, round object, fully prepared to chide himself and his overactive imagination.

This time, however, the movement in the blue orb on the paper was undeniable. He drew a breath again and before he realized what he was doing, he involuntarily dropped the scroll. It fell to the prison cell floor with a soft thud and rolled back up on its own as if it were a live creature instead of just an inanimate piece of paper.

Had he really just seen what his mind thought he had?

Was he losing his grip on reality?

The image on the scroll before he dropped it quickly came back to him like he was seeing it happen again. As he was unrolling the parchment, his eyes had been magnetically drawn back to the symbol at the top of the paper. The ball, itself, had turned an even lighter shade of blue, but that wasn't what had gotten to him. The reason he'd dropped the scroll had been because of something much more than swirling colors in the middle of the beautiful ornament on the paper.

For a split second, he thought he had seen a pair of eyes in the middle of the pale, blue haze that filled the ball... and he was certain they had been looking directly at him.

And they weren't just any eyes...

These eyes had been brightly glowing, orange, flame-colored eyes.

Nivri's eyes...

Was that possible?

After clearly seeing Nivri's face up close and personal during his last encounter with the evil sorcerer, the man knew he would recognize those blazing, orange eyes anywhere. Was the evil, black clad creature capable of doing such a thing? Would he be able to put his eyes into anything he desired, anytime and anywhere? The man had heard stories of powerful sorcerers and wizards who used to roam the lands, each wanting to be stronger and more powerful than the other, but those were just stories...

Weren't they?

There had to be some other explanation for what he had gone through in Nivri's chamber the previous day. He was certain there was some logical reason for the manner in which he had been lifted up off the ground as the creature in black stood by, watching. The pressure he'd felt on his back, incessantly pushing him down onto the floor, feeling as though he would soon be pushed into the floor, through the floor, if the pressure didn't stop...

His rational mind had been telling him time and again over the past two days that there had to be some reasonable explanation for all these things. The problem was that, unfortunately, it hadn't told him what the explanation was, and the man was getting tired of trying to figure it out.

Suddenly doubting he had seen a small portion of Nivri on the scroll before him at all, he bent down and picked the tube up off the floor, hesitating only slightly before beginning the task of unrolling it again. Although he continued to doubt he had really seen the sorcerer's evil, pumpkin-colored eyes glowing in the center of the crystal ball, he couldn't help but notice the unmistakable beating of his heart in his chest. In spite of his doubt, it was definitely beating faster…

Not surprisingly, his focus was immediately drawn to the symbol at the top of the page as he resumed unfurling the scroll with hands that now shook with nervous anticipation. The man didn't let his fear stop him as he continued to unroll the scroll. After a few seconds, he began to make out the picture of the hazy, light blue crystal ball, just like it had been before. As his gaze lingered on it, his heart began beating even faster when he realized that there, directly in front of him, was the unmistakable pair of glowing, orange eyes, staring directly up into his own brown ones.

He stopped unrolling the scroll and nervously held it out in front of him, his arms fully extended. Unsure of what to do, he remained motionless as his mind raced. He tried to think of what his next step should be in this bizarre situation.

"Human," a familiar, unwelcomed voice whispered.

His imagination began spinning and he thought for a split second that the voice was coming right out of the paper. Could it be coming directly from the eyes on the scroll?

"Nivri," the man answered back quietly.

As the sorcerer's name died on his lips, the man shifted his outstretched arms to his right, still holding the partially opened scroll away from his body. The orange eyes staring at him remained within the crystal ball, but as he moved the scroll slightly, the glowing orbs adjusted themselves within the circle of blue in order to maintain their focus on him.

"Your curiosity is predictable, human," Nivri's voice whispered. This time, however, it sounded as though the quiet, unsettling voice was everywhere around him.

"If you continue unrolling the parchment, you will see just what it is I am offering," the voice continued.

The man frowned slightly. He could almost hear a slight snicker as the voice continued.

"If you have any questions, I have made myself available to you and will be happy to answer them. Perhaps, in time, you will be able to return the favor and answer some of my many questions as well…"

The man's own eyes squinted with doubt at the picture on the top of the scroll. He did not trust Nivri, whether he was standing physically before him or was simply a pair of eyes somehow looking at him from a picture in the middle of an ordinary piece of paper. In no way, shape, or form did he trust the darkly-clad, pain-inflicting creature.

The man silently continued to unroll the scroll, trying his best to ignore the eyes as they watched him from the top of the page. Although he tried to appear very nonchalant about it, he found it very difficult to do.

"Nivri," the man began, "I am a man who respects a person's individuality and privacy. Can you please do the same for me and give me a few moments to read whatever it is you have given me? Perhaps I could read it without you hovering over me?" He struggled to keep the sarcasm out of his voice.

The sorcerer's eyes closed slightly. As the man watched the smaller, orange orbs buried within the larger blue one, he thought he could hear an evil, mocking laugh that was undoubtedly directed at him. The laugh sounded as though it was coming either directly from the paper or somewhere behind it.

"Do you find me that unnerving, human?" Nivri asked as he refocused his gaze on his prisoner.

"I would like a few moments of privacy if you don't mind," the man answered, ignoring the sorcerer's question.

"Very well then," Nivri answered, after giving it some thought. "I will allow you a few moments to read. If you have any questions, call my name and I will reappear."

With that, the glowing eyes instantly disappeared from the crystal ball on the picture. With a sigh, the man realized he was again looking at the drawing of a plain, round object, filled with a light blue haze.

As the man stared at the parchment, he noticed his hands were shaking. Thankfully, it was subtle enough he thought it unlikely that someone walking by his cell at that moment would have noticed anything odd about him. Not that they had much foot traffic in this part of the castle, but if someone *had* been walking by, they would simply see a prisoner standing calmly and quietly in his cell as he examined an unremarkable piece of paper.

The man noticed the effect the sorcerer's eyes had on him, however, and this bothered him. Feeling uncomfortable, he closed his own eyes and took a deep breath as he tried to throw an imaginary black veil over his nervousness. After several deep breaths, he opened his eyes again. Feeling as though his emotions were somewhat back under control, the man began to unroll the scroll.

His wide, dark brown eyes scanned the words written on the yellowed and wrinkled parchment he held in trembling hands and, not surprisingly, his mind doubted their meaning. Every few sentences, his gaze would drift back to the crystal ball symbol at the top of the page, but, true to his word, Nivri's glowing, orange eyes did not reappear.

With lingering doubts, the man continued reading. The words had been scrawled on the rolled paper in an obviously hurried hand.

"The following agreement is between the owner of this grand castle, Nivri, and the human who currently resides in the lower level of said castle.

"I agree to release the human if he will agree to the following terms and conditions:

"One – he will leave without question.

"Two – he will agree to a meeting with me, in order that I may assist him with any memories he may have of his time spent here. I cannot release him unless he agrees to speak to no one about anything he has seen while a resident in my humble castle. My assistance with this is mandatory, and if this condition is not agreed to, this entire agreement will be considered null and void.

"Three – he will not return to the Castle Defigo unless invited.

"If said human agrees to these terms, he will call for the guard, who will give him ink and a quill. He will sign his name below, and, after meeting with me, will be released immediately."

The man looked up from the paper in disbelief. After all the harassment and anger he'd experienced from the psychotic sorcerer over the past few days, out of the blue he was now going to be released?

This was unbelievable…

"Human, are you okay?" Zacharu asked quietly from the adjacent cell.

"Yes," the man answered in a low voice.

"What's happening?" Zacharu asked. "Are you still working on what you were working on before?"

"No," the man answered. "Orob brought me something."

"I couldn't see what he had in his hand," Zacharu said. "What was it?"

The man considered his new friend's question for a few seconds, unsure of what to do. As he grappled with the question of how much to share with Zacharu, he heard a familiar voice in his head whisper something that surprised him.

"Take him with you."

"Draco?" the man thought, but there was silence. He waited a few seconds for the mysterious creature to say more, but it only repeated itself before it fell silent.

"Take him with you."

The man hesitated for a few more seconds before answering his friend.

"It was a scroll."

"A scroll?" Zacharu asked in a questioning tone. "What's it for?"

Again the man hesitated briefly before he answered.

"Well, according to what's written on it, I'm about to be released."

Zacharu was silent as the prisoner's words sank in. The prisoner had said "I'm about to be released", not "we're about to be released."

"Zacharu," the prisoner began, but he was quickly interrupted by an obviously disappointed voice in the cell next door.

"It's okay," Zacharu said rather curtly. "I get it…"

"No, Zacharu, don't be that way," the man said. "I'm going to do what I can to get you out of here. I can haggle with him I think.

I'll tell him to release you with me."

"What?" Zacharu answered in a harsh, surprised whisper. "Are you out of your mind? If you anger him, he may change his mind and not release you at all! Don't lose your chance! If he's going to release you, go while you can…"

"Orob!"

The man's voice echoed off the dungeon walls, startling Zacharu.

"What are you doing?" Zacharu questioned, more harshly this time.

The prisoner ignored him as he called out again, "Orob, please bring me to Nivri!"

At the sound of his name being called, an iridescent image of the sorcerer immediately appeared in the rear corner of the prisoner's cell.

"You called?" the image asked.

Hearing a voice behind him, the prisoner whirled around and was shocked to see a transparent, ghostly apparition standing near the back wall, just a few inches away from his bed. Like the sorcerer, the apparition in his cell was clad in all black, and the man wasn't surprised to see two glowing, orange eyes looking at him.

"I would like to meet with you to discuss your proposal," the prisoner said to the ghostly image that floated just above the floor.

"Very well," the image replied in a smug, satisfied tone. As the man watched, the ghost slowly began swirling like a cloud of fog on a breeze for a few seconds before it disappeared into nothing but thin air.

"Human, what are you doing?" Zacharu repeated, completely unaware of what had just transpired in the cell next door.

"Please don't worry about me," Zacharu continued. "I'm sure it won't be long before I'm released and allowed to continue on in the castle as I had been. You must take this opportunity to go on your way. Hopefully, you will find your family…"

His words faded away as the sounds of footsteps were heard coming closer to the lower area of the castle. The man stepped away from the door of his cell, certain he was the object of this visit.

"Human," Zacharu began again, but the man spoke harshly in response.

"Hush!" he hissed.

Orob approached the prisoner's cell from the shadows of the tunnel that led to the upper floors of the castle. A set of shackles lay slung over one shoulder and his keys jangled loudly at his waist. The guard stopped and stared at the prisoner through the bars of the cell for a moment as if trying to communicate his thoughts to the tall, dark-eyed man. In one swift motion, Orob removed the cluster of keys from his belt and found the right one. The cell door unlocked with a squeak and a clunk, and the guard wasted no time before lifting the thick bar from its home on the outside of the door.

"Do not test me, prisoner," the guard muttered through clenched teeth. The man nodded in response, but said nothing.

"Give me your arms," Orob ordered. As the door to his cell swung open, the man held his arms out to the guard. Orob reached up and slid one set of shackles down from his shoulder and immediately wrapped a wrist restraint around each of the human's wrists. As they were locked into place, the man looked at Orob, but still said nothing.

For some reason, this interaction with the beagon felt different than those before it. The man couldn't quite put his finger on the exact difference, but he sensed a definite change in the guard. He was certain that if he tried to ask Orob what was going on, the only response he would likely get was a grumble. In spite of this he decided to try anyway.

"Orob," the man began.

His words left him when he heard a strange growling sound. The man didn't realize what it was until, without any warning at all, the beagon pushed him roughly up against his prison cell wall.

"Silence!" the guard ordered as he growled again.

Startled, but not wanting to upset Orob more than he apparently already was, the man nodded once to indicate he understood. No other words were necessary.

"Do not move," the guard ordered as his dark eyes flashed

angrily below course, hairy eyebrows.

Again, the man nodded and did as he was told.

Orob, certain the human would obey, turned and stepped out of the prisoner's cell, then turned left. He stopped and glanced at the human briefly and said, "Heed my warning, human, for I am not playing games."

Without waiting for the man to reply, the guard turned quickly and made his way towards the cell to the left.

"Stand up," the man heard Orob order Zacharu before he heard the familiar jangling sound of the large jumbled mess of keys at the guard's waist. He also heard the familiar sound of a key turning in a lock, the accompanying squeak, and the expected grating sound as the horizontal bar on the outside of the prison cell was lifted and set down on the cold, stone floor. The man obediently remained where he was and tilted his head to one side in an attempt at hearing the goings on next door.

"Come here," Orob ordered. The man wasn't surprised to hear the sound of a second pair of shackles as they were moved from Orob's shoulder.

"What are we doing?" Zacharu questioned, but the only answer he received was a muffled snort before Orob turned to look back at the previous cell.

"Human, come to me!" the guard ordered, ignoring Zacharu's question. Without a word, the man did as he was told and made his way out of his cell. Orob and Zacharu were standing just outside of Zacharu's cell, waiting for him.

The prisoner stopped next to his friend and looked at the guard expectantly. Orob glared angrily at each of his prisoners in turn for a few seconds before he finally spoke to them in a harsh, authoritative whisper.

"Do *what* you are told, *when* you are told to do it, and do not ask questions. Is this understood?"

The human was confused by the guard's odd order, but nodded as Zacharu said, "But I don't under…"

"Silence!" Orob grumbled through clenched teeth. The guard towered over Zacharu and suddenly leaned down, glaring at the shorter of the two prisoners.

"If you refuse to do as you are told, I will place you back in your cell and will let you ROT with the vile rodents who live down here in the dungeon!" Orob hissed.

Zacharu stared up at the guard and the man could see the smaller creature was now shaking with fear. He felt bad for his friend but felt helpless to do anything for him.

"Do… you… understand?" Orob said, pausing between words to emphasize the undeniable fact that he wasn't joking around.

Without waiting for Zacharu to answer the guard, the man laid a hand on Zacharu's shoulder as his restraints clattered together.

"Yes, Orob, we understand."

The guard stared down at the dwarfed figure next to him for a few more seconds before raising his narrowed eyes to look at the prisoner.

"Then let's go," Orob ordered as he pointed in the direction of the tunnel leading to the upper floors in the castle. The prisoner grabbed Zacharu by his arm and whispered his own command.

"Come on, Zac!"

Zacharu nodded, still shaken by the guard's reaction to his question. He walked in obedient silence beside the man as they made their way around the dungeon and up the ramp. Orob followed behind them, nudging the prisoner with the thick, wooden club he carried in his right hand. Although their hands were shackled together, both Zel and Zacharu were thankful that their feet remained unbound.

As the two prisoners made their way up the ramp leading to the upper levels of the dungeon, the man suddenly realized with dismay that after all the excitement involved in the guard preparing them for another journey into the upper regions of the dark, damp castle, he had forgotten, yet again, to get a look at the creature in the cell adjacent to his.

The mysterious creature being held there would, unfortunately, have to remain both unknown and unseen for a little while longer.

FOUR

The prisoners walked in silence as the guard prodded them up the dimly lit ramp. Just past the halfway point, Orob whispered to them in a raspy, quiet voice.

"Stop here."

Without question, both prisoners did as they were told. When the human glanced over his shoulder to look back at the guard, he was surprised to see Orob applying pressure to one of the many square stones in the passageway wall. To his astonishment, a hidden door opened inward just a few steps away. As far as he could tell, it led into a dark, gloomy tunnel.

"In here," Orob said in such a low voice it could barely be classified as a whisper. "Quickly!"

Zacharu was closer to the wall than the human, but the man did not hesitate to push the smaller prisoner through the doorway. He immediately stepped through it behind him.

"Hey!" Zacharu protested in a harsh whisper, thankfully remembering to keep his voice down.

"Keep moving, Zac" the human said, practically breathing down Zacharu's neck. "I'm right behind you."

Orob stepped into the passageway behind both prisoners.

"Wait right there."

The man and Zacharu stopped and turned to look back at the guard. Although the ramp leading to the upper floors of the castle had been dimly lit, it was nothing compared to the dingy, poorly lit tunnel Orob had brought them into. The prisoners watched in silence as the door to the former passageway closed quietly behind them, completely blocking the ramp from sight.

"Continue on," Orob said as he waved them to move deeper into the tunnel.

"Can we wait a moment for our eyes to adjust?" the man asked quietly.

Zacharu surprised him when he answered, "I think I can see the tunnel fairly well. I'll lead, if it's okay with you?"

He looked back at Orob who nodded.

Zacharu led the way and the man followed close on his heels. Not surprisingly, Orob remained only a step behind. They wound their way through the shadow filled tunnels for a few minutes before Orob growled his next order.

"Stop."

Both prisoners again did what they were told. Within seconds the man heard the familiar jingle of the key ring attached to Orob's waist.

"Give me your hands," the guard ordered gruffly.

Since the man was closer to Orob, he was the first to obediently hold out his hands. Although there wasn't much light in the tunnel, it didn't take long for the guard to find the keyhole on the shackle. He inserted his key and turned it, opening first one wrist restraint, and then the other. The man stepped back in order to let Zacharu move closer to Orob and the guard repeated the ritual. In less than a minute, the two prisoners stood before the guard completely unrestrained.

"Continue walking straight through until we pass three more intersections," Orob ordered.

Without a word, Zacharu turned and continued leading the way. When they found the third intersection, Zacharu stopped and turned back to the guard for guidance.

"There," Orob said as he pointed with his club, "just beyond the next turn, you will find a very dark, very short and narrow side tunnel to your left. Take it, and after twenty steps or so, you will find a ladder…"

The man raised an eyebrow and looked at Orob with a

questioning stare.

"Orob..." he began, but the guard held up his hand.

"Go up the ladder to the end – it will take you to an opening that leads to the outside. As you surface, you will find yourself inside a shallow, uninhabited, and partially hidden cave. There you will each find a sword and shield, as well as some fresh clothes and food," Orob explained.

"But..." Zacharu began, but again the guard held his hand up, silencing the prisoner.

"Remember your word to do as you are told!" Orob hissed angrily. "Go now, before it's too late!"

Zacharu glanced around the obviously empty tunnel as the man laid a hand on Orob's arm.

"Thank you," Zel whispered in a gentle voice. "I don't know why you are doing this, but whatever the reason is, thank you."

Orob nodded and reached into a small, black bag at his side. As the man watched in silence, the guard withdrew a light colored object and held it out to the taller of the two prisoners. The man held his hand out and the guard quickly, but gently, laid the object in the wide, outstretched palm.

As soon as the item touched his skin, the man felt his heart begin to beat faster. In the dimly lit tunnel, he recognized the drawing of the amulet on the alia leaf he'd left in his prison cell the previous day – or had it been the day before that? He smiled at the gesture and looked at Orob with silent thanks. He tucked the alia leaf into his shirt then nodded once at the guard before turning to nod at his fellow prisoner. Without another word, the two prisoners walked side by side in search of the narrow tunnel that would bring them face to face with freedom.

FIVE

Tonia stood as still as a tree while she stared at the creature moving toward her, afraid to hear whatever it was he was struggling to say. A moment ago, when he was trying to reassure them in hopes of finally gaining their trust, he had said something that brought back a memory from her past.

Her father, Uncle Andar, Tonia, and her brothers had gone hunting for valley quail a few years ago when they stumbled across a young growlie cat that was dragging a rabbit carcass across the rocks of a nearby hillside. As soon as it realized they were nearby, it anxiously dragged its kill by the neck in an attempt to take it to higher ground where it would likely try to dine in peace. When Tonia commented about how sad it was that the rabbit's revised purpose in life was to provide nourishment to the growlie cat, her father tried to console her by saying a single sentence to her.

"It is as it was meant to be."

It wasn't the exact statement the muck dragon had just said, but it was close enough.

Tonia saw this as a sign. Her father had been missing for the last year, and she and her friends were lost in this strange, unfamiliar world. In spite of this, it was as though her father was speaking to her from wherever he might be.

"It is as it was meant to be."

Staring into the muck dragon's eyes, Tonia began to shake with emotion as she whispered the three words the muck dragon had not been sure he would ever hear.

"I trust you."

The words weren't just coming from the young girl's mouth – this time he was certain they were coming directly from her heart.

As soon as her whisper faded into silence, the girls noticed movement in the mouth of the tunnel just above the muck dragon. The large, black spheres hovering against the ceiling suddenly started to twitch as if they were sharing in a group seizure. Within seconds, each one began to extend a half a dozen or more long, thin appendages from either side of its round, dark body.

"Watch out!" Tonia called out as she drew her sword and pointed at the above them.

"Kennard, over your head!"

The muck dragon glanced upward nonchalantly, apparently unconcerned about the activity happening almost directly over him. Just as Tonia realized what the dark objects were, Kennard spoke directly to her.

"Your friends in this world come in many shapes and sizes. Even better than that, they are not all dragons... or frogs, for that matter."

Tonia's sword began to tremble with fear at the scene taking shape above them and her mind struggled to accept what she thought she was seeing. As her trembling erupted into full-fledged shaking, Kennard spoke to her in a soft voice as he tried to reassure her that the creatures in the darkness above were their friends.

"Don't be frightened of them," he said calmly as fear filled her wide, brown eyes.

"Tonia," Kennard said to the panic-stricken young girl as she took first one step backwards, then a second. When her friends realized what was happening, they also drew their swords in uncertain defense.

Tonia didn't hear the muck dragon. Instead, both her mind and body were nearly overwhelmed with fear as she stared at the impossibly large arachnids in the dark space above them. As the three shadowy shapes shifted their positions, a familiar feature became obvious.

Each of the dark, round balls had a single pair of large, glowing, yellow eyes.

"Tonia!" Kennard said more forcefully this time. "It's okay. They are our friends."

"Tonia," Diam said quietly. "Remember what Nicho said back in the cave about the small spider we found on the ceiling in the room where Micah tripped? He said it was a glow spider and as far as he remembered, they were harmless."

"Yes!" Kennard agreed, "that's exactly right! These *are* glow spiders and they *are* harmless!"

Tonia stared doubtfully at the trio of hairy, spindly creatures above them, her sword trembling in her hand.

"Tonia, you said you trusted me," Kennard said reassuringly, "so please, trust me."

The young girl struggled to tear her eyes away from the creatures overhead, but eventually she forced herself to glance briefly at the muck dragon before returning her fearful stare back toward the spiders. Her sword was still drawn and shaking, but not as much as it had been a moment before.

"Tonia…" Kennard said quietly.

She moved her gaze back to the muck dragon, this time for a few seconds longer. Although the urge to watch the spiders was strong, she fought against it with every ounce of will power she had.

"You promise?" she asked. Her voice filled with doubt as she waited for his answer with baited breath.

"Yes… I promise," Kennard said.

The three girls stared up at the spiders for another long moment before Tonia slowly lowered her sword and returned it to its sheath. Following her lead, Diam and Kaileen did the same.

"Why are they here?" Tonia asked quietly, afraid to hear the answer. She continued nervously watching the spiders as two of the large, hairy creatures began stretching out their long, spindly legs. The third arachnid remained motionless as it curiously watched the activities below.

"They are here to help," Kennard said quietly.

"How?" Diam asked. She knew how much Tonia hated spiders and was certain her friend was having a difficult time even looking at the creatures above them in spite of the fact that they were at least twenty feet away.

"They will help you get to where you need to go at the top of the tunnel," the muck dragon explained.

Tonia suddenly came to life and glared at Kennard.

"Have you lost your frog-hopping mind? There's no way I'm going to accompany a single spider, much less three of them, anywhere! Especially not if it has anything to do with dark, unexplored tunnels!"

Kennard looked at her calmly.

"Okay. How do you propose you get up there, then? Do you have a few thousand feet of vines hidden somewhere in any, or all, of your bags? If you do, I'm sure our spider friends will be happy to carry one end of it up to the top of the tunnel and tie it off for you so you can climb it, one at a time, to the top..."

Tonia considered this and looked at Diam. They both knew they didn't have any tarza vines with them, especially any which would stretch from here to who knows where.

"I'm assuming your silence means you don't have enough vines, if any at all, to do the job, so let's try to think of something else," Kennard said as he stared off into the darkness. He dramatically placed one of his curled up front feet under his chin as if deep in thought.

"If we were to agree to accompany the spiders into the tunnel above," Diam began, "how would we do it?"

Kennard looked at her and smiled.

"Well, since the boat is out of the question, the next best mode of travel would be to either have you wrapped up in webbing and carried up," he said as he glanced at Tonia, "or we could effectively have you each ride to the top."

"Oh, joy," Tonia said sarcastically. "We could go from being lost adventurers to spider riders, all in the same day..."

Diam ignored her friend as her eyes squinted part way into the tunnel overhead before she dropped her gaze to the floor.

"You said I would need to wear the ring at the top of the tunnel, right?" she asked as she looked up at the muck dragon.

"Yes, that is correct," Kennard nodded.

"Okay, well why don't we have one of the spiders take me up to the top? Once I get there, I'll use the ring to get the amulet, come back down, and we can be on our way!" she suggested with surprising enthusiasm.

Tonia turned and stared at her best friend.

"What? Have you lost *your* mind now, too?" she asked as she shook her head from side to side in disbelief. "What would possess you to go up there alone?"

"Tonia," Diam began, "we both know you hate spiders, and I just can't see…"

Tonia raised her hand, interrupting her friend as her eyes blazed.

"No! I don't care how much I hate spiders! I won't allow you to go up there by yourself!" the younger girl said in a harsh, loud voice.

"Well what do you suggest we do then?" Diam yelled in angry response. "We don't have a lot of choices here, you know?"

"Why don't I go?" they heard a soft voice ask, and both girls turned to look at Kaileen.

"No!" they both said in unison. After a few seconds, Tonia looked at Diam and chuckled.

"Listen to us," she said quietly as she smiled at her friend. "I'm sorry, Diam. I didn't mean to yell at you."

"Same here," Diam said. "But Tonia, Kennard said I need to wear the ring up there, so I'll just go up and do what I have to do…"

"No," Tonia argued stubbornly. "I can't let you go up there alone. If you're going, I'm going with you."

"But…" Diam tried to argue.

"Diam, I can handle it," Tonia said. "I have to…"

"Then I'm going, too," Kaileen said. "I don't want to be left here alone…"

Diam smiled at the kalevala and rubbed her back.

"Thanks."

"Very good," Kennard said as he looked at Tonia. "I'm very proud of you for working through that!"

After smiling and nodding at each of the girls, he added,

87

"Well, are you ready?"

"As ready as we'll ever be," Diam offered as she threw a reassuring glance at her friends. After a few seconds she whispered to Tonia, "*You* can do this!"

Tonia nodded. When she set her mind to something, she could be as stubborn and focused as anyone else, but those darned butterflies were still fluttering around in the pit of her stomach like a horde of bees circling a giant honeycomb.

"Very well," Kennard said. "Let's get ready!"

As soon as he said this, the dark shapes clinging to the ceiling overhead began slowly making their way down the side walls of the passageway. Each time one of their eight legs made contact with the side of the tunnel and dug in to gain footing, a faint, muffled, rustling sound of sorts could be heard in the silence that filled the area around them. The arachnids continued climbing downward until they finally stood on the floor a few feet away from the girls.

Their large, round, glowing eyes reminded Tonia of the soft flames in a small campfire, changing from yellow to orange as each of the spiders slowly glanced from one girl to the next. Short, straight hairs poked outward all over their round, black faces, but their bodies appeared to be covered with a shorter, odd-looking material that looked more like fur instead of course hair. The long, sharp mandibles hanging down from each spider's gaping mouth twitched as if in anticipation of a meal.

Now that the trio of arachnids could be seen more clearly, the girls couldn't help but notice how each one appeared to have a wide, high-backed saddle of sorts resting firmly across their thoraxes. Each of these contraptions was strapped securely around their round, black bodies with thick, dark vines.

"Are those saddles?" Diam asked Kennard with surprise.

"And are they for us?" Tonia tacked on immediately after.

"Yes," Kennard answered. "As I said back at the puddle, we have been anticipating your visit. Our friends here were prepared for your arrival in hopes that they would be permitted to do their part in getting you where you need to go."

Changing the subject, the muck dragon asked, "Have you ever ridden a horse before?"

After gazing into the closest spider's eyes for a few seconds, Tonia tore her own eyes away and focused on Kennard.

"Yes. Not very often, but yes, Diam and I used to ride sometimes."

Diam agreed silently.

"Very good," Kennard said, "then consider what you are about to do as being nothing more than just a simple ride on a horse."

Tonia glanced at Kaileen as her face clouded with questions.

"Hang on a minute... Kaileen, you don't even know what a horse is, do you?"

Kaileen shook her head.

"No, but it's okay. I understand the concept, I'm sure."

"Are you sure you're okay with riding up there with us?" Diam asked.

"Yes, of course," the kalevala answered. "I'm with you both no matter what we must do."

She smiled reassuringly at her friends as Tonia mouthed, "Thank you."

"Very well then," Kennard said as he hopped next to the closest spider. "Why don't you come here and climb onto this one?"

The muck dragon looked at Kaileen and waved her over.

"Can I keep the torch as we go up the tunnel?" the kalevala asked as her voice shook with sudden doubt.

"Of course," Kennard said. "You will not only have the light from the torch, but you will also have the company of our glowing-eyed friends as well."

Behind the frog, a chorus of squeaks suddenly erupted from the area on the other side of the large rock which blocked their path. Without being prompted, a large number of gray rats hopped up onto the rock then scattered themselves around both the girls and the spiders.

"Wow," Tonia said quietly as she watched the scurrying rodents dart around the tunnel.

"No, the spiders won't eat the rats, although they very easily could," Kennard said, reading her mind. "These arachnids are different from most and prefer to feast on things like tree branches and mold that may be growing in different tunnels throughout the underside of the mountain."

"Hmm," Diam said as she nodded her head. She moved to stand next to Kaileen, being careful not to step on any of the rats around their feet.

"Kaileen, give me the torch so you can climb on."

The kalevala did as her friend suggested then moved toward the spider until she was right next to it.

"What do I grab onto?" she asked nervously. "I don't want to hurt it."

Kennard laughed.

"No, no, don't worry about hurting the spiders. They are a lot tougher than they look. Just grab a handful of fur and pull yourself up," Kennard suggested.

"Here," Tonia said as she took a few tentative steps forward until she was standing right next to her friend.

"Step into my hands and I'll boost you up."

Tonia bent over and clasped her hands together until her fingers were securely interlocked, creating a step for her friend. Without any further hesitation, Kaileen grabbed a handful of fur on the spider and lifted her bare foot into Tonia's makeshift step. As she pulled herself up, she felt her friend's hands rise up, giving her the boost she needed to get her right leg up and over the spider's back. As her backside landed in the saddle, the spider bounced a bit then stood quietly, waiting for the others.

"Okay?" Diam asked the kalevala.

"Yes," Kaileen answered. Diam smiled at her and handed back the torch.

"Tonia, you next," Diam then said.

"Nuh uh, you first," Tonia argued. She didn't think it was necessary to admit she didn't want to be on the spider any longer than she needed to be.

"Tonia," Diam said in a whiny, scolding tone. "You need to go first because you're shorter than I am. It will be harder for you to get into the saddle than me."

"Don't knock me because I'm shorter than you!" Tonia said argumentatively, but it was quite obvious the two girls were used to teasing each other. Kaileen sat quietly on her spider with her hands twisting and turning the spider's downy fur as she watched her friends. After a moment, she turned and glanced at the muck dragon. Surprisingly, he was watching the girls work together with an amused expression on his face.

"Ummmhmmm!"

Kennard cleared his throat, which sounded oddly like a very poor attempt at a frog-like '*croak*'. Diam and Tonia both stopped their bickering to look at him.

"Are you okay?" Kaileen asked in a worried tone, afraid something was wrong with their amphibian friend.

"Yes," he answered as he tried to disguise his embarrassment with a smile. "I was trying to get your attention."

Tonia giggled.

"Well, you certainly did that!" she said before turning her attention back to Diam. As if they were never interrupted, the two friends resumed their earlier conversation.

"Okay, Diam, I'll go next," Tonia said. She tried to sound defeated but didn't succeed very well.

"Okay," Diam said as they both made their way over to the spider behind Kaileen's.

Tonia stopped a few steps away, obviously nervous about what she was about to do.

"Trust us," Kennard encouraged her quietly as the young girl glanced back at him with nod of uncertainty.

"You'd better help me quick before I lose my nerve," Tonia whispered to Diam as she walked the final few steps toward the spider.

As soon as she reached the spider's side, Diam quickly bent down and made a stirrup of sorts with her interlaced fingers in the same manner as Tonia had done for the kalevala.

"Up you go," Diam said playfully as she boosted Tonia up and onto the spider's back.

While Tonia had been standing next to the abnormally large spider, her stomach lurched nervously and she almost lost her nerve. She took a deep breath in an attempt to calm down. She knew she needed to be strong, but having to be this close to not only a real spider, but one that was much larger than she'd ever dreamed she'd see, was almost too much. Like Kaileen, she

91

grasped a handful of the creature's fur as she prepared to mount it. She paused for a few seconds, surprised at how soft the texture felt in her hands when she suddenly found herself being boosted upward. As she landed in the saddle with a muffled *plop*, she looked down at her friend.

"Thanks."

Relieved Tonia didn't lose her cookies, Diam whispered up to her, "Are you okay?"

"Yeah, I'm dealing with it," Tonia said quietly as she took another deep breath. She closed her eyes for a few seconds as she tried to encourage the gigantic butterflies in her stomach to shrink down to moths.

"Your turn," Kennard said to Diam. "Do you need my assistance?"

"I'm not sure," Diam answered as she took the few remaining steps to get to the only unburdened spider. When she stood by its side, she peered into one of the creature's dark, round eyes and said, "I hope you're ready."

Without making a sound, the spider nodded once and leaned partially onto its side in order to make it easier for Diam to climb up. Understanding the creature's cue, Diam reached across the top of the spider's back and grabbed a handful of fur. Without further hesitation, she pulled herself up. As she slid into position, the spider leaned back in the opposite direction until it was upright again.

"Thanks," Diam whispered as she patted its side.

"Well done," Kennard said happily. "You're almost ready!"

Diam glanced back at Tonia with a worried look, but didn't ask the question that was written all over her face. Tonia nodded and gave her friend a look of reassurance.

"I'm okay," she mouthed.

"Alright, now that you're saddled up and ready to go," Kennard said enthusiastically, "let's talk about what happens next."

The frog hopped a few feet forward so he could be somewhat in front of the three girls.

"Our rodent friends will be accompanying you as you go in search of the Dragon's Breath amulet. They will not only guide you with their glowing eyes – they will also provide you with a warning system if they see anything that may be a cause for alarm.

"Once you reach the top of the vertical tunnel, you will likely find the air is not only thinner, but also much colder. If this is the case, you may need to permit our spider friends to wrap you in their webbing in order to keep you warm."

"Oh, boy," Tonia said quietly. In spite of her obvious unhappiness with the current topic of conversation, she turned to Kennard and tried to smile.

"I know, I know – trust you…" she said.

"Exactly," Kennard said. "I understand your apprehension, young one, but you must understand something. It is quite obvious that you do not care for spiders, but while you are in here, they are your friends, okay?"

Tonia looked at the frog with a measure of uncertainty, unable to hide either the doubt or nervousness covering her face. In spite of this, she nodded. No one could make the queasiness in her stomach go away or her pounding heart settle down just because they told her to believe something she felt she could never believe in a million years, but she could definitely try her best. All she could do was hope it would be enough.

With a nod, Kennard continued.

"When you reach the top of the mountain, you will probably be in a near-freezing environment, quite likely with temperatures that could make a wooly bear shiver. There might even be snow."

He stared at the girls for a few seconds as his words sank in.

"And I assume you are not prepared to handle this type of weather, am I correct?"

"Yes," Diam answered before Tonia could. "You're correct. We are definitely not prepared for any kind of cold weather."

"Alright then, since that is the case – if you suddenly find yourselves in the middle of a blizzard, what alternatives do you think you have?" Kennard asked.

Tonia sighed.

"I know," she said with a nod of defeat. "I understand what you're saying, but I don't have to like it."

"You say true," Kennard agreed.

"What do we do when – if – we retrieve the amulet?" Kaileen asked.

"Bring it back here and we'll continue through to the other side of the mountain," the muck dragon answered. "Once we get that far, I'm sure the dragon guard will be waiting for us."

"But… how will it know?" Kaileen asked.

"It will know because it will be able to see in my mind that we've recovered the gem!"

Each of the girls could hear the undisguised confidence and excitement in his voice.

"The saddles you are sitting in may seem a bit uncomfortable at the moment, but this is because they were designed with vertical climbing in mind," the muck dragon continued with another change of the subject. "If they were ordinary saddles, you would likely slide right off as the spiders began their ascent. However, because they are as wide and curved as they are, they should be very comfortable for you once you begin your trip up the tunnel."

"What can we expect when we arrive at the top?" Tonia asked as she focused on their upcoming journey instead of her mode of transportation.

"To be honest, I really don't know," Kennard answered with a frown. "Obviously, I can't accompany you, and things have changed quite a bit in this world since I've been cursed with living in the body of a frog instead of my true, dragon skin.

"It is rumored that the amulet is hidden in the cave of the snow bear, but I've also heard another story about it being hidden in an ice dragon's lair. Both stories indicated that it was hidden somewhere at the top of this mountain, so I'm not really certain what you will find once you arrive at your destination."

The muck dragon's gaze shifted from the girls to the tunnel over their heads. Cool air spilled down from the darkness above and swirled around them, although nothing but a ring of black could be seen beyond the mouth of the tunnel.

"You can be certain that the spiders and the rats will do whatever they can to help you in your journey, but you also must understand that much of what must be done depends on the three of you," Kennard said quietly.

"And of course, as I said a short time ago, if you fail, we all fail," he added.

Tonia nodded and looked at Kaileen.

"Are you ready to lead us?" she asked the kalevala.

"Yes," Kaileen said proudly.

"Is there anything else we need to know?" Diam asked Kennard.

The muck dragon shook his head negatively and sighed. He shook his head back and forth, sighed once more, then looked up at the girls as an obvious spark of something burned deep within him.

"There *is* one more thing, and I can't believe I almost forgot!"

The spiders were all shifting their weight slightly among each of their legs, obviously anxious to begin their ascent to the top of the mountain. The girls hardly noticed as they waited for Kennard to continue.

"When you arrive at the top, your first priority is to be very cognizant of danger – I'm certain there will be many shadowy places, such as nooks and crannies, for things to hide in…"

"Of course," Tonia reassured the dragon. "Especially if the amulet *is* up there somewhere, whoever put it there wouldn't have left it unguarded, would they?"

"Not likely," Kennard agreed. Again his eyes wandered to the tunnel overhead and the girls saw him stare into the darkness for a few seconds, deep in thought.

Diam wondered what the muck dragon was doing. Was he listening for something? Looking for something?

Before long, he turned to look back at the girls as his gaze focused on Kaileen.

"Look for a bag while you're there," he said quietly.

"A bag?" the kalevala asked with a frown. "What kind of bag?"

Kennard closed his eyes briefly as if trying to remember some missing part of a conversation.

"I can't be certain, but before I was changed into this… this… odd amphibian, I remember listening to some of the elder dragons as they discussed ways for our kind to fight for our freedom. Not all sorcerers are bad, and Scurio was one of the good guys. Many

95

moons ago, he used some of his magic to create a very special kind of dust called dragon dust, which he then placed in a large, sealed pouch. This dust can be used as a special defense against bad magic."

"Dragon dust?" Diam murmured as thoughts ran through her mind of Scurio using his magic to create the special powder.

"What does the pouch look like?" Tonia asked.

"I've never seen it so I can't be certain, but I've heard that if you see it, you will know, because it is decorated with the colors of the rainbow," Kennard explained.

"Like the stones," Diam whispered as Tonia nodded her head.

"Wow," Kaileen agreed.

"Unfortunately, there is nothing more I know to tell you," the muck dragon said, "other than to say that although I can't physically accompany you on the next step of your journey, I will be with you. I will be able to read your minds, of course, and Tonia, I may even be able to communicate with you as well."

The young girl nodded and turned to Kaileen.

"Okay then, lead the way."

"May the magic of the dragons accompany you, now and always," Kennard said quietly. "I will be waiting for your return..."

As if on cue, the spiders straightened and began making their way to the far wall. Without looking back, they each began climbing up the wall that would lead them into the tunnel above, one at a time. Kaileen's spider was in the front while Diam was in the middle. Tonia brought up the rear. It didn't take long for her to shift in her saddle in search of a more comfortable position. While doing this, she held onto the spider's fur on both sides of its round, warm body. After a few seconds, she glanced back to look at Kennard. He was sitting down in the same place he had been in when they left him. A small, reassuring smile covered his toad-like face.

She hoped she would see him again, sooner rather than later.

Six

The pair of prisoners made their way cautiously into the short, nearly pitch black tunnel. For a few seconds, they walked side by side, but eventually Zacharu took the lead. It wasn't long before he began whispering questions to the man, who silenced him with a hushing noise. They could barely see where they were going in the dark tunnel, so the man didn't bother placing his index finger in front of his closed lips to emphasize their need to be quiet. He was certain Zacharu understood the meaning of his wordless gesture, especially when the odd creature fell into an abrupt silence and remained there. It didn't matter anyway – Zacharu was now walking slightly in front of him, leading him through the darkness, so it's not like the shorter of the two prisoners would have seen his gesture even if the tunnel had been illuminated by some form of lighting.

It didn't take long for Zacharu to find the ladder Orob had described. As he grabbed one of the wooden upper rungs and began to step on a lower one, the man placed a large, strong hand on his shoulder.

"Wait. Let me go first," the man whispered from just inches away from Zacharu's ear.

Zacharu nodded without saying anything and obediently moved to the side of the ladder to allow the human to ascend into gloomy pocket overhead.

As the man slowly pulled himself up the rungs that led to some unseen, mysterious destination, his mind became a whirlwind of questions.

Why had Orob done this for them? Why would the guard risk his life to free them, especially after Nivri agreed to free him after wiping out his memory of his stay in the castle? Was it because Orob wanted to free Zacharu as well, and perhaps the guard knew Nivri would never agree to it?

As he continued to ponder the recent turn of events, he placed hand over hand and pulled himself methodically upward. After a moment, he glanced up and detected a very dim light in the tunnel looming overhead. He began to move faster, pulling himself towards the light as his heart thudded deep within his chest. Beyond the sound of his own heartbeat, the only other thing he heard was the faint sound of Zacharu climbing the ladder somewhere below him. The higher he climbed, the more he could feel cool, fresh air drifting down from above, swirling all around him like a mystical caress. He opened his mouth and took a deep breath as he made his way up the final ten rungs. The cool night air, so different from the stale air that filled the dungeon area of the castle, felt wonderful on his tongue.

Ah, this is what freedom tasted like.

He smiled.

After pulling himself up countless roughly designed ladder rungs, the prisoner came to a halt when he surfaced exactly where Orob said he would, in a partially hidden, dimly lit cave. He stopped abruptly as his head broke the surface. He glanced around with cautious eyes, allowing his focus to rove from one side of the cave to the other. Once he made sure the coast was clear, the man hastily climbed the rest of the way out of the tunnel. Without a sound he turned and reached down, grabbed Zacharu's outstretched arm and lifted him out of the hole. As soon as Zacharu was steady, the man released his arm and looked more closely at the area around them.

He was relieved to see the cave appeared to be deserted except for a single, flickering torch jutting out of the far wall. Leaning against the wall beneath the burning stick were two swords and two shields, two belts with sheaths, and a flat, square rock.

Resting on this rock were two bulging brown leather bags. One sword and shield set was obviously larger than the other, which was a good thing since the size difference between the human and non-human creature was quite significant.

The man cautiously made his way over to the cluster of items and picked up one of the bags. He opened it and dumped the contents out on top of the rock, taking a few seconds to shuffle through the contents. He quickly identified the items to be some kind of dried meat, a pair of rock sparkers, an odd-looking torch and a bottle of unmarked liquid. He opened the bottle and smelled the mysterious contents. He looked at Zacharu, shrugged and hesitated briefly before taking a small sip – it was water.

"I guess he wasn't kidding," the man said quietly as he took another small sip before offering it to Zacharu, who refused with a curt shake of his head. The man nodded and closed the bottle, then bent down and picked up the larger of the two belts. He immediately fastened it around his waist then grabbed the larger of the two swords and sheathed it without giving it much thought.

"I don't think we should stay here," Zacharu whispered cautiously as he joined the man. He turned a nervous glance back at the gaping hole in the floor then snatched the other belt from the pile. He secured it around his waist then took possession of the remaining sword and placed it in his own sheath. Like the man, he appeared to be very comfortable with a weapon.

Once his sword was secure, Zacharu turned his attention to the remaining leather bag on the rock. Without speaking, he opened it up and glanced inside. With a curt nod of his head, he closed it securely, slung it over his shoulder, and looked up at the man expectantly.

"I agree," the man finally answered quietly before turning his own attention toward the opening of the cave. A solid, uninviting darkness filled the area just beyond the entrance.

"I think we'll be safer out there than we are in here, especially knowing the lower part of the castle is just below us. I'd feel more comfortable if we got as far away from here as we can get right about now," the man whispered.

Zacharu nodded and whispered, "I'm ready when you are."

The man nodded.

"Let's go."

They turned and headed toward the mouth of the cave, focused on the darkness beyond. Neither of them looked back. If they had, they might have seen the single pair of dark, curious eyes watching them just below the opening where they had surfaced just a few minutes before.

SEVEN

After guiding his prisoners to the secret ladder leading out of the Castle, Orob immediately turned headed back the way he had come. When he reached the hidden doorway, he stopped and listened for footsteps in the hallway on the opposite side of the wall, but heard none. He quickly opened the door, stepped into the passageway, and silently closed the opening behind him.

Since it was such a late hour, only a few guards walked the halls of the castle. He made his way through the passageways in the lower tunnels and eventually came across two guards meandering around, obviously killing time. As he approached them, one of the guards turned and headed in his direction. Orob made eye contact with his fellow guard and nodded a single, respectful nod. Without hesitation, the guard returned the gesture. Once he was past the guard, Orob held his breath as he listened to the receding footsteps behind him. He sighed with relief as the footsteps eventually faded into silence. Hearing this, he turned down another tunnel. When he reached the end, he took a deep breath and entered the room to his right – the Guard Room.

After entering the long, narrow room, the door swung shut behind him. A few dozen faces looked up at him as he made his way silently across the room to the long table near the far wall.

"Is it done?" one of the guards asked.

Without waiting for a response, the guard raised a deep, brown bowl to a pair of dark, hairy lips, and then slurped noisily at the contents. As he did so, a few thick drops of liquid dribbled down his hairy chin and fell noiselessly to the shadowy void between the table and his body. When he lowered the bowl back to the table, the guard ignored the dark green colored mustache pasted on top of his ebony and chestnut facial hairs. After a brief delay, he licked his lips and stared at the newcomer with no emotion on his burly face.

Orob glanced into the bowl and allowed his eyes to linger on a thick green gruel – the usual, it seemed. In spite of this, his stomach grumbled, but he ignored it. He didn't have time to think about eating right now.

"Yes, it is," Orob answered. "We must move quickly."

His fellow guards, all beagons like him, stood up and began quietly gathering their things. The guard eating the soup remained seated as he picked up his bowl and raised it one final time to his lips, tipping his head back and slurping noisily as he emptied the contents of the bowl into his mouth. He then lowered the bowl and set it down on the table with a *clunk*, wiped his liquid mustache away with the back of one large, hairy hand, then stood up and made his way to a bag sitting on the floor next to the wall behind him. As he leaned to pick up the bag, he released a long, loud belch.

"Ah, my compliments to the cook," the guard said with a satisfied smile to no one in particular. The other guards in the room chose to ignore him.

When the eating guard raised the bowl to finish his soup, Orob noticed something that instantly caught his attention. On the table beneath the bowl, his hungry eyes spotted a thick piece of apparently forgotten, dried chickenbird. Once the soup-eating guard walked away from the table, Orob considered this a sign of rejection concerning the piece of meat. His stomach grumbled, more loudly this time, in anticipation of the small and obviously discarded piece of food. In Orob's eyes, it was a meal, no matter how small, and he quickly snatched the piece of dried meat from the table as his mouth began watering in anticipation of sustenance. He took a quick bite then glanced around the room at his fellow guards. A few were watching him silently, waiting for a sign. Others continued gathering their things, mumbling quietly to each other in the flickering torch light that filled the room with a soft, yet unwelcoming, pale, yellow glow.

"I must do one more thing before we go," Orob said quietly. "I wanted to let you know that part one has been completed. As soon as I do this last thing, we will be ready."

Without waiting for a response, the guard turned and headed back toward the door. On any other night, any normal night, a large percentage of the guards currently gathered in the guard room would have been sleeping, but tonight was definitely not a normal night.

Tonight their lives would change forever.

EIGHT

Each of the girls held onto a clump of thick, velvety spider fur as the large, lumbering arachnids made their way up the vertical wall in single file. They traveled in silence for a short time until Diam thought she heard Kaileen whimpering ahead of her.

"Kaileen, are you okay?"

"Yes," the kalevala answered quietly.

Although she tried to sound brave, Kaileen couldn't help it when she hastily shoved the flaming torch into the darkness in an attempt to illuminate the pit of blackness surrounding them.

Diam shrugged and turned to look back over her shoulder. "Tonia?"

"Yes," her friend answered, understanding Diam's concern and loving her all the more for it. "I'm fine."

Diam turned and stared ahead as her spider methodically carried her higher and higher into an unseen world of darkness filled with unidentifiable shadows. She smiled as she thought about how riding a spider was quite different from riding a horse... which was probably a good thing, because if her mount decided to take off and start running up the tunnel, Diam was certain she would go flying out of the makeshift saddle. Even worse than that, the ground here was a heck of a lot further away than the ground would ever be under a horse.

That settled it. She wrapped both hands deep into the spider's fur as her thoughts drifted to the piece of jewelry she carried in her pocket. Kennard said she would know the right time to wear the ring when they reached the top of the tunnel, but Diam was afraid she really wouldn't know when that time would be. Could she just put it on and wear it so it would be in place when, and if, the right time ever arrived?

She sighed. She definitely didn't want to turn into a million dust particles floating down onto Kennard's head before this strange day was through. She had too many things she wanted to do with her life! Places to go! People to see!

...Spiders to ride!

The accompanying rats climbed the walls in an disorganized frenzy, zigzagging this way and that as their glowing red eyes added extra lighting to areas of the tunnel both above and below the spiders. Every so often a small group of rodents would wander away to explore much smaller tunnels and crevices as they traveled, but for the most part they stayed with the main group as it slowly wound its way higher and higher toward the upper reaches of the tunnel.

"It's getting colder in here... can you feel it?" Kaileen asked as she swayed back in forth in the saddle with the gait of her spider. She didn't need to look back to know her friends weren't far behind.

"Yes," Tonia replied.

As she followed her friends and their spiders, Tonia remembered what Kennard had said about the possibility of the spiders needing to wrap the girls with webbing to keep them warm. How in the world would they do that if they were thousands of feet above floor level? Would the spiders take turns spitting gossamer strands through the air, aiming for each girl where she sat in the saddle? She dismissed this thought as a rather dumb idea on her part and decided not to worry about it until it happened, *if* it ever happened at all.

They traveled in silence, minus the squeaking rats and flickering torch flame, for quite a while when an opening mysteriously appeared ahead. It was behind a wide rock that jutted like a misplaced finger on the right side of the tunnel. Instinctively, the first spider climbed around the rock and turned into the opening with slow, cautious steps. Once it was standing on the flat surface, it paused and searched the area for any signs of trouble. As expected, the remaining spiders were just a few paces behind.

"What are we doing?" Diam asked as her voice shook with uncertainty. Tonia and Kaileen looked at their friend as she spoke, immediately noticing how thin streams of white mist exited Diam's mouth with every word. The temperature in the upper area of the tunnel had dropped significantly – enough so that they could easily see her breath.

The small group of explorers allowed their roving eyes to survey the nearby area, noticing the flat, somewhat open area had no other visible entrances.

"Tonia?"

The voice in her head startled the young girl and she jumped in her saddle, squeaking with surprise. Both Kaileen and Diam glanced over to see what was wrong, which Tonia caught out of the corner of her eye. It only took her a second to recognize the voice and she quickly reassured her friends that she was okay.

"Hang on – Kennard is trying to talk to me."

"Yes?"

"The spiders tell me you have reached the landing that is close to the top. Is this correct?" Kennard asked.

Diam and Kaileen watched Tonia as she stared into the flickering torch flames as if in a semi-trance. She nodded her head every once in a while as she continued her silent conversation with the muck dragon, located somewhere in the shadows far below.

"Very good," Kennard said. "Do you see a large, flat rock next to the wall somewhere near where you are?"

Tonia tore her eyes away from the amber colored flame to look around the shallow cavern. It only took her a few seconds to spot the rock. It was near Diam.

"Yes."

"Good," the muck dragon said. "This is where a large part of the trust I asked you for comes into play, my friend. Are you up for it?"

Silence filled the mental conversation for a few seconds as

Tonia hesitated.

"Yes, I'm ready."

Down below, Kennard breathed a silent sigh of relief.

"Very good. The next part of the plan is for each of you to climb down from your spider, put on any layers of clothing you may have stashed away inside your bags, and then allow the spiders to wrap their insulated webbing around your bodies in sections."

"Mmmmmmmm."

Tonia's muffled, unhappy response echoed throughout the small, gloomy cavern in a tone indicating she didn't care for the muck dragon's suggestion. Although she did not like it, she knew it would be useless to argue. She understood this was something that just needed to be done.

"Suck it up!"

Micah's voice whispered to her from somewhere in the back of her mind, and in spite of the uncomfortable situation she was in, she found herself smiling.

Diam and Kaileen watched their friend in silence, heard the strange sound she made from somewhere deep within her throat, and then saw her odd, unexplained smile.

"That must be some conversation," Diam whispered to Kaileen, who nodded with a chuckle. Fortunately, Tonia didn't notice.

"Once you have been clothed and insulated against the cold, you should be able to climb back on your mounts and proceed the rest of the way to the top of the mountain," the muck dragon continued.

"Okay," Tonia answered in her mind while out loud she added, "We need to dismount."

"Um, okay?" Diam replied in a confused tone, but before she could ask any of the questions that were beginning to fill her mind, Tonia answered the most important one.

"We need to move over to that rock and climb down," she said as she pointed at the nearby stone. "Then we need to put on any extra clothing we may have with us."

Understanding the conversation between the girls, Diam's spider moved in order to be directly next to the rock to make it easier for Diam to climb down. As it carried her the short distance to the stone, the taller, dark-skinned girl looked over at Kaileen and frowned when an unfortunate thought filled her mind.

Before Diam and Tonia left their village, they had each only grabbed one change of clothing because neither of them had any idea they'd be in the predicament they were in now. As a result, neither of them had a spare set of clothes for the much smaller friend they'd made acquaintances with back in the cave.

"You can wear my long sleeved shirt," Diam offered.

As soon as she finished speaking, Diam felt her spider flinch beneath her as it waited expectantly next to the large rock. She rubbed its smooth, bulky neck and hastily climbed down. When she felt solid ground beneath both feet, she wasted no time before moving to the far side of the rock. When she was safely out of the way, she pulled her bag off her back and immediately began rummaging through it.

"And my leggings," Tonia offered as Diam's spider moved away from the stone and Tonia's took its place. In a few seconds, Tonia stood next to Diam and began digging through her own bag for clothes.

"Even though we're going to put on additional clothing..."

She stopped mid-sentence and took a deep breath, hardly able to believe she was actually going to suggest the next step in the plan with as much calmness as if she'd just said to her mother, "I'm taking the mud puppy for a walk..."

Diam looked at her friend, sensing her unease.

"We need to allow the spiders to wrap us in their webbing to help insulate us from the cold," Tonia finished in an obviously uncomfortable tone. "Our clothes alone won't protect us."

"It's okay," Kaileen said softly as she looked from Tonia to Diam. "I'll just let the spiders work their magic on me. You can keep your clothes."

"Are you sure?" Diam asked.

"Certainly," Kaileen answered as she patted her spider on its side.

Tonia's spider moved out of the way to allow Kaileen's to move next to the rock, and both Diam and Tonia helped the height challenged kalevala climb down.

"Oh, it feels wonderful to get down and stretch," Kaileen said as she extended both arms out in front of her. As she spoke, the torch she still held threw a mixture of long and short shadows dancing across the far wall of the cavern.

"It sure does," Diam agreed as she raised her arms over her head, clasped her hands together and stretched upward.

Within a few minutes Tonia and Diam had put on their extra sets of clothes then turned their attention back to the spiders. While the girls continued chatting, each of the three arachnids spaced themselves out from each other as they stood guard.

"What's next?" Diam asked Tonia quietly.

Tonia closed her hand into a fist and raised an index finger into the air, signaling for Diam to wait.

"Are you ready?" Kennard asked in Tonia's head. After glancing at her friends and fellow creatures, the young girl nodded her head even though the muck dragon couldn't see the gesture.

"Yes."

Diam saw Tonia silently move her head and figured she was probably talking to Kennard again, so she waited patiently for the wordless conversation to finish. She glanced at the spiders noting how they stood like lifeless statues in the shallow cavern. As far as she could tell, not even a single hair moved on any of them.

Were they even breathing?

"Okay," Tonia said out loud. As her voice echoed around the small group, she turned and faced the spiders.

"Aranea!"

The trio of arachnids immediately jolted to attention and turned around to face the young girl where she stood tall and completely erect, directly in front of the rock.

"Are you prepared to help us on the rest of our journey?" she asked their friends with many legs. Each spider nodded its head and raised and lowered its front right foot – up, down, up, down – stomping loudly on the cavern floor. The repetitive motion created a strange chorus of dull, thudding echoes around them.

"Very good," Tonia said, looking from one spider to the next and nodding her approval. Kaileen and Diam watched the amazing transformation of their friend from an arachnid-fearing young girl to an order-toting young woman.

Tonia turned a pair of blazing, auburn, confident eyes toward the kalevala.

"Kaileen, please stand near the edge of the rock and follow my directions."

Kaileen nodded as Diam slowly shook her head in astonishment. She was completely baffled, in a good way, with the surprising changes in her best friend.

"Diam, take the torch from her so she can do this without worrying about dropping it," Tonia ordered.

Without a word, Kaileen handed the torch to Diam and moved to the edge of the large, flat stone.

"Okay," Tonia said as she took a shallow breath and tried to gather her thoughts.

"Hold your arms straight out at your sides, like this."

Tonia demonstrated by holding her arms out away from the sides of her body, forming herself into a 't'.

"At the same time, spread your legs until they're about shoulder's width apart."

Kaileen did as she was told while Tonia smiled and nodded.

"Yes, like that," Tonia said before turning back to the spiders.

"Aranea, we will call you in number according to how we traveled up the tunnel."

Looking at Kaileen's spider, she said, "You will be Number One." Without waiting for any acknowledgment, she pointed at Diam's spider she said, "You will be Number Two, and mine will be Number Three. Understood?"

The girls and spiders all nodded their understanding.

"Good. Aranea, very carefully work together and wrap our friend in a warm layer of your silky webbing, please."

Each of the spiders nodded, stomped its front right leg on the ground as a sign it acknowledged the order, and took its place next to the rock. As the girls watched, the center spider turned slightly until its back side was facing Kaileen while the two outer spiders remained facing the kalevala. The middle creature dropped the front part of its body downward and lifted its back end up slightly, then slowly began spraying a smooth, gentle

110

stream of webbing from its abdomen. As the gossamer strands flowed toward Kaileen, each of the outer spiders used their front legs to control the stream, guiding it first around one wrist, then her torso and eventually down each leg. As the stream reached the end of her second wrist, the spiders then guided the line of webbing backward, adding a second layer of insulation expertly over the first. As soon as they ended at the first wrist, the flow of webbing stopped and the spiders waited patiently for the next girl.

"Wow," Diam said quietly. "That was amazing."

Kaileen remained motionless, almost afraid to move, but after a second or two she finally looked down at her friends. Except for her hands, feet, and head, she was completely wrapped in a glistening sheet of white silk.

"Am I done?" she asked in a quiet tone.

"Yes," Tonia answered as she moved toward the kalevala.

"Diam, let's help her down."

Diam moved quickly to join Tonia and together they helped lower Kaileen down to the rocky floor of the cavern.

"How does it feel?" Diam asked. She was both curious and surprised to find that the insulation was soft and relatively dry, not sticky, which was the complete opposite of what she expected.

"Strange," Kaileen answered quietly, "but much warmer, for sure."

As if to emphasize the difference, the kalevala took a deep breath and exhaled a few puffs misty air from her mouth. Small gray clouds of vapor appeared in the air and quickly dissipated.

Tonia smiled at the kalevala's reaction, nodded, and then turned to her other friend.

"Diam – you next."

"Yes, ma'am," Diam answered in a teasing tone. She handed Tonia the torch before climbing up onto the rock. Kaileen and Tonia stepped back to let the spiders do their work.

In a few minutes, Diam was wrapped much the same way Kaileen had been. When the spiders were through, the older girl¬ jumped awkwardly off the rock, landing almost silently on the dusty cavern floor.

"Be careful!" Tonia scolded before handing Kaileen the torch.

With a brief, motherly frown towards Diam, she prepared to climb up onto the rock.

"I'm fine," Diam answered when she suddenly gasped.

"What's wrong? Tonia asked in an alarmed tone as she looked down at her friend. Diam was digging frantically at the area around the upper front part of her thigh.

"The ring!" Diam answered as her voice shook nervously. "I have to be able to get to the ring!"

She clawed at the webbing in the area where her pocket would have been. After a few seconds she finally managed to find a narrow gap just wide enough to reach through. She dug her fingers into the thin space in the webbing and smiled with relief when she felt the cool piece of jewelry.

"Wow," she said with a sigh. "These spiders are smart! They left me a way to get to it!"

"Good," Tonia nodded as she climbed onto the rock.

Although she was still a bit nervous about letting the spiders wrap her up in their webbing, she knew she needed to trust Kennard. The air in the tunnel had been continually growing colder the higher they climbed. Like her friends, she had also begun shaking a few minutes before they had stopped and she understood that if they didn't do this now, it probably wouldn't be long before they were very uncomfortable from the cold.

They needed the spiders and, although she would never in a million years admit it to anyone, she was glad they were here.

In a few minutes, all three girls were sufficiently covered with the shiny, white webbing. With their insulation job completed, the spiders spread out in the cavern standing protective sentry in the shadows.

Diam giggled and Tonia looked at her, puzzled.

"What's so funny?"

"We are," Diam said. "Do you know how silly we must look?"

"Yeah, I do," Tonia said. "Can you imagine how much Micah would totally harass us if he were here?"

"Oh, don't even go there," Diam said with a knowing wave of her hand. "He would be totally merciless, I'm sure!"

The girls laughed together and Kaileen smiled. She had only been with Micah briefly in the cave before they stepped into the rainbow portal, but she could just imagine how much fun he would be to have around – well, providing she didn't give him anything to harass *her* about!

"Let's get ready t…" Tonia began when she suddenly stopped in mid-sentence.

Diam stared at her friend and realized that this time Tonia's expression was different than before. The last time she'd been having a mental conversation with Kennard, her gaze wandered off as she stared distantly at the flickering torch flame. This time, Tonia's face and eyes were filled with a mixture of both fear and surprise. The rats wandering around the cavern suddenly began emitting a high-pitched, squealing alarm as soon as they understood what Tonia was being told. The softly glowing red eyes on each of the rodents quickly brightened to a fiery crimson, and all of the ruddy colored creatures ran toward the place where the girls had been standing next to the rock.

"Tonia, what is it?" Diam asked.

Without waiting for Tonia to answer, Diam instinctively wrapped her hand around the handle of her sword as the all too familiar butterflies began moving like tidal waves deep within her belly. As soon as she heard the tension in Diam's voice, Kaileen unsheathed her own weapon and took a few steps forward in order to be closer to her friend.

The spiders immediately came to attention and each stomped a front foot on the ground, creating muffled thuds that could barely be heard over the crescendo of rodent squeals filling the cool air of the cavern. This time, instead of stomping a few times and stopping, however, the spiders carried on with this repetitive motion for nearly a full minute before stopping in unison.

From where she stood next to the rock, Tonia appeared not to hear or notice the actions of the spiders. Instead, her eyes were partially closed as she concentrated on the voice in her head. Just a few seconds after the spiders ended their odd stomping behavior, the young girl suddenly came back to life.

"Aranea, protect us!" she shouted as she extended her arms out from her sides. The spiders immediately responded by jumping like fat, black frogs across the cavern floor toward the girls.

"What's happening?" Kaileen asked. Although fear could be heard in her voice, the kalevala didn't hesitate to raise her sword in a defensive posture. She stood close to Diam as her eyes darted nervously around the room.

After issuing the order to the spiders, Tonia leaped off the rock and landed with a thud next to her friends. In seconds, the spiders had the girls surrounded, nearly smothering them with their furry backs as they forced them into a tight circle. The spiders immediately reared up in a defensive posture as Tonia and Diam simultaneously drew their weapons.

"Kennard has warned me that there is movement at the top of the tunnel," Tonia quickly explained. "He can't see what it is, but he definitely senses some kind of activity above us. He said our newly acquired insulation may provide some measure of protection if there's a conflict, but he can't guarantee it..."

"But why..." Diam began.

Tonia interrupted her friend before she could finish by shaking her head, indicating she didn't know. After a few seconds she said something that made each of their hearts skip a beat with an unnerving mixture of both fear and nervous anticipation.

"Whatever is up there is heading directly for us."

NINE

Zel and Zacharu struggled to make their way through the cool, shadowy forest for a long time before they finally took a chance at having a quiet conversation. Although they couldn't see many details in the dense plant life around them, every so often they saw an opening in the trees overhead – a window to a strange world above which held countless tiny, blinking stars. After a while they reached an area with a vast cluster of rocks in all shapes and sizes. It was here they finally stopped to rest.

"You know, for a while there I was really questioning whether or not I'd ever see life outside those darn dungeon walls again," the man with a sigh of happiness as he stared at the twinkling lights over them.

"It sure is beautiful out here."

"Yes," Zacharu agreed, "and the fresh air is almost as sweet as a spring flower."

Zel nodded and leaned back against a large rock formation. After sitting in comfortable silence for a few minutes, the smaller of the two prisoners finally spoke up.

"What do you think we should do now? Did Orob tell you anything about where we should go or what we should do?"

"No," the man answered as he closed his eyes, enjoying the cool night air. "I'm wondering if we should rest here, at least until daybreak, so we can determine which direction we're traveling in."

Eventually he opened his eyes and stared up at the trees.

"If I could see the full sky, I could get a pretty good idea, I think, but since I can't see more than just a few stars, I really have no idea which way we're going."

"I think we should head west," Zacharu offered in a quiet, relaxed tone.

"Why is that?" Zel asked as turned to look at his friend.

"I don't remember," Zacharu answered, smiling sheepishly. "It just seems right that west is a good direction."

"Well, let's rest here for a bit before we move on," the man suggested. "You try to sleep for an hour while I keep watch, then I'll sleep while you keep watch."

"Fair enough," Zacharu said before shifting his smaller body into a more comfortable position. The man was amazed to hear his friend softly snoring a few minutes later.

Although the forest was fairly dark and full of shadows, the prisoner's eyes had adjusted quickly to the scarce light and he was able to see the area around them quite well. Numerous tall trees surrounded them on all sides, including the area directly overhead, which seemed very odd considering they were in a decent sized grove filled with nothing but rocks. As he looked more closely at the canopy overhead, he realized the uppermost branches on the trees stretched out an extraordinarily long distance from the base of the trees themselves. This seemed quite strange to him and he told himself he might get a better look at the upper reaches of the trees after sunrise. He had no way of knowing by the time the shadows of night had evaporated into the light of day, his mind would be in totally different place. The celebration of his recent freedom would be soon shattered with unforeseen tragedy and overwhelming grief.

After a few moments, the man lowered his eyes to ground level and peered around, but other than countless shadows and the cool night air, he didn't see, hear, or feel anything out of the ordinary. He allowed his gaze to move from one shadow to the next as his mind wandered back to his recent time spent in the castle and Nivri's insatiable insistence that there were magical abilities in his family.

116

Could there be something there that he wasn't aware of? His wife? His children? His relatives? His neighbors? Could some of them, or all of them for that matter, have possessed some form of magic or special ability that he hadn't seen, felt, or heard about?

He sighed. If anyone from the village possessed any special abilities whatsoever, he had totally and thoroughly not seen a single, solitary sign – at all.

After allowing his thoughts to focus completely on his wife and children for a while, he woke Zacharu up for his watch. They chatted for a few moments as Zacharu woke up before the man attempted to get comfortable against the rock he'd earlier claimed as his own. After a short time, he did manage to doze, but it was not a restful sleep. Before he knew it, Zacharu was returning the favor, shaking him awake.

"Are you ready to continue?" Zacharu asked in a low whisper. Crickets answered him in the distance but neither prisoner noticed.

"Let's eat a little something before we move on," the man answered as he shook his head. They enjoyed each other's company for a while as they ate, and before they knew it they were preparing to leave.

"I really hope Nivri doesn't send his minions out after us," Zacharu said quietly.

"I'm sure he will," the man answered, "just as soon as he realizes we're both missing."

This led them both to think about Orob, and the questions surrounding the circumstances for their release surfaced in both of their minds again.

They walked in the direction they believed was west without saying anything. Once they had moved beyond the rocky area where they took their break, the terrain changed to nothing but forest, and after walking uphill for quite a while, they finally stopped to catch their breath. Just as Zacharu was about to talk to the man, they heard a branch snap behind them.

The man spun around and without thinking about it, defensively drew his sword. His eyes darted from side to side, scouring the nearby area as his pulse thudded like a gust of unending wind through his ears. Although he was certain he had heard something crack in the brush nearby, he saw nothing but trees and shadows around them.

"Put down your weapons," a booming male voice suddenly called out from somewhere in front of them, but Zel continued to hold his position. As soon as Zacharu heard the deep voice, he drew his own weapon and planted his feet firmly into the ground next to his friend.

"I said, put down your weapons," the deep, growling, insistent voice ordered. It carried through the trees and echoed around the forest like a rumble of thunder.

"Who are you?" Zel called out. "My friend and I mean no harm."

Silence filled the forest for a few long seconds as Zel and Zacharu waited for a response from the mysterious owner of the voice. Just when they thought the unseen speaker might have gone away, the surrounding quiet was suddenly broken by a chorus of crackling branches and crunching leaves.

"Back to back!" Zel whispered harshly over his shoulder and immediately turned to push his back up against Zacharu's.

Peering into the shadows, Zel's stomach became a clump of tangled knots when he realized they had been completely surrounded by at least a dozen tall, weapon wielding warriors!

Ten

The girls huddled in the center of the ring of defensive spiders with their swords drawn and each of their hearts beating wildly with fear.

"I don't like how this feels," Diam whispered in a shaking voice.

"I don't either," Tonia agreed, "but I think it's a little late to be thinking about that now…"

Kaileen remained silent, cocking her head in concentration as she listened to the muffled, rhythmic sound echoing through the tunnel. They waited nervously as the approaching sound slowly increased in volume.

"Whatever it is, it's flying," Kaileen whispered in a worried, distressed tone.

"Flying?" Tonia asked.

"Bats?" Diam added inquisitively.

"I'm not sure," Kaileen answered as she shook her head, "but after hearing birds flying in the cave where I used to live, I'm pretty sure the sound I'm hearing now is very similar."

The spiders rocked slightly in their sitting positions as the uppermost six of their eight legs waved slowly through the air as if warding off insects in slow motion. Their amber eyes glowed brightly, illuminating the cavern and allowing the girls to better see their immediate surroundings.

119

Most of the rodents that had accompanied them to this point were in the cavern with them now, their squeaks intensifying in anticipation of an almost certain battle. Some clung to the walls near the entrance of the tunnel, which continued toward the top of the mountain, while others scurried around on the floor just on the outskirts of the oddly shaped circle created by the girls and their eight-legged friends.

"Okay," Tonia muttered quietly and, after repositioning herself, she spoke directly to her friends.

"Kennard says we need to stand with our backs to the center of the circle," she said as Diam and Kaileen followed her instructions without question.

"He also said he thinks he knows what's coming, and that we must aim for their tails."

"Their tails?"

Diam couldn't help but ask the obvious question.

"Yes," Tonia answered. "I think we're about to see something we've never seen before."

"Oh, no," Kaileen said quietly.

As if in response to her words, dozens of dark shadows swarmed into the upper area of the cavern from the tunnel above.

ELEVEN

Zel and Zacharu had their hands on their swords as a gruff, angry voice called out a warning from somewhere beyond the circle of strangers. It appeared that the armored, unidentified shadows had them completely surrounded in the darkness.

"If you draw your weapons, you will no longer be a part of this world, so draw only if you do not value your life," the mysterious voice warned from somewhere behind the circle of strangers.

"Don't," Zel whispered to Zacharu as understanding suddenly filled his eyes while his gaze moved from the shadowy faces of one warrior to another.

The whites of the eyes of each of the men surrounding the two prisoners stood out in sharp contrast to their dark, mud-caked faces. As far as Zel could tell, the skin beneath the mud masks appeared to be hairless. Some of the warriors held different sized swords, others held spears with jagged blades, and still others held rocks large enough to crush a skull with ease in their wide, hairless hands.

Were these warriors what they appeared to be?

A sudden movement a short distance away caught Zel's eye. When he glanced in that direction, he noticed the tall, shadowy shape of yet another warrior standing alone next to a large tree. The brawny silhouette wielded a long bow across his back and stood with his feet apart atop a wide, horizontal tree trunk. It was obvious he was prepared to fire a loaded arrow, if necessary, in the blink of a firebug.

"Who are you?" the warrior leader asked with an unmasked air of confidence. His voice was deep, husky, and completely lacked any signs of humor or welcome.

"My name is Zel and this is Zacharu," the man answered as he nodded to the smaller creature at his side, sounding every bit as confident as the warrior leader. Zacharu was quite surprised the man's voice wasn't shaking with fear.

"We mean no harm," Zel added, making sure his hands were nowhere near the handle of his own weapon.

The head of the silhouette's shadow moved with a nod before the unidentifiable figure jumped from the log and moved with long, direct strides toward them. The warriors standing between the shadowy figure and the former prisoners silently parted as the leader passed. As the figure got closer, Zel noticed he was carrying an unsheathed sword.

"And you come from where?" the approaching figure asked quietly.

"I come from a village called Uncava," Zel answered.

"And your friend?" the leader prodded as he stopped just a few feet in front of them.

Now that he was closer to them, the pair of former castle prisoners could see that the leader wore a light-colored band around his dark head. The sharp ends of a couple of long, upright feathers were tucked securely within the band. Although he didn't have much experience dealing with leaders of different tribes, the feathers indicated that this newcomer was some type of chief.

Zel remained silent as he waited for Zacharu to answer the leader's question. Although he had become fairly well acquainted with the strange creature during their shared time the castle, he didn't really know where Zacharu was from so he had no idea how to answer the most recent question. After giving it a bit more thought, Zel decided it wasn't his place to answer anyway, even if he *did* have the answer.

"I come from Defigo," Zacharu answered in an uncertain tone

as he tossed a nervous glance up at Zel.

"Defigo?"

The single word was harshly voiced and full of silent questions, and although shadows filled the space around them, Zel couldn't help but notice when the leader lifted an inquisitive, hairy eyebrow. In a few seconds, the raised line of hair above the leader's eye slid into a downward angle as the questioning expression was soon replaced with one of anger. Zel turned his attention briefly to the faces of the warriors around them and was unnerved to see the same look of unrest mirrored in every pair of staring eyes.

"We were being held prisoner there," Zel explained as he raised his right hand defensively.

"Why?" the leader growled with suspicion.

"I… I don't know," Zel answered quietly as memories of the multiple interrogations and beatings he endured in the throne room flashed with brilliant clarity through his mind. "Nivri thought I had knowledge of some kind of magic. I tried telling him I didn't, but…"

His voice trailed off as the leader abruptly moved toward him, stopping just inches away. Zel stared into the leader's dark eyes, trying to read what he saw there. Although he didn't want to appear defensive, he couldn't help but rest his hand on the butt of the weapon dangling at his side. He wanted to make it clear that if they were about to do battle, he would not go down without a fight.

As the pair of tall, dark figures stared into each other's eyes, Zel suddenly thought he heard an odd, growling sound coming from somewhere deep in the warrior's throat.

"Why are you here?"

Zel hesitated briefly as his uncertainty with their situation changed to defensive anger. He didn't even blink as his next words flowed from his mouth like a slow, clear yet raging river.

"I'm trying to find my way back to my family and I don't know where *here* is. I only know that I was just held prisoner in the bottom of some wretched castle for more days than I could count, I was beaten and prodded for information that I don't have, and I was jailed in a cell with little food, water, or company," Zel answered as his dark eyes flashed with anger.

"I don't know why I'm here," he continued with obvious exasperation. "If I did, believe me when I say I would be happy to tell you about it." He extended his hands as he shrugged his shoulders. "Unfortunately, I don't know much so I have little to share with you."

He continued to glare at the leader as he added, "If you don't like my answer then either let us go or kill us now."

He lowered his hands back to his sides and his fingers twitched on the handle of his sword, a sign which didn't go unnoticed by the nearby warriors. Those wielding swords of their own took a step forward and held them mere inches from the man, prepared to inflict serious injury if he made the wrong move towards their leader.

The warrior wearing the feathers raised his hand as a silent gesture to his men without breaking his stare with the former prisoner.

"What about the magic?" the leader asked quietly. "What do you know about magic?"

"I know nothing!" Zel growled in angry frustration. "I told Nivri I didn't know anything about magic and I tell you the same thing!"

Zacharu had never seen his friend this angry before and as he listened to the conversation between the two men, he found he wasn't surprised. He'd heard stories about ways The Master had used special techniques to get what he wanted from a few unfortunate residents of the castle, but he'd had no idea about the cruelty of some of those techniques. He sighed knowing he could no longer deny that he now knew far more than he'd ever imagined – or cared to know.

The leader continued to stare into Zel's eyes while he considered the prisoner's words. After a moment, he extended both his hand as well as an invitation.

"How would you like to join our group?"

Zel stared back at the leader, completely caught off guard by both the change in attitude and unexpected gesture. Where he thought he had been on the verge of battling for his life, he found he was being invited to join an unfamiliar group of experienced and somewhat intimidating warriors. He didn't have to look for Zacharu's approval as he slowly nodded his head. Although he was surprised at the turn of events, he was thrilled to know he and Zac wouldn't be traveling alone anymore in this strange, unfamiliar world.

Zel gripped the leader's hand firmly and shook it as a smile spread across his face.

"My name is Simcha," the feather laden figure said.

Zel nodded.

"Nice to meet you, although the circumstances are a little strange..."

"Yes, but you must understand there is much danger in this world. Not long ago we could have... welcomed you more openly. Unfortunately times have changed, however, and I'm sure you can imagine one can't be careful enough," the leader replied. After a few seconds, he added, "But when it comes to fellow humans and their friends, we try to make exceptions."

Zel smiled with relief, thrilled to hear that his earlier observation was right.

Humans!

TWELVE

As countless dark shadows darted like lightning into the cavern around them, Tonia yelled a single word to her friends and fervently hoped they could hear her over the drone of what seemed like thousands of miniature drums beating all around them.

"Defense!"

No sooner had she said this than one of the dark shapes emerged from the tunnel and headed straight for her. Tonia raised her weapon in defense just as she heard a mysterious hissing sound coming from her left. Out of the corner of her eye, the young girl caught sight of an odd white line as it streamed horizontally from one area of the cavern to the other. The line originated from an undefined black blob next to her and moved directly toward one of the converging shadows as if being pulled by an invisible pair of hands. She immediately realized the black blob was one of the spiders and the streaming white line was a narrow jet of milky liquid being ejected from the mouth of the arachnid. She watched in amazement as the wet line struck the approaching shadow and knocked it out of the air. The goo covered creature landed on the stone floor with a thump and immediately began screeching and writhing in pain.

Tonia found that she didn't have time to look at the spider, or thank it, for that matter, because in the air directly behind the place where the now dead flying creature had come from she saw at least a dozen more flying demons. Like the last one, these were also heading straight for her. She began swinging her sword from side to side in short, rhythmic arcs. She remembered Kennard's instruction to aim for the tails so she did. She swung at them over and over, taking down one, two, then five of the flying creatures.

"Aim for the tails!" she reminded he friends as she heard them waging their own battles behind her. Although they were in a fairly small area, it felt as though they were doing battle in a completely different room or universe. Swinging her sword from side to side, the young girl focused intently on what she was doing. Soon everything around her disappeared except for her sword and the next creature she would slice through.

The battle waged on for only a few tense minutes but it felt like endless hours. The girls fought bravely, swinging their blood-laden blades as they tried to protect themselves and each other from the dark, flying ghouls. They fought side by side with the trio of spiders who sprayed countless streams of toxic fluid onto the airborne fiends as they flew by.

Once the devilish attackers had nearly been defeated, Diam took a chance to look at Tonia. Before her eyes made contact with her friend, they moved across two of the spiders and she gasped in surprise at what she saw. Two of their arachnid friends had some of the odd-looking flying creatures walking around on their backs. What was worse, it didn't take long for her to realize the remainder of the invasive creatures were about to spring on her friend.

"Tonia, look out!" Diam called out frantically as she jabbed her sword in the direction of one of the shadowed, long-tailed creatures.

Trusting her friend, Tonia jumped out of the way just as two of the flying minions lunged directly for her. As soon as they realized they missed their target, the onyx oddities turned sideways and took flight. Without a moment's hesitation, Tonia darted forward and swung her sword. Her reward for her quick reflexes was a creature sliced in half, and she stared proudly as it fell to the cavern floor with a muffled thump. The separated halves of the dying body twitched and bounced uncontrollably across the dusty floor for several minutes, leaving trails and puddles of black ooze on the ground in their wake.

The second flying creature turned back toward Tonia and almost managed to make it to the young girl before it suddenly dropped out of the air like a rock. From somewhere beside her, Tonia caught sight of a perfectly aimed stream of liquid death as it struck the invading creature in mid-air. The jet of toxic webbing nailed the creature with another thump and knocked it into the far wall of the cavern. Instead of slumping to the ground and writhing in pain, the carcass of the minion fought within its poisonous crypt for a few seconds before all struggling ceased. It remained stuck to the wall like a splotch of black and white wax, bubbling with toxin, not life.

"Wow," Kaileen whispered as she caught her breath. "I've got to tell you, I've never been in any battle like that before!"

The girls looked around the room and quickly realized their once beautiful, glistening armor of webbing was now covered with an array of dark splotches and smears.

"What a sight we must be..." Diam began as she looked at her friends. "Is anyone hurt?"

Tonia and Kaileen shook their heads as Tonia turned to inspect one of the defeated creatures that was lying in the dust a few steps away. Just as she bent down to look at it, the creature twitched and glared up at her, baring its fangs.

"What is this thing?" Tonia whispered. She leaned cautiously away from the injured creature, worried it may have the ability to spray some kind of poison at her.

The black figure on the floor was nearly a foot long and appeared to be some strange mutant animal, an odd combination of possibly a bat and a snake. It had the head of a bat, including a short, stubby nose and wide, pointy ears, as well as a similarly shaped back and wings, but this is where the resemblance ended. Just behind the wings, the dark, finely haired body morphed into something else as it stretched into the elongated, coarsely scaled body of a snake that eventually narrowed to a fine, double-end at the tip of the tail.

While she stared with pity at the creature lying helplessly in front of her, it growled a menacing snarl at her and its tail began to quiver. Tonia didn't notice the shadow approaching behind her, and just as she was considering running her sword through the mangled oddity to put it out of its misery, a thin stream of liquid fell down on it from somewhere behind her, turning it into an instant puddle of goo. In less than a second, they heard a partial high-pitched squeal, an almost whispering, bubbling sound, and then silence.

Tonia turned to look up at the dark, eight-legged shape standing over her.

"They must be destroyed," a somber, yet now familiar voice said in her head.

"What was it?" she asked again, directing her question to their friend who was waiting for their return at ground level.

"Those, my dear, were one of either Nivri's or Lotor's experiments," Kennard answered. "I think you could see it was a combination of a bat and a snake. Left alone, it very likely would have healed itself."

The voice fell silent in her head but after a few seconds, came to life again.

"All surviving creatures of darkness must be destroyed. If you see any lying around where you are, you must either have the spiders spray them with their venom or use your weapons to remove their heads."

"But..." she mentally argued, but Kennard immediately silenced her.

"Tonia! You must trust me! If you do not destroy any surviving creatures, they will hunt you down!"

The young girl nodded and relayed the grim information on to Diam and Kaileen. They then spent the next few minutes destroying any creatures they found alive and removing the heads from all of them once they were deceased.

"No one is hurt, right?" Tonia asked as she looked at all members of the group. Thankfully, everyone appeared to be fine.

"Good."

In her mind, she asked Kennard if it was safe to continue their journey.

"Yes, as far as I can tell it is safe now. Mount up and proceed to the top of the tunnel as soon as you can. We are running out of time so you must move quickly!"

"Running out of time for what?" Tonia asked, but the muck dragon did not answer. Instead, he gave her quiet instructions.

"Go now. Go with the dragons and do what you were destined to do..."

Tonia listened as the muck dragon's voice faded to a whisper before it disappeared completely. After a moment, she turned her attention to the spiders where they stood quietly, again on all eight legs, waiting patiently for their next order.

"Come on, girls. Let's mount up so we can get this amulet and move on to the next part of our journey," Tonia said, her new-found confidence rising.

With renewed energy, she climbed up onto the rock before helping Diam and Kaileen join her. One at a time, the spiders moved into place as each of the girls climbed aboard. As soon as they were settled, the large, black creatures made their way in silent procession back to the tunnel. Without saying a word, the small group continued moving toward the top of the mountain in search of their destiny.

THIRTEEN

When Zel realized his suspicions about the band of warriors before them were correct, he nearly had to sit down. This group of face-painted, weapon-wielding men that had them surrounded was not just a group of males – they were *men!* Men! Humans!

"We understand more than you think," the leader said to Zel after they shook hands. He then turned to Zacharu and extended his hand in the same respectful manner. Zel's fellow prisoner from the castle nodded briefly and shook Simcha's hand, introducing himself.

"Zacharu."

"Come," the lead warrior said. "Follow me back to camp. We will talk there."

With a single nod, Simcha turned and lead the way back through the parted group of warriors. After a slight hesitation and brief nod at Zacharu, Zel followed.

They wandered through the shadowy darkness and eventually found themselves entering a camp hidden in the center of a thick bramble of bushes. Zel and Zacharu followed Simcha through a partially hidden entrance and it wasn't long before the ground suddenly sloped at a downward angle. The only sound heard was multiple muffled footsteps as the group of men followed Simcha through an enclosed passageway beneath a wide, bush covered hill. After a few hundred feet, the tall, narrow tunnel suddenly opened up into a large room lined with boulders and debris. Branching off the sides of this unexpected cavern were a few other tunnels.

Zel glanced around at the strange, natural design of the tunnel and soon discovered it had a familiar shape to it…

The shape was that of a spider.

His focus moved from the shape of the cavern to what he soon saw in the middle of the cavern – a bright, blazing fire. A large group of men sat around the fire on smooth, wide rocks that bordered the pit, and they looked up as the larger group approached. The sitting men didn't appear to be alarmed at the pair of new, unfamiliar faces being brought into their home. Although the arrival of strangers was a rare event, it did happen every so often. The group of seated men silently watched the arriving figures fill the room for a few seconds before continuing on with their previous conversations.

"This is our home," Simcha said proudly. "And these," he added with a broad gesture of his hand towards the men around the fire, "are my brothers."

Zel and Zacharu nodded respectfully towards the other men in the cave, while Zel quickly did a head count. There were fifteen men in the current room besides himself and Zacharu, but there were also a few dark tunnels leading off the room where other men might be. He was surprised to see so many other humans in a place so close to the castle.

"Please, have a seat," Simcha offered as he removed his armor and set down his weapons. Zacharu couldn't help but stare at the leader for a moment before he found himself asking a question.

"Your armor is quite different from anything I've ever seen."

He hesitated, almost embarrassed to ask the question that was bothering him. In the end, he decided to just ask.

"Is it made from… turtle shells?"

Simcha chuckled as Zel and Zacharu sat down on a vacant rock not far from the blazing fire. Although it was very warm outside, there had been an obvious chill floating through the dark tunnels as they made their way to the underground cavern. The fire blanketed the room with a very comfortable temperature and glow.

"Yes it is!" Simcha replied a booming voice that echoed through the surrounding tunnels. "And you may not know this, but they are not just simple shells from ordinary turtles – they are raguon turtle shells, which are incredibly strong! They make a *wonderful* addition to any type of battle gear!"

Zacharu considered this for a moment, then asked, "May I ask where you get them from? I see you have quite a few shells covering your chest armor, and I also noticed quite a few of your warriors are wearing them also."

Simcha smiled.

"If you are a fan of raguon turtles, you need not worry," he explained. "The castle is not far from here and turtle meat, especially fresh turtle meat, is a favorite of the castle inhabitants. The shells we use in our armor come from what we find when the castle cooks are finished with them."

Zacharu nodded with understanding as one of the men began passing around a pia bowl filled with small red apples. Zel and Zacharu helped themselves to two pieces of fruit each then Zacharu passed the bowl onto an unnamed warrior next to him.

"You have water?" Simcha asked Zel.

"Yes, we each have a pia bottle of water," the man answered.

"Very good." Simcha nodded. "Let us discuss some business then, shall we?"

Zel nodded and took a bite of his apple. Although the fruit was smaller than what he'd become accustomed to back in his home village, the flavor was sweet and satisfying. His stomach grumbled loudly as he swallowed.

"Mmmm," he mumbled in approval as he quietly licked his lips. "This is delicious."

"Your belly agrees with you," Simcha smiled.

Changing the subject, the warrior leader asked, "You were a prisoner in the castle?"

Zel had taken another bite of his apple and didn't want to talk with his mouth full, so he nodded quietly as he methodically chewed his piece of fruit. After a few seconds, Zacharu answered for him.

"Yes, we were both prisoners, although we came to Defigo

133

under totally different circumstances."

Zacharu told them about how he used to work in the castle, cleaning and organizing certain rooms within the mansion for Nivri. He went on to explain how he unexpectedly found himself moved to the lower area of the castle when he discovered a strange note in one of the rooms.

"Tell me about this note," Simcha encouraged quietly.

"It was written by a sorcerer named Scurio," Zacharu began.

"Yes, I've heard of him," Simcha said with a series of short, understanding nods. No one seemed to notice that a few of Simcha's fellow warriors also nodded.

"Go on."

"The note said he'd lost one of his prized dragons and he was offering a reward for the creature's return."

"Did it say the name of this creature?"

"No," Zacharu answered. His eyes focused on the fire as he searched for an answer between the gyrating yellow and orange flames while he considered the question. In a moment, his almond shaped eyes looked up from the licking amber tongues and scanned the warriors' faces before he continued.

"I was in the castle for many moons. During my time there, I sometimes overheard discussions among other members of the castle. Sometimes I would hear stories referring to the birth of a special dragon, and at other times there was talk about a magical dragon that had been born to save this world, but had mysteriously gone missing..."

His voice drifted off as distant memories of these stories floated through his mind like lazy smoke from a campfire.

"I know of this dragon," Simcha said, startling Zacharu from his thoughts. The former prisoner's eyes closed slightly and his face curled into a frown when the leader of the warriors suddenly stood up. All eyes stared at Simcha as he clasped his hands behind his back and began slowly pacing around the room.

Zel studied the warrior as he wandered in a counter-clockwise circle around the group of men. Simcha seemed to be uptight about something but Zel had no idea what it might be. If he had known Simcha for more than just a few hours he might understand the leader's posture and expression, but he didn't.

As he waited to see what else the leader might say, Zel finished his first piece of fruit, licked juice from his fingers, and began eating the second.

"If it is the same dragon we are speaking of, which is very possible, then his name is Gruffod. If it *is* him, then without question he is indeed a very special little dragon," Simcha continued.

"Have you heard of him?" the leader asked as he turned to look at Zel with a curious stare.

Zel didn't need to consider the warrior's question. He immediately shook his head in reply.

"Gruffod? No, I haven't heard of Gruffod. I have, however, heard of another creature I think you might be interested in..."

Simcha stopped pacing and stared directly at the prisoner. "Go on."

"When I was in the dungeon of the castle, Zacharu was in a cell on one side of me," the prisoner said. As he stared into the fire, Zacharu offered a silent nod from beside him. "In the cell on the other side, as I'm sure you've already guessed, was another prisoner."

"Did this man give you his name?" Simcha asked curiously. Before Zel could answer, the leader returned to his stone near the fire and sat down.

"I don't think it was a man, and yes, he gave me his name."

Zel tore his gaze away from the mesmerizing, flickering flames and looked at Simcha.

"He told me his name was Draco."

Many of the warriors around the fire gasped in surprise as a thick shroud of silence fell across the room.

"Did you say Draco?" Simcha repeated in a low, questioning tone.

"Yes," Zel answered. "Now, you must understand I never saw this creature, not even once, but he said his name was Draco. He also stressed that I needed to find a way to help him get out."

Simcha leaned forward and placed his hands on his knees as he stared deep into Zel's eyes.

"Did he tell you anything more?"

Zel nodded, realizing he was sharing some obviously very

important information with this renegade band of humans.

"He said something about how he comes from a special bloodline. He explained how he had been able to control his growth for a while but he's getting weaker every day, and can't control it anymore. He also said his body is growing again and he must escape from the prison before he grows too much. He stressed that if he doesn't escape from the prison in time, evil will reign in this world unlike anything any of us have ever known."

Zel had been looking directly at Simcha as he explained what his fellow prisoner had told him when he suddenly felt an overwhelming need to stand up and walk around. Without a word, he did just that. He slowly paced around the room, lingering at the mouth of the tunnel entrance, staring into the inky blackness beyond.

As the man paced around the room, Simcha turned around and faced the other former prisoner as his questioning continued.

"Did you hear the conversation he speaks of? Or were you being kept in another room?"

Zacharu looked at the warrior and nervously shook his head.

"I was in one of the prison cells directly next to him," the dwarfed creature answered as he nodded in Zel's direction. "Unfortunately, the only part of the conversation I heard was the part *he* was speaking."

As he said this, he pointed at his former fellow prisoner.

Simcha's focused, green eyes suddenly widened with understanding as he began moving again, heading straight for Zel. Simcha's abrupt relocation worried Zacharu, but when he glanced at the warriors around the fire, he noticed with relief that they seemed to be listening without any signs of undue concern.

"Zel," Simcha said as he placed a strong hand on the prisoner's shoulder. "This fellow unseen prisoner in the cave – did he tell you what he was?"

Zel turned a grave, worried face toward Simcha and shook his head in slow motion.

"No, he didn't give me many details about anything other than the situation he's in. Unfortunately, the last time we were taken from the dungeon I was a bit nervous about seeing Nivri again. As a result, I completely forgot to look into the cell as Orob led us up the tunnel toward the upper floors of the castle."

"I see," Simcha said as his hand slid back to his side. He nodded with understanding then turned away and slowly paced back toward the fire.

"Why do you ask?" Zel asked as his eyes followed the path of the human leader.

"I ask because I think you may have given us something we've been looking for – the missing piece in our puzzle," the leader answered.

"What piece was that?" Zel asked as his brows furrowed with confusion.

Simcha sat back down on his stone and smiled at his guests.

"That piece is called Gruffod."

Zel looked at Simcha and shook his head in denial.

"No," the prisoner argued. "He didn't say his name was Gruffod – he said his name was Draco."

"Indeed," Simcha said with a knowing nod. "Do you know what the term 'draco' means?"

As Zel considered his question, Zacharu quickly answered.

"Dragon."

Simcha nodded.

Zel's amazed stare moved from Zacharu's face to those of the other men in the crowd. His focus finally settled on the leader's eyes and lingered momentarily.

"Dragon?" he whispered quietly, afraid to believe the words. The dragons were all gone, weren't they? None of the villagers had seen any of the ancient flying creatures at all in more years than he dared to count.

"Yes," Simcha said with a satisfied smile. "I'm certain that your fellow prisoner was Draco, also known as Little Draco, and ultimately known as Gruffod..."

Simcha stood up with a sudden motion of excited authority, "Warriors! Tonight we sleep; tomorrow we head to the castle to rescue our dragon!"

A great burst of echoing shouts filled the cavern and attached tunnels as an electric charge permeated the air. Remnants of the outburst echoed through the shadows before fading away in the distance as Simcha raised his hand for silence.

"Now we must sleep so we may be well rested before tomorrow's journey. Zel, Zacharu – you may both sleep here by the fire. The rest of us will sleep in our assigned spaces.

"Lacsar?" Simcha directed his focus to one of the short, stocky warriors with a raggedy mess of blonde hair streaked with black patches. "Please stay with our guests in case they need anything during the night."

"Aye," Lacsar answered with a nod of acknowledgment.

"Good night," Simcha said.

Without waiting for a response, the leader of the band of humans turned and made his way down the first narrow tunnel to the left of the cave entrance.

"Good night," Zacharu replied, but Zel said nothing. He was thinking about their conversation and still struggling to believe what he had heard.

Draco was a dragon?

And not only was Draco a dragon – from what Simcha implied, Draco was Gruffod...

Gruffod, the dragon!

FOURTEEN

Once they were well on their way again, Diam muffled a chuckle as she turned her head partially over her shoulder and asked Tonia the question she could no longer keep to herself.

"Was that Kennard you were 'talking' to back there?"

"Well, who else would it have been, you ninny!" Tonia answered sarcastically.

"Oh, I don't know," Diam teased. "First it was the turtles in the cave, then the crazy bat, and now a frog who thinks he's a dragon. For all we know, you could have conveniently found another mental playmate and forgotten to tell us…"

Her voice drifted away as she pretended to stare off into space.

"Diam!" Tonia scolded her friend, "You need to be nice to me! I can't help it if I can hear voices, you know…"

"Oh, yeah?" Diam taunted her. "And what if I don't want to be nice to you? It's not like you can do anything from back there!"

Diam laughed at her witty response as Tonia scoffed at her.

"I could have left you to be a meal fit for a spider back when you were an insect you know…"

Tonia stopped mid-sentence when she suddenly felt the spider beneath her rumble like an earthquake. Before she could react, she heard an accompanying low, menacing growl. Diam turned to look back at Tonia with a surprised expression.

"Did your spider just growl at me?" she asked suspiciously.

"Ha!" Tonia said as she patted her spider's side happily. "Maybe that will teach you to play nicely with others!"

"Hmmph," Diam grumbled before facing forward again.

Ahead of them, Kaileen rode in silence, extending the flaming torch away from her body in hopes of chasing away the gloomy shadows that stubbornly filled the tunnel above. Although they'd lost a few of their fellow rats during the battle with the flying creatures back in the cavern, many of the remaining rodents continued to scale the tunnel walls, partially lighting the way for the group as they continued their seemingly endless ascent.

The higher they climbed, the colder the tunnel grew, and although the torch didn't provide the best light, they could easily see clouds of condensation rhythmically pooling in front of their faces as they exhaled. Each of the girls was thankful they had their fashionable webbing armor – it definitely would have been difficult to withstand the colder air without it. The air also thinned and their breathing became slightly more difficult as they moved higher and higher into the tunnel, but it was too late to worry about little things like that now.

They had been traveling for a while when something in the tunnel above caught Diam's eye.

"Hey girls, is the tunnel lightening up a little ahead or is it just me?" she asked in a loud whisper.

Kaileen had been looking at the shadowed walls and Tonia had been dozing in her saddle. Both girls immediately focused on the tunnel ahead, and as if reading their minds, the spiders began to slow down.

The kalevala peered around the torch and after a few seconds, she nodded.

"Yes, I think so," Kaileen agreed. Looking back at the girls behind her she asked, "Should I put the torch out?"

Tonia thought about this for a moment before answering her.

"No, but I think maybe you and your spider should fall back a bit," Tonia suggested. "Let Diam and I move ahead of you, or hand the torch back to me, since I'm in the rear. I don't think we want to draw attention to ourselves just yet by marching into an unknown area with a blazing beacon of light."

"True," Diam agreed.

Kaileen rubbed the side of her spider encouragingly and asked, "Can you fall back, please?"

The spider obediently moved to the side of the vertical path and allowed its fellow arachnids to pass by.

"Thank you," Kaileen said as she again rubbed the spider's side.

"Aranea!"

The sound of Kennard's voice erupted in Tonia's head, causing her to jump in her saddle with surprise.

"Tonia, stop for a moment."

Before the young girl could repeat the muck dragon's order, each of the spiders stopped their forward motion.

"What's wrong?" Kaileen asked with a look toward her friends. "Why did we stop?"

Tonia needed to only say one word for the small group to understand.

"Kennard."

"Tonia, have one of the spiders extinguish the torch for now. They can use their webbing, which will allow you to re-light it whenever you need it. The spiders still have the ability to spray venom if anything less than favorable calls for it, and trust me, they will not hesitate to use it as they see fit," Kennard explained as a bodiless voice in Tonia's head. "Be wary about trusting anything you find at the top of the tunnel, young one, except for the amulet itself... IF you are able to find it at all..."

"Okay," she answered in her own mind before focusing her attention on Diam and Kaileen. As expected, her friends were patiently waiting for an explanation. Tonia quietly relayed both the dragon's instructions and warning to them in a low, hushed voice.

"Carry on," Kennard's voice added when she was finished.

"Let's go," the young girl said as her eyes drifted towards the opening above them.

The tunnel widened as it neared the top of the mountain, and the spiders naturally moved from a single file formation to a side by side approach. Before they continued on, however, Kaileen held out the torch and Diam's spider shot out a short, wide stream of sticky, gray webbing at it. The action extinguished the flame in less than a second with a *hiss* as multiple wisps of steam threaded their way through the cold air toward the ceiling like thin, ghostly snakes. With this part of Kennard's instructions accomplished, the spiders moved cautiously forward.

The higher they climbed, the more the lighting in the tunnel changed from black to gloomy gray from the mysterious light source above. When they were just a few feet away from the top, the spiders slowed the speed of their approach to a snail's pace. Worried that a second wave of the dark, flying creatures might attack without warning, each of the girls wordlessly drew their swords.

Just before reaching the crest of the ledge, the spiders stopped. The girls waited nervously as each of the arachnids peered into the gloomy, gray void at the top of the tunnel.

"Hold on tight," Diam whispered.

The spiders held their position for a few seconds before they began creeping forward again. Each of the girls dug their free hands deeply into their respective spider's fur and held on as the arachnids lumbered warily over the edge of the opening. Once the arachnids stood on solid, horizontal stones, they peered cautiously around the dimly lit enclosure, eventually making their way into the center of the room. The open space ahead of them appeared to be nothing more than a large, open passageway, which led to one door to the left and another to the right. Each of these two doorways was arched as if it was part of a larger circle, with a path encompassing the entirety of the upper cavern. Wisps of ghostly, white air hovered and swirled above the floor beyond the doorways and spilled out into the area around each of the arched openings.

Looking at the roof overhead, the girls could see cracks in the ceiling which allowed light to enter the main passageway. Although light in dark spaces was generally seen as a good thing, in this case, the light above was the cause of the gloomy atmosphere all around them. Countless drops of water descended from somewhere above, pooling in various puddles on the floor nearby. Tonia stared at the areas of liquid around them, wondering briefly why they didn't converge into one giant puddle, but after a few seconds, she realized. Instead of expanding as more drops fell into the puddles, the standing water escaped into dozens of cracks at the base of the cavern wall with the assistance of an uneven floor.

"This isn't what I expected," Diam whispered as her eyes roved around the dimly lit area.

She turned her attention to their rodent friends, which were scurrying all around the room. Many of the rats were sniffing enthusiastically around the floor as well as investigating cracks and crevices in the walls, while others disappeared through the arched doorway to the right. Those unafraid of the unseen were immediately swallowed by the swirling fog in the next room.

"Let's climb down and check it out," Tonia suggested in a soft whisper.

Without waiting for a response, she dug into her spider's fur with both hands, swung her right leg over the arachnid's abdomen, and slowly slid to the dusty surface below. As she did this, her spider lowered its entire body to the gray cavern floor to assist her with her dismount. In less than a second, both of Tonia's feet were planted firmly on the damp, cold ground.

"Thank you," she whispered as she patted her spider on its side before turning towards Kaileen.

Diam quickly followed Tonia's lead. Within seconds she was at her best friend's side just as Tonia was reaching up to assist the kalevala dismount her spider. The two girls worked together, lifting the shorter member of their group and setting her gently on the floor. In the blink of a firebug the three girls were standing next to each other.

The girls remained on guard as they wandered to the left, examining the eerie cavern for signs of life or activity. The glow spiders watched the girls for a few seconds before they caught a strange scent. As if driven by a single mind, all three spiders turned and moved toward the passageway on the right. Each of the two groups became engrossed in their own thoughts, neither one realizing they were separating themselves from each other as they did so.

Diam was the first to reach the arched passageway leading into a very cold and much larger room to the left. After staring into the room for a few seconds, she captured Tonia's attention when she whispered something to her friends in an excited voice.

"Wow, Tonia! Kaileen, look at this!"

Diam stepped through the passageway. After a brief hesitation she began making her way toward a large, sparkling statue near the center of the far wall. Above the statue, a long, jagged gap in the ceiling opened the way for brisk, cold air and melted snow to drip into the cavern. Streams of ice cold liquid cascaded like wet sands following some unseen, vertical path directly down onto the statue's head. After a silent landing, the wetness then drizzled a short distance down the body before eventually freezing in time, creating a thick layer of ice from the topmost part of the statue's head to the floor.

Diam stood before the icy sculpture and stared up at it in awe, amazed to see something both so beautiful and unexpected in a place such as this.

The frozen structure appeared to be a completely solid, massive ice sculpture of a sparkling gray dragon. It stood upright, on all four legs, with its wings splayed out on either side of its thick, muscular body as if frozen in the middle of a major battle. It stood at least ten feet tall, from the top of its head to the stone floor beneath it, and it had an impressive wingspan of at least that much, if not more, from wingtip to wingtip.

The solid, glistening creature glimmered with thousands of tiny diamonds as narrow rays of moonlight filtered in through the large crack above, shining almost directly down on the massive beast.

"Isn't it amazing?" Diam said quietly as Tonia and Kaileen joined her just steps away from the flawless, almost iridescent sculpture.

"Wow," Tonia breathed in agreement as she slowly walked around the entire statue.

The mammoth beast was definitely eye catching in both size and appearance. Tonia's mouth hinted at a satisfied smile as she stood frozen in front of it, staring at it in hopeless wonder.

"I wish we knew who sculpted this beautiful thing," Diam said, voicing her obvious amazement.

As the three girls fell into a comfortable silence, they suddenly became aware of the sound of running water somewhere nearby.

Curious, Kaileen broke her gaze away from the ice creature and slowly walked around the cavern until she was at the back side of the beast. Once there, she quickly located the source of the sound.

"Hey, look at this," she called out to the others.

When Diam and Tonia joined the kalevala, they noticed a narrow wall of melting snow that was continuously running down the entire length of the wall behind the sculpture. As it reached the floor level, it puddled up into a wide, shallow pool and eventually made its way into a gaping, four foot high tunnel in the wall. Beyond the entrance to the tunnel, all they could see was yet another pool of darkness.

"I wonder where that goes," Diam offered as she pointed at the mysterious tunnel. She stretched her neck towards it, but found herself unable to see much in the moist darkness.

"You *would* wonder about something like that," Tonia chided her friend.

"Wait a minute," Diam said with obvious agitation. Before looking at her friends, she had to forcibly break her eyes away from the tunnel in order to scan the walls and floor around them.

"What is it?" Tonia asked, nervous about what her friend was about to bring to her attention. With Diam, she just never knew what to expect next.

"The rats," Diam said quietly as her gaze expanded across the floor to the nearby walls.

"What about them?" Kaileen asked with a confused frown.

"Where are they?" Diam asked quietly. "Where did they go?"

Tonia nodded her head as understanding filled her mahogany colored eyes. She and her friends were the only live creatures in the room.

"And the spiders," she added with obvious concern. "What happened to them, too?"

"I think they went the other way," Kaileen said, vaguely remembering seeing the spiders looking towards the other door off the last room. She shook her head as the all too familiar butterflies began fluttering around in the pit of her stomach.

"Maybe we should go find them," Diam suggested quietly as she began to step away from the pool of cold water.

In Tonia's head, she suddenly heard Kennard's distant voice

whisper a warning.

"Careful..."

Just as she was about to pass the warning on to her friends, the three girls began to hear an odd, cracking sound which echoed loudly through the cavern. Tonia turned to investigate the unnerving noise and quickly realized where it was coming from.

The lifeless ice sculpture beside them was beginning to crack!

Fifteen

Zel and Zacharu got comfortable around the fire and talked about the day's events for a few minutes before they both fell silent and eventually drifted off. When sleep finally overtook his tired, worn out body, Zel drifted into a dream.

"The amulet," a voice whispered in the darkness all around him. There was no light in the dream and no face to the voice – his dream simply consisted of a soft, soothing male voice whispering to him from some distant somewhere.

"The amulet," the voice repeated. "You must save us."

"Us?" he asked as his eyes rolled back and forth behind closed eyelids. "Us, who? Where are you? *Who* are you?"

"Take the amulet to Immolo and save those of us who will surely perish without your help..." the mysterious voice continued before drifting off into silence.

"What amulet?" the prisoner asked as he twitched and flexed his arm in his sleep. "What castle? Who are you?"

The mysterious voice, so eager to speak to him just seconds before, now remained strangely silent.

"Hello?" he asked in his dream. The sound of silence was almost deafening.

Surrounded by complete darkness and no sound, the man twisted his body this way and that as he searched for any source of light. For endless seconds, he saw nothing, until a faint glow from the corner of his eye caught his attention.

He froze in place when the faint glow in the distance slowly grew into a pair of familiar, iridescent orange circles. A large lump formed in his throat when he realized they were approaching him much too quickly. He tried to turn and run in the opposite direction but his feet suddenly felt as though they were filled with rocks, glued helplessly to the dark yet solid ground. He looked down to see why his feet wouldn't move, but of course saw nothing but an infinite puddle of blackness. His eyes darted to his right, and as his heart jumped up to accompany the lump in his throat, he realized the blazing orange eyes were nearly on him...

And they looked angrier than ever.

His final thought was, "This beating is going to be a doozy..."

He jerked awake with a muffled cry as Zacharu rolled on the blanket next to him and bumped the man's arm. Zel reached for the sword that was not at his side, his thick mind muddled with sleep and confusion. As sounds of the crackling fire and Zacharu's sleeping form came into focus, the man remembered he'd taken his sword off and laid it on the cavern floor next to him. While his heartbeat slowly dropped back down to a regular rate, he began questioning his surreal dream.

Why was he dreaming about an amulet? Was it the same amulet he'd drawn while in his prison cell? And those eyes – why was Nivri coming toward him in the dream? Was he coming to take him back to the castle? Back for more torture?

He could just imagine how angry the sorcerer would be, or likely already was, when he realized his favorite torture toy was no longer in his cell. Thinking of this reminded him of Orob – the guard who had given him his freedom. He didn't understand why the odd creature had released him and Zacharu, but it was too late to worry about the guard's fate now.

What was done was done.

As his mind continued to dust away the remnants of the dream, the man glanced over at Lacsar with a sheepish expression. The warrior was staring at him across the room. Lacsar nodded and returned a half smile. Zel didn't know if the warrior knew Nivri as up close and personal as he did, but he appeared to at least understand.

Zel could just imagine that Lacsar must have had his share of vivid, not-so-pleasant dreams during his lifetime. He was certain many of the men living in this hidden cave, if not all of them, would probably have some very interesting stories to tell if given the opportunity.

He sighed and decided to try to sleep again. Even if he couldn't sleep, hopefully the rest would do him some good. He closed his eyes and listened to the flickering cracks and pops of the fire in the center of the room. It felt good to be in front of a fire again – it had been entirely too long since the last time, and being here brought back many fond memories of his family and village…

Eventually, the sound of the flames and warmth of the fire relaxed him, and soon, he was fast asleep. It felt like he had only closed his eyes for a few seconds when he was startled awake by the sound of running footsteps. He opened his eyes just in time to see everyone around the fire jumping to their feet as Lacsar drew his sword.

Zel and Zacharu picked up and drew their weapons without worrying about consequences. When feeling defensive, old habits were hard to break.

"Simcha," a breathless, male voice called out in the darkness of the tunnel entrance as an unfamiliar warrior suddenly emerged into the cozy cavern. Tall and red faced, the warrior nodded at Lacsar before stopping just inside the tunnel leading to the leader's sleeping quarters.

Zel and Zacharu found themselves immensely relieved when Lacsar returned his long, narrow sword back to its sheath. The warrior looked at the visiting humans and nodded toward the newcomer.

"He's one of us," Lacsar said to the visitors in a reassuring tone.

With a joint sigh of relief, Zel and Zacharu returned their weapons to their original locations. A few seconds later, Simcha emerged from his tunnel with a wild mop of tousled brown hair and sleep filled eyes.

"What is it?" the leader asked in a harsh, groggy tone. He stopped a few feet away from the newcomer just as he finished buckling the long, black leather belt which housed his own weapon around his hips and somewhat rounded waist.

"Sir, there is talk about an upcoming battle flying through the hillside like a wildfire," the breathless warrior said as he knelt down briefly on one knee, a sign of respect to his leader.

"What kind of battle?" Simcha asked as he softly touched the messenger's head with the tips of his fingers. The touch was gentle, almost loving. After a few seconds he drew his hand away. His brown eyes clouded with thought as they narrowed into a pair of tight, horizontal slits. With a nervous glance around the cavern, the messenger stood and continued telling his story. It wasn't long before other warriors began filling the area around the fire like a swarm of bees flying toward a large pia bowl of honey.

"Nivri," the messenger mumbled in a nervous, hushed tone. He took a deep breath as his eyes again scoured across the faces of his fellow warriors. When his focus landed on the pair of visitors, it lingered there for a moment before returning back to Simcha.

"Word outside is that Nivri has been angered for some reason. More importantly, it is believed he is about to try to claim one of his amulets."

Simcha nodded and mumbled something that sounded like, "Ah, the amulets," then he turned and began pacing silently along one of the cavern walls. In a moment, he turned back and headed in the direction he'd come from. His dark eyes moved directly back to the messenger, filled with concern.

"Did you happen to hear who has possession of the amulet, and which one it is?" the leader asked. The hushed sound of his voice danced through the group along with intermittent crackles from the fire in the center of the room.

"I can't be certain," the messenger answered, "but rumor has it that a group of children have rescued the Tear."

When Zel heard this, he was quite surprised to find it piqued his complete attention.

A group of children have rescued the amulet? How many were involved and how old were they? They must be older children if they could take on the feat of gaining possession of an amulet! Ideas wound through his head as another, more important question came to mind...

How in the world did these children, whoever they were, happen to stumble across something as special as an amulet?

Not surprisingly, this question led him to thoughts of his own children. He would hate it if they found themselves in a world such as this, rescuing a special gem as important as the one being discussed apparently was. He smiled; thankful his own children were safe back in the village. His smile grew as he thought of his wife, knowing she would never allow them to wander off on such an adventure!

He kept his thoughts and questions to himself as the conversation in the now crowded cavern continued.

"Did you also happen to overhear when this unexpected event will take place?" the leader asked the newcomer in a low, contemplative tone.

"Creatures outside everywhere are gathering together as we speak. From what I could tell, it is anticipated the battle will happen sometime around sunrise," the messenger reported.

Simcha nodded and stroked his chin, deep in thought as his eyes scanned the crowd. After a moment, he stood up straight and placed his hand on his sword, a sign of unwavering authority.

"We must also prepare for battle... immediately!"

The warriors responded without any hesitation. They quickly turned and dispersed, working strategically to gather both armor and weapons.

In the blink of a firebug only Zel, Zacharu and Simcha were left standing in front of the fire. Lacsar stood near the far wall, watching quietly. Turning to the newcomers, the leader asked a question that caught both of the former prisoners totally off guard.

"Will you fight with us?"

As surprise flooded into his eyes, Zel turned toward Zacharu and gave his friend a lingering, imploring look.

"It is not an order – it is a request," Simcha added humbly.

Zacharu returned the look to his friend and fellow prisoner. After a slight hesitation, he offered a brief, nearly undetectable nod of his head.

Zel wasn't surprised by Zacharu's response, and after

151

thinking for a few seconds, he turned to Simcha, ready to voice his thoughts.

"I'm not sure how I know this and I do not feel this coming from you, but I definitely feel the answer to your question has already been decided for us."

As Simcha listened in silence, Zacharu smiled and nodded. When Zel saw this, he turned to the warrior leader and offered their final answer.

"Yes, we will fight with you."

"Thank you, and welcome to our band of warriors," Simcha said. He hugged Zacharu and Zel then and proudly shook each of their hands with a firm, sincere grip.

"Prepare them," Simcha said to Lacsar. The warrior guard had been standing a few steps away as he waited respectfully for the outcome of the conversation between the three remaining men.

With a brief nod of approval regarding the recent events, Simcha turned and retreated back to his sleeping quarters. Lacsar watched his leader depart down the dark tunnel, and after a few seconds, he began searching for some suitable armor for their newly appointed warriors. Once being fitted with armor, helmets, and metal masks, the entire group made their way to the tunnel leading to the outside.

None of the armored warriors had any way of knowing the event before them would be one of two epic battles they would be part of, the outcome of which could quite possibly lead to something they all looked forward to more than anything else in the world.

Freedom.

SIXTEEN

When the initial cracking sound echoed through the cold, wintry air like an out of place crunch, Tonia was the first to discover where it was coming from. By then, Diam had already turned toward the archway they'd entered through.

"Um, I think we should get out of here... like, now!" Diam shouted in alarm. She glanced at her friends as she turned and headed back toward the archway when something suddenly moved above her head.

"Diam, don't move!" Tonia screamed.

Completely trusting her friend, Diam responded by freezing where she stood, just shy of the entryway. It wasn't a second too soon. As she stabilized her balance, a thick, black object slammed down in front of the entrance just inches from Diam's feet, crashing into the floor with a ground jarring thud. The doorway was completely blocked.

Diam turned to look at Tonia, her wide, brown eyes filled with surprised thanks. The thick slab of stone would have crushed her like an alia leaf if she hadn't stopped when she did.

"That was close," she said. Just as she caught Tonia's gaze, a piece of ice from the sculpture cracked and fell to the floor, shattering in hundreds of glistening pieces like a shower of shooting stars.

"Get away from it!" Diam shouted to her friends as she drew

153

her sword.

While this was happening, it didn't take long for Kaileen to see that the entryway on the other side of the room was still open.

"Over there!" she called out as she pointed at the door.

Without hesitation, the three girls began running toward the opening as more ice cracked and fell from the glistening statue. Before they could reach the doorway, however, another thick chunk of black stone slammed down in front of this entryway as well.

They were trapped.

"Tonia, listen to me!" Kennard's voice boomed in her head.

Without thinking, Tonia clapped her hands over her ears, not realizing it would do her no good. Before she could answer the muck dragon, he gave her one final piece of advice in a voice that was different than it had been any other time he'd communicated to her. As she listened to her unseen friend, his voice began quickly fading away, almost as if it was being carried in the opposite direction by a gust of wind in the valley.

"Remember the ring..." she heard him say before his voice fell completely silent.

"Kennard!" she called out to him frantically, but she somehow knew she would receive no answer. Whatever was going on was blocking their communication.

They were on their own.

"Tonia?" Kaileen asked. As she drew her sword, she glanced nervously at her friends.

Their adventure was certainly more than she'd bargained for when she agreed to join them, Kaileen thought as one corner of her mouth twitched with the shadow of a smile.

"I'm okay," Tonia said over the sound of tinkling ice shattering on the crystalline cave floor. "Kennard was trying to talk to me, but I can't hear him anymore."

The girls stared at the crumbling statue, helpless to do anything but watch as hundreds of lines crept like vines through every part of the icy sculpture. At the rate the ice was cracking around the massive body, it wouldn't take long before the beast broke completely free of its frozen prison.

Tonia drew her sword as Diam asked, "What did he say?"

"I'm not sure," she said as she shook her head in disbelief. "Something about remembering the ring..."

Diam's eyes widened as she reached toward the webbing covering her waist and hip, searching for the nearly invisible gap hidden there.

"Oh, no," she said in a panicked voice. "Tonia, I can't find it!"

"Diam," Tonia said calmly. She struggled to get her friend's attention as she placed a cool, unwavering hand on Diam's web-covered arm. Diam briefly locked eyes with Tonia and could feel her friend's energetic touch as soon as Tonia's hand made contact with her. She took a short, quick breath, and immediately calmed down.

"Take your time, Diam – it's there. It has to be," Tonia said in a reassuring tone.

Diam nodded and took another deep breath. Without looking at her friend, she began searching again, and like magic, the opening appeared to move by itself. There it was – the two inch long opening she was looking for. Without a second's hesitation, she dug her fingers deep into the somewhat secure opening, searching for the one and only item that should be there. She breathed a sigh of relief as her fingers brushed across the small, cool piece of metal.

"It's there," she whispered. Her voice was calm and soft.

"Good," Tonia said. She nodded as she turned her attention back to the shiny, crackling sculpture across the room.

"What do we do?" Kaileen asked as the large chunk of ice from the entire back side of the dragon's left wing suddenly dropped and smashed on the floor. It shattered in millions of pieces, shooting ice pellets directly toward the girls. Without a word, they tried to protect their faces by ducking their heads into the crooks of their arms.

"Ouch!" Diam shouted when a piece of the broken sculpture bounced off the floor and made painful contact with her head.

Although their extremities were covered with protective webbing, their heads and certain other areas of their skin were still exposed. Unfortunately, when it came to small pieces of ice flying at them from across the room, it was quite obvious that a few of those which came in contact with body parts, in spite of being covered with webbing, were very likely going to be felt.

"Keep watching the creature while I check something," Diam whispered to the others. Without waiting for an answer, she turned and began inspecting the wall around the doorway.

"What are you doing?" Kaileen asked as she kept her eyes on the crumbling sculpture.

"I'm looking for a way out," Diam answered.

"Oh, no," Tonia said as her voice shook with fear. "I think it's moving its wing…"

Diam glanced briefly at the dragon before hastening her search for an exit. The creature was definitely moving its left wing – just a little bit, but any movement was BAD movement! She frantically ran her hands along inner and outer edges of the cold, dark block that looked much like a giant slab of marbled stone. She was hoping to find some sign of a switch, lever, or anything that might give her a clue as to how the door worked, but frowned when she found nothing.

As the dragon slowly moved its left wing, more ice along the rest of its body cracked and splintered. Without warning, the beast jerked its other wing backward. The movement hurled an unexpected, large, round chunk right toward the girls.

"Diam, duck down!" Tonia called out as she quickly reached back and grabbed her friend's web-covered back in an attempt to pull Diam to the ground. Again trusting Tonia's reaction, Diam did as she was told, dropping as low as she could just as a large piece of ice shattered on the upper part of the black slab blocking the doorway. It shattered into hundreds of pieces directly over the girls' heads on impact.

Diam's head was very close to Tonia's and she looked at her friend with a sigh of relief.

"Thanks – that was a little too close!"

Tonia nodded as the sounds of cracking ice began to grow infinitely louder.

"Come on," Kaileen said. She turned and began scooting along the cave wall, heading away from the dragon. Diam and Tonia followed her, each wielding their weapons the entire time. When they reached the farthest point away from the dark gray creature hatching from the ice, they stopped and looked back at the sculpture.

The dragon was slowly moving its head from side to side as shards and chunks of frozen water fell to the floor at its feet. Once its massive wings became free from the ice, the dragon lowered them to its sides. With a surprise flick of its tail, the final pieces of its icy cocoon dropped to the ground with a splintering crash. The dragon blinked a few times as if struggling to see, then suddenly turned and stared directly at the girls.

"You do not belong here," the beast hissed as he glared at the intruders.

The girls watched helplessly as the impossibly alive creature stretched like a cat waking from a long nap. As soon as its stretch was completed, the beast turned and began methodically making its way directly toward them!

SEVENTEEN

Whispers filtered through the winding halls of the castle as Orob walked through the lower levels of the cold, gloomy fortress. He was about to take part in an event he never dreamed he would be part of, but before that happened, he had to make one final, hasty stop. He spoke to no one as he walked quickly from one castle passageway to the next until he finally stopped in front of a plain looking, single wooden door on the level just above the dungeon. He glanced first to his right, and then his left. The passageway was empty in both directions.

Just as he was about to knock on the closed door, it creaked open.

Nivri had an impressive array of unusual looking creatures doing his bidding throughout the castle, some more different than others. Not surprising, their sizes ranged from quite small to extremely large. The creature looking at him through the opened doorway now was somewhere in the middle, just larger than Zacharu, yet not quite the size of the human prisoner had been. As far as Orob was concerned, the creature staring at him with an expectant expression was delicate, beautiful, and wonderfully feminine.

He smiled at her as his heart thumped loudly in his chest.

"It is time."

She nodded and offered a hint of a smile before stepping

into the passageway, then closed the door softly behind her. Her hands were empty, but he wasn't surprised – she didn't need to bring anything but herself.

They walked in silence back to the guard room, he with his slow, awkward gait, and she with the grace of a princess. She wore a thin, light pink, floor length dress, its jagged edges wafting around her. On her feet she wore dark pink slippers made from thick, expensive satin. As they walked quietly together, side by side, her long, straight, calico hair flowed as if being blown by a gentle breeze coming from somewhere ahead of her. Orob stood easily a foot taller than this delicate creature at his side, but they walked together as if they were equals.

Orob finally spoke when they arrived at the Guard Room.

"Wait here."

She nodded, watching him as she stood next to the wall. Orob pushed the door open slightly and poked his head inside while his body remained out in the passageway. He mumbled something the female creature couldn't hear, and within seconds, the door was thrown open and a large group of guards spilled out into the hall. When they saw the salmon colored female waiting there for them, their eyes lit up with appreciation and they nodded respectfully. Without a word, every one of the armor-clad warriors stepped aside, making room for the rest of the exiting guards to join them.

Orob stood just outside the door, waiting patiently for his fellow guards to file out of the room like ants on a mission. As soon as all the guards were accounted for, he nodded and whispered a final command.

"Let's go."

Muffled, excited mumbles of approval moved through the group as they and their mysterious female companion made their way through the winding castle passageways until they reached the narrow tunnel with the hidden staircase. One at a time, the guards climbed their way up the ladder until they all stood in the dimly lit cavern at the top. The final member of their group to emerge from the tunnel was their petite, almost angelic looking, female companion.

"We must move quickly now," the vision in pink purred in a

low, authoritative voice that jingled like bells in the wind.

The gathering of hairy, dark skinned guards stood watching her for a moment, each caught up in her beauty. Light from the lone torch in the cavern glinted off her hair like firebugs in the forest on the darkest of nights. Like her hair, her wide, hazel eyes also sparkled in the dim, flickering torch light. Her locks were decorated with various colors of small, round beads, strung in wide arcs from the front to the back. Long, narrow, pointed ears sprouted from either side of her hair, and from the lobe of each of these dangled a single, pink earring.

Focusing on the task ahead, Orob nodded at the group before he turned and led the way westward along a barely recognizable path. Outside of the cave, the cool night air greeted them as the large group of castle inhabitants followed the trail of the former prisoners. After a while, Orob stopped along the edge of the trail to wait for their female companion as he waved the rest of the guards on. He nodded at the passing guards and suddenly realized they had accumulated quite a procession of creatures, each with hopes for a world that would most certainly see overwhelming darkness, death, and misfortune in the near future unless something was done to change it.

He could only hope they would all live to see this change. He also knew without a shadow of a doubt that if change was going to happen, it would have to happen soon.

The end of the line of stoic looking beagons came into view, and as the final creature approached, Orob couldn't help but smile. Passing him was a decent sized group of armored, weapon-wielding guards making their way together up a barely discernible path. Each stoic looking warrior in his group understood and was fully prepared to do battle against an evil worse than any of them had ever experienced. They were all heading toward something none of them could see the result of, and bringing up the end of that line of frowning, hairy beasts was a dreamy, beautiful angel in pink.

This brought him to their newest member. Although she appeared to be a lithe, harmless female creature that wouldn't harm a firebug, Orob knew better. He had complete confidence she would be an asset to their small band of warriors. She was a mesmerizing, graceful creature that was prepared, like the rest of the warriors, to throw away her entire life, everything and everyone she'd ever known, to support a belief, a memory, of something as uncertain as this.

"You're certain of the impending battle?" Orob quietly asked as she approached him. The smile on his hairy face was quickly replaced by a frown of consternation.

"Yes, absolutely certain," Aseret answered as Orob turned and fell into step at her side.

"How long do we have?"

While he waited for her to answer, he attempted to catch a casual glimpse of her from the corner of his eye. They had long been acquaintances in the castle, but only over the past few weeks had they really gotten to know each other. At first glance, it would appear the beagon and the naiad were as different as the moon and the sun, but some friendships bloom in spite of the differences between appearances or species.

"From what I've been able to pick up from others of my kind, a storm is coming," she said as her eyes focused on the guards ahead. "I have requested immediate assistance from anyone I can think of, but only time will tell whether or not they will support our cause."

Orob grunted in understanding.

"We must hurry to the lake," she said as she turned to look at him. The guard held her gaze for a moment.

"The sun will rise soon," she added softly before falling silent. There was no need for more words – Orob understood her message.

With a nod, he pulled his dark, serious eyes away from hers. Although her own eyes were gentle when looking at the guard, their centers began to glow with a bright, yet thin, pink ring as her thoughts focused on the seriousness of their situation. Seemingly unaffected by this change, Orob lowered his head and picked up his pace along the uphill, rocky path, intent on moving to the front of the line of guards to lead them to the place where, soon, life and death would converge as one.

EIGHTEEN

The girls held their swords tightly as they began pushing back against the wall behind them. None of them were surprised when it didn't budge.

"I love you guys," Tonia whispered to her friends, keeping her wide, brown eyes focused on the large, gray creature as it continued its slow, taunting approach toward them. The dragon slowly smiled in anticipation, and as they watched, the smile melted into tooth-filled, evil snarl. It was hard to miss the two wide rows of long, white teeth that nearly spilled out of the beast's mouth.

"Love you, too," Kaileen and Diam replied in unison, ignoring the intimidating sounds coming from the approaching dragon. As the shallow echoes of their voices disappeared, each of the girls found it difficult not to focus on the unfortunate sounds of the approaching beast that swirled around the room like a wind storm.

A low growling, much like that of an angered dog, rumbled from some place deep within the belly of the dragon. As the approaching creature took one slow step after another, its long, black claws scraped on the uneven, rocky floor. The distance between the beast and the girls narrowed slowly until it stood about fifteen feet away, where it suddenly stopped.

"You definitely do not belong here," the dragon whispered

through clenched teeth as its eyes twinkled with anticipation, "but may I admit that I'm glad you are?

"As you can imagine, I've been trapped in that cold, icy layer of skin for quite some time. Now that I'm finally free of those physical bindings, however, I feel as though I must voice my gratitude to you for freeing me."

Its mouth curved into a tight smile as its eyes narrowed into wide, twitching slits.

With nowhere to run, the girls bravely stood their ground. They held tightly to their swords and stared at the beast as they each struggled to think of what they should do.

"Yes," the dragon nodded, "I will thank you once for freeing me, and then I will thank you twice for volunteering to be my first meal in a very, very long time…"

Kaileen glanced at Tonia as she raised her sword in a brave display of strength. Her eyes glared at the beast, and when she finally spoke, her words expressed the intense defiance each of the girls felt.

"Not without a fight, you won't," she hissed.

Tonia's next words were directed to her friends as her eyes remained focused on the gray creature that stood smirking at them with black eyes filled with confidence.

"Spread out!"

As if expecting her instructions, Tonia's friends immediately reacted. Kaileen moved quickly along the edge of the wall until she was near the dark hole in the tunnel, while Diam moved in the other direction and headed toward the other archway. After seeing which way her friends were going, Tonia smiled at the beast, but her smile did not reach her eyes.

"If you attack one of us, the others will slice you to shreds," she said with a wry smile. "You may succeed in killing one of us, or maybe all of us, but you will not do so without sustaining significant damage… I promise you that."

The dragon watched the girls as they spread out around him, surprised by their maturity and ability to focus this well when faced with a situation that most grown men would run away from like cowards.

"Are you volunteering, then?" the beast asked Tonia in a

voice that almost sounded like a purr. It stared hungrily at her as it took another slow, grating step toward her. Diam and Kaileen mimicked each of the dragon's movements. As it took a step toward Tonia, Diam and Kaileen took a step toward it. The dragon sensed their movement and smiled with satisfaction. This could prove to be one of the most delightful battles he'd seen in centuries! His smile widened as he ruffled his wings into a more comfortable position across his back.

"You want me to volunteer?" the young girl hissed again as she raised her sword to eye level. Across the room, Diam's heart skipped a beat as she watched her friend.

Tonia was a great friend and Diam loved her to death, but when she got the determined, glazed look in her eyes that she had right now, Diam knew without a doubt it wasn't a good thing. When she was both angry and focused, Tonia was a force to be reckoned with, as Diam was sure Micah would happily attest to. She helplessly watched her friend with both pride and fear as Tonia stood one on one, face to face with a creature she'd dreamed her whole life she'd see. Under different circumstances, this would be a dream come true for her friend, but in the present time and place, it was anything but a dream.

It was more like a nightmare.

"I volunteer to do my very best to gouge out your eyes with my sword if you so much as even think about harming me or my friends," Tonia replied without attempting to mask her anger as she answered the dragon's question.

Diam's mind raced as she tried to think of anything they could do or say to stop the dragon's advances on her friend. After a few frantic seconds, the only thing she could think of would be to step forward and somehow coerce the dragon to come for her instead, but she had nothing to offer...

Or did she?

"I love the frisky ones," the dragon mumbled with a cocky shake of its head. He began to drool in anticipation as his eyes focused on the young girl standing in front of him... so brave... so tasty! His sharp teeth glistened as warm saliva oozed down their lengths.

"You should have been around centuries ago to teach men

how to stand tall and proud, instead of cowering before me like screaming, helpless children as I devoured them."

The dragon turned his head to the left, then the right, as he looked around the room. For a few seconds, his dark eyes lingered on the blocked passageways.

"And, it's quite fortunate for you... since you have no way out of here. I will be more than happy to save you from a long, painful death of cold starvation after being trapped helplessly in this cave..."

Without waiting for her to respond, the ancient creature lunged at the young girl. Instead of watching the actions of the other two girls in the room, the dragon completely focused on thoughts of a fresh, warm meal. Just before he left the ground, an unexpected, bright flash of light illuminated the cavern from somewhere behind him. Thoughts of consuming the young girl were suddenly replaced with both surprise and curiosity. Distracted, the beast miscalculated the distance to the girl and crashed into the wall before falling to the floor with a thud and a cry of pain.

Tonia dashed to the right as soon as she realized the dragon overshot his jump. As if in slow motion, she waited for the moment the beast would land on the ground so she could make an offensive move of her own – aiming for his head, his eyes. She was so focused on her thoughts of damaging the beast as quickly and effectively as possible that she failed to notice what was happening on the other side of the room.

"Aaaaaaaaaaaargh!"

The dragon cried out in pain as he took a breath and slowly got to his feet. With blazing, angry eyes he whirled around to look for his intended victim just as an unexpected movement across the room captured his attention.

"Diam?" Kaileen called out as both she and the dragon stared at the place where the other girl in their group had been standing just moments before.

The young girl with the curly black hair had disappeared. In her place stood a ghostly, dark haired stranger in a flowing, white gown.

"You will not harm these girls," the ghostly woman said

165

sternly to the dragon in a feminine, firm voice that echoed like a song around the cavern.

The woman held her right arm behind her back, and as the dragon stared at her, she slowly moved it until it was extended out in front of her. In her hand she held a beautiful, gold scepter. At the top of this exquisite, beautifully carved rod was a faceted, purple stone that shone like the brightest star on the blackest night, chasing away any shadows lingering around the cavern. Without waiting for the beast to answer her, the woman waved the scepter in a wide arc before pointing it in the dragon's direction. An instantaneous, electric ray of red and blue jagged lines spewed from the tip of the scepter, shooting across the cavern. Before anyone knew what was happening, the dragon was crying out in pain.

It had been struck on the left side.

The dragon turned and charged the ghostly woman as thick, blue liquid began oozing from the wound on its side.

"No!" the beast cried in anger and pain as another ray of light struck him, this time in the front right leg.

Behind the beast, Tonia smiled at the opportunity as she raised her sword in preparation.

"Attack!"

Kaileen hesitated for only a second before she began running straight for the large gray creature. Her aim was focused on its right side while Tonia charged from the left rear. As the dragon lunged at the ghostly figure that stood without fear in the place where Diam had been just moments before, the apparition suddenly rose into the air where it hovered just above Tonia for a moment. Before the dragon realized what was happening, another electric bolt of light shot through the air. This time, the damage occurred on its left wing, which was still tucked tightly against his side.

The force of the impact drove the damaged creature into the wall of the cave. In the blink of a firebug, the dragon slumped to the floor. There was no mistaking the beast's anger and pain as it growled loudly, shaking its head as it attempted to regain its bearings. The pupils in the creature's eyes expanded and contracted for a few seconds as it struggled to focus. Eventually, he turned to look for the ghostly woman, eventually spotting her a few feet off the ground. The beast took a deep breath, preparing for a fiery roar, as a red hot, screaming pain raged without warning through its left side.

The beast reflexively turned to the left just as Tonia withdrew her sword and plunged again.

Forgetting about the ghostly figure, the dragon threw its head back with a roar of agony as it swung around to the left. It was now totally focused on pummeling its attacker with its neck and tail. Tonia anticipated this and stepped away just in the nick of time. The beast threw her a hateful glare and growled just as Kaileen plunged her own sword into the dragon's right thigh. Again the dragon howled in pain and began to turn his head in the other direction when another red and blue bolt of light struck him on his left side. The beast collapsed where he stood, breathing heavily, then glared up at the ghostly white figure. A complete look of pure hatred washed across its face before it closed its eyes and began howling with both anger and pain. Kaileen ran around the back side of the beast and joined Tonia a few feet away from the dying creature.

"You must finish it," the ghostly woman said to Tonia in a soothing, gentle voice. She gave the young girl an encouraging nod as she descended gracefully back to the ground.

Tonia stared at the thick river of dark, blue blood running from the wounded beast as it lay next to the wall. She took a hesitant step backward as the dragon began to tremble, afraid it was somehow working its way up to another attack. The injured creature struggled to raise itself up for a few seconds before collapsing again into a bloody heap on the cavern floor. The girls watched in amazement as the vile monster slowly rolled over onto its right side as if being pulled by unseen large, gentle hands. Finally, after a few seconds, the only movement from the massive body came from the sporadic rising and falling of its sides as it struggled with each slow, labored breath.

While she stared at the dying dragon, Tonia finally replied to the ghost's suggestion that she needed to finish the job.

"How?"

Although she tried to sound confident, she whispered the

question with visible uncertainty.

"I will restrain it, but you must plunge your sword deep into its heart," the woman in white answered.

Without waiting for the young girl to lose her nerve, the ghostly apparition suddenly extended her hands, palms out and facing the dragon. The scepter she'd been using just a few moments before was now nowhere to be seen.

The girls began to hear a low pitched whining sound when the vision of a pale, white blanket appeared out of thin air. Like a leaf falling out of a tree on a gentle autumn breeze, the blanket floated slowly downward until it completely covered the dragon. The beast either didn't see this white, translucent blanket or didn't care. It remained where it had collapsed, almost lifeless.

Tonia stared with doubt-filled eyes at the ghostly woman. Feeling the young girl's hesitation, the woman in white nodded her reassurance.

"You must," the ghost encouraged.

"Do you want me to do it?" Kaileen asked from somewhere behind her. Without waiting for Tonia's answer, the kalevala took a step toward the dragon.

"No!" Tonia shouted as her hand shot out to restrain Kaileen. "I can do it."

She turned back to the ghostly figure with a solemn frown and reddened eyes.

"Is it the only way?"

The dark-haired woman nodded.

"But why in the heart?" she asked. "It seems so... final... to aim for the heart."

"It *will* be final," the woman answered matter-of-factly, "but I'm sure you know the heart of the beast holds the heart of Euqinom."

Before she could reply, Tonia suddenly heard a different, yet familiar voice in her head.

"Tonia."

Tonia squealed with surprise before she realized she recognized the owner of the voice.

"You must defeat the dragon in order to retrieve the amulet."

When there was no immediate response from the girl, the

muck dragon added, "You must defeat the dragon in order to *save the dragons.*"

"But it's a dragon," she answered in her mind, unable to believe she would have to kill the only dragon, or the only dragon that actually *looked* like a real dragon, that she'd ever seen. It wasn't just part of a myth or a story told to the villagers in front of a crackling campfire. This was the real thing, the real deal...

A real dragon.

"Tonia, it appears to be a dragon, but it's really not. Its only purpose was to protect the amulet," Kennard said reassuringly.

"You must finish it soon, young one," the ghostly woman's soft, excited voice prodded as it echoed off the cavern walls. "Finish it before the spell of restraint wears off."

"Do it now," Kennard ordered. "Tonia, do it now, before it's too late and we all perish!"

Finally convinced, Tonia nodded and took a step toward the dragon. As she approached it, the beast twisted its head so it could look directly at her. When it spoke, its voice was both staggered and raspy.

"You...

"Are...

"Not..."

The young girl stopped just a few feet away from the dragon as it closed its eyes and struggled with another breath. She waited for a long moment, and when she was sure it would be silent, she began moving again. As a flurry of emotions battled within her, she took one slow, hesitant step toward the dragon, then another. Without warning, the beast raised its head a few inches and opened its eyes again. It locked eyes with the young girl, staring at her with an intense, fiery hatred as Tonia stood in silence, just inches away from its injured side. As she thought about what she was about to do, she suddenly felt an eerie, icy chill shoot up her spine that bristled the hairs at the nape of her neck.

"You are not... the chosen one," the beast eventually whispered, its cold glare locked on the young girl.

For a long moment, Tonia couldn't move. She struggled with the idea of what she knew she must do, but didn't know if she had the strength or ability *to* do it. Just when she was about to turn toward the ghost and walk away in defeat, the dragon suddenly dropped its head with a thud and exhaled a long, shuddering, dying breath.

"Now!" the ghostly woman ordered, jolting Tonia out of her reverie. "Hurry, before it's too late! You must pierce the heart before the beast is gone… before the amulet is gone and no longer attainable!"

"Now, Tonia!" Kennard ordered with a booming voice. His order echoed like thunder between her ears, filled her heart, and consumed her soul.

Without giving another thought to the dying dragon's final words, Tonia wrapped both hands around the hilt of her sword, raised it over her head and thrust it down into the side of the beast's wide, dark chest with everything she had. She felt the sword first puncture the dragon's skin then enter the chest cavity. In the blink of a firebug, the outer edges of her palms were finally lying against the beast's bloody side.

The dragon did not offer any signs of resistance as Tonia begrudgingly followed the orders she was given. When she looked down, she was surprised to see that her sword had pierced the dying beast's side nearly all the way to the hilt.

"Again!" the ghostly woman ordered from somewhere behind her now. "You must cut out the heart!"

Focused again on her task, Tonia stood over the dragon as she wiggled the sword from the gaping hole she'd made in the side of the creature's chest. She took a quick breath and plunged the sword downward yet again. She heard the thick skin ripping and felt the chest cavity crunching as bones broke from the force of the impact. After repeating this procedure one more time, she thought she had enough of an opening to get to the large vessel nested behind the scales, muscles, and dark, sticky blood.

"Diam, Kaileen, help me," Tonia called out as she dropped her sword to the floor beside her. Without waiting for her friends, she fell to her knees and began using her hands to pry the lifeless beast's chest cavity apart. In an instant, Kaileen was on her knees at Tonia's side, digging and clawing at the dragon's chest with focused determination.

Although the large, gray creature was no longer breathing, the girls began to see a soft, blue glow emanating from somewhere deep within the its corpse. Kaileen dug her hands deeper into the dragon's body, searching for treasure. Eventually, the light shone a little brighter, then a little more. Just when she thought she couldn't dig any further, Kaileen saw that the blue light had strangely begun to change to a smaller, piercing white light. Seconds later, Tonia began to move a large chunk of dripping heart muscle.

"Grab it," Tonia told her friend breathlessly as she shoved the muscle to the side. "Grab it while I separate it. Hurry! I don't know how much longer I can hold it!"

It took a few seconds for Kaileen to manipulate her much smaller hands around the brightly shining object, but eventually, she began gently removing it from the dragon's chest cavity. As her blood covered hands withdrew from the body, the only thing both girls could see was a beautiful, bloody gem.

Silence filled the cavern as they stared at the glowing stone, mesmerized by its dazzling brilliance and beauty in spite of the dark, blue blood smeared across nearly every part of its surface.

"It's beautiful," Tonia said quietly as her eyes slowly filled with tears. For a long time, she had doubted there really was an amulet hidden in this cave. Nevertheless, she still felt compelled to carry on with their quest. Relief washed over her as she realized everything Kennard had told her was true. She could no longer doubt this was the item they'd come here to get.

She sniffled and wiped her eyes with the upper part of her arm, then repeated the process for her nose. She took a deep breath and turned her palms upward, staring at her abnormally dark colored hands. Her lower arms and hands were almost completely covered with sticky blue blood.

"Tonia?" Kaileen asked quietly, almost afraid to intrude on her friend's thoughts, but feeling she had no choice.

Tonia looked up at Kaileen, whose face was bathed in soft, whitish-blue light from the glowing gem she held snugly in her lap. The kalevala was staring at her with a worried expression.

"Yeah?"

"Where's Diam?" Kaileen asked nervously. "I noticed earlier she wasn't standing in the place where she had been, but then the dragon went after you. Now that we don't have to worry about the dragon anymore, I don't see her anywhere, and I don't know where she went."

When Tonia looked around the room, her eyes were first drawn to both of the arched doorways. They were still completely blocked by the black marble slabs. Then something else caught her eye, and the sight made her heart jump into her throat. The only other figure in the room was the ghostly form of an angelic woman – the one who had just been guiding Tonia through what she needed to do with the dragon. The woman shimmered in a pale, white light, a few feet away, as she watched them in complete silence. Tonia felt a knot settle in the pit of her stomach when she realized she didn't see Diam anywhere in the room.

"Diam?" she called out as she picked up her sword and got to her feet, the amulet momentarily forgotten. The echo of her voice was the only answer she received.

"Diam?" she called again, louder this time. Her nervous eyes darted from one side of the room to the other. When she still received no response, her focus returned to the ghostly apparition.

The dark haired, luminescent female figure was smiling at her.

"What?" Tonia asked, scowling at the stranger, obviously offended by the expression on the woman's face. Her friend was missing and this woman was smiling about it? She shook her head as her worry changed to anger.

Tonia looked around the room again. It only took a second or two for her to finally admit to herself her friend was no longer anywhere in the cavern. Kaileen stood at her side, about a foot away. As Tonia's eyes again focused on the ghostly figure, she realized the apparition was standing in the same general location where they'd last seen Diam.

"Where is she?" Tonia asked accusingly. With glaring eyes she took a step toward the woman. As she approached the partially transparent figure, the smile slowly began to fade from the apparition's face.

"Where did she go?" Tonia growled. "You've been watching what's been going on in here the entire time, haven't you? You must have seen where Diam went!"

The ghost simply shook her head in denial as Tonia called out for her friend again.

"Diam? Where are you?"

Ignoring the ghost temporarily, Tonia made her way over to the dark tunnel entrance by the shallow pond.

"Diam!" she called into the tunnel. Again, the only answer she received was her echoing, insistent voice, repeating her friend's name over and over before fading away into silence.

She turned back to the ghost as her grip on her sword tightened.

"Where... is... she?" Tonia hissed. She glared at the misty figure as she headed directly toward her.

When Tonia was just a few feet away, the woman held her hands out toward her, indicating she wanted her to stop. Strangely, instead of facing her palms outward, towards Tonia, the ghost faced her palms toward herself, so the backside of her hands faced the approaching girl.

The gesture meant nothing to Tonia, who knew she couldn't bear to lose Diam, her best friend in the whole world. She couldn't be gone – she had to be here somewhere, so they could leave together! They'd manage to retrieve the amulet and now they could leave, couldn't they?

Without thinking, Tonia glared at the ghost's face as her own face flashed a mixture of emotions – first fear, then anger, and eventually determination. Tonia wasn't thinking about what the woman had done to the dragon. All she could think about was standing nose to nose with the stranger. She was totally focused on showing the ghost she was serious about her friend! She wanted nothing more than to find Diam so they could leave. Then, once they found her, the ghost could have this cold dragon crypt all to itself!

As she focused on the creature's eyes, something shiny on the ghost's finger suddenly caught Tonia's eye. When she realized what she was looking at, the young girl immediately froze in place as her eyes bulged with complete and totally unexpected surprise.

On the ring finger of the apparition's left hand was a sparkling, beautiful ring. As Tonia stared at the glittering piece of jewelry, she could see swirling white clouds swimming across the surface of the round, magnificent green gem in the center of the ring.

Tonia choked on her breath, unable to believe her eyes! The ghost was wearing the ring they'd found in the cave!

Nineteen

Zel and Zacharu trailed at the end of the group of warriors as they carefully made their way down to the lake. The moon continued to light the sky with its colorful hues, but it wouldn't be long before the sun crested the eastern horizon with the dawn of a new day.

Once they were well on their way, Simcha continued his earlier discussion with the messenger and eventually determined the impending battle would happen sometime after the sun was up. Since time was of the essence, they took no breaks as they headed toward their destination.

Eventually, Simcha stopped them and ordered them to don their full battle gear, including shields and face masks. Many of the warriors had their masks and shields strung across their backs, and stopped briefly to help each other. After a few minutes, the warriors, including Zel and Zacharu, were walking again, but this time they were fully armored, head to toe.

"We will be able to see the lake once we make it around that hill," one of the warriors said as he pointed to the barely visible gray, rocky hillside in front of them. The path they were following took them on a slight decline, and from what Zel could tell, they still had quite a distance to travel before they reached the bottom. The path was narrow and the group of warriors had no choice but to follow each other single file as they trudged on.

They passed the large hill, but it was too dark to clearly see the lake in the distance. They continued on in silence as the hill was replaced by a thick expanse of brush, when suddenly, an unfamiliar voice called out to them from somewhere in the nearby shadows.

"Halt!"

The human warriors instantly stopped and drew their swords, raising their shields defensively in front of them.

"Who goes there?" the deep, emanating voice called out from somewhere behind a nearby bush.

"We pass in peace," Simcha answered firmly as he stood his ground alongside his warriors.

"What is your name, soldier?" the deep, authoritative voice demanded.

Zel noticed that Simcha hesitated for half a second before he answered.

"I am Simcha."

The sound of rustling leaves and twigs suddenly filled the air as abnormally large, shadowy forms began to take shape everywhere around the human warriors. Some materialized from deep within the bushes, while others appeared farther along the path. As Zel turned his head, a slight movement behind them caught his eye. He cringed when he realized it was a dozen or so of the dark, armor-clad beings.

They were surrounded!

Zel was standing close to one end of the bushes, where a tall, masked creature suddenly emerged from the shadows. In one hand, the dark figure held a battle axe with a massive blade. In the other it held a glittering, silver shield.

Not all of the human warriors were wearing their helmets. Instead of donning their head gear when the rest of the group had done so, these men had chosen to wait until they got closer to the lake before putting on the heavy, somewhat uncomfortable, head pieces. The shadowy figure that had just emerged near the bushes, close to Zel and Zacharu, was also close to some of these non-helmeted men.

"Grrrrrrrrr," the deep voiced stranger growled as he surveyed the group of humans.

"You!" his voice boomed as he pointed at a thin, unmasked, blonde haired man in the center of the group of men. "Weren't you being held captive in the castle?"

Without waiting for an answer, the deep voiced newcomer turned and began pushing his way into the crowd of men, heading straight for the fair-haired human.

"What are you doing?" Simcha asked as he turned to head back toward the commotion. He didn't get very far because the path became suddenly blocked by three large, axe wielding warriors.

The blonde-haired human stood his ground as the tall, hairy warrior approached.

Zel remained silent as he watched the scene unfold in front of him. As the hairy guard spoke to the blonde human, he detected a familiarity that he couldn't quite put his finger on. He'd been held prisoner in the castle for more days and weeks than he cared to admit, so how could it be that any voice outside the castle would be familiar to him?

He shook his head in denial. The possibility of his knowing anyone outside the castle walls in such an unfamiliar world was totally unlikely, he told himself. There was no way he'd recognize the voice of strangers out here...

Although the humans were both outnumbered and outsized by many of the dark figures that surrounded them, the tension in the crowd was intensifying at an astounding rate as the dark figure continued stomping through the leaves as he headed directly toward the fair-haired human.

"How did you escape from of the castle, prisoner?" the dark, armor clad warrior asked the blonde man as he stopped abruptly just inches away from him.

"Tell me how you escaped!" the voice boomed.

The tension among them was as thick as mud. Angry whispers raced through the crowd of humans and just when a battle seemed eminent, the nagging voice in Zel's head suddenly gave him the surprising answer to his question.

"Orob!"

The tall, dark warrior towering over the human whirled around as he searched for the voice calling his name. Had it come from the outer edge of the crowd?

"Orob, it's me," Zel said hastily as he pulled off his helmet. "The man you are speaking to is Lacsar. He didn't escape from the castle – he was released."

"Hmmph..." the warrior grunted in response.

"A few weeks ago, he was released into this world with no food, no weapons," Zel explained. "Nivri thought it would be more entertaining to hear stories about how this man died at the hands of some hungry beast than to let him die somewhere within the walls of the castle."

Zel knew he risked being recaptured and returned back to the castle, but he trusted Orob. He also believed, no matter what had happened in the castle, the beagon had a good heart under his thick skin and mat of scruffy hair. He hoped more than anything the beagon would not let him down... especially now.

"Orob, we could really use your help," Zel pleaded as he made his way towards the former guard.

"Help?" Orob asked curiously as he passed a narrow-eyed glance at the blonde man.

Simcha had been listening to the conversation and finally managed to push his way through the crowd. He didn't stop until he was standing next to Zel.

"Many of my men are former prisoners of the castle, and each one was released for one reason or another. That, however, is neither here nor there."

Orob stared at the armored human leader standing right in front of him. Without a word, the castle guard removed his helmet then gestured at the human leader.

"Let's be men and speak to each other face to face," the guard said as he pointed at the leader's helmet. "I like to look into the eyes when I have a conversation with someone, especially when the conversation is as important as this."

Simcha nodded his approval. In one swift movement, he removed his helmet and tucked it safely under his arm.

"Agreed," the human said as he held his right hand out to the guard as a peace offering.

Orob smiled and shook the human's hand.

"Orob, this is Simcha. Simcha, Orob," Zel said with a quiet

sigh of relief. It looked like they weren't going to have a bloody battle after all, he thought with a small smile.

"What are you doing out here?" Zel asked his former guard. It seemed very odd to see the beagon outside the gloomy castle walls... very strange, indeed.

Orob knew quite well how his former prisoner felt about Nivri, so he only briefly hesitated before offering an explanation.

"We got word of an impending battle," the guard explained curtly as his eyes scanned the group of mostly unfamiliar humans.

"A battle?" Simcha asked as he scratched his chin in an attempt to sound surprised. "What battle? Where?"

"We've been informed that there will be a major battle sometime after sunrise down near the lake," Orob explained.

Simcha nodded his head in understanding as he considered the guard's words. After a moment of thoughtfully rubbing his chin, he finally asked, "And Nivri is involved, yes?"

Orob nodded his head, but before he could offer any kind of response to accompany his gesture, Zel spoke up excitedly.

"We heard the same thing..."

As the former prisoner considered the implications of what he'd just heard, he hesitated. After a long moment, an unfortunate thought suddenly occurred to him.

"Orob," he began. He didn't attempt to hide his concern as he stared at his former guard. "Are you planning on fighting with Nivri or against him?"

Orob considered Zel's question before offering a surprising, single-worded explanation.

"Against."

Zel's eyes lit up with disbelief as he passed a hopeful glance at Simcha.

"Orob," Zel continued, "I've got a crazy feeling when the sun rises in just a few hours, a lot more will be at stake than simply one warrior battling another."

The armored guard stared at his former prisoner in silence as he considered his words.

"Orob," Zel added as he rested is hand on the guard's hairy arm, "help us try to save this world. Help us fight for innocent people and creatures everywhere. Stand up with us as we try to make a difference. We may not be able to beat him, but Orob, we've got to try! You more than anyone should know this..."

The prisoner stared at the beagon with a pleading expression. The air was thick with tension as the guard stared back at him with his wide, unreadable eyes.

"Orob, please..."

Zel's voice was barely a whisper in the cool night air. Silence surrounded them as the large group of men waited for the guard's response, if any, to Zel's request. Not wanting to give up, Zel turned and passed a hopeful glance at Simcha. The human leader nodded once while waiting for the beagon guard to answer.

While twilight began to slowly chase away the shadows of night, Orob's eyes surveyed the mixed group of silent men and beagons standing in a loose circle around them. He understood this was a rare opportunity, and if he knew Nivri at all, this would be the only chance they would have of defeating the darkly cloaked creature while he was still the weaker of the two sorcerers. He, more than anyone else, had no doubt that they had to make their move, if a move was to be made, before Nivri he had the chance to recover any of the missing amulets.

It was now or never.

After sharing a long look with Simcha, Orob turned to Zel and gave him his answer.

"Today, we fight together."

TWENTY

For a long moment, Tonia stood frozen in place as she stared at the narrow, silver band that encircled one of the apparition's long, thin fingers. She slowly tilted her head as she stared disbelievingly at the familiar piece of jewelry, suddenly lost in the beautiful shade of green and soft white clouds swirling in the center of the olive colored stone. Although she would barely remember this later, for a moment she felt as though she might somehow fall helplessly into the center of the ring, and she just knew she would be happy to do so. Time stood still for the young girl until she eventually heard a familiar voice somewhere in the distance, calling her name. With much effort, she shook her head in an attempt to escape her reverie.

"Tonia, what is it? What's wrong?" Kaileen asked, unaware of how much she had startled her friend.

Tonia's head snapped up as her eyes changed their focus from the ring to the woman's white, ghostly face. Confusion flooded across her milky, brown eyes as she tried to understand what was happening.

Before the ice dragon had come to life, she had been certain Diam was carrying the ring in her pocket. Later, when they split apart to make separate, more difficult targets for the dragon, as far as Tonia knew, Diam still had the ring in her pocket. But then things began happening entirely too fast... especially when the dragon turned and headed straight towards Tonia. This abrupt change in the beast's path had led to Tonia totally focusing on the approaching creature instead of watching Diam or Kaileen anymore.

She frowned.

Now, Diam was nowhere to be found and in her place stood this strange, ghostly vision who was posed as still as stone along one wall of the cavern. Worse than that, the female stranger was wearing a familiar ring on her finger...

The same ring that had been in Diam's pocket just a short time before...

"Where is she?" Tonia asked the ghostly woman. She couldn't help but ignore Kaileen's question as the fear and confusion that had settled in the pit of her stomach slowly transformed itself into anger and frustration.

"Where is Diam?" she said again with an undisguised growl. Her almond-shaped eyes slowly narrowed into thin, angry slits.

"Where is my friend!"

Without waiting for an answer, Tonia began making her way over to the ghostly figure, tightly clenching the handle of her sword in one of her hands.

"Tonia... don't!" Kaileen shouted as understanding filled her worried, dark eyes. Realizing what she was about to do, Kaileen began walking quickly toward her angry friend.

The ghost watched Tonia's reaction as the sword-wielding girl slowly closed the distance between them. Thankfully Tonia was too focused on the ring to notice how the woman's gray, thin lips spread into a slow smile. With no sign of resistance, the ghost began to speak in a soft, feminine voice as she offered an explanation for Diam's odd disappearance.

"What you see is not as it seems."

Tonia stopped less than two few feet away from the ghostly figure as her heartbeat thudded like a hammer in her chest. For a long moment, she could only stare at the vision in white with wide, questioning eyes.

Kaileen, still nervous about what her friend was about to do, spoke to Tonia in a soothing tone as she slowly approached her from the right side. The last thing the kalevala wanted to do was to surprise her friend while she was angrily holding her weapon out as if she was going to slaughter the dragon again.

"Tonia..."

Although the young girl's eyes darted toward the kalevala to indicate she recognized the smaller girl's presence, most of her attention was on the glowing woman before her.

"Ohhhhhh, not you, too!" Tonia shouted as her eyes glared at the ghost. "Do NOT talk to me in riddles – especially not now!"

She passed another quick glance at Kaileen before allowing her gaze to briefly scan the room. She didn't realize that she had completely overlooked the softly glowing object which was still in the kalevala's hand. Tonia's blazing, angry eyes brushed across Kaileen then turned back to the ghost and stared at her accusingly. When she began to speak, her voice cracked as it rose with obvious distress.

"Where... is... my... friend?" she asked as she stressed each word. "What have you done with her?"

The ghost lowered her arms to her sides and nodded her head.

"She is safe," the partially transparent form answered as she continued smiling down at the young girl.

Kennard's voice suddenly reappeared deep within Tonia's head.

"Tonia, let her speak. She must tell you some very important things before she leaves..."

Tonia jumped, startled to hear the muck dragon's voice again after such a long stretch of silence. After a moment, she looked at the ghost with her face covered in doubt like a wide, dark storm cloud – thick and full of intertwining clouds.

"Tonia..." Kaileen said worriedly as she gently touched her friend's arm. She tucked the amulet in her pocket in case she needed to catch her friend, who looked almost as though she might pass out any minute.

Struggling to control her emotions – fear of the unknown, anger at the situation, and relief the dragon was no longer a threat – Tonia finally nodded and reluctantly lowered her sword.

"Please... where is she?" she asked quietly as her eyes slowly began filling with emotion. She struggled to maintain her composure as the liquid, horizontal lines confined by her lower eyelids threatened to spill down her cheeks in the blink of a firebug.

"She *is* safe," the ghostly figure repeated. "She will return when I leave."

"But I don't under..." the young girl began to argue when the woman held up her hand, stopping Tonia in mid-sentence.

"I know," the ghostly figure said gently, "but I must talk to you before I leave."

Kaileen touched Tonia's arm as a gesture of encouragement. With an exhausted sigh, Tonia offered a half-hearted smile to the ghost.

"Go ahead."

"Thank you," the woman said quietly.

"First and foremost, let me explain who I am. My name is Alyshana..."

"Wait," Tonia said as her eyes shot open, wagging an index finger up and down repetitively in the ghost's direction. "We've heard that name before..."

"I remember! You're the wife of that wizard..." Kaileen offered in a slightly doubtful tone.

"Yes!" Tonia said as she nodded at the kalevala. She wiped her unshed tears away with her fingertips then added, "That's it. You were the wife of that sorcerer... what's his name?"

Alyshana smiled at the girls as they tried to remember the story they were told earlier.

"Scurio... my Scurio," the woman whispered as a ghostly tear of her own trickled down her wispy, gray face. When it reached her jaw, it froze in place for half a second before it floated like a tiny, round feather to the cavern floor. Instead of splattering on the colorless rock near her feet, the tear disintegrated into a thousand tiny dust flecks before blending invisibly in the cool air around them.

"Scurio, my husband, and I lived happily for countless years until I was taken away from him. He gave me the ring many moons ago as a token of his love."

She paused for a moment as her memories brought her back to a time and place that only she could see.

"The day I was kidnapped, I was wearing the ring."

It didn't take long for her to shake her head gently as she stared beyond the nearby rock wall. Before she could say anything else, Tonia jumped in.

"Wait a minute," the young girl said in confusion as she turned toward Kaileen. "Didn't the monkey say something about someone else having possession of the ring? I don't remember him saying it was her, though." She pointed at the ghostly figure hovering just above the floor of the cavern.

"Do you remember who he said had it?"

Kaileen shook her head as Alyshana spoke again.

"Was it Amandalyn?"

"Yes!" Kaileen nodded with renewed energy as she looked at Tonia. Although the kalevala was sure the name was right now, Tonia was still shaking her head.

"I don't understand. If it was taken away from you when you were captured, how did Amandalyn get it?"

"Do you know anything about Amandalyn?" Alyshana asked in a soothing, soft tone. Both girls shook their heads.

"Amandalyn was a wood nymph who was also a very good friend of mine. At some point after I was taken prisoner, I was finally allowed small patches of time to be outside.

"One day, I was sitting in the grass close to a tree, enjoying the rare treat of sunshine and fresh air. Guards were constantly nearby, but on this particularly beautiful day, they were kind enough to give me a little more space than usual. After sitting in the sun for a few moments, I heard a small noise coming from the nearby tree. At first, I didn't see anything, but eventually a small patch of leaves moved and I saw Amandalyn peering at me through the branches.

"I nearly panicked when I saw her because I had no doubt if any of the guards realized she was there, they would do everything in their power to destroy her.

"At this point, I had only been a prisoner for a few weeks, but I constantly worried that Lotor would become suspicious of my ring. When I saw Alyshana in the trees, I knew this would probably be my only chance to get the ring away from Lotor and his castle.

"I gave her a barely perceptible nod as I slipped the ring from

185

my finger. Before it was too late, I carefully tossed it toward the trunk of the tree while some of the guards were chatting with each other. Amandalyn quickly understood she needed to retrieve the small piece of jewelry, and once I was certain she had it, I got up and made my way over to the tree to smell some of the flowers. The guards closely watched me, but thankfully left me alone as I fingered an assortment of nearby buds. When I got close enough to Amandalyn, I whispered to her, telling her to take the ring and hide it someplace where Lotor would never find it. Then I ordered her to leave and never come back."

"Did she?" Tonia asked quietly.

"Yes, she left with the ring just in time. Within seconds, one of the guards decided I'd had enough fresh air for one day."

"What happened to it after that?" Kaileen asked curiously. "How did it get in the cave?"

"I know not," Alyshana answered with a shake of her head. "I have never seen Amandalyn again, but if I ever do, I would love to know the rest of the story."

The apparition raised the bejeweled hand to her chest and stared down at the sparkling ring on her finger. She smiled as she allowed a wave of unspoken memories to wash over her. After a moment, she clasped her hands together in front of her waist.

"What about Diam?" Tonia asked.

"Your friend is still here – you just can't see her," Alyshana explained. "When I leave, she will return.

"Before that can happen, however, we must discuss the amulet."

Remembering the acquired gem, Tonia's eyes widened with fear.

The amulet!

Her mind raced as her eyes darted around the room. She remembered they had recovered the white stone, but couldn't recall what had happened to it after that.

Had they lost it?

"It's okay, Tonia," Kaileen said reassuringly when she noticed her friend's distress. "I have it in my pocket."

The kalevala patted her upper thigh.

Tonia exhaled a long, loud sigh of relief and smiled at Kaileen.

"Whew! That would really stink if we were to leave the amulet behind when we left, especially after everything we went through to get it!" she whispered.

Kaileen nodded. She was about to reply when the ghostly woman shifted her position to just a few inches above the stone floor. From her new location, she continued her story.

"The amulet must be returned to a dragon guard," the ghostly figure said as her eyes turned serious. "You must get it to a dragon guard… do you understand?"

"Yes… I guess so," Tonia answered. "But how will we know…"

"I will help you find one," Kennard answered.

Tonia nodded and raised her gaze to the pair of dark eyes. The ghost was staring at her.

"Kennard will help us," she said quietly.

"Very good," Alyshana said with an approving nod.

The white figure paused as she turned to look at the floor for a few seconds, lost in thought.

"Let's see," she finally said, more to herself than the girls. "The amulet, the ring…"

"What about how we get out of here?" Kaileen asked as she looked around the room. The two doorways were still completely blocked by the thick, black marble slabs. Certainly, none of the girls, or all combined, would have the necessary strength to move them.

Tonia tilted her head upward until she was looking at the wide crack in the ceiling. Beyond the crack, the stars were no longer visible. Instead of seeing the blanket of darkness, the black, night sky was finally being repainted with just a hint of grayness. Twilight – it was almost morning.

"Is there any way you can lift us up there?" she asked as she pointed at the jagged opening overhead.

The ghost shook her head in denial without following Tonia's eyes to the area above them.

"Unfortunately, I can't," the apparition answered. "It's almost time for me to go, but before I leave I must tell you one more thing.

"The ring on my finger is, in fact, the ring Diam had in her

187

pocket. Although you didn't see her do it, because you were dealing with the dragon, she placed the ring on her own finger, which summoned me here," Alyshana explained.

"She did?" Tonia asked in amazement.

Her friend had been terrified to wear the ring before, and Tonia found herself struggling to believe Diam had actually done it willingly. But the ghost and the ring were here, so Diam must have done something, right?

"Now that I have been freed from the center of the ring, I can come back again if you need me," Alyshana continued.

"But what about Diam? Where is she?" Kaileen asked quietly. She glanced at Tonia and shrugged. They were both afraid to hear the answer, but they understood the question had to be asked. They had to find their friend before they could even consider leaving this place.

"She will be here in a few moments," Alyshana said with a smile.

"Tonia," the ghost said as her focus turned directly toward the taller of the two girls. "Listen carefully, for there is something you must remember.

"When you leave this place, the wheels of time will begin turning quickly. Everything will begin happening much faster than you would expect."

Tonia nodded but said nothing. She sensed that the ghostly apparition's words were important before they were spoken. She could feel the tension in the air again – it was as thick as the stones surrounding them.

"When things start happening and you feel there is no hope, you must say my name in order for me to appear," Alyshana explained. "Can you remember this?"

Her dark eyes stared, first at Tonia, and then shifted to Kaileen.

"You must remember," she said again.

"We will," Tonia said as she glanced nervously at the kalevala. She was relieved when she saw Kaileen nod.

"Very good," Alyshana said.

Satisfied with their answer, the misty figure reached into and behind what appeared to be a large, solid rock on the wall to her left. Her hand disappeared behind the stone for a few seconds then slowly withdrew as a cacophony of colors spilled onto her hand and extended up her arm. As she pulled her hand away from the rock, the girls could see that the ghostly woman's fingers were wrapped around a multicolored, glowing cloth bag.

"Wow," Tonia said quietly. "It's beautiful."

"It has the same colors as the portal from the cave," Kaileen whispered in a strange, monotone voice.

Alyshana nodded.

"You must take this with you and use it against the evil you will be soon facing."

She held the bag out to Kaileen, who stood without moving for a few seconds, mesmerized by the beautiful colors. Alyshana waited patiently and smiled when Tonia gently nudged her friend. With a shake of her head, Kaileen finally moved forward. When she was just a few inches away from the ghostly figure, the kalevala held her hand out, palm up, and Alyshana dropped the glowing bag into it. It landed with a quiet, muffled *whoop*.

Kaileen nodded as she stared at the rainbow colors swirling around her hand.

"Thank you," she whispered as she moved back to her place beside Tonia.

"Put it in my bag," Tonia said as she turned her back toward her friend. The kalevala opened Tonia's bag and gently dropped the glowing pouch containing the dragon dust inside.

As soon as the girls stood side by side again, Tonia heard a strange noise. For a split second, she thought it sounded like a high pitched squeal in the distance, but it was hard to tell exactly where it was coming from. Her eyes darted nervously around the room, lingering nervously on the defeated beast. She was thankful when she realized it was still a lifeless, motionless heap on the cavern floor. She shook her head as her thoughts drifted back to what the ghostly apparition had been saying.

"You said we need to take the amulet to a dragon guard, whatever that is, but how are we supposed to get out of here?"

Tonia frowned as she repeated the question from a few moments before. They wouldn't be bringing the amulet anywhere if they couldn't find a way out, and as far as she could tell, the only real option they had was the dark tunnel by the small pond of water.

The dark tunnel with the running water in it…

Running water that came from a place at the very top of the mountain…

The place where not so long ago an angry, frozen dragon had been standing guard…

An ice dragon.

"Oh, yeah," she thought. "That sounds like a wonderful plan."

She shivered as she stared at the ghostly figure, she decided once and for all she didn't like this, not one little bit.

TWENTY-ONE

The mixed group of humans and warriors gathered their things and continued making their way down toward the lake. When they still had about one more hour's worth of a hike to the bottom of the mountain, Simcha stopped them in an area where there was a fairly large group of tall, thick trees and bushes.

"Let's rest here for a while," he said with quiet yet firm authority.

There was no sound of argument from anyone in the group, man or creature. None of them had gotten enough rest before they began this excursion. At this point, even a brief cat nap would do them some amount of good.

"No fire," Simcha ordered. Not surprisingly, he was quickly greeted with a chorus of unhappy but understanding grumbles. He knew his men were tired. As a result, he wanted to attract as little attention to them as he could during this brief resting period. They all needed to save their energy for what could be a long and tiring battle...

He looked around at his fellow soldiers and eventually focused on a small, shadowed group of men standing around one of the taller, nearby trees. He stared at them intensely for a moment until he realized it was the lead castle guard and his former prisoner. As he listened, he could just make out certain pieces and parts of their conversation as they chatted under the cool blanket of twilight.

Simcha remembered back to the time, long ago, when he also had been a prisoner of the Castle Defigo. Like one of the newcomers to their modest sized group, he, too, had been questioned and tortured by Nivri. In addition to this, neither he nor this man had answers to the questions the sorcerer repeatedly asked him. He understood the frustration Zel talked about when he explained his situation. Simcha also found he wasn't surprised to hear the echo of just a few familiar questions...

"What kind of magic is in your family?"

"What special abilities do you have?"

"What can your children do that others can't?"

Oh, yes, the questions had all been the same... but then again, apparently so had the answers.

One strange thing about this whole situation was how each of the humans in his group had, at one time or another, been former prisoners of the Castle Defigo. Each had been accused of having special powers in their family, and each of the men had vehemently denied knowledge of any such powers.

Although Orob had been Zel's castle guard, he hadn't been the guard for all of the humans. Some of the other guards had supposedly just disappeared one day... never to be seen again.

Simcha sighed as he settled down against his tree to rest, quietly watching and listening to Orob and Zel as they continued their conversation in hushed whispers.

*****

"Orob," Zel began as they sat together on a large, gray rock. It was just the two of them and they weren't paying attention to anyone else around them. "Why did you release us?"

The guard remained silent for a moment as he glanced over at Zacharu. The strange creature looked as though he was sleeping already in the leaf litter a few feet away.

The guard sighed.

"I did it because in my heart I felt it was the right thing to do," he answered quietly. "I'd been at Nivri's side far too long, and I've seen and heard far too much..."

He paused as he turned to look at the human beside him.

"I simply couldn't do it anymore."

Although his gruff voice was quiet, it was firm.

"But why now?" the man pushed on. "Why today? Why not yesterday, or last week? Why did you decide today was the day to release us?"

Orob sat quietly, staring off into the gloomy predawn shadows as he pondered Zel's question. The man thought the guard hadn't heard him and was about to repeat himself when Orob shifted his foot, causing the leaves under it to crackle and crunch from the movement.

"The time just felt right," he answered abruptly before falling back into silence.

"Orob..." Zel voice was quiet and pleading. "Please, Orob, tell me – why now? Did I do or say something to influence your decision? If it wasn't me, was it Nivri? Or someone else?"

The former castle guard concentrated intently on moving his foot back and forth through the leaves, obviously uncomfortable with the topic of discussion. After a long pause, he lifted his eyes and turned to look at Zel.

"Answer a question for me," the guard said quietly.

"Anything," Zel answered, glad he was finally making some kind of headway. He might not end up with the exact answers he was looking for, but at least they were making a little bit of progress.

"Remember when you were in the throne room with Nivri the last time and the monkey came scurrying in with something in its hand?" Orob asked quietly.

Zel closed his eyes and let his mind drift back to the time and place the guard was referring to. Orob saw the human's mouth twitch with the memory. In his mind, Zel could almost see the brown, furry creature running past the dragon statues with the light brown item clutched in one hand, waving it in the air for all to see.

"Yes," he answered quietly as he opened his eyes.

"What was that item?" Orob asked as his thick, hairy eyebrows furrowed into a partial scowl.

"It was an alia leaf," the prisoner answered quizzically. Where was Orob going with this line of questioning?

"And on the leaf was a…" the guard said as he paused, leaving the end of his sentence dangling like a piece of fruit on a tree.

The image of a bright, red apple suddenly flashed into Zel's mind.

"Strange," he thought as he wondered where the image of the apple had come from. Was he hungry already? No, that wasn't it. He had no idea where the mental image of the apple came from and quickly shook his head to clear it away. Instead, he focused on the conversation with Orob and nearly panicked when he realized he had forgotten the question the former guard had just asked.

He took a deep breath and the question came back. Relief washed over him as he looked up at his former guard.

"An amulet was drawn on the leaf," Zel answered. He suddenly had a vision of his cell, the gloomy atmosphere, and the mysterious picture of the beautiful, charcoal colored gem.

"Who drew it?" Orob asked quietly.

Zel stared at the guard for a moment as his mind filled with a jumbled mess of questions.

Why was Orob being so inquisitive? Was he Nivri in disguise? Had the sorcerer cast a spell on his former guard so he could manipulate information out of him? Zel scowled at the guard, who immediately understood the gesture.

"I'm simply curious," the guard explained as he stood up and paced around the rock. "The amulet was beautifully drawn."

"Yes, I agree," Zel said quietly. "But Orob, you were the one who brought me the charcoal and the unmarked leaves, so you more than anyone should know the answer to your question!"

"I know what I brought you," the guard nodded with the hint of a growl, "but I also know it doesn't necessarily mean you were the one to create the drawing."

Zel nodded as he considered this. After a moment of thought, Zel looked at Orob and nodded.

"Well, for what it's worth, I do not remember drawing the amulet, but my hands were covered in charcoal as if I had. The picture meant nothing to me."

Orob stare of curiosity began to curve into a scowl. When he saw this, Zel suddenly felt the need to clarify.

"By that, I mean I didn't recognize it – I'd never seen such a gem before, so I'm having difficulty believing I could have possibly drawn it..."

Orob nodded. After a few seconds, he said something that surprised the man.

"I suspected as much."

Zel stared at him with his mouth open.

"You *suspected* this?" Zel asked in amazement. He stared at the guard as he shook his head and frowned in confusion.

"Well, if you had any idea I was going to say what I just said, why were you even questioning me about it in the first place?"

The two figures stared at each other across the rock with serious, flashing eyes.

"I asked because I wanted to know what you'd say," Orob said matter-of-factly.

Zel continued to shake his head as Orob continued.

"I also brought it up because that was the main reason why I decided to do what I did," the guard explained. "I got the impression you were being questioned about something you weren't familiar with, even though the amulet on the alia leaf came from your cell and you had charcoal under your nails."

"I don't un..." Zel began. He stopped mid-sentence when he saw the look Orob was giving him. It was serious and focused directly on him.

"You are the one," Orob said quietly as he brought his face closer to the man's.

"What?" Zel asked quietly. He had no idea where Orob was going with this.

"You are either in denial or you really don't know," the guard answered as the left side of his dark mouth lifted into a crooked smile. "Yes, of that I am certain, and I suspect it is the latter..."

"Orob, whatever it is you're implying, I'm totally lost," Zel said. On the ground next to the rock, Zacharu shifted in sleep then became still again. Zel watched his friend quietly for a few seconds as his mind raced.

The one...

Which one?

Had Orob lost his guardly mind? Had he been in the castle with Nivri too long? Perhaps he had been damaged by some miscalculated spells?

Orob snorted as he tried to muffle a chuckle.

"You really don't know... do you?" he asked.

Zel shook his head.

"No."

"Tell me one thing, man to man," Orob said as he leaned against the rock.

"Okay," Zel answered, unable to hide his curiosity.

"Your family," Orob began quietly, and then stopped with a long sigh. He pondered how to ask the question without making his former prisoner worry he was being spied on.

"What about my family?" Zel asked as his eyes narrowed into defensive slits.

"Do they have powers?" Orob asked quietly. He decided there was no easy way around the question, so he may as well be direct and just ask it.

Zel looked at his former guard as his eyes flickered with caution and mistrust. His heart began beating faster as he remembered the last time he had been asked this question. Not long afterward, the beatings began. He stared at Orob and waited, determined to fight if it came down to the same result this time. He refused to be tortured anymore for something he didn't have the answer to...

"You are the one."

Orob's words echoed in his mind, but this time, instead of being just empty words, they flickered like a star in a dark, moonless sky.

"You are the one."

"What kind of powers are in your family?"

Orob's voice, Nivri's voice... they both echoed in his mind, almost at the same time, like twins asking the same question. The man closed his eyes and pushed his fists to his temples, willing the voices to go away.

"You are the one."

Suddenly, his eyes shot opened and he glared at the guard.

"Orob, tell me what you mean by 'I am the one'?" Zel insisted as he grabbed the beagon's arm.

196

Orob smiled and patted the man's hand.

"It is simply just that. Although you may not yet know it, or understand it, I am certain. I can feel it."

"Feel what?" the man asked in a harsh tone.

He realized too late that his voice was too loud in the cool night air. In the gloomy shadows a short distance away, they suddenly heard someone clear their throat. Zel and Orob both turned to see Simcha staring at them as he quickly made his way over to the rock.

"Is there a problem here?" the tousle-haired leader asked as he placed his hand on the handle of his sword.

"No," Zel answered. "I apologize for my rudeness. There is no problem."

He looked at Orob, who nodded and smiled at the human leader.

"It is your own choice whether to sleep or not sleep, but you must keep your voices down so others can rest," Simcha admonished them.

Zel nodded.

"I apologize."

"We will," Orob agreed.

Simcha hesitated for a few seconds as his eyes moved cautiously from Zel to Orob. Satisfied they would quiet down, he nodded and headed back the way he had come.

As Simcha walked away, Zel glared at the beagon.

"Explain yourself," he hissed, but Orob smiled knowingly and remained silent.

"Orob, come on!" Zel begged. "Please explain yourself? Explain what it is you feel..."

The guard sat down in the leaves and made himself comfortable as he leaned back against the rock.

"Sit," he said, quietly patting the leaves beside him.

Zel sighed, suddenly tired from the long day. He knew they should get some rest, but he wouldn't be able to even think about resting until he had the answer to the question that was gnawing at him like a forest beaver chewing on a log.

He leaned against the rock and slid downward, landing in the leaves with a crunch. He grunted then looked at Orob with wide, expectant brown eyes.

"You are the one," Orob said again with a smile.

Before Zel could ask for more information, the guard obliged him.

"I sensed it the last time you were in the throne room," the guard continued. "I don't know how and I don't understand it, but somehow you were able to hide it."

Orob smiled and nodded appreciatively, then patted the man on the back of his shoulder.

"You hid it from Nivri that you are the one he's been looking for," the guard said quietly.

"But I'm not," the man argued as he shook his head in denial. "I don't know anything about any magic, either in my friends or family."

"And that is the beauty of it," Orob said with another smile. "If you truly don't know, that would explain why you were able to keep it so well hidden."

He nodded knowingly before adding, "Yes, I'm certain if you had known what he was talking about, he would have gotten what he needed from you one way or another. Then, when he was satisfied he had all the information you would share, willingly or unwillingly, he would have likely tortured you beyond belief before killing you."

Zel sat staring at Orob with intense disapproval.

"So you're saying I made out in the end?" His whispered question was filled with sarcasm. "I was only really tortured a couple of times, but if I'd have given him what he wanted, he would have taken every bit of it, and then killed me as a token of his appreciation?"

"Yes," Orob answered in a knowing, eerie tone.

"Great."

Zel shook his head in disbelief.

"Trust me, human," Orob said with a smile. "Before we are through here, you will know, and accept, you are the one."

Zel's head suddenly felt as if it had overflowed with a combination of doubt and exhaustion so he closed his eyes. He needed to get some sleep. Maybe they were wrong about the impending battle, but if they weren't, everyone needed to be ready to fight the good fight. He sighed and pushed every piece of the previous conversation out of his head. Surprisingly, it didn't take long before he was sound asleep.

Twenty-Two

"The dragon guard will find you once you are out of the cave," Alyshana replied quietly.

"But how will it know where we are? Will it be waiting for us as we get out, or will it be somewhere in the tunnels below?" Kaileen asked as she glanced at Tonia.

"Tonia, I have already summoned the dragon guard," Kennard answered from somewhere far away. "I will direct it to me once you and your friends have returned to ground level."

"Kennard's taking care of it," Tonia answered.

She was just about to smile at Kaileen when suddenly a loud, screeching sound filled her ears. She closed her eyes and instinctively raised her hands to either side of her head in an effort to block out the sound. After a long second, the shriek began to fade away, but when it happened again, she realized it wasn't a noise in the cavern…

It was in her head.

"Tonia!" a fast, high pitched voice cried out. The sound filled her head and nearly brought her to her knees with surprise. When recognition finally hit her, she straightened her neck and dropped her hands as her eyes scoured the room.

"Tonia, what's wrong?" Kaileen asked nervously. Although she had experienced this before, it was still very strange that her friend could hear noises and voices that she couldn't.

"The bat," Tonia answered without looking at the kalevala. "I hear the bat – it's calling out to me."

"The bat?" Kaileen asked with a frown. "You mean the bat from the cave?"

"Yes," Tonia answered as she began walking around the cave in search of the small, dark colored mammal. The walls and ceiling of the cavern were also dark, and if the bat was hanging around here somewhere, chances were she'd never see it...

Unless, of course, he began flying around...

"Where are you?" she asked out loud.

Her gaze briefly examined the rocks jutting out of the ceiling, then changed to focus on the countless crevasses scattered here and there within the borders of the cavern. After a moment, her eyes finally settled on the now familiar, ghostly figure next to the wall. Alyshana was still there, watching and listening, but she was fading away fast.

"Watch out!" the bat suddenly cried out again, this time causing her to jump in surprise. "Danger! Danger! Danger is coming!"

"What danger?" Tonia asked as she quickly drew her sword.

"I must go now," Alyshana whispered, barely loud enough for the girls to hear. "If you need me again, say my name..."

"Wait!" Tonia called out as she reached out to grab the woman's gray, fading arm. "Don't leave yet!"

Unfortunately, the apparition either didn't hear her or couldn't respond. With soft, nearly transparent eyes, Alyshana began fading away into a thin, pale cloud of white mist. The cluster of fog slowly crawled upward along unseen, vertical steps toward the topmost part of the cavern. As Tonia stared at the white wisps floating toward the gaping crevasse above them, something small and dark suddenly caught her attention. She focused on the black shadow as it darted into the cavern through the crack in the ceiling. It descended and flew in sporadic circles around them and she had a difficult time focusing on it as it darted quickly this way and that around the room. Both girls nervously watched the new, dark figure as it suddenly changed direction and began flying in a counter clockwise rotation around them.

Although Kaileen couldn't hear the anything besides the soft, rhythmic sound of wings beating in the chilly air, she sensed something was not right. She stood close to Tonia as they watched the small, flying figure shoot around the room like a wild bird.

"You must leave!" Nayr ordered in Tonia's head. "No time to talk… no, no, no! You must leave now!"

"But how?" Tonia asked. "How are we supposed to leave?"

"There, there, there!" Nayr said as he circled the place on the opposite side of the room. It was the dark tunnel in the wall of the cavern.

"But I don't want to get wet!" Tonia argued. "Isn't there another way? The air up here is freezing and the water will be incredibly cold! Besides, we can't go yet! We can't leave without Diam!"

A voice directly behind her made Tonia jump nearly out of her skin.

"I'm right here."

"Diam!" Tonia cried, immediately recognizing the voice. She whirled around to face her best friend and grabbed Diam into a bear hug. She almost started crying as relief washed over her.

"Are you okay?" she asked as they broke apart long enough for Kaileen to give Diam a hug as well.

"Yes," Diam answered.

"Hurry, hurry, hurry!" Nayr interrupted. The bat was flying diagonally from one end of the room to the other before changing his flight pattern to circle the girls.

"What's it doing?" Diam asked with a frown.

Her question died on her lips when her roving eyes found the broken and blood smeared remains of the ice dragon near the wall. She cocked her head to the side, unable to believe she'd missed anything, yet unable to deny the mangled remains of the gray beast on the floor of the cavern. Her questioning eyes squinted partially closed, which in turn caused her eyebrows to furl into a deep, worried frown.

"It's the bat from the cave," Tonia explained as she pointed at the only apparent opening in the room. "He wants us to jump through that hole to escape."

"He does?" Diam asked as she shook her head in confusion. She had no idea why she was at such a loss about what was going

202

on, but somehow knew now was not the time to ask questions.

Tonia saw the look of confusion that covered her friend's face, and just as she was about to try to explain what had happened, numerous giant clumps of snow began falling through the gaping fissure in the ceiling above them.

"Watch out!" Kaileen cried as she jumped out of the way. Less than a second after she moved, a large amount of cold, thick snow landed in the exact place where she'd been standing. It hit the ground with a muffled thud. The impact vibrated through the floor of the cavern like an earthquake.

"Wow, that was close!" the kalevala called out as Tonia and Diam moved to a different part of the cavern that wasn't under the opening in the ceiling.

"No, no, no!" Nayr cried in Tonia's head. "Danger is coming! It's coming now! Into the tunnel! Into the tunnel! Go! Go! Goooo!"

Tonia instinctively raised her hands to cover her ears again, but dropped them as soon as she remembered the voice was coming from somewhere in her head. She looked at her friends sheepishly.

"He says danger is almost here, and that we need to go into the tunnel – now."

Just as Diam was about to ask for more information, a loud, long, cracking sound filled the cavern from somewhere overhead. The girls looked up just in time to see a long, jagged piece of the crevice above them suddenly falling through the air.

"Watch your eyes!" Diam cautioned loudly as the piece of snow covered rock landed on top of the pile of snow that had preceded it just a moment before. If the snow hadn't been there to cushion the fall, the girls would certainly have been hurt from the impact of the stone shattering on the cavern floor. Luckily, the snow protected them from danger…

This time.

Tonia looked up to see where the enormous piece of stone had come from. It didn't take her long to see that the crack in the ceiling was much longer and wider now than it had been.

Diam was staring at the mess on the cavern floor when she noticed Tonia had stopped moving. It was almost as if her friend was frozen in place. She looked at Tonia's face before following her line of sight upward, across the cavern walls, eventually stopping on the area just above them. As she stared at the newly renovated gap in the ceiling, she clutched Tonia's right arm.

"What is that?" she whispered, but Tonia didn't hear her. All she could hear was Nayr screaming at her, at them, to leave, leave, leave now... hurry, hurry, hurry!

As the three girls huddled on one side of the gloomy cavern floor, the world above them suddenly began to change. Beyond the crack in the ceiling, the sky had lightened considerably, and was now a mesmerizing combination of mostly pale gray and pastel pink colors. On any ordinary day, seeing the first remnants of sunrise might have made Diam and Tonia happy, but today was definitely not one of those days. On the other hand, if it had still been full dark outside they never would have seen what they were seeing now.

All three of the girls stared at the scene unfolding overhead in total disbelief.

Partially blocking their view of the sky was a very large, dark, and ominous looking creature. It was raking at the opening as it struggled to make the entryway large enough to fit through. It bit into the rocky ceiling, moving its unbelievably huge, dark head up and down as it struggled to secure a section of the rocky crag in its wide, gaping jaws. A few seconds later, part of the crevasse broke off with a crunch. The dark creature wasted no time before discarding the jagged rock into the open cavern below without any signs of worry or care as to where the dangerous chunk of stone landed. The creature repeated this action a few times until the long, narrow crack had been substantially widened.

Before they knew what was happening, the dark, multi-legged creature was suddenly falling, falling, falling until it landed in the middle of the slushy pile of snow and rocks with a resounding thump. The girls felt the ground rumble beneath them as if they were experiencing a powerful earthquake, and they each stared at the creature in wide-eyed disbelief. In seconds, the small group of girls had their swords drawn in spite of the fact that nothing should have fallen from that height without incurring some kind, if not numerous, injuries.

Tonia stared at the long, black creature, unable to believe it could be what she suspected it might be. Her eyes darted around the room for a few seconds when she realized, surprisingly, that the bat had finally fallen silent in her head.

Could the blessed silence mean that the danger was over?

Maybe their dark, warm blooded, airborne accomplice had given this creature – this much too large, much too strange creature that looked like a giant, long-tailed scorpion – too much credit?

Maybe the distance from the ceiling to the floor had been too much for the abnormally large arachnid?

And maybe, just maybe, it had died when it landed with a painful, thunderous thump?

Diam released her frightened grip on Tonia's arm and took one short, hesitant step toward the scorpion.

"Wow, have you ever seen a bug as large as this?" she asked in astonishment.

Before either of her friends could answer her, the dark creature lying on the rocks in a heap began to move.

Twenty-Three

Aseret lingered at the edge of the group of men and stared off into the dark shadows of the forest. It had been a long time since she'd seen these woods, and there was no mistaking it felt good to be here again. She closed her eyes and took a few deep breaths, inhaling slowly before softly allowing the fresh air to exit through her lips and re-enter the cool, night environment. She could hear crickets and puddle hoppers chiming their nightly songs in the distance, which made her smile with happy memories from when she was a young naiad. When she turned her head, she caught the welcoming scent of pine needles on some of the trees as well as the thick, musty aroma of the clustered expanse of nearby tree trunks. Another couple of deep breaths led to yet another smile as she even detected the damp, organic odor of millions of nearby mushrooms.

She was almost home.

She was happy none of the soldiers were watching her, but if they had been, it wouldn't really matter. Ignoring the scattered bodies resting amid the leaves and on the rocks around her, she turned and faced the nearby birch tree. In the pale light of the moon, the normally white skin on the woody plant appeared gray and speckled. She smiled as she wrapped her hands around the trunk and began to climb, pulling one hand over the other along the back side of the tree. The smooth bark felt wonderful against her skin as her bare feet conformed to the rounded trunk, lifting her higher and higher with every pull. She took another deep breath – noting that even the birch bark smelled wonderful!

When she'd made it halfway to the top, she stopped and swung herself over one of the long, wide branches. With a leg on either side of the branch, she leaned back against the trunk and stared out across the tops of the much shorter line of trees. Shadows of desolate, leafy branches reached out in all directions against the dark of the night sky. Many people as well as creatures wouldn't have been able to see this, but she could. Her eyes adjusted quite well to darkness. It was one of her better traits.

For quite a long time she'd been forced to live in the castle without enjoying the freedom she now had. She was completely aware that she was taking a chance with her decision tonight, but felt in both her heart and mind that she really had no choice. If Nivri got his way after the sun rose in the morning, her family would be doomed. The black-clad owner of the Castle Defigo had threatened to destroy her family and friends if she were to ever leave on her own, but at this point, she figured it was useless to worry about it anymore.

She also fully understood that it was not just her family that was in jeopardy. Every creature in Euqinom may be doomed…

Besides, Nivri must know the entire world outside of Defigo was vibrating with discussion and preparation for the impending battle, mustn't he? And if he did, certainly the self-centered sorcerer would be so wrapped up in his own problems, planning out his battle strategies, that he likely wouldn't even consider the fact that one of his former minions had jumped ship and left his harem.

She sighed as she felt the cool, night air brush her cheek, her arms, her bare feet. At least he probably wouldn't think about it today. Tomorrow, after the battle, if he managed to survive the battle at all, would likely be a different story. This would be when the evil sorcerer would likely look back at those former members of his castle, his guard, his spell creators – yes, that would likely be the time he would notice they were missing.

She sighed again as she chided herself. Now was not the time to worry about what Nivri might or might not do when he found out about the choices she and other former castle residents had made today. The time to worry would be *if* they made it through the battle.

She looked down at her dainty, feminine hands, as she wrung them together, over and over in the soft moonlight, while she considered her plight. Hopefully, by the time the battle was over, an arrangement would have been made, and her family and friends would be far enough away from the one place the sorcerer would go looking for them. Yes, if they were lucky, there would be no trace of them, whatsoever.

If Nivri somehow managed to survive the impending battle, she hoped more than anything that her family and friends, all of them, would be gone like a fleck of dust on the wind – gone and instantly forgotten.

A sudden bristling noise from somewhere behind Aseret startled her. In a flash she had jumped to her feet as her previously unseen wings shot out from their hidden location on her back. She was prepared to jump into the air at a moment's notice…

"It's me," a soft, childlike voice whispered from a nearby treetop. Aseret stared nervously in the direction of the voice. It sounded quite familiar, much like a voice from her past, but she was afraid to hope. She knew how tricky Nivri could be…

With her heart beating like a drum in her chest, Aseret shifted her weight on the branch so she could peer around the trunk of her tree.

"It's true," the voice whispered softly from the darkness just in front of her. Her eyes darted from tree to tree when suddenly they found what they were looking for. There, a few trees away, she saw a small, waif-like creature peering at her through the darkness. A pair of beautiful, nervous eyes, very similar to her own, was staring at her like the reflection in a pond on a beautiful summer's day.

"Ilamet?" Aseret asked in a quiet, hesitant tone, afraid to trust the vision before her. She stood frozen in place, staring at the pale yellow eyes. They were staring at her with just as much curiosity and caution as she felt.

The head which housed the familiar pair of eyes nodded slowly – once, twice, a third time – then the hiding creature moved out from behind the wide, dark tree trunk. Wings similar to Aseret's own flitted quietly behind the newcomer like those of a butterfly, but much faster as the smaller creature hovered in the air. Aseret could hear the rhythmic wing beats and couldn't help but smile.

"Is it really you?" the larger, pink eyed creature asked the obviously nervous newcomer. The creature did not answer her – it just stared at her through wide, uncertain eyes.

"Ilamet, is it really you?" Aseret repeated, afraid to believe this fragile creature, one of her own, wasn't a figment of her imagination.

Ilamet finally offered a silent answer by moving her head in a slow, methodical, up and down motion. Then, without a word, she darted straight towards Aseret, stopping to land silently on a branch just a few feet away from the larger, winged creature.

Aseret smiled with stunned disbelief. It had been years since she'd seen her younger sister. In spite of this, Ilamet looked much the same as she used to, except she was quite a bit taller than she had been when Aseret left home. The larger naiad held out her arms as tears poured from her softly glowing, pink eyes. Without further hesitation, the smaller naiad cried out with relief and astonishment as she flew into those waiting arms she'd thought she would never feel around her again.

"Shhh," Aseret crooned as she cradled her younger sister close against her. She held Ilamet tightly, gently rubbing her long, flower soft hair, waiting patiently as the smaller naiad shook with both relief and racking sobs. It seemed like yesterday when Aseret had lived with her family, taking care of Ilamet and her brothers, instead of living in the cold, dank castle on the hill. As she held her younger sister securely in her arms, she was overwhelmed with love and thankfulness because she was able to be here now, sharing the emotion and warmth she remembered from so long ago.

"I can't believe... it's really you," Ilamet whispered against Aseret's neck a moment later, after she'd finally calmed down enough to try to speak. "You're really alive..."

"Yes, I am. I'm right here," Aseret said as she soothingly stroked her sister's flowing, honey-colored locks. She closed her eyes and smelled the familiar sibling smell emanating from Ilamet as a sudden thought struck her...

Both Ilamet and her younger brother, Omeret, had inherited the straight, blonde locks, while their other two brothers, Dilanet and Ponduet, had each gotten curly, brown hair. Aseret was the only one who'd been given combination of the two – multi-colored hair.

Although many from their clan had seen this rare trait as a gift, it had actually been a curse in disguise, for it had been her calico colored hair that had captured Nivri's attention. As soon as he saw her hair, he knew there was something different about her. This was when he made her the offer she simply couldn't refuse...

She could choose to come to the castle and live as one of his future readers, or she could choose to stay with her family. If she chose the castle, she would have food, shelter, and a life most creatures outside of the castle only dreamed about. However, if she chose the latter...

Well, she didn't. She chose to move to the castle, almost immediately, in order to prevent any harm to her friends or family. Nivri had given his word he would forget about her family as long as she stayed with him. To his credit, he did keep his word, but nothing like that, especially from the likes of him, came without a price.

Her family was told she was dead – killed by some freak accident near the castle. She knew this and hated the pain her family must have gone through when they were told the atrocious lie, but what could she have done? Her hands were tied...

She smiled across the top of her sister's head, focusing on one of the nearby stars.

Revenge would be sweet...

*****

They sat on the wide, birch branch as darkness faded into the beginnings of sunrise, catching up for a little while on each other's lives. They chatted about many things until Ilamet eventually touched her sister's arm and stared at her with sad, glowing eyes.

210

"What?" Aseret asked, suddenly alarmed. "Ilamet, what is it?"

Ilamet suspected she knew how her sister would react when she told her the news she'd been keeping to herself since they'd been reunited, but she also knew she couldn't keep the news from her either. There had been too many secrets kept over the past few years, and the chain had to be broken. It had to be broken right here, right now.

"Ilamet?" Aseret questioned quietly.

She had been swinging her legs beneath the branch of the tree casually, almost carefree, just a moment before, but now she stopped their motion and allowed them to dangle limply beneath her.

"Whatever it is, you can tell me," Aseret promised as she touched her younger sister's chin, drawing the pale, thin face upward so she could look in the sad, amber-colored eyes.

"Tell me," she whispered as she offered her little sister a reassuring smile.

Ilamet closed her eyes for a moment before her head slowly nodded in answer. She took a deep breath then began sharing the information she knew her sister would not want to hear.

"It's the others," Ilamet said quietly as she stared into her sister's focused, completely pink eyes. "They're coming."

"Coming? Coming where?" Aseret asked in confusion. As her mind raced, she saw the serious expression on her sister's face and suddenly understood.

"No!" she shouted, a little too loudly. Below them, some of the guards shifted in their sleep.

"No, they can't," she grumbled with a frown. Aseret began shaking with anger and quickly stood up on the birch branch. She stared at her sister in disbelief for a few seconds before her wings began beating rhythmically in the cool night air. She jumped off the branch and darted in circles around the tree in distress.

"They can't come here," she said in an argumentative tone in response to the silent, wide-eyed stare her sister was giving her. Ilamet watched quietly as Aseret flew around and around, dealing in her own way with the news she had just received. As the younger naiad stared into the leaves below, she quickly shifted when the branch she was sitting on suddenly moved from the weight of her sister rejoining her.

"Ilamet," Aseret said as she grabbed her smaller figure's shoulders. "They can't come here. You must go home, right now, and tell them they can't come here…"

"It's too late, Aseret," Ilamet said as she reached up and gently wiped a lone tear from her sister's cheek.

"Why?" Aseret demanded. "Why can't you go home now, fly like the wind, and tell them to stay there? It can't be that hard…"

"No," Ilamet said as she shook her head from side to side as if to emphasize her negativity. "You're right. It wouldn't be that hard, but they've already left. There's no one there to listen."

Aseret stared at her sister, shocked by her words.

"We heard about the upcoming battle and decided to come here so we could be close to the castle."

"But why?" Aseret asked, thoroughly confused. She didn't understand why her family would come here and put themselves in danger knowing there was about to be a major battle in a matter of hours.

"I don't understand…" she said as she shook her head in disbelief.

Ilamet laughed lightly. Although it was a tense moment between the two naiads, Aseret couldn't help but smile. The sound of her sister's laughter reminded Aseret of tiny, tinkling bells in one room in the castle.

"You're silly sometimes," Ilamet scolded her older sister as she playfully nudged her arm. "They're coming here now because if Nivri and the rest of his minions got themselves tied up in a major battle, what better time would there be to try to rescue you from the castle?"

Aseret blinked at Ilamet as she considered her words, staring at the younger naiad for a moment until understanding finally flowed across her face.

Her family would be here soon – and they were coming here to rescue her from Nivri.

She tousled Ilamet's hair before giving her a big, reassuring sisterly hug.

"I don't need rescuing, thank you very much! However, as

soon as I've done what I've promised to do, we're going to gather everyone together and leave. We'll find some place far, far away, and make a new home for ourselves – all of us, okay?" Aseret asked as thoughts of the future filled her head.

Ilamet nodded, happy to have found one piece of her life again, after too much lost time had passed.

Unfortunately, things don't always go along as planned.

Twenty-Four

The small group of females stood frozen in time and space as they stared in disbelief at the long, dark creature lying motionless across the stone floor just a few feet away. The scorpion appeared to be nearly as long as the dragon had been, although it didn't have wings stretching out across the floor and it definitely wasn't as wide.

The girls were startled into shocked silence when they saw one of the creature's feet begin to tremble ever so slightly. Although it seemed a bit farfetched, such a movement might be explained by the arachnid's body reacting to such a recent and tragic death. Diam turned to look at Tonia with wide, unbelieving eyes, and it didn't take long for any of the girls to entertain the possibility that the creature was only injured and not dead. As if to reiterate this idea, another extremity on the same side began moving with a similar jerking motion and even more intensity. Within a few seconds, each of the arachnid's other feet were lurching and jerking from side to side as well as up and down. The girls stared in dumbfounded disbelief as they huddled close to each other, and Tonia grabbed Kaileen's cool hand as the creature's thick, black tail suddenly began to move.

The scorpion's entire body had been lying flat against the snow and rocks, but within a minute or so, the slightly twisted, segmented tail began to slowly curl up, up, up, until it eventually

214

hung over the arachnid's thickly scaled back. As the tip of the tail curved under itself, back then forward, then back under again as if the scorpion was flexing a muscle, the wide, front claws on the creature also began to open and close repeatedly as the abnormally large arachnid slowly came back to life.

"It's not dead," Diam whispered as she grabbed Tonia's arm. "Tonia, it's not dead!"

As the echoes of Diam's voice resounded off the surrounding walls, the giant scorpion lazily turned the front half of its body directly toward her. Glowing red eyes glared at the girls from the front of the arachnid's torso where the front claws joined at the body – an area that would be home to a face if the creature actually had one.

"You!" the trembling creature growled in a low voice that rumbled around them like low, distant thunder. Strange clicking sounds wafted in the air between the scorpion and the girls.

"Is it clicking its teeth?" Diam thought as the creature suddenly shifted its position and lunged in her direction.

"No!" she shouted as she hopped backwards, nearly tripping over shattered pieces and chunks of the ice dragon's former crystalline tail. As she stumbled around the broken shards, she stepped in a large puddle of melted ice and snow, splashing cool water up onto her foot and leg, but she didn't notice. Instead, she quickly glanced backward to be sure the ice dragon wasn't somehow coming back to life to join the scorpion. She breathed a quick sigh of relief when she realized it remained nothing but a motionless heap on the other side of the room.

"Split up again!" Diam called to the others as she extended her sword toward the multi-legged creature. It made no noise as it moved its head in slow motion from left to right in uneven palpitations. Tonia and Kaileen followed Diam's suggestion as the kalevala began frantically searching for a way out of the room.

"We need to get out of here," she said to her friends as her dark eyes darted back to the archways. Both were still blocked by the thick, black stones.

"Tonia," Kaileen began as she turned toward the younger of her two friends, "I think..."

She was interrupted by a low, growling sound coming from

somewhere deep within the scorpion's throat.

"You..." the dark, segmented figure purred as it turned its full attention to Kaileen. "Ah, yes! You are the one who has the stone – the special little stone – the one that is no longer protected by the ice dragon!"

Kaileen clutched the hilt of her sword tightly in one hand while her other hand moved to protectively cover her thigh. She couldn't tell if the amulet was glowing anymore and was afraid to look down at it. After a moment, however, she realized it didn't matter because the scorpion apparently was well aware, without any signs of doubt, that she carried the special piece of rock.

"You will not touch her," Diam hissed protectively, but the creature ignored her. To their dismay, the scorpion lifted its head slightly, curved its thick tail nearly into a complete circle over its back, and slowly turned its armored, segmented body directly toward the kalevala.

"Kaileen!" Tonia called out to her diminutive friend. "Get out of there!"

As Kaileen shot a glance back at her, Tonia pointed toward the dark hole in the wall with her sword, shouting the words with her weapon that she was unwilling to say out loud.

Kaileen shook her head negatively from side to side. Although she'd spent most of her life in a cool, dark environment, with all shapes and sizes of creatures lurking around her, she refused to venture into the dark tunnel by herself. She couldn't imagine going in there without her friends. In fact, if she had her way, she *wouldn't* go without them.

"Yes!" Tonia ordered when she saw the kalevala's reaction. "You must!"

Inch by slow inch, the scorpion continued dragging its injured body across the cold, stone floor toward Kaileen, completely focused on the one who carried the amulet. It didn't matter that she was the smallest of the three creatures here, it only mattered that she had the stone in her possession. She was the one who carried the all important amulet, the single piece of the puzzle, for now, that would take him one step closer to his master...

Lotor.

Kaileen stepped back – first one step, then another, as the

scorpion continued moving toward her. The only weapon she had was her single bone sword. She knew if she ran at the creature in an attempt to turn the tables, attacking it instead of the other way around, it would probably take half a second for the scorpion to use that pointer, that thick, sharp pointer at the edge of its tail, and thrust it right through her tiny body as easily as running a stick through a mushroom in the cave. Then what? Then what would happen to her? More importantly, what would happen to the amulet?

That's when she had an idea.

She could lead the scorpion along the outer edge of the cavern so Diam and Tonia could escape. If she was going to die, she would do what she could to save her friends. Besides, if she died, it wouldn't really matter since all of her friends, her family, and any other creatures of her kind had all been slaughtered in the cave when the soldiers came looking for the red amulet. If she didn't survive this part of the journey, it would be okay, because there was no one for her to go home to.

She was the last of her kind.

Diam and Tonia watched from separate sides of the ice cold room as the scorpion crept closer and closer to Kaileen. They both knew they had to do something, but also realized that neither of them, or all of them for that matter, would be any match at all for the segmented beast crawling across the cavern floor, in spite of its injuries. Tonia's frightened eyes found Diam's across the back of the scorpion, and Diam shrugged, unsure of what to do. As their minds collectively raced for some idea, some clue about how to handle the situation, Kaileen silently made the decision for them.

The kalevala quickly moved backwards until she could feel her shoulders pressed against the icy cavern wall then she darted to the right as she led the scorpion away from the dark tunnel. As she began closing the gap between herself and Diam, her eyes made brief contact with the oldest girl and she flashed her a reassuring smile.

"Kaileen, what are you doing?"

Diam's shout of concern echoed around the room as she frowned at the kalevala. Within seconds, her eyes clouded with

217

the sudden realization of what their friend was about to do.

"No, Kaileen! Go back! Go back and get into the tunnel!"

"Kaileen, go back!" Tonia shouted from across the cavern. "You're going the wrong way!"

Not wanting to turn her back on the approaching creature, Kaileen took careful steps as she continued backing towards Diam.

The scorpion ignored their conversation. He knew where the amulet was now and he was determined to take possession of it. Besides, he sensed their hesitation concerning their only way out of the cavern, which suited him just fine. Let them continue discussing their options. This would conveniently allow him the time he needed to move closer to his goal. If he could only get close enough to inject just the smallest amount of poison...

"Kaileen!" Tonia yelled, angry now, from across the room. "Turn around right now and go into the tunnel!"

"No," the kalevala calmly argued as she shook her head to emphasize her answer. "You two go and I'll catch up. I'm the one he wants, so it just makes sense for both of you to go first."

Kaileen slowly continued narrowing the gap between her and Diam as her plan became clear in her mind. She looked back over her shoulder at Diam and smiled.

"Go, now, before it's too late."

Diam stared at the kalevala with a mixture of doubt and disbelief.

"I'll be okay," Kaileen said encouragingly as the scorpion continued crawling toward her.

"Go!" Kaileen yelled suddenly, hoping to scare her friends into action. "I promise I'll be right behind you, but you must go first!"

Tonia watched Diam and Kaileen from across the room, wondering if she could possibly do the same thing with the scorpion that she'd done with the dragon. The more she thought about it, the more her better judgment told her what she didn't want to hear – this time it wasn't possible. There was something about the scorpion's stinger at the end of its tail that worried her. Although the black beast had been injured in the fall, its tail was mighty long. She had a feeling the sharp, poisonous end would

218

find her even if she somehow managed to land far enough away from it.

No, somehow she didn't think it would be possible to ambush the scorpion like she had the dragon.

"Tonia!" Kaileen called out, startling the young girl out of her thoughts. "Please – go now! I will not go unless you both go first, and I really don't think you want my death on your hands, especially not now…"

For a split second, Kaileen's thoughts took her back to the cave, when Ransa, dear Ransa, had offered the ultimate sacrifice right in front of her. Her best friend, the small snake who very easily could have been one of her worst enemies, had grown on her like fungus grows in damp, cool places. As a result of this odd, unexpected relationship, instead of being an enemy as nature had likely planned, Ransa had become something much, much closer to her heart. The little brown snake had quickly become the equivalent of a soul sister.

Sharing the same parents, as odd as that thought was, could not have made them any closer than they already were.

Memories of Ransa allowed other memories, those of the other one, to flood into her mind like a tidal wave.

Muscala.

The other reptile.

The infinitely evil, arrogant snake that had done the unspeakable, the *unthinkable*, which in turn changed their lives forever. The giant snake had lived in the cave for as long as she could remember. He was the cause of the recent pain filling her heart, her mind, her entire being. In the blink of an eye, Muscala had turned his total attention on her dear friend, Ransa, with the glare of death written all over his reptilian face.

It was like a bad dream that she couldn't escape from. The scene in the cave came back to her over and over again, running through her mind as if she was seeing it happen right in front of her… the snake turning and coming toward her, smirking at her because she was cornered and had no where to run, then a flash of brown flying through the air… Ransa to the rescue! Her unremarkably sized reptilian friend didn't hesitate for a second when she lunged at the much larger reptile, who really made

Ransa look more like a snakelet than a fully grown snake.

When it came to Ransa, the difference in size didn't matter. What mattered was friendship, love...

And ultimately sacrifice.

Ransa had sacrificed her own life as the ultimate sign of love and friendship for Kaileen. She had given up everything to save her friend, and now, just a few days later, the kalevala found herself ironically facing a surprisingly similar situation. She was staring into the face of another dark, evil creature in a cave, which was glaring at her with the look of death. Although, like Muscala, this creature was stalking her – for now – Kaileen could not, *would* not if she could help it, allow the same situation to happen again. She also refused to let this creature change its mind and go after one of her friends if it decided they just happened to be an easier target.

No, even though she would like nothing more than to get out of this place, Kaileen would gladly give her life for her friends; much like Ransa had given her own life. She'd had frequent thoughts over the past few hours about how she could go on and live out the rest of her life in a whole new world, with the new friends she'd made, partly as a result of the tragedy in the cave...

Partly because she had lost her best friend.

But now she had serious doubts about whether or not she would make it out of the cave alive. How ironic would it be to live her whole life in one cave, then finally make it out for a very brief amount of time, only to find herself faced with the very real possibility of death inside a totally different cave? Although her brief time outside the cave, with fields, trees, and fresh air all around her, had been wonderful, she would do what she could to try to stop fate from striking twice in nearly the same number of days.

Life was full of irony, wasn't it?

Diam turned to look at Tonia and she saw her friend waving frantically for her to join her. Without a word, she ran to move closer to her friend, and together they headed for the opening in the cavern wall.

"Kaileen?" Tonia called out. "Come on, now! Don't make us wait too long!"

The scorpion focused solely on the small, dark creature standing next to the wall. Its plan wasn't really to kill her – it would only do that if it had to. It really wanted nothing more than the amulet. But this small, dark creature that held the gem didn't look like she would give up the amulet without a fight. No matter, though. It didn't care if it killed the one who held the gem, or her friends for that matter. It just wanted the amulet – it wanted it so bad it could almost taste it.

And it would get it.

The creature clicked its mandibles at Kaileen. She jabbed her weapon in its direction and glared at it with heated determination in response.

"Mine," the arachnid whispered in the gloomy light of the cavern. "Soon, it will be mine…"

With a nod to no one, the scorpion suddenly began increasing its pace. The short, thin legs on either side of its elongated body began to move quicker as if trying to keep time with a silent drumbeat that marched alongside another creature named Greed. It did its best to shorten the distance between itself and the lone amulet.

Diam and Tonia stood at the entrance to the tunnel, ready to jump in at a moment's notice.

"Kaileen, come on!" Diam whispered waving frantically at Kaileen as the kalevala slowly inched closer to the tunnel.

"Please, Kaileen, hurry!" Tonia whispered.

When the scorpion recognized the kalevala's intentions of joining her friends near the shallow pool of water, it began shifting in that direction in an effort to block her path. As the gap between the scorpion and the tunnel lessened, it began to look as though Kaileen might not make it to the opening in the tunnel after all.

As Tonia and Diam watched with nervous trepidation, the scorpion began rapidly closing the gap between them. Just when they thought it might be too late for the kalevala to make her move, a familiar, dark shadow suddenly shot out of the tunnel and began darting around the upper area of the cavern.

"I bring help!" the flying creature cried as it circled in a wide arc around the room. "You must go! Move, move, move!"

"Move?" Tonia asked in confusion. "Move where?"

For a brief moment, Diam found that her eyes were locked on the approaching scorpion as though she was temporarily frozen in place. She held her sword out in anticipation of an attack.

"No, no weapon..." the bat cried out. "Move away from tunnel!"

Without questioning the bat's suggestion, Tonia and Diam stepped to either side of the tunnel entrance.

"Tonia," Kennard said in her head, "the spiders will help you."

"What?" Tonia asked in surprise.

She didn't realize she'd said the words out loud instead of in her head until she saw Diam giving her a funny look. "But we got separated from the spiders once we arrived in the cavern. They won't be able to do us any..."

Just then, a large, furry, black blur brushed past her and headed directly for the scorpion. The injured arachnid was just feet away from Kaileen now.

"Yes! Yes!" the bat cried gleefully as it narrowed its flying range to bring it somewhat closer to the action. Across the room, Kaileen stopped moving and stared at the new arrivals.

Not just one, but all three of the spiders that had accompanied the girls on their earlier journey sprang into the cavern from the tunnel, one immediately behind the other. The scorpion, which was still totally focused on the smaller member of the group – the one with the gem of gems, the stone of stones – was caught totally off guard by the reinforcements. The arachnid was so caught up in its thoughts of acquiring the amulet that it didn't notice the spiders were even in the cavern until one sprang roughly onto its back.

This was the beginning of just one of the major battles that would happen over the next few hours.

When the scorpion felt the odd sensation of something landing on its scaly backside, it turned abruptly and squealed in both anger and surprise. As it turned, it hooked its tail forward and downward, piercing the spider's thick fur and skin with a thump. The spider cried out in pain, but held on tightly. In seconds, the other spiders were joining their comrade, attacking the segmented arachnid with everything they had.

"Kaileen, go, go, go!" the bat ordered as the kalevala stood frozen in place. She was glad the scorpion was no longer coming after her, but felt horrible when she realized the first spider was seriously injured. She couldn't tell if it was her spider or one of the others, but it didn't matter. All three of the battling balls of fur were their friends, and it pained her knowing something very bad was happening to it. As she stood watching the battle between the dark colored creatures, she felt helpless and almost completely overwhelmed.

When Diam realized the kalevala wasn't going to move on her own, she sheathed her weapon and ran back to get her. They couldn't leave without Kaileen, and although it appeared as though the scorpion would lose as a result of being outnumbered, it had a huge stinger on its tail that likely carried quite a punch. She glanced over at the battle in the center of the room as she ran towards Kaileen. The spider that had been the first to jump onto the scorpion's back was now lying off to the right. It crumpled into a heap before rolling slowly onto its side, its legs twitching as the poison sped through its veins like a wildfire. She could only hope its death would come quickly.

When she reached the kalevala, she didn't hesitate for an instant and grabbed her arm. Kaileen was staring at the battle scene as if in a trance. The bat, although still flying around the room, had finally fallen silent.

"Kaileen, we have to go!" Diam pleaded as she leaned down to speak in the kalevala's ear. "Go, now!"

Without waiting for an answer, Diam tightened her grip around her friend's arm and pulled her, almost running, toward the tunnel.

"No!" the scorpion cried when it saw the dark figure running away with the amulet. It called out again as it angrily watched the girls head straight toward the tunnel through one of its red-ringed eyes. The other eye had been torn from the socket in the battle and was hanging down the side of the creature's face like a juicy, red tomato.

Kaileen snapped out of her trance as Diam pulled her toward Tonia, who was waiting next to the tunnel entrance.

"Go now, go now!" the bat cried as he flew tight circles just inches above the girls' heads. He was flying so close to them they could hear his quick, repetitive wing beats. It sounded almost like someone was beating rapidly on a pair of tiny drums just inches behind them.

"Go, before the creature follows!" the bat shrieked. Then, before any of the girls could respond, he suddenly darted into the dark tunnel ahead of them and disappeared.

Without waiting for any further encouragement, Diam picked Kaileen up and shoved her into the tunnel. The kalevala began to say something that may have been the beginning of an argument, but before she could, she disappeared into the darkness as the water and the incline carried her away from the cavern.

"It's cold!"

The sound of the kalevala's protest echoed away until there was only silence.

Tonia glanced at Diam and nodded.

With a return nod, Diam quickly climbed into the tunnel. The water was uncomfortably chilly on those few places where bare skin was exposed, but surprisingly, the remaining places, the ones covered with spider webbing, remained dry. As she began sliding away, she tried to turn back to see if Tonia was following behind her. She frowned when she realized the tunnel was curved and all she could see was darkness.

Tonia, standing alone at the tunnel entrance, turned and stared at the ongoing battle between the spiders and the scorpion. The first spider was no longer twitching on its side – it lay motionless where it had fallen and she was almost certain it had succumbed to its venomous wounds. Although she'd never been stung by a scorpion, she had heard other villagers talk about people they'd known who had been stung by them. She suspected it could be pretty painful, especially if the scorpion was a large, mature one. Those who were stung didn't always die from the stings, but given the size of the arachnid in the cavern and the amount of venom it likely had built up in its tail, she could only assume the worse when it came to the extent of the spider's battle wounds. The other two spiders continued to put up a valiant fight with the arachnid, although one of the spiders had lost two of its legs.

The girl with the straight, chestnut-colored hair decided it was probably best not to wait to see what the final outcome of the battle would be. She felt bad that she hadn't assisted their eight-legged arachnid friends, but she knew the odds were against her and she would probably be hurt or killed if she tried. With a regretful frown, she slipped into the tunnel and as she began her own journey into the unfamiliar tube of darkness, she thought of the irony of the situation.

Spiders – she had hated all sizes and kinds of the eight-legged creatures her entire life. As a result, she had spent much of her life being afraid of them.

Today, not only was she no longer afraid of spiders, she'd found herself feeling closer to them than she'd ever dreamed possible. Even better than that, those same creatures she'd spent her whole life hating and misunderstanding were now in the middle of a battle for their lives, in part because of her. They were the ones prepared to sacrifice their lives for her and her friends.

As a single tear rolled down her grimy, pale face, Tonia mouthed a word of thanks to the surviving creatures battling the scorpion. Without looking back, she pushed herself into the tunnel and allowed herself to be carried away into darkness.

TWENTY-FIVE

After entering into his secret chamber, Nivri ambled through the winding, gloomy tunnel until he came to the end. Here the passageway opened up into a small, round room, which was separated from the tunnel by a thick, black satin curtain. As he reached the cloth barricade, he shoved it aside without stopping, and immediately moved toward the single chair in the center of the room. Behind him, the curtain whispered back into place like a faint whisper in the wind.

In front of the chair was a small, square, wooden table, on top of which stood a pair of clear, solid dragon statues. The statues were placed about two feet apart and faced each other as if they had been frozen right in the middle of an intense staring contest. The dragons themselves were nearly identical except for one obvious difference. The tail on the left dragon curved behind it to its left, while the opposing dragon's tail curved to its right. In the position they were in, they were mirror images of one another.

The spell room, which is what this room was called, was lit by only two torches – one mounted on the wall to the left of the entryway and another directly opposite, mounted on the wall to the right. The room was completely silent except for the sound of the flickering torches.

Although this room was much smaller than the glorious throne room in another part of the castle, the floor here was layered in similar, although smaller, cool marble tiles. Nivri walked silently across these tiles as he made his way to the chair. When he was just a few inches away from the dragon statues, they jumped to life as they lit up with a soft glow the color of daffodils. The sudden change in their color was not coming from the statues themselves, however. The welcoming glow originated instead from the sorcerer's flaming, orange eyes.

Nivri was angry, and as he sat down, his hands gripped the arms of the chair to steady him. Once he was settled in the chair, his hands remained wrapped around the end of the wooden arms, each one clenched in a death grip.

Those boys, those rotten boys! Not only had they escaped the bears he'd sent after them, they'd managed to get one of his bears killed! And not only was one of his most prized and feared bears killed, it had been the smartest and strongest of the three bears to boot!

His eyes widened as he focused his gaze on the torch flickering on the wall to his right, thinking about the day's events. His anger began to flow through his veins like gallons of boiling water. As a result, the color of his eyes slowly changed from glowing amber to a dark orange which soon bordered on the edge of blood red.

Nivri didn't like it when he wasn't in complete control of certain situations. He didn't like it one bit.

To make things worse, not only had the meddlesome boys escaped from the bears, they had also somehow managed to find their way successfully to the Castle of Tears. Then, to top *this* off, at this very moment the troublesome twosome were talking to the keeper of the Tear. If they managed to retrieve the Dragon's Tear amulet, they would have found two of the three missing gems.

He scowled as his thoughts drifted to the color red... the Blood. He'd heard the Dragon's Blood amulet had already been found and returned to the dragons. Although he didn't want to believe this, he sensed it must be true.

His eyes slowly shifted away from the flickering torch, along the stones in the wall, then across the floor until they finally settled on the dragon statues on the table in front of him. He continued to grasp the handles of the chair in a tight hold as he stared first at the dragon statue on the right, then through it. His eyes drifted closed as he concentrated on the boys, those meddlesome boys, and how they were ruining all of his plans to become the King of Euqinom!

He would soon have his revenge!

Nivri opened his eyes wide – they were now filled with a deep, blood red glow. Struggling to control his anger, he took a long breath and focused solely on breathing in, then out. Eventually, his eyes changed back to the deep, orange glow and he was able to breathe easier. When he realized his knuckles were aching on both hands, he loosened his grip on the arms of the chair and reached out to gently stroke each of the dragon statues in turn. They flickered a matching orange glow at his touch and he knew it was time.

The boys were in the Castle of Tears – he knew this like he knew his own name. Nivri closed his eyes then laid each of his hands on the respective dragon statue. It was time to recant the spell of fear.

As soon as the skin of his palms touched the dragon statues, they flickered quickly with a flash of soft orange light before brightening in intensity as the sorcerer's hands wrapped around the top of each of the dragon's cool, crystal backs. Each statue began shimmering with a deep, solid orange glow within just a few seconds.

Nivri's lips formed silent words as he dove into the spell of fear. His eyes rolled behind closed, wrinkled eyelids and his hands began to tremble. In spite of this, he maintained his hold on the dragons and focused completely on the scene taking place at the exact same moment deep within the Castle of Tears.

He could see them. There, in the middle of the castle, the boys were about to retrieve the amulet. As Nivri focused, he found himself looking at a somewhat blurry image of the smaller of the two boys. It was as if he was looking at the brat through a thick piece of glass, almost like some type of strange plate.

"No!" he cried in alarm when he realized the younger of the two boys had just beheaded the dragon in the castle. How could he do such a thing! How could he kill the dragon that lived there, no matter how grotesque it was from its deformities?

Then, as he watched the scene unfold from some dark place deep within his head, Nivri realized the dragon's dying body housed the missing amulet. This was when he heard the amulet as it used the body of the dragon to call out for help. He stared through the blurry doorway into the castle as the amulet magically reached out to the boy standing just a few feet away.

"*Save me.*"

Ah, yes, the amulet was calling to be rescued. Nivri wasn't surprised, and as he continued watching the scene in his mind, a plan began to form.

Now that he knew the location of the amulet and that its keeper was no longer alive to protect the beautiful, blue gem, he could send someone, perhaps Blaken again, his menial servant, to go retrieve it for him. Ah, yes, once he had the Dragon's Tear, he would only need to find the other two amulets. Then he could begin forming the spells to help him find the last piece of the puzzle – Little Draco. With the amulets and the dragon, he would be invincible!

He smiled at the thought, and could almost feel his impending success, but first, he had to get these meddling boys away from the carcass which held the amulet. He smiled as he turned his complete attention to the boys in the castle. He listened to their conversation for a few seconds and soon realized the boys were planning on removing the amulet from the dragon's lifeless body.

"Get out!" he yelled out loud as his own body flushed with angry heat. They couldn't take the amulet!

"I will hunt you down and kill every last one of you if you don't turn on your heels and leave this place RIGHT NOW!"

Through glazed, angry eyes, Nivri saw the dragon on the floor of the Castle of Tears as it quickly turned into nothing more than a pile of sand. He also heard a high pitched, squeaky voice, coming from somewhere beyond his line of vision. The unknown speaker was encouraging the young boy to use his sword to cut the amulet out of the dragon's chest.

"No!" Nivri cried out angrily.

The black-clad figure suddenly saw the gem as its beautiful, blue light began to slowly fade away. He understood the amulet's glow would disappear completely unless this young boy, the one

229

they called Micah, cut the amulet away from the dragon, but he couldn't handle the thought of the boy taking control of the amulet...

His amulet.

"Dare...

"You...

"NOT!" he growled, unable to help himself. He continued to stare at the boy through what he now understood was the blade of a sword.

His eyes were still closed, lost in concentration, while his hands tightly gripped the dragon statues as if he was holding on for dear life. He felt the strange sensation of being lifted, lifted, lifted as Micah raised his sword into the air. An instant later, as Nivri suddenly felt himself moving in the opposite direction, he understood this was it – Micah was swinging his sword downward. Nivri was helpless to stop the weapon's blade from flying toward the dead carcass in the middle of the castle floor.

"Noooooooo!" he cried, unable to help himself.

Nivri knew he'd lost this battle as his connection with the castle began to fade away. The boy, the one with a very special death wish, had succeeded in retrieving the amulet. He knew this without a doubt.

"Nooooooooooooooooo!" he cried again as his connection faded away into sudden blackness. The spell had been broken.

He opened his eyes and released the dragon statues, then dropped his arms to the empty spaces on either side of his body between his torso and the arms of the chair. He sat this way for a moment replaying the scene in his mind, until out of the blue he placed his hands on the arms of his chair and pushed himself to his feet. He raised his clenched fists over his head and vocalized his anger and frustration in a single word expression of disgust.

"AAAAAAAAAAAARGH!!!" he cried as he pumped his fists up and down in the air.

His eyes flashed angrily. They had the amulet! They had *his* amulet!

As the realization of what just happened slowly sank in, he collapsed back into the chair, gripping the arms for stability as he did so. Although he didn't notice it before, his whole body was shaking with anger.

He should have known it wasn't going to be that easy to recover any of the amulets, not a single one! He also should have known that those meddling kids would get in the way like a bloody thorn in his side, digging into his skin, piercing his flesh like a multi-pronged spear.

He growled under his breath.

Those kids! Those dreadful kids!

He should have sent some of his minions after them as soon as he received word that they'd come through the portals, but he had been too busy with other, more pressing matters. At the time, some things had been more trivial than others, and unfortunately, he knew he couldn't go back in time to change his reactions to certain situations.

He sighed as he tried to calm his nerves.

Who in their right mind would assume a group of children showing up here, in his world, would cause as much of a headache to him as these four had?

His sigh quickly changed to a snarl.

He knew this would probably never happen, but if he ever had the opportunity to meet the parents of those meddlesome kids, he would certainly enjoy enlightening them with new ideas concerning how to raise children the right way!

He shook his head and stared at one of the dragon statues on the table. Both pale colored sculptures were dull and lifeless, no longer throwing a soft amber light into the torch lit room.

His mind was spinning as he tried to accept that the boys had retrieved the amulet. He had to focus again! He had to focus his energy on the tiny island in the middle of the lake. He needed to verify that it was still standing.

He grunted.

Hmmph!

If those pesky adolescents had really taken possession of the amulet, the island would very likely be crumbling under their feet right now. The real question then would be, did they make it out of the castle in time? And if they had, did they make it off the island?

If they hadn't made it, what had happened to the amulet?

He had to focus – he had to see for himself. Once he knew the exact situation, then, and only then, could he plan his next move.

He leaned forward in the chair, and like before, wrapped one wrinkled, long nailed hand around each of the glass sculptures on the table. The instant his hands touched the dragons, they suddenly sprang to life, glowing with a familiar bright, orange light that lit up the room like sunset on the beach.

Nivri closed his eyes and focused on returning to the lake. The place behind his eyes became an overwhelming onyx before slowly fading to the deepest shade of charcoal gray. As he allowed himself to be carried across space, across time, he relaxed. He was searching for something, some catalyst that would allow him to see the area around the lake – the shoreline, the water, the castle in the center, resting on a bed of coarse sand like an enormous, brown shell. Like an invisible shot through the darkness, through the moist air hovering around the lake, he searched high and low as he considered both living and nonliving objects. This time, instead of putting himself back into the young boy's sword, which would surely get him nowhere since he was fairly certain it was tucked away in its protective sheath, he eventually found the perfect, although unlikely, host not far from the Castle of Tears.

A long-legged gray heron walked unsuspectingly through the shallow waters on the marshy side of the lake, searching for small fish and crabs for its predawn breakfast. As Nivri's essence entered the bird's body, he felt it tense up with a combination of surprise and fear. The feathered creature twitched and jerked for a moment as it fought the odd sensation consuming every nerve and muscle in its body. After a moment, Nivri forced the bird to relax and completely took over.

The bird lowered the upper portion of its body as if staring into the dark water around its feet before slowly raising its head and staring in the direction of the castle. Although this species of bird could normally see fairly well in the darkness, it had never been able to see long distances. Now, however, with Nivri's magical assistance, the heron peered across the water in search of something vaguely familiar. The eyes saw the choppiness of the water out in the middle of the lake, but it couldn't find what it was looking for. Was it looking in the wrong place? Just as it was about to take flight and begin an aerial search, a movement in the distance caught its eye.

There, in the center of the dark lake, the heron's glowing orange eyes were able to focus on the last remnants of the castle as they crumbled into the cool liquid surrounding it. The sand was collapsing in on itself, slowly in some places and quicker in others, as the lake swallowed the former home of the Dragon's Tear amulet. As it did so, it caused the water immediately around the former island to become rough and erratic.

The heron's eyes scanned the area around the former island. Would it find what it was looking for? Had the meddling boys escaped or were they finding themselves tragically trapped in hundreds of pounds of wet sand, somewhere below the surface of the lake? The bird focused on the water around the sinking island for a few seconds, and there, floating across the water not far to the right of the once beautiful castle, it finally spotted what it was looking for.

Those who had caused this entire mess!

An unidentifiable creature that looked much like a cat, as well as two human figures, were riding on the back of a two-headed dragon. Back in the spell room, Nivri growled under his breath, certain it was them. The heron's focus floated to the white figure just a few feet away from the others… a large, white dragon.

What was his name?

The bird shook his head as the name escaped him. It wasn't important, really. Now that Nivri knew where they were, he could focus on another spell. Yes, he would confront them with the spell of mist.

As quickly as he had taken over the bird's tall, thin body, the sorcerer removed himself from it. The heron stood as if in a daze for a moment, then looked down at the water trying to remember what it had been doing. Was it looking for fish? It thought so, but found it was no longer hungry.

Ignoring the activity across the dark lake, the heron pushed itself out of the water and flew off into the darkness, heading for a marshy field a few hundred yards away.

Back in his spell room, Nivri slowly opened his eyes. His hands remained around the dragon statues while he focused his complete attention on them and gathered his thoughts. After a moment, he began reciting the spell of mist. He knew, for this particular spell, he must channel one hundred percent of his focus on it if he wanted to be successful. If he did it correctly, he would materialize from the center of a large, white cloud in the exact place he wanted to be, which of course was right in front of those troublesome brats. If he could pull this off, he would literally be in two places at once, if only for a moment. Then, depending on their reaction and if everything went as planned, the brief amount of time it took for him to do this would give him plenty of time to take possession of the amulet.

All he would need were a few seconds. Less than a minute if things got tricky.

Yes, if he had his way, when he removed himself from the cloud and returned back to the spell room, his eyes would be open and his mouth would be frozen in an ear to ear grin. He had every confidence that when he finally returned from this brief journey, he would have a glowing, blue amulet lying in the palm of his hand.

TWENTY-SIX

Nivri sat in his chair with his arms outstretched, one on each armrest. His palms were open and facing upward as if each hand was frozen in a wave at the ceiling. Once he realized where the boys, those sniveling, conniving brats, were located, he had taken a moment to put on his black cloak – the one he'd carried in with him but had not worn until now.

He was planning a little trip.

His stoic expression melted into a sarcastic smirk as the wheels of planning spun around and around in his mind, endless circles chasing endless circles. As he made preparations, his fingers nimbly worked their way from the neck line of the cloak, securing it a little at a time. He was staring off into nowhere as he worked his way slowly from the top to the bottom, not paying much attention to his fingers as they worked, but then again, he didn't need to. He'd worn this particular cloak countless times, most recently just the previous day when he had called the uncooperative prisoner, yet again, to his throne room.

He scowled as his thoughts drifted to their most recent... discussion. Nivri knew he'd done a decent job of using his abilities to scare the prisoner, but the stubborn man had continually refused to give him the information he had been looking for. Not surprisingly, this last time had been no different than any of the others. The prisoner had repeatedly denied any knowledge about what Nivri was asking for – he didn't know what powers may be in his family – and, although it had taken quite a while, Nivri had finally relented to the idea the annoying prisoner might just be telling the truth.

He sighed.

Although he wanted nothing more than to retrieve the desired information from the prisoner, if his most recent guest didn't have the information Nivri was looking for, he may as well just let him go. After a bit of consideration, Nivri had finally decided to set the stubborn, unknowing human free. He would release him from the castle like he'd released previous prisoners in the past, convinced there must be someone else in this world that had the answers he was looking for.

He sent Orob to deliver a scroll with his terms of release to the prisoner earlier – he was adamant about wiping out the prisoner's memory before allowing him to leave and would not consider the release until this was complete. Just a little while ago he had been just about ready to summon Orob to bring the prisoner, but something more important had come up, as 'something' always did. As a result, the human's release would have to wait.

After concealing himself completely from neck to toe in the very special, satiny material, Nivri returned to his seat. He settled into the tall, wooden chair then closed his eyes, forcing any thoughts of the human into a far, darkened corner of his mind. He took a few long, deep breaths and began to relax. When his mind had finally cleared and his body was no longer tense, he slowly tilted his chin upward, ready to begin. He sat this way for several minutes, and eventually began mumbling to himself. On opposite sides of the room, the two small torches seemed to be competing against each other with their flickering flames, but Nivri didn't notice. Instead, his long, narrow face took on a gray, almost ghostly hue.

He resembled an upright, recently deceased corpse.

Without opening his eyes, the sorcerer twitched and leaned forward, wrapping his hands gingerly around each of the dragon statues. As his fingers slid around the fragile figurines, the lifeless objects began to glow with a bright orange light, but this time was different from the last. Since Nivri's eyes were still closed, he didn't see how the head of each dragon began to change from a bright, solid orange to a deeper, sunburned copper color that eventually changed again to a deep, dark red. This last color was strikingly similar to the color of fresh, human blood.

As the sorcerer concentrated on his spell, he began to feel the cool night air around him even though the spell room had no windows. In spite of this, his eyes remained tightly closed. He paused his indecipherable mumblings for a few seconds and took a deep, slow breath in, then exhaled.

He smiled. He could smell the dampness in the air, and yes, the water was very near now. If he concentrated hard enough, he believed he could just about taste it on the tip of his tongue.

A few more seconds went by as endless strings of unintelligible words flowed from his mouth like a river. The air around him began to turn cooler still as a thin blanket of wispy, gray fog suddenly appeared out of nowhere and surrounded the sorcerer in his chair. Keeping his eyes closed, he slowly stood up and pushed his lower body against the table while his hands remained firmly on the dragon statutes.

His mumblings, quiet at first, began to grow increasingly louder as the foggy cloud surrounding him slowly thickened as it widened. In less than a minute, he was completely encased by the cool, white cloud.

Nivri knew without a doubt his spell was working. He focused all of his attention on the scene coming into focus behind his closed eyelids, and without any indication he was about to do so, he fell silent. The darkness behind his eyes was slowly being replaced by sun above and dark, cool water below.

He felt the chilly embrace of the fog as it penetrated every part of the cloak. The cloudy mist brushed against every inch of his body, both covered and exposed areas, and his skin immediately responded by erupting in millions of tiny chickenbumps. As if he was right there next to them, he heard the sound of the water lapping gently at the side of the dragons as they floated away from the place where, not so long ago, the remnants of a once beautiful castle stood gracefully in the middle of the lake.

Most importantly, he heard the low, murmuring voices of the thieving brats.

They were moving across the water, congratulating each other and bragging about how they had actually done it – they actually had the amulet! They sounded like they were just a few feet away.

He frowned, but pushed away his anger and frustration, choosing instead to concentrate on the task at hand.

Concentrate…

His heart began to beat faster with the knowledge that it wouldn't be long before he had the amulet in his hand. Protected by the cloud, and within the cloud protected by the cloak, he smiled.

Now they had nowhere to run.

As he listened to the voices which sounded like they were coming from right in front of him, Nivri finally opened his eyes – they were blazing like the sun in a beautiful sunset. The glowing orange light painted the inside of his cloud the color of fresh carrots for just a few seconds before the cloud began to eventually darken. Nivri felt a bit disoriented for the length of a single heartbeat. Before the next thump of his heart, there they were, right in front of him.

Although he hid the smile on his face, he was beaming radiantly in his mind.

He stared at them from inside his cloud, letting their predicament register in each of their minds. Within a few seconds, he heard one of the dragons speak his name. He heard their hearts begin beating faster with surprise. Best of all, he smelled their fear.

Oh, yes, revenge would be sweet.

His eyes scanned the nearby dragons before settling on the boys like an eagle spotting a duck on a lake. They had nowhere to run.

One of the boys was obviously older and sat a bit taller than the other one, but it was the shorter, younger boy he was interested in.

"You!" he called out loudly.

Although his voice was loud and deep where he floated above the water, in the tiny room, it echoed around him, bouncing from one wall to another before fading away like a ghost.

"Give me my amulet NOW!" he ordered as he glared at the younger of the two boys. Nivri knew without a doubt that this minor boy, who incidentally had turned into a major thorn in his side, was the one who currently had possession of the amulet.

In the spell room, Nivri leaned forward in his chair. Although he physically didn't move his feet, the other sorcerer, the one hovering over the water, slowly began to float toward the boys.

When he realized the younger of the two boys wasn't moving – wasn't following his order to give him the amulet – anger pulsed through his veins like an earthquake.

He was tired of chasing these brats and needed to be done with it! If the boy wouldn't give him the amulet, he would simply have to take it!

Without wasting another second, Nivri released the dragon statue to his left and thrust his arm through the cloud surrounding him in the spell room. At the same, exact second, the sorcerer's left arm shot out of the cloud over the lake, reaching for the boy with the amulet. His arm extended horizontally above the water, palm up, as he waited impatiently for the boy to hand over the gem. As his fingers twitched anxiously, Nivri decided he would give the boy a few more seconds to do as he was being told. If he didn't, the dark cloaked figure would just have to grab the brat by the front of his shirt and drag him into the cloud. Then he would bring the boy back to the castle and take possession of *his* amulet.

Then the real torturing would begin.

"Give it to me," he growled. "Now!"

Nivri's patience was about as thin as it had ever been. He would give the boy three seconds before he accompanied him on the ride of his life.

One...

Two...

"No!" Micah yelled defiantly.

The boy's outburst caught the sorcerer completely off guard, but it wasn't enough to stop him. His eyes flashed as he imagined the torturous things he could do to this young thorn, and just as his mind was about to finish counting, something unimaginable and totally unexpected happened.

Before anyone, including Nivri, realized what the boy was about to do, Micah raised and lowered his weapon without a sound in what would later be viewed as both an offensive and defensive move. In the blink of a firebug, faster than even the sorcerer could withdraw his arm, the boy swung his sword with all his might. The arcing weapon caught the spell caster's arm halfway between the wrist and the elbow. Nivri watched helplessly as the boy's sky blue eyes widened in surprise, a full second before his separated limb fell into the water with a splash.

An instant, searing pain filled both his left arm and his head like a wild fire burning across millions of acres of dried forest, and the sorcerer immediately released an ear piercing cry of pain and anger. His body reacted to the unfortunate and unexpected violation and his arm retreated back towards his body. In less than a second the cloud in the spell room dissipated and the sorcerer quickly released the dragon statue with his right hand. Without thinking, he then used his good hand to grab what was left of his left arm, clutching it to his chest like a father consoling a tiny, scared child.

Blood, as black as night, gushed from the stump in spurts and rivers. Realizing the danger he was in, Nivri stumbled toward the flickering torch on the castle wall. As his pain filled eyes focused on the hungry flames, he suddenly exploded with a long, loud cry filled with agony, hatred and anger.

"You will pay!"

His damaged stump continued to spurt blood as he tripped and nearly fell head long into the thick and very solid stone wall. Since he was in a secret area of his castle, Nivri knew he would be in real trouble if he couldn't stop the bleeding quickly. He sat still for a moment, holding his oozing limb as his mind raced over, under, and through the pain, as he struggled to concentrate and figure out what he needed to do. His mind jumped from here to there and everywhere...

He had to get the amulet!

Those boys!

His arm!

Waves of blinding anger filled his mind and soul as he forced himself to concentrate. He had to stop the bleeding.

240

He wrapped an end of his cloak around his bloody stump and took a few deep breaths as his thoughts drifted back to the boys.

Those darn boys!

His heart raced again as he struggled to control his anger. After a few seconds, he gave in. It was useless. He allowed anger to consume him.

Revenge.

The only thing he wanted was to hurt the one who had hurt him so badly, so viciously! He squeezed his damaged arm close to the severed end (which hurt like a mud puppy!) with his good hand, trying to stop, or at least slow down, the bleeding. At the same time he also tried to focus on the boys, the lake, and the amulet. All it would take was a few seconds, just long enough for him to dart through the foggy cloud, grab the boy with the amulet, and bring him back here.

He just needed a few seconds...

He closed his eyes and tried to focus on rebuilding the cloud around him when he suddenly felt a whoosh of air as something in the other world completely disrupted his concentration. He instantly knew that the veil of fog he had begun forming, surprisingly with some success, had rudely become disorganized like the smoke from a camp fire in an unexpected gust of wind. The result was his concentration being shattered into a million pieces. He released his arm, forgetting about the blood still shooting out of it in a heavy stream, and screamed up at the ceiling.

"Nooooooo! My am-u-letttt!"

Frustrated, exhausted, and suffering beyond belief, Nivri suddenly remembered his bleeding arm. He wrapped his fingers around the end of it once more in an attempt to stop the incessant spewing of blood as he also struggled to regain his composure.

"I must forget the amulet for now," he told himself in his most authoritative voice. "I must focus only on my arm..."

Forgetting where he was, his eyes darted around the room in search of someone, anyone, who might be able to help him with his wound first, and his damaged ego second. He wasn't surprised to find there was no one around to help when he remembered he had been alone in the spell room. He very briefly considered attempting to cast a spell on himself to help with the pain, the bleeding, or anything else at this point, but his nerves were like a screaming, raging lion in both his head and his entire left side, clawing and biting at him, one jagged, excruciating piece at a time. In his current condition, he was almost certain he would not be able to concentrate enough to get the spell out right.

He couldn't take that chance. He growled in pain, took a deep breath, and tried to focus.

No, he definitely didn't have time to try to conjure up a spell. Before he did anything, he had to stop the bleeding, and he had to stop it now. As he knelt on the floor, still holding his blood-soaked, throbbing arm against his chest, his blurry focus crept up the wall as he concentrated on getting to his feet. The flickering torch, a few feet over his head, faded in and out of focus on the closer of the two walls. He had an idea and grunted loudly as he struggled to pick himself up off the floor.

The torch...

He didn't like his options, especially the one directly front and center in his mind, but knew he had to do something to stop the bleeding, to stop infection, to stop...

He paused for five seconds to breathe and focus. When he was ready, he continued on as his mind proceeded to spin with ideas.

Or rather one main idea...

He knew, without a doubt in his screaming, frenzied, shocked mind, if he was going to do it, he had to do it fast... before he lost his nerve.

Focused on one thing and one thing only, his right hand released his left arm. He stood up as straight as he could and pushed the black fabric of the cloak away from his damaged limb. Once he knew the cloak would stay put, he then pushed what used to be a loose, billowing shirt sleeve carefully up and over the stump. When he'd gotten the sleeve past the raw part of his arm, he quickly pushed it up past the elbow in an effort to get any flammable material away from the fleshy, bloody part of his arm. His sleeve had been cream colored when he'd first come into the spell room, but now it was stained with black spatters as dark as the darkest night.

He felt himself growing faint, but he focused everything he

had on stopping the bleeding. He paused for just a few seconds as he tried to control his lightheadedness.

He didn't need anyone to tell him he was running out of time.

He inadvertently lowered his left arm as he reached up with his right for the torch. Too late, he realized the left side of the cloak floated lazily downward until it had completely covered the stump. As the material brushed across the edge of his damaged forearm, he screamed in pain. Blood, still spurting from the wound, soaked the edges of his black cloak, but the color blended in perfectly. Nivri steadied himself, moved the cloak out of the way, raised instead of lowered his arm this time, and grabbed for the torch a second time. Once he had it in his shaking right hand, he dropped back down to his knees. He felt his eyes begin to lose focus as he brought the torch down toward his bloody stump, suddenly totally aware this would probably be more painful than anything he'd ever experienced in his long life. He also knew, somewhere in his pain-filled mind, this was something he must do if he wanted to survive – if he wanted to get his revenge on that boy… those boys… those troublemakers that had done this to him.

For just a moment, his eyes completely focused again, and as rage filled every cell of his body, his eyes began to glow a bright, blood red instead of a soft, luminous orange. He stared at the flickering flames for a half a second as dark, sticky blood continued to spurt from his arm. Finally, without giving it another thought, he moved the top of the torch directly toward his open wound. Seconds before the flame cauterized what was left of his arm, the sorcerer yelled four words at the top of his lungs…

"I…

"Will…

"Kill…

"You!!!"

As his words turned into self-inflicted, tortured bellows of anguish, hatred, and pain, the sorcerer dropped the flaming torch near the wall and collapsed into unconsciousness.

*****

When Nivri woke up a little while later, his injured arm was absolutely throbbing. It burned like a flaming, raging dragon heart beating in the middle of a wide, open, unprotected chest after it had been pierced with hundreds of thousands of poisoned, flaming swords. This brought him back to reality quicker than dunking his head in a bucket of freezing lake water ever could have.

It took him less than a second to realize he was lying on his stomach in the middle of the cold spell room floor. He struggled to focus as he turned his head slowly to the right, facing the wall-mounted torch. The other torch, the one he'd used to stop the bleeding on his arm, was still licking at the air, flickering just a few feet away from his right hand. Although he couldn't see his damaged and certainly blackened left arm, he knew it was stretched out somewhere in front of him.

He moaned against the cold, stone floor as he grappled with his options. He certainly didn't have many, and the more he thought about it, he admitted to himself that he really only had one…

Getting up was going to be fun.

If his strange sense of humor had even an inkling of an opening to peek through the window of pain in his arm, he might have tried to attempt a sarcastic chuckle. Instead, all windows and doors were closed. Perhaps later he would find some humor in something – anything – going on, but right now, the Humor family household was closed up as tight as a yarnie clam. There was no one home.

He slowly moved onto his right side as his entire body, but mostly his arm, argued with spiked flares of pain. He rolled another rotation like a wheel across the spell room floor and eventually found himself next to the little table in the middle of the room. After struggling to pull himself into a sitting position with only one arm, instead of the usual two, he finally managed to grab onto the table with his right hand and slowly pull himself to his knees. He sat in this position for a moment as he waited, willing the nausea and light-headedness to go away.

What had he gotten himself into now?

As he pondered his situation, he thought he felt his left

244

thumb itching and reached over with his right hand to scratch it, stopping just as he realized his thumb was gone. So was his hand and the bottom half of his lower left arm.

He growled angrily, vowing under his breath to find that troublesome young boy and make him pay with something far worse than a thumb, a hand, or an arm.

He would make him pay his life.

Nivri knew he couldn't dwell on either the boy or his missing arm right now – he had other, more important things to think about. He would re-visit both of those topics another time. Instead, he had to return to his throne room so he could move forward with working out plans for bigger and better things…

Things like revenge.

He took a deep breath and got to his feet. When he was certain he wasn't going to pass out, he turned to leave the room. He glanced back at the torch lying on the floor and his eyes passed over the dragon statues. Both of the crystal figurines were still on the table, staring at each other like nothing out of the ordinary had happened. He considered taking them with him, then realized if he wanted to take them he'd have to tuck one under his left arm and carry the other with his right hand. He didn't want to take a chance on dropping one. Separating them was not an option because part of their magic came from the energy between them as a mirrored pair.

His arm throbbed like a giant, blazing heart, reminding him he couldn't waste any time. He looked toward the spell room doorway and cringed as the pain flared up in his left arm. He decided to leave the dragon statues on the table for now.

Besides, he reassured himself, he would be back. Once he went back to his throne room and took care of a few things, namely his damaged arm, he would return. Then he would go find those meddling boys! He would find them and teach them a lesson, a very harsh and direct lesson, that neither one of them would ever forget. Then, once he gained possession of the stone, he would return to his dragon statues and show them the amulet.

In spite of the pain coursing through his body, he smiled. He couldn't wait to see the reaction of the crystal dragons when he held the amulet out to them! Perhaps once he showed them he had the Tear in his possession, the statues would work with him to show him where the remaining amulets were hidden?

He glanced down as his left arm, almost afraid to look closely at it. The edges of the wound appeared to be scorched and bumpy, almost like a piece of chickenbird meat that has been held over a hot campfire for entirely too long. The skin partway up his arm had also blackened, but that was a small price to pay in order to avoid bleeding to death! Thankfully, it looked as though he used just enough of the torch flame to stop the flow of black, sticky blood before he had passed out.

He glanced back down at the dark stone floor where he'd collapsed. Of course there was quite a trail of blood from the table to the wall where he'd retrieved the torch, but it looked as though he hadn't bled much more once he'd cauterized the wound. He considered himself lucky, because if he hadn't stopped the bleeding before he had passed out, it was very likely he would have bled out *while* he was passed out.

Of course, if that had been the case, he'd be dead now.

Sometimes big miracles come in small packages...

He turned and cautiously brushed his way through the spell room doorway, winding his way hastily back up the dark passageway. It took every ounce of strength and determination to focus on what he was doing and where he was going, instead of giving into the pain he felt coursing like thunder through his entire body. He held his damaged arm under his cloak, careful not to brush the wound with the material, and was relieved when he saw only a scattering of creatures here and there along the way. Most of the bodies he spotted were guards, roaming the tunnels of the castle or performing their rounds. He thought it best that he spoke to no one as he scurried through the gloomy, dank passageways until he reached one wooden door in particular.

He pounded on the door with his right fist, unaware of the time and totally not caring. It didn't matter what time it was or what any of the residents of Defigo were doing – he had things he needed to do and he needed to do them now. If his minions were sleeping or busy when he called upon them, so be it.

He was about to pound impatiently on the door again when it creaked open and a pale, thin, feminine face peered out at him from the darkness between the door and the frame.

"Aseret," Nivri said quietly. He made sure to keep his damaged arm beneath the cloak as he greeted the female who stared wordlessly at him. The last thing he needed right now was for rumors to start flying through the castle like a horde of wild, buzzing flies.

"Yes, Master?" the naiad answered quietly as she waited for him to continue.

"Prepare the castle residents for battle," the black clad creature ordered sternly. As her eyes met his, she held her breath, but tried her best to not let it show. Anger was completely pasted across his ravaged, dark face, especially in his wide, black eyes. She briefly also thought she could sense something else – some other form of emotion – but was unable to pinpoint it and then it was gone. As her heart began to beat faster, she felt as though she could smell – no, feel – anger pouring out of his very soul, filling the doorway, the passageway, the entire castle.

"For what time, Master?" she asked as she quickly recomposed herself. She straightened and threw her shoulders back, focused and ready to act without another word. Her mind raced as she wondered what had happened to cause this strange, unexpected turn of events.

"Have them meet me at the west entrance of the castle in one hour," he said sternly.

Without waiting for her response, Nivri turned and headed down the hall toward the throne room. Before he did, however, the naiad saw him flinch. In case he turned back to look at her reaction, she nodded her head once, a sign of acknowledgment as well as respect, then closed the door softly.

The end of the long passageway loomed ahead and Nivri cringed as pain shot through his arm, but he forced himself to show no signs of trauma in his expression. He walked quickly to his throne room, again not speaking to anything or anyone he encountered along the way, which, thankfully, were few. When he finally reached his destination, he entered through a side door that was strictly for his own use. In a small back room off of the main entryway, beyond the chair at the front of the room, was another, much smaller room that was used for storage. Over recent years, a portion of this room had also grown into a small medical area, which was used occasionally when he tortured his victims a little too... harshly.

It was to this part of the room where he headed now to treat his burnt, throbbing arm.

After locating the necessary medical supplies – ointment and gauze to name a few – Nivri sat down on the bench next to the supply table and went to work on his arm. He clenched his teeth as he washed the wound with a cold, bubbling liquid, carefully dried it, and gently applied ointment to the edge as well as the blackened area at the bottom of the stump. Once the end was shiny with medicine, the sorcerer carefully wrapped the remains of his arm. This proved to be most challenging, forcing him to use his teeth and chin to hold things in place the best way he could. When he was done, he had a treated, albeit not very beautiful, bandaged arm.

Nivri stood in the doorway of the medical room looking into the throne room. He stared beyond the statues of dragons frozen in flight and across the beautiful, glistening marble floor tiles, until his eyes finally focused on the two large, thick wooden doors that served as the main entrance to this room. *His* room. Beyond these doors he could hear the constant sound of footsteps as his minions made their way through the main passageway to the western side of the castle. They were the footsteps of a mighty army, indeed.

In spite of the throbbing, burning pain in his arm, he smiled.

His troops, his minions, were congregating in preparation for battle.

"I'm coming for you," the sorcerer whispered. Venomous hatred exuded from his pores as he made his way back to the chair that waited for him, front and center, in the throne room. He needed to meditate for a few minutes before joining his mighty troops in the west wing of his fortress. Careful not to bump his newly bandaged arm, Nivri sat down, got comfortable, and closed his eyes.

Although his physical eyes were closed, the eyes in his mind were wide open. He saw the large, white beast, floating next to the smaller, two-headed dragon. On the back of the stranger of the two creatures, he saw the abomination that had caused him so much grief – so much pain.

Two boys, one with short, straight hair and the other with short, curly hair, were sitting on the back of the two-headed dragon. The straight-haired figure sat a bit taller than the other, and the sorcerer assumed he was the older of the two. Nivri memorized their faces, hair, and clothes, committing the images to his mind as if burning them there like a mental tattoo.

After a few minutes, satisfied with his meditation, Nivri leaned forward and used his good arm to push himself up. As he made his way past the large dragon statues frozen in various flight positions throughout the room, he focused on the wooden doors ahead of him. He didn't see the dragons, and he didn't see the doors.

He saw the boys sitting on the dragons…

He saw their faces…

He saw their eyes, staring at him as if he wasn't there, one with blue eyes and one with brown…

Oh yes, he saw them… he saw them very well.

"I'm coming for you," he whispered as he roughly pulled opened one of the large, wooden doors.

He exited the throne room and made his way to the western edge of his castle.

As thoughts of revenge and success filled his mind, he smiled with anticipation.

Twenty-Seven

After her initial protest about the water temperature, Kaileen rode down the dark, wet tunnel in silence. As she slid through the darkness, her tiny heart beat faster than it ever had in her life. She knew yelling as she slid down, down, down, wouldn't do her any good, except maybe to let her friends know, when she stopped screaming, that it was probably because she'd slammed into a stone wall and broken her neck. On the flip side of that thought, if she did scream and somehow managed to make it down to the bottom of this strange, downhill slide, what kind of creatures might be waiting at the bottom for her after hearing her yell the entire way down?

After a few more seconds of controversial thought, she decided it would be much smarter to travel down the slide in silence so when she finally made it to the bottom – she was trying to think positive – she would quickly find a place to hide until her friends joined her.

The ride only took a minute or so, but when you don't know what's waiting for you at the bottom of such a situation, it makes it feel more like ages. Sometimes the tunnel curved to the left, then to the right, and sometimes it went straight, but eventually, a particularly long slope evened out and she slid to a stop.

As she caught her breath, she quickly realized she had no idea where she was. Thankfully, because she was a kalevala who had spent most of her life living in a lightless environment, it took almost no time at all for her eyes to adjust to her new location. She turned to look back up the tunnel, and thought she heard something moving in her direction, so she quickly jumped up to get out of the way.

Hopefully, her friends would both join her sooner rather than later.

She stood off to the side of the slide, waiting patiently for her friends. In less than a minute, a dark shape shot into a view, sliding to a stop in the same general location where she had stopped just a moment before.

"Kaileen?" Diam called out quietly.

"I'm here," the kalevala answered from the shadows to Diam's right.

"Whew, I'm glad you made it okay," Diam said as she carefully moved to the edge of the rock slide. "I can't see a thing – where are you?"

Kaileen couldn't see perfectly, but could see her friend's shape in the darkness. She took a step towards her and placed her hand on Diam's wet, web-covered arm.

Not expecting to feel something touching her, Diam muffled a partial scream of surprise.

"Sorry," Kaileen apologized. "I guess I should have warned you I was going to reach out for you."

Diam took a deep breath to steady her pounding heart.

"It's okay," she said. "I should have known you were going to do that."

Although Diam couldn't see her reaction, Kaileen nodded, and gently pulled her friend toward her.

"It's too bad the torch isn't lit anymore," Diam said.

Kaileen chuckled.

"I don't think it would have survived the splashing water on the ride down the slide."

"Sorry about shoving you into the tunnel," Diam said apologetically. "I didn't mean to be so rough with you, but I needed to get you moving so we could get out of there."

"It's okay," Kaileen said, accepting her apology with a sigh. "I'll admit you surprised me, but I understood why you did it.

251

I'm sorry I kind of froze up there." She pointed toward the tunnel without thinking that Diam wouldn't be able to see the gesture. "I hated seeing what was happening to our spider friends…"

"Me, too," Diam agreed. They waited in silence for a moment, each in their own thoughts.

"Where's Tonia?" Diam asked in a worried tone. "She should have been here by now."

As her eyes adjusted to the darkness, she leaned back toward the tunnel and called up to her friend.

"Tonia?"

They both held their breath and listened for a moment, but all they heard were the echoes of Diam's voice ascending upward in the dark hole and running water as it moved toward them down the sloped tunnel.

"Tonia?" Diam called again. She waited a few more seconds, but Tonia didn't show. Now she was really starting to worry.

Just as she was about to suggest heading back up the slide to find their friend, they both suddenly heard faint squeaking sounds coming from somewhere behind Kaileen. Diam nervously drew her sword in one hand and held Kaileen's hand with the other, but quickly discovered the weapon wasn't necessary. Around the corner of the tunnel, multiple pairs of glowing red lights suddenly appeared, and Diam released a tense sigh of relief.

"Wow, you scared us," she said to the dozen or so rats that were now scurrying around at their feet and up the nearby walls. Just when one rat in particular squeaked loudly in reply, they all froze. A sudden, nearby, splashing sound echoed through the darkness.

"Tonia?" Diam asked quietly, hoping it was her friend.

An alarming thought occurred to her. What if it wasn't her friend? What if, instead, it was the dreaded scorpion? She shivered at the thought, knowing they would be in a world of hurt if the pointy-tailed arachnid joined them now.

"Yes!" Kaileen cried happily a half a second before Tonia answered her friend.

"Of course, it's me, Diam! Were you expecting someone else?"

"Not really, but the way things are going for us so far, I'm not sure I'd be surprised by much of anything anymore," Diam answered in a stressful voice.

Tonia carefully lifted herself up off the slide and looked around. Thankfully, more rats had joined them, and their dimly glowing eyes lit up the room with a soft, welcoming red glow. It wasn't much, but at least they could now make out each other's profiles in the room.

"Are you okay?" the new arrival asked her friends. They nodded.

"Are you?" Diam asked in return.

"Yes," Tonia answered, "but I think we should get moving in case the spiders lose the battle up there. It was two on one when I left, but I don't want to press our luck."

"Where do we go from here?" Kaileen asked as her eyes examined the room.

"I think I can help you with that," a familiar voice said from a dark corner of the tunnel.

It was Kennard!

The girls heard him hopping slowly towards them, and within a few seconds, his shadowy figure appeared just a few feet away.

"Is everyone okay?" he asked. Although his voice was a bit raspy, it was also tender with obvious concern.

"Yes, I think we're all fine," Diam answered. When she took a step toward Tonia, she stumbled on something on the floor.

"Oh," she said as she caught herself. She leaned down to see what it was she'd tripped over, and found the torch Kaileen had been carrying earlier.

"Is this your torch?" she asked the kalevala.

"Yes," Kaileen answered. "I'm sorry. I set it down not realizing you were going to trip over it."

Tonia pulled her bag off her back and looked at it in the dim, red light provided by the rats. She sighed. She didn't need to see it to know it was dripping with water.

"Oh, darn! I was hoping we could light the one I had in my bag," she said as she held her dripping bag out in front of her. "Unfortunately, we'll need to let it dry out a bit first."

"Great," mumbled Diam. "What are we going to do with two wet torches? They won't do us any good wet, at least not until they've been out in the sun to dry for a while."

She looked at the multitude of shadows around them.

"And I think that could be a little bit of a problem while we're in here," she added wryly.

"It's okay," Kennard said in a weak, reassuring voice. "The rats will help light the way for us for now, and thankfully, if I remember right, the end of our journey through the mountain isn't too far away from here."

As their eyes adjusted to the dimly lit room, Tonia and Diam could finally see their amphibious friend a few steps away. Tonia stared in Kennard's direction for a moment and realized there was something hanging down around his neck and chest.

"What's that?" she asked as she reached out to touch the long, dangling item. As her fingers brushed it, she realized it was part of what remained of the harness he'd worn to pull them in their makeshift boat.

"Oh, that," Kennard began, "is something I will not be needing any longer. Could you please lift it over my head and take it off of me?"

"What happened?" Diam asked as she moved over to help Tonia.

"Well," the frog began, "I'm sure you can imagine there was no way I could have made it here with the boat we were using."

As if he was asking them a question instead of making a statement, the girls nodded their heads.

"Well, while you were in the upper cavern, I had our rodent friends assist me with my predicament," Kennard continued. "They chewed through the vines until I was free of the boat. Once that was done, I was able to continue on past the blocked part of the tunnel in hopes of finding you somewhere on this side.

"I realized there was a tunnel over here when the spiders came back down the other tunnel and headed this way. Of course, they traveled much faster than I ever could – well, in the body of a frog..."

Kennard stopped and looked around the gloomy cavern.

"Speaking of the spiders, where are they?"

Tonia looked at Diam and Kaileen, then turned to face Kennard.

"It wasn't good," she said quietly as she turned to look back toward the sloped tunnel she'd slid down just a short time before.

"Why? Tonia, what's wrong?" Kennard asked. Although he could sense a problem, he couldn't see far enough into her mind, into any of their minds, to fully understand what had happened.

And then, in the blink of a firebug, he got a glimpse of a long, angry scorpion as it battled two of the large, black glow spiders, and there, a few feet away from the scene of the fight, lay what was left of the third spider.

"Oh, no," Kennard said quietly as he shook his head with sadness and shocked disbelief. "I had no idea."

"We defeated the ice dragon," Tonia said proudly, but a second later the tone of her voice changed from pride to sorrow. "But the scorpion… it dropped right out of the ceiling and headed straight toward Kaileen. It wanted the amulet and no matter what we did or said, it wouldn't stop. Then, out of nowhere, the spiders came and jumped right into battle with it. They saved her… they saved us."

She shook her head sadly as she struggled to accept what had happened in the cavern above. Seeing her distress, Diam gently touched her friend's arm.

"We tried, but there was nothing we could do," the older girl said quietly.

"I understand completely," Kennard said as he offered an encouraging nod, "and I'm sure you did everything you could – everything you had to."

"I think we should go," Kaileen interrupted in a gentle, yet firm tone. The others looked in her direction.

"Before the scorpion comes after us," she added solemnly.

"Yes, we should go," Kennard agreed. "When the remaining spiders make it down the tunnel, they will be able to follow us by our scents."

"Don't you mean 'if'?" Diam asked quietly, her soft voice full of doubt.

"No, I mean 'when'," Kennard said, smiling at her in the gloomy light. "Now, more than ever, we need to think positively, don't you agree?"

Diam nodded in silence as Kennard continued.

"Now, follow me, and we'll find our way out of here."

Without a word, the girls found themselves again following the muck dragon, but this time they were walking instead of being pulled behind him.

TWENTY-EIGHT

Zel woke to the sound of low voices. He stretched, but kept his eyes closed, hoping to drift back off to sleep. In a matter of seconds, he admitted to himself the chances of that happening were slim to none.

At first, he thought the voices might be those of his children and their friends as they tried unsuccessfully to chat quietly while sitting around a crackling, late night fire. He dozed as the voices buzzed around him like insects in the distance, close enough to know they were there, but far enough away to not understand the words. Eventually, he took a deep breath and listened a little more closely. It didn't take him long to realize the voices didn't belong to children at all – they were adult voices. He also misidentified the familiar crackling sounds of what he'd thought was a fire, which he'd heard countless times during his life. Instead, they were the sounds of dead, dry leaves being crunched under foot. In fact, the more he focused on the sound, the more he realized it sounded like not just one foot, but many feet.

He cracked an eye open and took a long, slow breath, in through his nose, out through his mouth. Nope – no fire.

When he fully opened his eyes, he first found himself staring up at numerous tall, leafless trees. The jagged canopy towered over him like faceless, skinless abominations, reaching out their countless, long, skinny arms to smother him with scratches and

257

pokes instead of kisses. He blinked and the scary, nightmare creatures were simply trees again. Beyond the trees, he could make out a calm but dark, charcoal-colored sky. He lazily rubbed the last remnants of sleep out of his eyes as he remembered where he was, which led him to turn his head toward the direction of the voices.

About thirty feet away stood a small crowd of men, and there, on the outer edge of the makeshift circle, he could just make out Zacharu. His short, strange looking friend turned and acknowledged him with a nod, then turned his attention back to the group of men he was listening to.

Zel got up, brushed himself off, and passed a hasty, yet observant glance around the camp. Without giving it too much thought, he became one of the leaf crunchers as he walked across the wide bed of dry leaves to join the others. He suddenly paused and took another look around the area they'd chosen to rest in – he was the last one up!

"We'll be heading out in just a few minutes," Simcha said to the group, nodding respectfully at Zel as he joined them. "I'd recommend everyone have a quick bite to eat, as it may be the last one you have for a while. I suspected we're going to be a tad bit busy in a very short time..."

Movement out of the corner of his eye caught Zel's attention. With his hand on his sword, which he'd fastened securely at his side as he'd made his way toward the group of men, Zel turned to see what it was. He quickly understood the movement that captured his attention was from not just one thing, but two. There were two creatures making their way down the wide trunk of a very tall, nearby tree.

Both creatures, which appeared to be female, were climbing down feet first. They moved one hand, one foot, then the other hand and the other foot in almost perfect harmony. The first of these creatures had a beautifully mixed dark-colored, long, straight hair, and was dressed in light-colored clothing. She was fairly thin and taller, more mature-looking, than the second, smaller creature. The latter creature, whose hair was just as straight, but lighter colored and shorter, was dressed in similar, yet darker clothing. When the first creature reached the ground, she immediately reached up, grabbed the smaller creature under the arms, and lowered her lovingly to the ground.

"Ah, there you are Aseret," Orob said as he walked toward the taller of the two female creatures. He hugged her gently before turning his attention on the smaller female. She was partially hidden by Aseret and was quite obviously shy.

"And who might this be?" Orob asked, his gruff voice full of curiosity as he leaned slightly toward the two females in an effort to pick up the scent of the newcomer.

"This is Ilamet," Aseret said. She smiled as she placed a protective hand around the back of smaller female, pulling her closer and slightly forward. After a few seconds, she turned and leaned down to talk to the smaller creature.

"It's okay, Ilamet. They are friends."

Not convinced, Ilamet remained where she stood. Her wide, green eyes stared at the armor covered, hairy creature with flaring nostrils. Although Orob was not very tall for one of his kind, he towered over the smaller, green-eyed creature that had completely captured his attention.

Aseret's eyes scanned the crowd until she found Simcha. She nodded once at the leader of the humans before her gaze turned back to Orob.

"Ilamet is my younger sister," she began, again hugging the smaller creature closer to her. "I haven't seen her since... well, since I became an involuntary guest at the beautiful Castle Defigo."

Her eyes flashed an angry, bright salmon color for a split second before clearing. "Ilamet and I were sitting up in the tree, catching up with each other, while everyone rested."

"Ahh," Simcha said with a knowing nod as he moved toward the elder naiad.

"I thought I heard soft voices floating around on the breeze. Now I know where they were coming from."

As he approached her, the elder naiad's eyes darted through the crowd of male creatures surrounding them.

"I'm sorry if we were too loud..."

Aseret threw a grim glance at her sister before she dropped her eyes nervously to a pile of nearby brown and yellow leaves.

"Perhaps we should have gone somewhere else to talk, but I didn't want to move too far away from everyone. I wanted to remain watchful over those resting below while we talked."

"It's quite alright," Orob said, taking control of the conversation. "We appreciate the fact that you had our safety in mind."

Aseret raised a thankful look to Orob before turning her gaze back to Simcha.

"My sister, Ilamet, would like to join us."

Simcha stared at her with a look filled with both caution and surprise, as the curve of his wide, dark eyes slowly followed his mouth into a frown. He was not familiar with Aseret or her kind, whatever that may be, but the thought of bringing a younger member into their group before they headed into what could easily be the most important battle of their lives, especially one as young as the smaller of the two female creatures standing before him, made him very nervous. He did not want to be responsible for anyone's death as a result of the impending battle, especially not any human, or creature for that matter, that was barely more than a child.

"How old is she?" Simcha asked before Orob could say anything. They needed more information about this beautiful, fragile-looking creature before they could answer either way.

Aseret nodded as she pulled Ilamet out in front of her. The younger naiad resisted for a few seconds before finally allowing herself to be moved to her new location. Obviously still nervous, Ilamet kept her head down.

"Although she looks young, I assure you she is a mature female. Our kind comes in a variety of heights," Aseret said quietly. "Do not let the appearance of youth and innocence fool you."

She smiled mischievously at Simcha.

"And if you allow it, she will not be the only addition to our group. There will be others of my kind – other naiads – that should be here very soon," she said as she raised her head and addressed the entire group of warriors. "They will join us in the battle, and believe me when I say they will join us willingly and proudly."

Mumbles erupted through the group of men as Simcha raised a hand for silence before turning back to Aseret.

"Are you certain of this?" he asked, eyeing the younger of the two sisters warily. He was still uncertain of her age or the need for her, one so young, to be here – to face death in order to save lives.

"Perfectly," Aseret answered with the hint of a smile. "My sister told me so."

She turned and glanced at Ilamet, who returned a nervous glance to her older sister before addressing the small crowd in a small, tinkling, elf-like voice.

"Yes, we heard about the impending battle and I came to find my sister. The others, our brothers, our friends – those like us – are now on their way. When I last spoke with them, they said they planned on being here before sunrise," the shy creature explained before falling silent.

Aseret glanced upward as she tried to see the sky through countless lines of the black, leafless branches of the surrounding trees.

"The sun will rise soon," she said quietly. "We must head down to the lake and position ourselves while the cover of darkness protects us."

With that, Orob clapped his hands together, *clap, clap, clap.*

"You heard her, men. Up and at 'em!"

The former castle guard glanced at Simcha, who nodded his wordless agreement.

"We head out in five minutes!" Orob said with refreshed authority. He turned and made his way through the group of men, heading back to the tree where his things were piled on the ground in a disorganized heap. Just before he reached them, he noticed a tingling, almost electric feeling in the air that had not been there last night. Something was about to happen, and whatever that something was, it would be big – probably bigger than anything any of them had ever seen or experienced before.

His mind took him back to the castle, back to the throne room, where he'd witnessed many times just how angry and evil his former master could be, especially when he wanted something.

He grunted with disapproval. A few of the nearby warriors

glanced his way but Orob didn't notice. Although his eyes roved around the area on the ground where he had scattered his belongings, his mind was in another place and time. It had taken him for a surprise ride down memory lane, behind tall, damp stone walls, and across marbled, tiled floors.

There were a few times when Orob had seen Nivri torture some of the castle's prisoners nearly to the brink of death when he didn't get the answers he was looking for, and this made him think about his most recent prisoner. Orob raised his eyes to glance briefly at the taller of the two prisoners – the human, the one who called himself Zel. He was one of the lucky ones, and although Orob suspected the human knew this, he wondered if he *really* knew just how lucky he was.

He grunted again as thoughts flew through his mind. The human, sensing Orob's curious gaze, turned and looked at his former guard. Orob gave the man a brief nod, then quickly turned back to finish packing up his things. Yes, this one – this prisoner, man, human – whatever he would be called – was special, of that Orob was certain. He didn't know how he knew this, but he had no doubt he was right.

His thoughts suddenly drifted in another direction – this time to the day ahead. The former castle guard suspected he may not survive the upcoming battle with his former master, but he would fight the valiant fight and go down in a blaze of glory if he had his way about it. He had been one of Nivri's most respected guards for many moons during his years in the castle. As a result, he was certain that, after getting over the initial shock of seeing his first lieutenant on the opposite end of the battle line, Nivri would come for him.

Orob smiled when he thought about Nivri's almost certain reaction to the situation. After seeing countless prisoners on the receiving end of the sorcerer's anger and fury, it would be quite different to see Nivri on the other side of that jaded, torturous coin. This time, instead of being the torturer, the glowing-eyed sorcerer would finally be a not-so-helpless victim, being attacked and tortured by others when he certainly wouldn't feel it was deserved or called for.

The former guard chuckled to himself as he picked up his bag and slung it over his shoulder.

Yes, Nivri would likely not handle being on the receiving end of things on the battlefield very well, but this was certainly something that had been a long time coming. Orob had no doubt his former master would be angry at the strange turn of events, which would likely cause him to go into torture mode to the infinite degree. But knowing Nivri as he did, and Orob certainly hoped he knew the sorcerer as well as he thought he did, when his former master became over-the-top angry at the situation, there was a chance, small as it may seem, the creature with the glowing orange eyes and thick, black heart would be unable to cast the spells he would surely try to cast.

Orob could only hope...

Nivri would be angry, hateful, and very likely out for blood. Orob had a strong feeling both in his heart and his mind that he would be the first in line for any, or all, of those lovely reactions from is former master...

Yes, he completely expected Nivri would be angry...

And he was certain, beyond a shadow of a doubt, that it wouldn't be pretty.

TWENTY-NINE

For a short time, two boys, three dragons, and a single yarnie cat traveled in silence as they headed in the direction of the rising sun. The large ball in the sky was just beginning to crest above the top of the eastern line of trees, glittering along the top of the water like millions of tiny stars.

After a few minutes, Nicho frowned and turned to look back at his brother.

"Hey, Micah?"

"Hey, Nicho…" Micah answered in a teasing tone as he gave his brother a tired smile. It had been a long day already and, unfortunately for those who are tired beyond the point of exhaustion, it had just begun. Heck, it had been a long couple of days. How long had it been since they'd slept? Not just dozed, like a couple of little kidlets in the village, but really and truly slept? They needed to rest their tired minds and exhausted bodies, or exhausted minds and practically dead bodies. Either way, one thing was obvious…

They needed to sleep.

Soon.

He didn't know about Nicho, but Micah had already made a promise to himself that when he finally did sleep, he would sleep like the dead. Ah, yes, uninterrupted sleep would be bliss!

"What's up, bro?" Micah questioned as he forced himself to

concentrate on the day, not on the sleep to come. He tilted his head to the side to try to see his brother's face for a second, which had turned forward again. Micah knew that look – Nicho was stewing on something. As his brother turned back to look at him, Micah saw his mouth was set in an unmistakable frown.

"This could mean trouble," Micah thought.

"Did you see where the bat went?" the older of the two boys asked as his eyes scanned the horizon. It was much easier to make out the shoreline and distant trees now that the day was dawning with sunshine. It was especially easier to see what was around them in the absence of the thick bank of fog that surrounded them the night before.

Was it just last night when they had crossed the eerily dark and growling body of water on their way to the Castle of Tears? It seemed like a lifetime ago.

Micah saw Nicho's brown eyes scan the horizon nearly full circle and wondered where his brother was going with his question. He watched Nicho for a few seconds in silence, and then followed the direction of his only brother's gaze as he took in the area around the lake.

To the north was a mountain range where the particularly tall and jagged peak of one mountain was partially covered in a brilliant, unblemished white blanket of… what?

Snow?

There was something odd about the snow covered mountain, but Micah had other, more important things, on his mind right now than dwelling on what might be covering the top of a distant, raised piece of land. Instead, he turned his head slightly as his eyes continued to explore the horizon, slowly canvassing the outer edges of the lake.

Next to the snowy mountain, he saw what appeared to be a wide, never-ending brown valley, and next to that, another lower, smaller stretch of a mountain range lay in the opposite direction of the first. Between the two mountain ranges, directly opposite the brown valley, he saw what appeared to be a long, yet fairly narrow, stretch of shoreline. A long line of shrubs stretched parallel to this, and beyond the low bushes was another, much smaller mountain range.

His eyes returned to the stretch of shore at the edge of the lake. Was that a beach?

His focus moved from the shoreline back to the water, and he smiled. If he stared at the countless, blinking firebugs shimmering across the top of the water for much longer, he was certain it would put him to sleep. Micah pondered how this strange, unfamiliar world seemed so peaceful in the light of day, yet the ghosts and goblins hidden by sunlight could be so plentiful at night...

"No, I don't know where the bat went," he finally answered.

"Have any of you seen him?" Nicho asked their dragon friends.

As the rest of the group shook their heads to indicate they hadn't seen the small, flying creature, Micah added, "The last time I saw him was after we retrieved the amulet. He was flying out of the castle before it collapsed in on itself."

"Yeah, same here," Nicho agreed with a brief nod, "which is exactly what I thought. So the last time we saw him was before the sun came up. I wonder if he needed to go hide somewhere during the daylight hours? I mean, bats are nocturnal, aren't they?"

"I think so," Micah nodded.

Beneath them, the boys suddenly felt the muscles along Zig and Zag's back tighten, raising them slightly higher into the air. As the swimming creatures drifted to a stop, both boys focused their attention forward, looking at the separate heads belonging to the single body of the dragon they rode on. Both heads had turned and were looking towards the west.

"What is it?" Micah asked quietly, sensing the unmistakable tenseness in the air.

Although Zig and Zag had stopped their eastward progress, Lemures was still drifting slowly forward along the two-headed dragon's right side. Without a word, the white dragon continued his course for a few more seconds, then made a half circle rotation around the front of the boys until he was on their left. He stopped about twenty feet away and facing in the opposite direction.

"Shh," Lemures said quietly.

The ghostly dragon drifted to a stop next to Lemures and sat

266

as still as stone. Uncertain about what was happening, the boys each unsheathed their swords then sat at attention. Although Zig and Zag had stopped swimming, the muscles along his back were pulsing in quick, repetitive movements.

Was he trembling?

Suddenly, Lemures rose up on his back end and extended his wide, ivory colored wings completely away from either side of his body. As the boys watched, the dragon's partially transparent, shimmering skin suddenly shifted in opacity until the entire beast's body was no longer transparent at all. Right before their eyes, the ghostly dragon's body became one solid color.

"Get behind me," Lemures hissed as a cool breeze began to blow across the water, creating small, shallow crests across the top of the lake. Lemures focused his stone cold gaze on the sky in the west as he said this. Without a sound, Zig and Zag immediately moved through the water until the two-headed dragon was positioned close behind the larger, white dragon.

"Arm yourselves!" Lemures ordered.

Without turning to look at the others, he began moving his wings slowly forward and backward, in wide, long arcs. Micah, sitting behind Nicho, scooted as far forward as he could, until there was not a millimeter of space between him and his brother. When he noticed the distance between them had increased, Ragoo quickly got up and moved closer to Micah, but instead of sitting back down, he remained standing as he waited for whatever would happen next.

Micah peered around Nicho's shoulder, looking westward. All he could see was a valley on the far side and mountains to the southwestern corner of the lake. His focus moved to their immediate area – Lemures was still flapping his wings as if he was about to fly away, and Flamen...

Where was Flamen?

The smaller, younger dragon had disappeared.

"What is that?" Micah heard Nicho whisper. He quickly looked up and turned his attention back to the western edge of the lake. What were they looking at?

As Lemures lifted himself out of the water, sprinkling liquid droplets across everyone and everything around him, a dark shadow began to take shape in the distance. Although quite a few landed on them, neither Micah nor Nicho noticed the water droplets from Lemures' departure from the lake – they were focused intently on the shadowy shape over the water.

It was long, dark, and very large. As it moved closer, they could see it had bright, fiery red eyes. Micah's breath caught in his throat.

It was heading directly for them!

He grabbed the back of Nicho's left arm and looked up at Lemures. The white dragon was hovering just above and in front of them, his massive wings beating in slow motion.

"Boys, when I tell you to go, dive into the water and do *not* question me!" Lemures whispered harshly toward Nicho and Micah. Before they could even acknowledge his statement, the ivory-colored dragon turned and roared at the approaching shadow. In response, the black, flying beast lifted his own head up and growled right back.

Nicho held on tightly to Zig's neck.

"If he tells us to jump, I'll go right," he whispered over his shoulder at Micah.

"Okay," Micah said quietly as he stared at the approaching beast.

The black creature began to weave slightly to the left, then to the right, as it continued barreling through the air like an arrow. It was coming right at them and wasn't slowing down.

"It's a flying snake," Nicho said in disbelief, not realizing he'd spoken out loud.

As his voice traveled across the continuous cool breeze, the approaching viney shadow heard him. Instead of leaving its death glare focused on Lemures, it suddenly turned to adjust its target and stared at the two larger figures on the back of the smaller dragon. As soon as the creature changed direction, Nicho realized the mistake he'd made by speaking out loud. In seconds he saw the creature's nightmarish, yet unmistakable smile of confidence spread across its ugly face.

"There you are!" the flying snake creature hissed as it headed straight for the two-headed dragon.

When Lemures heard Nicho's voice, he suspected the

approaching creature would change its course and head directly for the boy. With a loud warning growl and a change of wing beats, the large, white dragon shifted his own position until he had placed himself directly in the snake creature's path.

"Now!" Lemures called to the boys. They immediately responded to the dragon's voice by diving into the cold, dark water. In seconds, they surfaced on either side of the two-headed dragon and quickly looked around for the approaching creature.

It had stopped its forward motion and was now hovering above the water roughly twenty feet away.

After a few seconds, Nicho realized the cool water around him, although a bit choppy from the incessant wind that had come out of nowhere a few minutes ago, was vibrating just below the surface. Suspecting he knew what it was, Nicho touched the right side of the two-headed dragon, which was Zig's half of the odd creature's body. He felt the scales along the side of the dragon vibrating with large, chattering tremors. He glanced up at Zig and saw exactly what he suspected – the timid dragon's face was completely covered in fear. Zig's half of the dragon was shaking almost uncontrollably, but to his credit, the less confident dragon was not crying and begging to hide like Nicho expected he would be. This surprised him, especially after seeing the way Zig had cowered in fear when he realized they were actually going to the Castle of Tears the previous night!

"Give them to me," the red-eyed snake growled as he hovered just above the water, keeping a safe distance. As Micah watched it, he could see an unmistakable look of hunger in the creature's eyes, but he wasn't sure if the look was caused by the desire for food or death – the death of the boys!

The snake-like figure glanced at the younger boy with hot, glaring eyes for what felt like forever. The creature panted as it hovered over the lake while streams of white, slimy bubbles foamed around its mouth and fell into the water, landing with an interrupted *hiss*. Thin wisps of a winding, smoky vapor floated lazily from the snake's nostrils, ascending up and away from the creature's nose for a half a second before being swished away by a combination of the morning breeze and the air turbulence from the flying dragon's wings.

"Grrrrrrrrrrrrrrrrrrr," the snake growled. "I said, give them to me!"

With this sentence, clumps of bubbles spewed from the snake's foam covered lips. The bubbles combined with slime from the shadowy creature's mouth and fell to the water below.

"If you know what's best for you, you will leave right now," Lemures warned as he glared at the hovering newcomer.

"Leave, and I will let you live," he added.

The bubble-faced creature broke its intent gaze from the boys and turned to look at Lemures, whose bright, yellow eyes glared right back.

"Stay, and you will surely die," Lemures warned.

"Arrrrrrrrrrrrrrrrrgh!" the dark creature cried in fury as it began moving again. It darted to its right in an attempt to move around the white dragon as it focused on the boys. As soon as he saw what the intruder was planning, Lemures struck out to his left with his muscular, white neck. He aimed for the snake creature's long, onyx tail as it whipped from side to side in the air behind him.

Would he move fast enough to catch it?

Crunch!

He missed! In an instant, Lemures turned to the right in preparation for the snake-like creature's return path. He growled as his eyes focused on the black beast. He was surprised to see it just a few feet away, heading straight toward the boys for a second attempt.

Wow, it was fast!

The shadowy creature had been focusing on Nicho before, but as he narrowed the gap between them, his ruby red eyes finally caught sight of Micah.

"You!" the creature yelled as recognition filled his wide, reptilian face.

The snake changed course and flew in wide, counterclockwise circles, which took him a safe distance away from the group of friends as he plotted out his next move. Zig and Zag suspected what was about to happen and quickly began turning in the same direction in an effort to both face the dark creature head on as well as to push Micah around so he would be shielded by the two-headed dragon's body.

Lemures realized what was happening as soon as he saw the snake's full attention focus on the younger of the two boys. He roared at the creature again in an effort to break its concentration, but it was no use. The large, white dragon knew he had only a few seconds to make a difference! The snake's focused behavior was something Lemures had seen before... it was now on a suicide mission.

Kill or be killed.

The flying snake halted its circling movements for a few seconds, then suddenly turned and headed straight for the young boy.

From the other side of the dragon, Nicho also realized what was about to happen. Without giving it another thought, he put his sword in his mouth and quickly began climbing up onto the two-headed dragon's back. He had to do what he could to save his brother!

Out of the corner of his eye, Lemures saw Nicho moving next to Zig and Zag, but he chose to focus his attention on the attacking creature. More steam flew out of its flaring nostrils, and its eyes began glowing with a deep, vibrant light the color of blood. More bubbling, corrosive saliva fell noisily into the water in a splattered, uneven trail across the lake.

Hiss... hiss, hiss, hiss... hiss, hiss!

Micah saw the snake heading straight for him and he knew there was nowhere to go but down. He had no idea how far down he could go, but what did it matter? The snake creature was coming at him from about ten feet or so above the water, which would give the snake the advantage. Chances were high that the shadowy creature would catch up to him faster than he could swim down into the depths of the lake. The only other option he could think of would be to swim beneath Zig and Zag, but knowing his luck, he'd end up getting clobbered by the swimming dragon's moving extremities – and that's one way he really didn't want to die.

He decided to stay where he was and do as much damage as he could to this attacking, evil minion, when suddenly he had another idea.

Certainly, this snake would be able to go into the water deeper and faster than Micah could go without a head start, but what if they were in shallow water? Micah didn't know how deep the water was in this part of the lake, but maybe luck would be on his side and it was shallower than it seemed to be? Perhaps he could just *appear* to try to hide below the surface from his current location, but instead he could turn and swim *around* Zig and Zag until he joined Nicho on the other side of the two-headed dragon's wide, floating mass? Would it work?

What did he have to lose?

Without another thought, Micah sheathed his sword and took a deep breath, then dove below the surface of the water. At first, he dove straight down, hoping to make it look as though he was diving for the bottom of the lake, but after a few seconds he turned and swam to the right in order to move behind and around the two-headed dragon.

Neither Nicho nor Lemures saw Micah disappear under water – they were both too busy focusing on the quickly approaching shadow of death. With short, wide wings and a long, flailing tail, the flying creature was quite an oddity as it flew.

Oddity or not, it was coming.

Lemures hovered in the air just a few feet in front of Zig and Zag, but the snake-like creature appeared to not see the solid white beast. Instead, the snake was staring intently at the area next to the floating dragon.

The place where Micah used to be.

"Perfect!" the creature thought. "Let him try to hide in deeper water. I'm more at home in the water than I am in the air. He is making my job easier!"

With that, the dark snake folded its wings into its sides and prepared to dive into the water after the boy.

"No you don't!" Lemures growled protectively as he lunged for the snake's tail, determined to not miss his target a second time.

Luck was with the white dragon this time around. As he struck out at the snake's thick, black tail, his jaws found flesh just as the gruesome beast was about to enter the water.

When the snake realized something had clamped down

272

on his tail, was *biting* his tail, he suddenly remembered the white dragon that had been hovering nearby. The odd creature whipped around as it prepared to lunge at the dragon, looking forward now to inflicting a wound of its own – a wound that would certainly cause death – but this time the snake made a fatal mistake. As it whipped its head to the right, it swung the front of its body directly in front of the two heads belonging to Zig and Zag. In an instant, each of the two heads followed Lemure's lead and clamped down on the snake's neck. Zig sank his teeth into the midsection of his neck while Zag caught the snake directly behind the head.

The snake cried out with a wail of defeat and anguish when it realized it was trapped in three different places. It wriggled its winding, flowing body as it tried to escape, but each of the dragons held it firmly in their strong, sharp-toothed mouths.

Seeing the perfect opportunity, Nicho quickly crouched on the back of Zig and Zag. In an instant, he was jumping – launching himself onto the writhing creature's back. He landed with a muffled thump, nearly knocking the wind out of himself with the impact. Before he fell off, he quickly wrapped his arms around the struggling snake's torso.

The boy glanced up at Lemures, who couldn't speak to tell him what should be done. Nicho was on his own, but that was fine with him. He knew exactly what he was going to do.

The older brother focused his thoughts and tightened his grip on the handle of his sword. Without any more hesitation, he plunged it into the side of the snake, causing the creature to thrash every inch of his wriggling body that wasn't being held in the jaws of the dragons. The snake cried out and tried to extend its wings in an attempt to fly away, which nearly knocked Nicho off.

He felt the snake tense up and realized if he had been five feet closer to the creature's back end, he would have ended up in the water in the blink of a firebug!

He felt the monstrosity trying with every ounce of his being to get away, so Nicho withdrew the sword quickly and plunged again, aiming for the heart. On a creature such as this, he wasn't certain where the heart would be, but it made sense it would be somewhere in front of the wings, didn't it?

Thick, black ooze ran out over his sword and covered his hand. For a split second, the boy worried the creature's blood may consist of the acidic slime dripping from its gaping, crying mouth, but luck was with him and it appeared to be just what it was – dark blood.

Nicho plunged his sword into the creature's side one more time, and its struggles finally began to subside. It cried out again, this time more in defeat than in pain, and as the life seeped out of the creature's body, Nicho sat up and looked around.

Where was Micah?

Suddenly, on the left side of Zig and Zag, they heard an odd, splashing sound.

"Nicho?"

"Micah!" Nicho answered, his hand still wrapped around the handle of his sword. The creature's blood covered most of his arm and was splattered across his clothes.

When he was certain the snake creature was dead, Lemures dropped the snake's tail. It fell into the lake with a splash.

"Nicho, you should jump into the water and wash off as best as you can. I'll take the snake and drop him into the middle of the lake."

With that, Lemures hovered in the air in front of the lifeless creature, taking the snake's upper neck in his mouth. He nodded at Zig and Zag once he had a firm grip, and the jaws from each of the two heads released their hold on the front of the snake's body. Lemures then lowered the carcass down towards the water so Nicho could slip off.

"What happened?" Micah asked as he peered around the front end of Zig and Zag. "Was I under water for *that* long?"

"We tag-teamed while you were goofing off," Nicho teased as he splashed around in the water, trying to wash off the snake's sticky blood.

"I guess I went deeper into the lake than I planned," Micah said with a frown. "It's a lot deeper here than I thought it was."

"Yes," Zag agreed. "It has to be, for the amount and different sizes of creatures that live here."

They watched Lemures as he hovered over an area near the

center of the lake then dropped the carcass into the water with a silent but visual splash.

"Is it okay that he's just dropping the snake's body into the lake like that?" Micah asked as Nicho joined him at his side.

The two-headed dragon partially submerged himself so the boys could climb back on. Ragoo was in the same place he had been earlier, although he was sitting now instead of standing.

Micah thought it was odd the yarnie was being so quiet, but Zag interrupted his thoughts.

"Nothing goes to waste here, young one. The snake's body will be used as food for the many aquatic creatures in the lake."

Nicho quietly climbed onto the dragon's back and Micah followed close behind, careful to keep his distance from the yarnie cat.

Flamen suddenly surfaced a few feet away. He looked at the boys as Lemures also rejoined them.

"Where did you go?" Nicho asked Lemures' son.

"I was afraid the snake creature would recognize who I am, and who I was, meaning that I used to be like him. If he would have seen me, he likely would have sprayed a generous amount of venom on us, killing us. Without my being here to distract him, the snake creature focused completely on Micah. He was consumed with the thought of taking the boy instead of killing him. I'm sorry if it seemed like I was abandoning you during battle, but I really felt it was in everyone's best interest to make myself scarce for a while," the young dragon explained.

"We understand," Zag offered as Lemures lowered himself back into the cool water just a few feet away.

"We must be on high alert," the white dragon warned. "It seems as though we are about to be a part of something much bigger than just a confrontation with a single creature."

"What do you mean?" Nicho asked as he passed a hand through his wet hair.

The largest of the three dragons looked from Nicho to Micah with wide, concerned eyes.

"According to some of our fellow creatures posted in various places around the outside of the Castle Defigo, Nivri and his troops are on their way."

"On their way? Where?" Micah asked, not understanding.

Lemures looked at the younger of the two boys, not surprised he didn't understand. He then turned to glance to the west for just a few seconds before returning his focus back to the boy.

"Here," Lemures said. "Nivri is on his way here."

Micah stared at the dragon as the words sank in. Nivri, the black-cloaked, orange-eyed, evil being was on his way here, to the lake.

"This is the day all creatures of Euqinom have been waiting for," Lemures said quietly. "Today is the day we fight for our freedom. Today is the day the battle begins."

*****

Ragoo groaned and Micah turned to look back at the yarnie. It was sitting behind him, the closest of the group to the dragon's tail.

"Ragoo, are you okay?" Micah asked in a worried tone.

The cat didn't answer. Instead, he sat staring down at the water as if in a daze.

"Ragoo?" Micah asked again as Nicho turned to look past his brother at the yarnie. He couldn't see much of the cat because his brother was in the way.

"What's wrong?"

Before Micah could answer, Ragoo began to rock slightly from side to side as if trying to keep the beat of some unheard drums with a slow, relaxing undulation. Just as Nicho was about to ask his question again, the yarnie cat suddenly toppled off the back of the dragon and landed in the water with a splash, instantly disappearing from sight!

"Ragoo!" Micah yelled. In a flash, the young boy reacted. As soon as the word was out of his mouth, he leaned to his right and dove into the water just a few feet away from the place where the yarnie cat disappeared below the surface.

"Micah!" Nicho called out. He was just about to follow his brother into the water when Lemures called out to him.

"Wait, Nicho! Let Flamen look for them!"

When Nicho looked to see where Lemures' son was, he realized the smallest of the three dragons had already disappeared below the surface in search of Micah and Ragoo. After almost a minute, Micah's head erupted from the water with a splash. He took a deep breath of fresh air, wiped his eyes, and frantically searched for the dragons. As soon as his eyes caught sight of his brother, he called out to him.

"Did he come up yet?"

"No," Nicho answered in a worried, solemn tone. He was about to tell Micah that Flamen was somewhere below them looking for the yarnie cat, but Micah was already gone, diving into the cool blue water once more as he frantically searched for his feline friend.

"Micah!" Nicho yelled as the two remaining dragons slowly circled the area where the boy and the cat disappeared.

All was silent for a few seconds when patches of bubbles suddenly began to explode in different locations across the top of the surrounding water. Without realizing his hand was on the handle of his sword, Nicho's brown, worried eyes turned to look at Lemures.

"Can't you go help them?" he asked worriedly. He tried to sound strong but was struggling to hide that he was almost on the verge of tears. "Lemures? Can't you?"

Before the white dragon could answer, Nicho looked up at Zig and Zag as each set of eyes darted between the boy, the white dragon, and the choppy water.

"If I jumped off, could you go look for them?" Nicho asked the two-headed dragon. "Please?"

"Nicho," Lemures said calmly. "Flamen has lived in these waters for quite some time now. If he can't find them, I'm sorry to say I don't think anyone can."

"No!" Nicho shouted in a gruff, angry tone, shaking his head in denial. "If you won't help them, then I will!"

Just as the older of the two boys was about to swing his left leg over the dragon's back and jump into the water after his brother, Micah's headed popped above the waterline again. He coughed a few times then looked around frantically.

"Micah, are you okay?" Nicho asked in a voice filled with both anger and worry.

Micah looked at his brother with fear-filled eyes. Before he could answer, he coughed again and tried to catch his breath. He was about to ask if anyone had seen any signs of the yarnie when Flamen suddenly broke the surface just a few feet away. Ragoo was draped across the lower part of the smaller dragon's neck like a soaked, motionless rag doll.

Micah's heart stopped when he realized his friend from the yarnie village wasn't breathing.

"Ragoo!"

Zig and Zag immediately paddled toward the swimming figures.

"We're going to partially submerge our body so you can get the yarnie out of the water," Zag said as he turned back and looked at Nicho. The older boy immediately felt cool wetness surround his foot before it crawled up his legs. At the same time, Micah grabbed onto Flamen's neck and the small dragon carried both the younger boy and the cat toward Zig and Zag until they were just inches away from the two-headed dragon.

"Ragoo!" Micah cried as he grabbed the motionless, water soaked yarnie cat by the neck. He was surprised at how weighty the cat's body had become now that it was wet, and he struggled to hand the unconscious yarnie to his brother.

Still sitting on the back of the two-headed dragon, Nicho had rotated his body around until he was facing the back end of the beast. The new position gave him more room to lay the yarnie cat down across the Zig and Zag's wide, thickly scaled back. He held out his arms and Micah grunted as he lifted Ragoo into the air. He gently swung the cat to his brother, leaning on Zig and Zag for leverage as he did so. As soon as Nicho had the limp yarnie safely in his arms, he gently laid the cat down on the dragon's back. Without a word, Micah immediately headed toward Zig and Zag's tail, where he scurried up onto the dragon's back and joined his brother. His blue eyes focused on the black and white striped yarnie cat, lying in a motionless heap across the dragon's back. A large, uncomfortable lump filled the pit of his stomach when he realized his feline friend was still not breathing.

"Ragoo!" Micah called out as he quickly took his place on the other side of the cat. He began rubbing the yarnie's head and slowly slid his hand down across the cat's back. As the thick blanket of unknowing fear covered his heart, the blue-eyed boy began to cry.

"Ragoo!" he sobbed as tears filled his eyes before spilling down his cheeks like round, liquid stars. As they followed the path of gravity, the tears landed in both the cat's disheveled fur as well as on the dragon's back.

Nicho ignored his brother's distress as he focused on helping their friend, but as the seconds passed, he realized he had no idea what to do for the cat. He had never studied medicine and definitely wasn't a mundunugu, but he knew for a fact if he didn't do something quick, his brother would probably hate him for the rest of his life. He had to do something...

Nicho began slowly rubbing the cat from head to tail, partly to offer circulation and partly to rub moisture out of its fur. After a brief pause, common sense finally took over and he had an idea.

He felt again along the cat's side until he found what he thought was a rack of rounded, narrow rib bones. He closed his eyes and struggled to remember something Uncle Andar told them during one of their many trips into the forests around the village as they hunted for both food and adventure. Like their mother and father, Uncle Andar was always trying to teach them bits and pieces about life. Nicho closed his eyes as he tried to remember something in a distant part of his mind, something that had happened just a few months ago while they were out on one of their excursions.

Micah was sniffling as he tried to hold back the tears, but Nicho didn't hear him. Instead of smelling the dampness of the surrounding lake, he smelled the nearby wall of evergreen trees. Beyond the scent of the forest, he could smell valley flowers where they bloomed in a myriad of colors, shapes and sizes.

Remember...

He opened his eyes and his gaze drifted to the sun sparkling off the water as he thought about the conversation he'd overheard in another time and place that felt like it had just happened yesterday. For some reason he was unable to remember now, and it really didn't matter, Tonia had asked a question about a skeleton they had found lying in the tall grass of the nearby valley.

He closed his eyes again, just briefly this time, as his mind tried to focus on the small, lifeless carcass they'd found. Although the skin was long gone from the skeleton, likely removed by worms and smaller bugs that fed off of carrion, the bony structure itself had remained almost perfectly intact. Not surprisingly, this had drawn the complete curiosity of his younger sister.

Hovering over the skeleton, Tonia had asked many question about the bones, especially the halfmoon-shaped ones that formed broken circles around a lot of empty space. Uncle Andar had patiently explained to Little Miss Curious (and oh, how she hated when he called her that!) that those halfmoon-shaped bones were called ribs. He further explained that the main purpose of the set of arced bones was to protect the heart.

In addition to protecting the heart, those thin, arc-shaped bones also protected the lungs, didn't they?

Nicho smiled as he remembered such times with his sister, his brother, his uncle and his father. He was so wrapped up in his memories of times past that he didn't notice his brother staring at him. Only when Micah called out to him in an angry tone, obviously upset that sibling appeared to be daydreaming while Ragoo needed their help, did he return to reality.

"Nicho! What are you doing?"

Nicho stared blankly at his brother for a few seconds before offering him a small, but reassuring, smile. His expression faded when he saw no indication of having the gesture returned to him before turning his attention back to the yarnie. Ragoo was lying on his side, still unmoving, and for a split second Nicho was certain the feline was dead. Without wasting any more time, he ran his hand along the cat's side. When he found the halfmoon-shaped structure he was looking for, he began pushing down on it.

He pushed once then stopped. He pushed again then stopped. Nothing.

"What are you doing?" Micah asked with confusion as he wiped more tears from his cheeks with the back of his hand.

Nicho didn't answer. Instead, he tried over and over to expel water from the yarnie cat's lungs as he struggled to save Ragoo's life. Unwilling to give up easily, Nicho soon found himself following some strange kind of rhythm – push, stop – push, stop – as Micah watched helplessly, still sniffling from less than an arm's length away.

Lemures and Flamen floated nearby, watching in wary silence as the older boy continued to work on the motionless feline.

"Be careful!" Micah warned cautiously, but Nicho ignored him. Instead, he continued to repeat the process, still unwilling to give up and not too concerned he was hurting the cat. Right now, his main concern was that it *wasn't* hurting the cat. If the yarnie was dead, it wouldn't matter anyway, but if it wasn't…

Without warning, Ragoo suddenly sputtered to life, and threw up what appeared to be the equivalent of a pia bottle full of clear, warm liquid over the side of the dragon. Nicho watched with surprise as Ragoo gagged, coughed, and threw up again. The entire time, the cat's eyes remained closed.

"Ragoo!" Micah shouted happily as he lovingly stroked the cat's head. "Ragoo, you're okay!"

But as Nicho watched the yarnie, he knew the cat wasn't okay. Although he was now breathing, the gagging feline wouldn't open his eyes.

"Ragoo? What's wrong?" Micah asked softly as he continued to gently rub his hand across the feline's head, down his neck, and along the length of his black and white striped body.

"Why won't you open your eyes? And what happened? Why did you fall into the water?"

Although Micah wasn't crying anymore, Nicho could hear in his brother's voice that a fresh onslaught of tears wasn't far away.

"Sick," Ragoo mumbled weakly.

The yarnie lifted his head as if he was going to throw up again, but after a few seconds, he laid it back down. The boys watched him in silence, both of their faces completely covered with worried expressions. After a moment, Ragoo lifted his head again, this time throwing up over the side of the dragon. When the yarnie stretched his neck out to vomit, Nicho noticed a strange, reddened area on the underside of the cat's neck.

When the wave of nausea finally passed and Ragoo appeared to be resting peacefully, Nicho decided that, although it might not be the best time to question the yarnie, he needed to. He was worried about the reddened area he had seen.

"Ragoo, I want to roll you over for a moment."

The cat nodded his head weakly, indicating his understanding. Although it wasn't much of a nod, it was enough for Nicho to see.

"Why?" Micah asked defensively. Although he was no longer crying, he had scooted protectively closer to the yarnie a few minutes before.

"Micah," Nicho said, "trust me, okay? Let me roll him over."

"But why?" the younger boy asked again in a slightly angry tone.

Nicho sighed. He knew how his brother could get when he was protective about something, and now was not the time to try to be a bullying big brother.

"There's something on his neck," Nicho whispered as he leaned closer to Micah. He looked down at the yarnie cat and pointed at the general area without touching it. The yarnie was now breathing steadily, but didn't seem very aware of what was going on around him.

Either he hadn't heard their conversation or hadn't cared...

Micah sat back and stared nervously at his brother before he turned his focus back to his feline friend. He leaned from side to side, looking the cat over from head to tail, but couldn't see anything out of the ordinary anywhere on Ragoo in his current position. Micah frowned and looked back at Nicho with a questioning look.

Nicho understood Micah's confusion and pointed wordlessly to the area of Ragoo's neck that was underneath him. Without a word, Micah nodded his understanding.

"Ragoo?" Nicho asked quietly.

"Mmm?" the yarnie replied weakly.

"I'm going to roll you over now."

"Mmm," the yarnie mumbled again.

Although he appeared to agree, the weakened cat did not offer any assistance. Instead, he remained motionless as if he were trying to sleep. Nicho rubbed the yarnie gently from head to tail before he turned to look at Micah.

"Help me," he whispered.

When Micah nodded, Nicho grabbed the yarnie's front legs while Micah grabbed the back. When Nicho nodded again they worked together to gently roll the cat over onto his back before completing the turn and rolling him onto his other side. Thankfully, the feline had been lying with his head to one side of the dragon and the tail to the other, so the move only required that they roll him perpendicularly along the dragon's spine. Nicho sighed with relief when he realized they didn't need to worry about him rolling off into the water again...

At least not yet.

As soon as they stopped moving him, the yarnie cat shifted slightly to make himself more comfortable. As he did so, Micah stifled a surprised gasp.

On the right side of the yarnie's neck, close to his shoulder, was a very obvious, bright red area about two inches in diameter. Small clumps of fur had fallen out in tiny patches around the affected area. When Micah reached out to gently touch the cat's neck, another small clump fell out and rolled down the dragon's side like a weightless ball of pollen. Micah watched as it landed on top of the sparkling water below before it floated away across the gentle ripples of the lake.

"Ragoo?" Micah asked quietly as he turned his attention back to the yarnie cat. The feline flinched when Micah's hand barely touched the fur in the strange, reddened area. "Ragoo, what happened to your shoulder?"

The cat appeared to not hear the young boy's question. Just as Micah was about to ask it again, the yarnie's eyes began to move from side to side as if he were having a dream. After a few seconds, they slowly fluttered open. With effort, Ragoo struggled to turn his head in an attempt to see the object of Micah's question.

"Last night," the yarnie said. He slowly relaxed his head as he realized the wound was in an area he couldn't see.

"No," Micah said as he gently rubbed his hand along the yarnie's body, encouraging him to lie still. "Don't look at it. It's just an irritated area that I... we... hadn't noticed until now. I was just curious about what had happened."

Micah hated lying to the yarnie, but felt deep down in his gut it was necessary. He hoped the cat didn't hear the worry in his voice or see it in his eyes. Micah suspected the cat wasn't seeing much of anything though – the yarnie seemed to be pretty out of it.

After a few seconds, he realized he needn't have worried about the yarnie seeing much of anything, because the cat's eyes had drifted closed again. Micah let out a silent sigh of relief.

"Ragoo, I want you to lie still until we reach land," the younger boy continued. The yarnie didn't move, but he was fairly certain the cat had heard him.

Micah nodded. "Good. Now that you're resting, can you tell us what happened?"

Ragoo kept his eyes closed and did not try to rise up again when he answered his friend in a scratchy, tired voice.

"Last night… the dragons… the battle…"

Micah looked at Nicho before glancing over at Lemures. The large, white dragon was floating very close to one side of Zig and Zag, while Flamen waded in the water on the other. The dragons were listening intently to the conversation between the boys and their pet.

As Nicho listened to his brother, his mind was racing. The battle, the dragons…

Suddenly, an idea struck him, and he decided to take a turn asking the yarnie a question.

"Ragoo, last night, did something happen to you during the battle we had with the mini dragons?"

Ragoo nodded, took a breath and shifted slightly before he answered.

"Yes… mini dragons…"

Micah thought Ragoo was done with his explanation, and he reached down to gently stroke the feline's side. He felt Ragoo take in another shallow breath, then he felt his own blood run cold when the yarnie added a brief, chilling end to the previously incomplete sentence.

"One… bit me."

THIRTY

The girls followed Kennard through a winding, dark tunnel for a while. The muck dragon was moving much slower now than he had been when they first entered the cave, but the girls figured this was because they were on foot instead of being pulled behind him in the makeshift boat. They carefully followed the dim, red eyes of the accompanying rats darting along the tunnel floor and walls, each of them searching for an exit. It was much warmer in the lower levels of the cave than it had been in the upper, snowy cavern, and in some places, the atmosphere seemed very stale and dry. They walked in silence for a few moments until Diam stopped them.

"Hey, hang on a minute," she called out as she wiped sweat from her brow with her forearm. "Kennard, do you think it's okay if we get ourselves out of this thick, confining, spider webbing? It did a great job keeping us safe from the ice dragon in the top of the cave, and it really kept us dry when we slid down that wet tunnel..." She stopped mid-sentence and tried tugging at the webbing on her arm. It barely budged. She looked at her friends with a frown. "I don't know about you girls, but I can guarantee you that I'm quickly going to do my best at imitating one of Tonia's stinky brothers if I don't get this extra insulation off soon."

Tonia chuckled and looked back at the muck dragon. It had

stopped a little ways ahead and was coming back towards them.

"Certainly, young Diam. Let's take a few minutes to rest while you help each other out of your 'insulation'."

The web covered figures found a narrow area of the tunnel with a few rocks suitable for sitting on. Using their swords as carefully as if they were handling newborn mud puppies, each of the girls worked to remove the dirt and grime covered webbing from their bodies. Diam was the first to be completely free, and she immediately went over to help Kaileen, who was the least efficient at using the sword as a large knife. The older girl smiled as she helped the kalevala remove her multicolored insulation, and soon Tonia joined them, offering her assistance from the other side of the kalevala. Before long, the three girls stood in a small cluster, still exhausted but much more comfortable than they had been just a few minutes prior. The tunnel floor around them was littered with various piles of dirty and discarded webbing.

"Whew, now doesn't that feel better?" Diam asked with a knowing smile.

"Absolutely!" Tonia agreed happily as she turned a mischievous eye towards the frog. "Well, as long as Kennard doesn't send us into any other upward tunnels to fight more unsuspecting and unfriendly ice dragons!"

As she cracked the joke, she realized if they *did* have to go up another tunnel, their furry, eight-legged friends were no longer around to get them there. They also didn't have the spiders to wrap them in protective webbing – hopefully they wouldn't need it again.

She sighed as she wondered if they would ever see the arachnids again.

"Let's go," she said somberly. None of the others needed to ask why her mood had changed so quickly. They understood without the need for words.

Kennard turned and continued leading them into the shadowy tunnel. The only sound heard was the scuffling of their feet along the dirty, dusty tunnel floor. It didn't take long before they realized they didn't need the narrow, red beacons of light provided by the glowing-eyed rodents anymore.

"Wait," Kaileen said as the others stopped in front of her.

"What is it? What's wrong?" Diam asked as she reached out to touch the kalevala's cool, dark-skinned arm.

"Up ahead. Do you see it?" she asked in a hushed voice.

The others strained their eyes as they stared straight ahead, but none could see anything except for the yawning, black darkness waiting for them, waiting to take them to nowhere. Diam was about to turn back to the kalevala to ask what she was talking about when she thought she got a glimpse of something...

Was that a vague hint of gloomy light in the darkness up ahead?

"I don't see anything," Tonia said quietly from where she stood less than a step ahead of Diam.

"Wait a few seconds and look again," the kalevala suggested.

Tonia leaned slightly to her left as she peered into the darkness beyond the motionless frog. She could hear his raspy breathing, but could barely see him. She held both her balance and breath as she squinted her eyes in hopes of making out something – anything – in the shadows filling the space of the tunnel ahead. By the tone of Kaileen's voice, it sounded like she thought she could see something ahead of them, but as Tonia continued staring into the darkness, she had no idea what it might be. There was just darkness up there – darkness and cool, likely stagnant air, waiting to greet them like it always did in her dreams...

But suddenly, as she tilted her head a little more in the other direction, a different kind of shadow caught her eye. Without giving it much thought, she placed her hand on Diam's shoulder to both balance herself again as well as to reconfirm that her friend was indeed still standing just a few inches away.

"What is it?" the now curious, brown-eyed girl asked with obvious excitement in her feminine, raspy voice. As the muck dragon turned back to look at her with the hint of a shadowy smile, she turned her question to him.

"Kennard, is that it?"

The muck dragon chuckled weakly before erupting in a round of coughing, which Tonia suspected was from the dusty environment they had created around them. "I do believe it may be," he struggled to say as he took a moment to catch his breath.

"Kaileen," he said turning to smile at the kalevala, "My

eyesight is pretty good, but you definitely saw it before I did!"

"That's what happens when you live in a cave filled with nothing but dark corners and tunnels your whole life," the kalevala replied as she smiled in the gloom.

Kennard nodded silently.

"Let's go!" Tonia said with a renewed spring in her step. She began walking forward again as she glanced back at Diam. She thought Kennard had continued heading toward the light, but didn't realize he hadn't until it was too late. After taking a few steps forward, she walked right into the frog, who was still sitting in the middle of the tunnel.

"Oh, geez, I'm sorry, Kennard! Did I hurt you?" she apologized as one hand covered her mouth. Without waiting for the muck dragon's answer, she added, "I thought you had already started moving again."

The first thing she noticed after realizing what she'd run into was how much the texture of the frog's skin had changed. Back at the puddle, she hadn't needed to touch it to see how wet and slimy it had been. Now, however, it was cool, smooth, and quite dry beneath her fingertips...

It was too dry...

"It's quite alright," the muck dragon said as he coughed again. "Bear with me though, for I seemingly can't move as fast as I once could."

The girls stared at each other as they suddenly remembered the sacrifice the frog was making in order to escort them from one end of the cave to the other.

"Kennard..." Tonia began. Her eyes met his and she paused. Even in the shadow filled tunnel, she recognized the icy glare he sent her way.

"I'm fine," the frog answered in a firm yet definitely weaker voice. "Now let's get moving, before something happens and I can't..."

Without waiting for a response, the dozen or so glowing-eyed rodents began making their way noisily toward the lighter end of the tunnel. Without finishing his sentence, the muck dragon turned and followed them. Diam's worried eyes met Tonia's as the younger girl shrugged her silent response. She laid a gentle hand on her friend's shoulder before turning to follow the dragon. They all knew that no amount of arguing would make a bit of difference concerning the fate of their guide, except, perhaps, to exhaust him more than he already was.

As expected, the tunnel continued to lighten as they made their way toward the gray circle of light. In less than a minute, they stepped through a roughly arched doorway into a completely different environment filled with cool, fresh air. Without meaning to do so, they each stopped and stared at the sight before them.

A round, pregnant moon was hanging nearly halfway down the colorless sky like an enormous, glowing beacon in the night. Its reflection flickered in countless shattered pieces across the center of a large body of water somewhere below, like a twin shaking in fear from its sibling above. Although the sky provided a mostly dark background to the moon, along the lowest part of the eastern edge of the sky a pale, thin, orange border was just beginning to peek at them above the tree line.

Tonia stood between Diam and Kaileen, and grabbed one of each of their hands in her own. She squeezed their palms tightly as tears pooled in her eyes for a few seconds before spilling like a mini waterfall onto her cheeks.

"It's beautiful," she whispered.

"Yes," Kennard agreed. "This is one of the many reasons why we are here."

They stood like silent sentries in the cool, morning air as they watched the exquisite birth of a new day. In the distance, the sound of birds welcoming the sun could be heard, their songs increasing in volume as more and more of the finely feathered creatures joined the chorus. In contrast, the travelers could barely hear the normal sounds that accompanied the darkness, such as crickets and puddle frogs. As the sun slowly began to paint the sky with its accompanying colors and light, the creatures of darkness silenced themselves and settled down for bed.

The girls didn't notice when Kennard slowly leaned to his right, away from them, and rested his wide, yellow-brown torso against the outside of the cave. The stones were refreshingly cool against his warm skin.

"What do we do now?" Kaileen asked as she gazed at the

beautiful, yet extremely large, colored orb hanging in the distant sky. Although she'd been in the valley outside the cave just the previous day (is that all it had been? Just one day?) she hadn't had the opportunity to see anything as beautiful as the sight in front of her right now. When Kennard didn't answer, she turned to look at the muck dragon. He was staring down at the dark body of water in the distance, seemingly mesmerized by the white lines flickering like millions of miniature, shiny fish across the top of the water.

"Kennard?" she asked as she tried to get his attention. The other girls turned toward the dragon to see why he hadn't answered the kalevala, when suddenly his body crumbled to the ground.

"Kennard!" Tonia shouted in surprise as she turned and immediately ran to his side. The other girls were next to her in half a second. While Tonia gently stroked the muck dragon's shoulder, Diam whispered the single question neither of the other girls had dared ask.

"Kennard, are you okay?"

"Listen well," he whispered hoarsely. His breathing was shallow as he struggled for air. He lay on his belly in a heap, and visibly forced himself to raise his head in order to look at his three female companions. In the end, the effort was too much for him. He closed his eyes and dropped his head back down to the ground, where it landed on the dirt and rock littered path without a sound. His sides expanded and contracted as he struggled with each shallow and irregular breath.

Tonia knelt beside Kennard's head and began gently stroking the side of his neck as fresh tears slid down her cheeks. One of the liquid diamonds fell and landed on the top of the muck dragon's nose with a soundless, explosive splatter. Although the muck dragon didn't open his eyes, Tonia thought she could detect a slight upward twitch at the corner of his mouth – a totally unexpected attempt at a smile. She sniffled in a totally unladylike manner and quickly smeared the betraying dampness away from her cheek with the back of her hand. As her emotions threatened to throw her into a complete emotional tail spin, she struggled – and failed – to express the words drowning in her heart.

Understanding Tonia's turmoil, Diam and Kaileen quickly dropped to the ground beside her. As they huddled together around Kennard's head, each of the girls understood what was happening. Worse than that, they fully realized they could do nothing to stop it.

The trio of teary-eyed girls waited for the dragon to continue his comment, but he chose to remain silent. Instead of saying anything else, he used what was left of his dwindling energy to struggle with the inhale and exhale of every breath. After a few seconds, Diam finally found the courage to ask the question they were all thinking.

"Can we do anything to help you or make you more comfortable?"

Again, the corner of Kennard's mouth curved slightly upward with a halfhearted attempt at a smile. It wasn't long before the curve melted back into its original position and he lay completely motionless.

Had he died?

Three pairs of wide, frightened eyes stared at the frog in disbelief. None of them moved as they waited for Kennard to respond. Just as Tonia felt panic on the verge of swallowing her like an ocean wave during a bad storm, the muck dragon's side slowly expanded again as he struggled to take a long, slow breath. The girls watched in silence as, instead of answering Diam's questions, the dying frog lifted his head slightly until it hovered just barely above the dirty path. With obvious effort, he moved his head to the left one inch, then changed direction and moved it two inches to the right.

That was his answer. They could do nothing to help.

The trio of girls stared at the frog with tear-filled eyes as they watched their friend struggle with his futile attempts at both breathing and communication. He was trying to shake his head negatively from left to right, but this simple task obviously required more energy than the muck dragon was able to give. His sides contracted with a long, slow exhale and Kennard eventually returned his heavy head to the ground. It tilted to the right as if he could no longer balance it, but he seemed to not care in the least. It rolled to the side like a lopsided pia seed until it eventually came to rest on a wide, round cheekbone.

The muck dragon's eyes remained closed as he took another slow, deep breath. When he exhaled, whispered words filled the nearby air as he tried talking again.

"The lake... go there... find the beach on the western edge. Find Teresia..."

As he ran out of breath, Kennard's one visible eye suddenly fluttered open. With a surprising burst of strength, he inhaled deeply, passed a glance over at each of the girls, and finally settled on Tonia.

"Kennard..." she began, but the words died on her lips when she realized he was struggling to say more.

"Find... brothers."

Without letting Tonia reply, he turned back to look at Kaileen.

"Don't be... afraid..."

He gasped for breath and his eye rolled erratically in his head. After a few seconds, he tried again.

"To... look... in the mirror."

The kalevala stared at the dying frog, not understanding his statement. Without hesitating, Kennard's dark, tired, one-eyed gaze cut to Diam.

"Ring... is yours."

"Kennard?"

Diam's single word was barely audible. The muck dragon lay still as his eye closed for the last time and he fell abruptly silent. He was almost out of time and they all knew it.

Tonia continued gently stroking Kennard's rough, dry neck as she struggled to whisper words through her tears before it was too late.

"Thank you for everything. Thank you for your sacrifice."

There was neither a dry eye nor face in the group as the trio of girls stared helplessly at their friend. After a few agonizingly long seconds, Kennard used his waning energy to force a small but unmistakable smile. With his eyes still closed, the muck dragon took one labored, final breath. As he slowly exhaled, he shared his final words.

"Save... us..."

And then he lay motionless.

Although they understood he was gone, the girls continued to stroke the lifeless corpse's skin as Tonia began to cry quietly. They held each other in the cool morning air, sharing tears and a certain measure of comfort, wishing things could be different, yet knowing it was too late for those kinds of wishes.

They held hands as they forced themselves to pick up the shattered pieces of their hearts. Within a few seconds, Kaileen noticed something odd was happening to the lifeless amphibian's body.

It didn't appear to be lifeless anymore.

"Uh oh."

The girls stared at the heap on the ground in shocked surprise as the frog's formerly lifeless skin suddenly began to twitch as if it had magically found new energy.

Was Kennard having some kind of afterlife seizure?

The girls jumped to their feet as if they had been burned, then leaned away from the carcass as confusion flooded each of their young, tear-streaked faces.

Was he coming back to life?

As they stared in dumbfounded amazement, the lifeless, yet undeniably twitching body of their amphibious friend suddenly wriggled erratically on the ground as it began to change shape.

"What's happening to him?" Diam asked with an alarmed frown. She appeared to not notice when her hand drifted to the handle of her sword.

Although they all had the same question, neither of her friends answered. Instead, as if responding simultaneously to a silent order, they hastily stepped away from the frog's body. From their new location, they couldn't help but stare at the carcass in utter disbelief.

It was writhing on the ground as if it was possessed!

Although his eyes remained closed, Kennard's head began to slowly change shape as if being molded by a pair of strong, invisible hands. The head changed from being wide and flat to more elongated and narrow. At the same time, a duplicate pair of unseen hands stretched the frog's neck forward and eventually moved to his torso. Previously short and wide, the body remained wide but, like the neck, it also began to lengthen. Just when the girls thought the body's transformation was complete, a strange appendage with a flattened end began emerging from somewhere along the back end of the carcass. The protruding limb slithered along the ground like a long, eyeless snake, away from the torso, as if trying to disappear back into the depths of the dark cave behind them.

"Oh... my gosh," Tonia breathed in stunned amazement when she finally realized what was happening.

"Do you see what I see? Do you see him? Is this really happening?"

"A dragon," Kaileen whispered with a nod. Without fear, she extended her hand out to stroke the completely reformed body.

"He's beautiful," Diam said softly.

She moved forward to join Kaileen, but just as she was about to complete the motion, she stopped. The kalevala's hand had frozen in midair and her eyes darted upward, full of alarm. Before she could voice any kind of a warning, a strange, unexpected sound filled the cool air overhead. Kaileen immediately took a step back toward the tunnel entrance, instinctively grabbing Diam's arm in one hand and drawing her sword in the other.

Tonia, who had been standing one step behind and beside Kaileen, froze in place when she saw the kalevala's reaction. She trusted their new friend's senses, and knew without a doubt something had distressed the odd yet gentle creature from the cave near Uncava. Following Kaileen's lead, Tonia also drew her weapon as she took a step backward. Her eyes immediately followed the kalevala's gaze toward the charcoal colored blanket overhead.

As dust began to swirl around them, the girls felt waves of cool air being pushed down on them in rhythmic pulses – *whoop, whoop, whoop!* The noise sounded like the beating of large wings, keeping in perfect time with the unheard song of Euqinom. Tonia heard Kaileen gasp in surprise as she finally saw what the kalevala saw – a very large, shadowy shape descending from just over their heads!

"Back!"

Diam hissed the command as she grabbed Tonia's shirt and pulled her backwards. The girls took cover in the tunnel entrance as they stared at the approaching creature, prepared to run back into the shadow filled labyrinth, if necessary. They stopped when they were side by side, just inside the tunnel.

"What is it?" Tonia asked in a quivering voice.

Before either of her friends could answer, the flying creature landed a few feet in front of Kennard's motionless, newly transformed body. When the landing beast's large, long-clawed feet were settled firmly on the ground just a few inches away from Kennard's partially opened, tooth-filled mouth, the new arrival folded its wings across its back. Without a word the beast turned to stare at the girls with dark, serious eyes. They, in turn, stared back, weapons outstretched and quivering as they waited nervously to see what the new arrival would do.

Was this dark, thickly muscled, unexpected visitor a friend or foe?

It was quite obvious the staring creature was another dragon, but it was nearly twice the size of Kennard. It was definitely large enough for the girls to ride, if needed, which would have been impossible with Kennard. Now that their friend had mysteriously transformed from a frog to a dragon, it was easy to see the differences between the two ancient creatures. Kennard was the much smaller and lighter-colored of the two, while the new arrival was much darker and more muscular.

And more alive.

"Ahh, you," the larger beast said. Its strong, gruff voice shattered Tonia's thoughts as it stared at the girls. "Yes, yes, yes… you are the ones. You are *definitely* the ones…"

"Yes," Diam answered with a confident nod.

Tonia turned her clouded, questioning eyes slightly to look at Diam, but her friend didn't appear to notice. She was standing tall and straight as if she was frozen in time. She was completely focused on the new dragon and returning the dragon's stare with an intense look of her own.

The larger creature's wide, nonthreatening eyes broke away from Diam and quickly found Kaileen. After lingering on the kalevala for a few seconds, its focus continued on until finally settling on Tonia. The new arrival ignored Diam's reply as it examined the trio of females.

"I see the resemblance," the dragon said eventually as it nodded its wide, thickly scaled head in approval.

Diam shifted her weight until she stood just slightly in front of her friends. Although she watched the dragon with nervous curiosity, she felt they were in no danger from this creature. In spite of this, she turned her head slightly to look at her friends. Tonia was just behind her and to her left, while Kaileen was beside her and to her right. If she needed to head towards the tunnel in a hurry, she didn't want to plow over her friends to get there.

As the dragon moved its head slowly up and down, still staring at the young girl, Tonia's eyes narrowed even further until they were nearly closed.

"Resemblance to what?" she asked. The cynicism in her voice caused the tone to rise with a mixture of excitement and trepidation.

The dragon stared intently at the young girl with the chestnut colored eyes, but did not immediately answer her. After a moment of uncomfortable silence, the large beast ceased nodding his head and became as motionless as a stone. Just when she was about to ask her question again, the beast surprised her by speaking with an unexpected note of humor in its voice.

"Silly girl! Resemblance to the ones we've been waiting for… the ones who have the power to save our world."

Before Tonia could ask anything else, the dragon turned and gazed mournfully at Kennard's lifeless body. It briefly lowered its head in a respectful gesture before returning its attention back to the girls.

"Sometimes appearances can be deceiving, can they not?" The dark dragon smiled a knowing, thin smile. "He was a good dragon, in spite of how he looked. His job here is now complete."

His sad eyes returned to Tonia before passing briefly across the other girl's faces. When his focus landed on Diam, it lingered there for a moment.

"Yours is not, however," he said.

With no indication that he was waiting for an answer, the dragon turned his attention in the direction of the mountainside. For a few long seconds it stared at the barely visible body of water at the bottom of the mountain, deep in thought.

"Follow the path, there," he finally said as he nodded toward a partially hidden opening in the bushes a few feet away. "It will lead you to a place that's safe and concealed at the south eastern end of the lake."

"But how will we know we're in the right place?" Kaileen asked in a doubtful tone. Tonia and Diam nodded as they stared at the dark dragon that nearly blended into the surrounding shadows.

"You will find as you follow the path it will eventually become very narrow. When you get to the place where you don't think you can go any farther, look for a group of wood nymphs."

The dragon paused as he tilted his head sideways, an obvious question filling his dark eyes.

"Do you know what a wood nymph is?"

The trio of girls stared at him with questioning expressions. After passing a glance at each other, Diam finally answered as she shook her head.

"No, I don't think we do."

"There are many different types of creatures living in this world, which I'm sure you can imagine and likely already know. Wood nymphs, and water nymphs, too, are just a few. All nymphs are generally on the smaller end in comparison to the varying sizes of creatures that live here, and although wood nymphs and water nymphs are the same type of species, there are subtle differences between the two.

"Water nymphs, also called naiads, thrive when living in or around water, while wood nymphs generally live among the trees."

The dragon stared off into the distance again for a few seconds before continuing.

"Seek out the wood nymphs at the end of the path. They are expecting you, and will help position you for the impending battle."

In the distance, a loud, squawking cry broke through the silent gloom like a ray of sunlight through a pitch-black cave. The dragon turned and looked in the direction of the sound, and although the girls couldn't see much in the surrounding shadows,

Tonia was willing to bet the beast standing before them knew exactly what it was looking at.

"Wait," Tonia said as she took a step toward the dragon. "What if they're not there when we get to the end of the path? How will we know how to find them?"

The dragon chuckled as he shifted his wings across his back. It was a strange sound in the cool air around them. It sounded very similar to patting a pile of large, dried leaves.

"You need not worry about things such as this. As I said, they are expecting you. Trust me when I say *they* will find *you*."

Tonia glanced over at Diam and frowned. Before either of them could say anything, Kaileen spoke up with words that surprised them.

"I understand."

Her friends stared at her in surprise.

"Very good," the dragon said with a smile. "As I'm sure you've heard, I am being summoned and must leave soon, but there is one more thing before I go."

His dark eyes slowly began glowing with a pale shade of green as his gaze passed across each of the girls. When his focus reached Kaileen, he smiled.

"I believe you have something for me?" he asked expectantly.

"I do?" she replied in a surprised, slightly frightened tone. She tightened her grip on her sword, which she still held at her side.

"Wait," Diam said as she stared at the dragon intently. "Are you the dragon Kennard told us about?"

The dark beast tilted his head slightly to the side and smiled.

"I must be," he answered as his eyes twinkled with tiny green specks. Although his words could have been taken sarcastically, it was obvious he meant them with only humor. "I was sent to meet you when you came out of the cave."

"Okay."

The tone of Tonia's voice was no longer defensive and she nodded. She remembered the conversation they'd had in the tunnel with the muck dragon, and understood the reason for Diam's questions.

"If you are the one who was sent to meet us, tell us more about

298

you," she said. Like Kaileen, she was still holding her sword, but kept it lowered at a downward angle.

"More about me, eh?" the dragon asked with a quizzical expression. He admired these girls for their brevity and thoroughness. They were the ones, indeed, he thought.

"What else would you like to know?" he prodded. "My name? My year of birth? My Master's name? My birth parents? My status among those of my kind?"

"Don't mock us!" Diam said harshly as her eyes flashed with anger. "We are trying to protect ourselves..."

Her face crumpled into such a deep scowl that the inner edges of her eyebrows nearly joined across the bridge of her nose.

"Forgive me," the dragon said as he lowered his head with regret. "I was only trying to lighten the moment."

"Why don't you put yourself in our shoes?" Diam continued as if she hadn't heard the dragon's apology. "Think about how we feel! We're in a strange world and don't know where we are, who *you* are, or who we can trust. Can you blame us for trying to be careful?"

Her eyes blazed with a mixture of anger, exhaustion, and frustration as she stared at the surprised dragon in the gloomy, predawn hour. Although she didn't realize it until later, the way she was feeling and reacting was very similar to the way Tonia had reacted back at the puddle when they had first met Kennard.

Had that only been the previous day?

"Humor is good," Tonia said as she placed a calming hand on Diam's shoulder. She nodded her understanding at her friend as her thoughts briefly turned to Micah and his constant antics. She shot Diam a quick smile, then shook her head, scattering the thought about her brother into sprinkles of memory as she forced herself to refocus on the dragon's still lowered head.

Diam nodded and took a deep breath as she struggled to contain her emotions. She had no idea where her outburst had come from, but it had obviously been brewing for a while.

All eyes turned to Tonia as she addressed the dragon.

"We need more information from you before we will do or say anything else. Take it or leave it."

"Why don't we start with your name and why you are here,"

Kaileen suggested. Although the tone of her voice was calm and low, there was no mistaking the seriousness of her words.

In the distance, the squawking creature cried out again, louder and closer than before. This time, instead of turning in the direction of the sound, the dragon raised his head and answered Kaileen in a calm, firm voice. He tried his best to hide the urgency from his tone, but each of the girls knew it was there.

"My name is Ronnoc and I am a Dragon Guard..."

He looked at them expectantly, unsure whether or not he should provide more information. He watched the girls exchange quick glances and hoped what he had given them would be sufficient.

"And what do you want?" Kaileen added. She needed to hear the dragon specify exactly what it was he had come for.

"Why, the gem," Ronnoc answered with a knowing grin. "The third and final amulet."

And there it was. Everything fit. This was Ronnoc, the Dragon Guard, the one who had come for the last of the three amulets. Kaileen glanced at Tonia and Diam, who nodded in answer. Without speaking it out loud, they each agreed they were certain that what the kalevala was about to do was agreed upon by all.

"What happens when we give it to you? What happens to the amulet? Where do you take it?"

The words flowed like an unstoppable stream from the kalevala as her face clouded with skepticism. Although it all seemed to fit together, she still needed to know just what would happen next.

"I will take it to the place of the dragons," Ronnoc said, "and the rejoining will begin."

"Rejoining?" asked Diam.

"Yes, we will use our dragon magic to put the three amulets back together until they have become one. If," he added, "it's not already too late."

Before the girls could ask any other questions, a screeching cry, much louder this time, echoed through the shadows only a few hundred feet away, causing the trio of girls to jump with surprise. The sound bounced off the nearby rocks and trees before rolling down the mountain, where it eventually faded away into silence.

"Now," Ronnoc said sternly, "I must leave. Please, hand over the amulet so I can go to my next assignment!"

"Kaileen, it's okay," a voice said quietly from beside her.

Without looking at Diam, the kalevala moved her head slightly up and down in an incomplete, partial nod. She carefully reached deep into her pocket and withdrew the somewhat familiar, round stone. Although it was not glowing like it had when they retrieved it from the chest cavity of the ice dragon, it did sparkle with countless miniature reflections of the fading moonlight.

"Put it in my mouth," the dragon said. He lowered his head and opened his mouth just wide enough for her to drop the stone into it.

"I will see you again, this I promise," the beast added as it watched Kaileen. None of them knew how soon this promise would become a reality.

The kalevala hesitated as the dragon continued in a harried yet gentle tone.

"Kennard was my brother. I give you my word on the Land of the Dragons that you are doing the right thing. Further, I also give you my word that I will return both him and the amulet to our home."

The kalevala stared into the still softly glowing green eyes, looking for hope, encouragement and truth. With an eventual sigh she took a few steps forward and dropped the gem into the dragon's waiting maw. As soon as she let it go, the beast's mouth began to shimmer with a radiant, luminous glow.

Behind her, Kaileen heard Tonia and Diam inhale a surprised breath.

"It's beautiful!" Tonia whispered.

"Thank you," the dragon muttered.

Without another word, its wide, muscular wings shot out from either side of its body then the beast nodded at the girls. After holding its wings out in a horizontal pose for a few seconds, it began to move them rhythmically up and down. As its dark body floated into the air, it hovered briefly over Kennard's corpse. The airborne dragon lowered itself down until its wide, broad feet touched gently on either side of the muck dragon's back. The

301

girls watched from just outside the mouth of the tunnel as the Dragon Guard wrapped each of its sharply-clawed feet around either side of Kennard's body and slowly lifted the carcass into the air. With one final nod toward the trio on the ground, the dragon headed gracefully into the direction of the rising sun.

Tonia took a few steps forward and gently caressed the kalevala's arm. Until she was standing right next to her, Tonia hadn't realized their friend from the cave was crying. A pair of narrow, glistening streaks had dampened her dark, narrow cheekbones.

"Are you okay?" Tonia asked quietly as Diam joined them. Kaileen nodded and quickly wiped the dampness away.

"He's gone," she mumbled.

"Yes..." was all Diam could say. She looked up at Tonia and both girls realized they each had tears in their eyes as well. They were all crying.

Kaileen sniffled and took a deep breath before she tried to speak.

"Come on, let's get moving. I don't think we want to be traipsing around out in the open once the sun has come up."

With that, she turned and began walking along the path leading down the mountain. Tonia glanced at Diam, gave her a quick hug, and both girls followed the kalevala.

They had been a lost group of three before they entered the tunnel on the other side of the mountain. With doubt that eventually grew into trust, they had become four. Now, in less than a day, they were back to being three again.

This was only the first of many lessons which demonstrate how people, and creatures, can come and go through our lives like the wind.

Thirty-One

A s Nivri made his way to the west wing of the castle, his mind raced like a tornado, ripping through a field of recent events he'd been less than privileged to take part in. The Dragon's Blood amulet, missing for longer than he cared to admit to anyone, even himself, had surfaced in a dark, desolate pit of a cave. As he thought about this tiny amulet that looked like nothing more than a simple red stone, his eyes squinted partially closed with the assistance of a deep, lingering scowl. The amulet, *his* amulet, had been returned to the dragons before he realized it had even been found.

He scoffed as his thoughts drifted to the image of the wingless creature that had failed him...

Muscala.

Once the general location of the amulet had been discovered, Nivri and Lotor had worked together to choose the serpent who really wasn't a serpent to be the guardian of the gem. The snake had been their only decent choice at the time. As soon as the decision had been made, they sent the snake through one of the magical portals to live in the cave near the small village.

Once he arrived, Muscala had been free to live in the cave. He'd also been given the freedom to torture the residents as much or as often as he needed or wanted. As long as he searched for and eventually found the amulet, neither Nivri nor Lotor particularly cared for the methods the snake used to do it. As time went on, Nivri's thinking changed slightly, and soon it became more about *his* amulet and less about *their* amulet. It came down to the simple fact that he wanted *his* amulet, and of course he preferred to have it sooner rather than later.

Hmph!

Nivri's scoff turned into a grunt of anger as his remaining hand opened and closed in methodical, angry clenches. He didn't seem to notice that only one of his hands was opening and closing like a claw, however. He was too caught up in his thoughts as he shuffled through the castle passageways, which he knew as well as the back of his own hand.

His good hand.

"How hard could it have been to live in the cave and scare the residents into providing the location of the special, blood-colored gem?" he thought angrily.

His mind was spinning with too many questions and too few answers when a sudden movement in the tunnel ahead caught his attention. His step slowed as he stared cautiously into the passageway.

A few of his men were standing in a small cluster, chatting in quiet, rumbling voices. As he passed the small group of armored guards, what he was doing and where he was going came back to him like a splash of cold water on his face...

As did the throbbing pain in his arm.

Was that his missing hand screaming like it was on fire? Were his fingers shrieking that they'd been smashed beyond recognition like a basket of tomatoes flung over the edge of a mountain to a jagged, rocky path below?

He stopped, closed his eyes and took a deep breath in an attempt to calm his frazzled nerves. He didn't notice how the chattering voices nearby faded into barely audible whispers as the guards curiously watched his odd behavior. Before any of them could ask if he was okay or needed anything, Nivri's eyes flew open and he turned to look at them with a scowl.

"Have you seen Orob?" he asked harshly.

He vaguely remembered sending his guard to deliver the scroll to the no good, shell of a man who had no useful information for him whatsoever earlier in the day. Had he also sent the guard to bring the prisoner to him for his mind erasing spell? He couldn't remember.

He sighed. If he had sent Orob to get him, they hadn't returned yet. This was probably for the best since he was in no position now to meet with the useless man anyway!

He had bigger things to worry about...

His questioning eyes passed briefly across the nervous faces of the soldiers before looking deeper into the passageway in search of his main guard. In an attempt to hide his missing forearm, he nonchalantly pulled his black, silky cloak around the front of his body, looking as though he'd been doing such a thing for years instead of less than an hour. There was no sense in upsetting his men by letting them know he was injured. Soon enough, they would find themselves in the midst of a battle that should take less than a few minutes – once those meddling children were killed or taken prisoner, it wouldn't matter if his guards knew of his body's unfortunate disfigurement. Although it would take some time, Nivri was certain he would learn to adjust to life without the lower half of his arm.

Besides, he thought positively, once he retrieved his amulets, all of them, his existing worries would be over. He could then concentrate on that *other* prisoner, the very special one, that he still had locked up in the lower level of the castle. Ah, yes, he would then be well on his way to using the scales and claws to his advantage. He had complete confidence when all was said and done, his powers and abilities would be everything he'd ever dreamed!

He stared into the tunnel and smiled as his mind drifted to yet another place. This time, it had taken him somewhere that was just at the end of his fingertips...

This time he saw himself where he had finally become the most powerful sorcerer in Euqinom.

Ah, yes, he liked this place!

Perhaps he could use his special powers to replace his missing forearm with something other than his old, plain, speckled, and wrinkled body part?

He didn't notice his guards watching him in silence as his

305

mind raced with endless possibilities – what would he most like to see at the end of his arm? What kind of tool could he most use? Countless ideas and plans for the future swarmed through his head for what seemed like hours...

A dragon's forearm?

He chuckled under his breath, suddenly remembering the small group of guards nearby and hoping they didn't hear. As if in somewhat of a daze, he looked up and saw them all staring at him intently.

"No, Sir," one guard answered curtly, interrupting his dreamy thoughts.

"Is there anything we can do for you, Master?" another hairy soldier questioned as he nervously shifted his weight from one foot to the other.

Nivri stared at them for a few seconds, amused by their obvious discomfort.

Without answering the guards, the darkly hooded sorcerer turned and headed toward the west end of the castle. Just when they thought he hadn't heard their questions, Nivri called back to them without stopping.

"Have Orob meet me near the west castle door... immediately!"

"Yes, Master," the guards answered in unison as Nivri disappeared around a bend in the passageway.

The guards looked at each other and shrugged. It was obvious their master was agitated about something, but most knew well enough to leave him alone when he got like this.

"What was up with him?" one guard named Dean asked quietly.

He was a tall, lean guard with a tousled mop full of black hair. He knew from firsthand experience that Nivri could sometimes hear them when they spoke to each other, no matter how careful they were about being quiet. After seeing the way the master had been acting a few moments ago, Dean had a feeling this time the sorcerer wouldn't hear much of anything between them. He had been too distracted with... well, with whatever he'd had going on in that gray-haired, black-cloaked head of his.

"I'm going to head down to the guard room to see if Orob is anywhere around," Dean said as he turned and headed down the passageway.

"I'll check the storage room," another guard said with a chuckle. "You know how much Orob loves to snack!"

The other guards cackled quietly and headed toward the west end of the castle. They had no way of knowing the next time they saw their friend and fellow guard would be on the battlefield, fighting alongside a dragon.

THIRTY-TWO

The former castle guards and small group of warriors stumbled into an area of lush, deciduous trees just a few minutes before the sun came up. Per Simcha's instructions, they had traveled in nearly complete silence for the last half an hour of their trek. Now, however, as they converged around a long, thin, rocky area in the center of the trees and once the all clear was given, the buzzing of low, chattering voices filled the air around them. Anticipation was building, that much was obvious. It wasn't that they were excited about going to battle – it was more that they believed in and understood what they were battling for…

Freedom.

The former castle guards knew there was a high possibility they could run into some of their old friends – castle residents who would fight to the death for their Master in spite of the sorcerer's less-than-moral activities. Murmured voices whispered of how this saddened them, but the owners of those voices also understood how, in battle, a certain percentage of death was practically unavoidable. They knew freedom didn't come either free or easy, regardless of how the word 'freedom' is spelled. It was also believed by everyone involved that one of the highest prices to pay for freedom was the loss of life – friends, loved ones, or enemies. A life was a life, regardless of which side of the drawn line it was on…

"Men!"

Orob cleared his throat repeatedly to get the group's attention then paused when he suddenly felt eyes boring into him from two figures to his right, just beyond his point of focus. He turned to see who the stares were coming from but quickly realized he knew before they were actually identified.

Aseret and Ilamet.

He hastily added, "and ladies..." before nodding an unspoken apology.

The two female naiads stared at the former castle guard for a moment before Aseret nodded her ascension, nearly blushing as she forgave him with the slightest, crooked smile. He nodded thanks and continued.

"It's time to get into position. Remain under cover as best you can and listen for my signal, which will sound like this."

Orob pulled a long, thin, cylindrical item from a place somewhere behind the armor covering his chest. He brought the item to his lips and blew gently into it, creating a soft but very audible high-pitched, almost musical sound.

"This is the sound you will listen for, but when it's for real, it will be much louder," the guard said. "Is this understood?"

Some within the circle of bodies around him nodded their answer, while a few others mumbled replies such as 'yes' and 'got it'.

Orob looked quickly around the circle then turned his gaze upward.

"Very well, then."

He withdrew his sword from his sheath and pointed it skyward. His fellow castle guards immediately did the same. Zel, unsure of what they were doing but feeling the need to participate as part of the group, also raised his weapon. Within a few seconds, every weapon was outstretched and pointing towards the sky.

"May we be blessed by the dragons on this fine morning," Orob said as he closed his eyes, "and may we have the strength, agility, experience, and numbers to make a difference today!"

He opened his eyes and looked at his men with an expression of excitement mixed with encouragement. He began pumping his weapon up and down above his head, jabbing at the dark, shadowy tree branches above. Careful to harness their enthusiasm, the rest of the group repeated Orob's weapon-pumping gesture and smiled at each other. After a few seconds, the excitement finally died down and the group disbanded as each soldier searched for a hiding place. Once there, they would wait patiently for the sign.

It was almost time for battle.

THIRTY-THREE

While they walked in a staggered, uneven line along the rocky, dirt-covered path, Tonia's brown eyes scanned the shadows around them. The first thing she noticed was the way the path itself had started out wide and flat just outside the mouth of the cave, but the further they walked, the more narrow and uneven it had become. As a result, where they had been walking side by side when they first began this part of their journey, they were now forced to walk single file.

The second thing she noticed was how the plant life around them had changed. The tall trees that had been hovering over them like looming, shadowy giants not far from the cave opening had been replaced by various levels of thick, leafy shrubs. These oddly shaped hedges lined the jagged, uneven borders of the narrow, winding path, and although they were physically much different in both height and thickness than the memory that suddenly flashed in her mind, she couldn't help but smile. Her mind carried her back to the countless times she and Diam had found themselves hiding from each other in and around rows and rows of tall, dried corn in the field near the village.

Memories like these came from a time when they were young and innocent… back before they knew what real fear, real death, and real loss were all about. At least death, as difficult and tragic as it may be to deal with, offered some measure of comfort with the closure it provided. Although there were no easy answers when it came to loss of life, the lack of answers for a loss *without* the finality of death was one of the most difficult things she'd ever had to deal with in her life.

She mentally pushed away the cluster of thought she was on and turned to focus her gaze on the shadowy figure at the head of the line. Ever since they began this leg of their journey, Diam had been leading them eastward, with Kaileen in the middle and Tonia bringing up the rear. It almost made sense to have Diam leading them since she was the oldest of the three girls, but when you put someone in an unfamiliar place, or a group of someones, it was like having the blind leading the blind...

Tonia smiled as her thoughts drifted to her mother. That had been one of her sayings, 'the blind leading the blind'. Tonia remembered how she had wondered what her mother had meant by it, and now she understood...

Boy, did she understand!

If only her mother was here so she could tell her as much...

As she trudged along at the end of the line, Tonia found herself surprised by an unexpected yawn. She rubbed her eyes afterward and admitted she was tired, really tired. In fact, she thought she was much more tired now than she'd been in a long time. Her legs ached and her arms hung at her sides like limp, lifeless flesh-colored caterpillars. They were all exhausted, of this she was sure, but she refused to be the one to ask to stop for a break. They were making progress, but she had no doubt that they weren't moving nearly as fast as they had been just a few short hours ago – or was it days?

She shook her head as she tried to quiet the endless voices which spoke from within. It didn't matter if it was an hour, a day, or a week, really. All that mattered was they needed to make it through the day... make it through THIS day.

She sighed.

Today was the day, not just *the day* but THE DAY... the day of the impending battle. Ronnoc had made it clear they must make it down the path to whatever place waited for them at the end as quickly as they could, before sunrise at the very least. She glanced eastward and felt reality hit her like someone had poked her with a stick – a very long, very sharp one.

On a normal day, during a normal sunrise, the sight before her would be beautiful and calming…

But not today.

Tonia slowed her pace and stared at the wide, thin, salmon pink line that was slowly kissing the edge of the blanket filling the night sky goodbye. The familiar line of sunrise that had been barely creeping above the lower edge of the sky just a short time ago had grown thicker and longer as morning approached.

Would they make it to the place at the end of the path in time?

She thought about Kennard – the odd puddle creature who had called himself a muck dragon. In reality, he was a frog that had finally turned into the beautiful dragon instead of the handsome prince, much like the bedtime stories their mother had told them over and over again when they were younger. She thought about how much their amphibious friend had sacrificed. She was certain they couldn't have made it through the dark tunnels of the cave without him and it made her extremely sad that they hadn't been able to save him.

Thinking about Kennard brought her back to the accompanying rats. As soon as they found the exit to the cave, every single one of the glowing-eyed rodents had disappeared into the night, leaving them alone with Kennard.

Where had they gone?

She sighed as her thoughts spun like a hundred spider webs in her head.

"Tonia?"

It was Diam. Ripped from her fantasy, Tonia looked up and saw her friends looking back at her, both of their faces covered with confusion and unspoken questions. They were waiting about fifty feet away, standing side by side next to a lone tree that was growing along the edge of the path. She began making her way towards them and found herself looking at the tree – it was nearly growing right out of the long wall of hardened earth. She suspected this was the lower edge of the mountain they'd just gone through.

"Are you okay?" Kaileen asked in a worried, almost motherly tone.

"Yeah, I am. I was just thinking."

Although Diam didn't ask for more of an explanation, Tonia knew the look on her friend's face. Diam wasn't satisfied her short, nondescript answer.

Tonia sighed. "I was thinking about Kennard, that's all."

As Tonia caught up to them, Diam nodded with understanding. Just as she turned to continue leading the way along the path, the three girls suddenly heard the sound of rapid, beating wings just above their heads. Without thinking about it they instinctively ducked and grabbed for their swords as their eyes frantically scanned the dark sky above.

They saw nothing.

"What was that?" Tonia asked in a shaky voice.

It was obvious she was nervous and she hoped it was the wood nymphs that had found them instead of some other unforeseen menace flying over their heads. Her thoughts suddenly flooded with worried questions.

Were the wood nymphs invisible? More importantly, would they attack if they didn't know who was approaching?

"There you are! I've found you! I've found you!" a rapid, high-pitched voice called from the shadows of the nearby trees.

Again, Tonia looked up, her hand trembling as it wrapped around the handle of her sword. Try as she might, whatever was flying overhead was lost in the shadows and too fast for her to spot. If it was the wood nymphs, she didn't want to hurt them with her sword, but if it wasn't, she would have to defend both herself and her friends...

What should she do?

"Diam," she whispered as she scooted to the left. "Do you see anything?"

"No," Diam answered harshly. Although her own hand grasped her weapon tightly, she kept it pointed at the ground.

"I see it," Kaileen said quietly.

Of course! Tonia chided herself for not remembering their friend the kalevala was used to seeing everything in the midnight darkness of the cave.

"What is it?" Diam asked when suddenly the voice called out to them again from the safety of shadowy trees ahead.

314

"Tonia! Diam! You must move quickly! Get to the place at the end of the path now! Right now! Hurry! Go! Go! Go!"

"The voice… there was something familiar about that voice," Tonia thought. She'd heard it somewhere before… or at least she'd thought she'd heard it before, but from where?

"Hurry! Hurry! Hurryyyy!" the frantic voice called out to them. "You must find cover at the end of the path before he seeeees you!"

Tonia looked briefly at Kaileen, then beyond the kalevala to Diam, as her brows furrowed into a scowl of confusion. Where had she heard that voice before?

Immediately, on the tail end of that question, another one followed…

How did it know their names?

"Now!" the voice screeched in its high pitched, yet commanding, tone. Just as she was about to identify the dark shadow, it flew just over their heads and headed in the same direction they'd been heading.

"The bat!" Kaileen said quietly as she glanced at her friends.

Tonia nodded and watched the dark shadow dart back over their heads in the opposite direction before making a quick turn to go back the other way.

"You're right, Kaileen! That *is* his voice! Do you recognize it from the cave?"

Diam turned to look at her friend in the growing light of the new day. She almost chuckled because Tonia apparently hadn't thought about the obvious…

"Um, I think you were the only one who 'heard' him before, so that would be a no, I don't think either of us recognize his voice," the older girl said with a teasing smile.

"Go! Go! Goooo!" the bat shrieked again.

"Come on," Kaileen said.

She quickly stood up as she put her sword back into its protective sheath. Without waiting for a response, she grabbed onto each of her friend's shirts and began pulling them both towards the end of the path.

"Let's go!"

Their earlier single file arrangement had changed, and now

Kaileen was leading. Diam followed while Tonia still brought up the rear.

Their weariness and sadness forgotten, for the moment, the girls walked hastily along the still narrowing path. They followed it as it curved around the mountain sharply to the right, and in less than a minute, they abruptly found themselves at a dead end. They stopped and Diam looked skyward. Sure enough, they again had tall, thick trees hovering over them.

"Where did it go?" Diam asked.

Three pairs of eyes scanned the area above them, but it would be hard to make out a small, flying object in the sea of dark shadows they found overhead. They listened but heard nothing. Even the wind was still.

Was the mysterious flying creature hanging from one of the branches above them, concealed by the surrounding shadows? Just when they thought the bat had disappeared, they suddenly heard the familiar fluttering of invisible wings circling over them again.

"Quick! Follow me! Follow me!"

Although they couldn't make out the small mammal's features, Tonia now recognized his voice.

Without waiting for them to answer, the bat darted into the narrow area between the side of the mountain and a wide, dense cluster of bushes at the end of the path. Before she could ask where it was going, the thinly furred mammal took an abrupt turn to the left and disappeared into the shadowy maw. She peered into the cluster of bushes through a dark, round opening, which faced the mountain, totally unseen from the opposite side.

Was this another hidden passageway?

"Hurrrrrrrrrry!" a screeching voice echoed from somewhere deep within the bush.

Without waiting for her friends to say anything, Tonia led the way through the narrow, nearly invisible entrance. She was nervous at first, because on the outside, the cluster of scraggly vegetation appeared to be approximately three feet wide and maybe four feet high, which was hardly large enough to hold all three girls and a flying bat. As she stepped through the entrance, however, she was surprised to see the inside area of the hiding spot was actually much larger than she thought it would be. She also quickly realized the bat had, not surprisingly, again disappeared.

Trusting their friend, Diam and Kaileen quickly followed Tonia through the uninviting opening. As soon as she realized where they were going, Diam almost half expected Tonia to lose her chickleberries when she noticed she was walking into a large spider web, or even worse, a spider's home! Instead, her spider-fearing friend had sauntered right into this unexpected place without a stick or even a glance back.

Diam smiled – she was proud of her best friend. It looked as though she had finally gotten over her fear of spiders!

As she thought about Tonia and her surprising accomplishment, Diam wasn't watching where she was going. As a result, she almost walked into Tonia, who was waiting for her friends just a few feet inside the opening.

"Are you okay?" Diam asked worriedly as she raised her eyes from the dark area around her feet to Tonia's face. Why had her friend stopped?

When her eyes reached the place where Tonia's should be, all she saw was a cluster of raven-colored shadows. Diam's first thought was that her friend's face had disappeared, but she quickly realized that wasn't it at all. She couldn't see Tonia's eyes because her friend wasn't looking at her – she was looking in the opposite direction.

"Follow me! Follow me!" the bat called out from somewhere ahead. His voice, although still high pitched, was not as loud as before. It was as if he had been swallowed up by the surrounding gloom.

Kaileen stepped into the shadow-filled shelter right behind Diam, who felt the kalevala's presence but didn't turn to look at her. Instead, her eyes focused on the ebony area ahead.

Initially, the older girl believed they were stepping into a slate, branchy area hidden deep in the center of a nondescript bush. If this would have been the case, simply standing would be extremely difficult for a single person, not to mention three. Instead, it felt as though they had stepped into a smaller cave, of sorts, where it was just as dimly lit as she had expected, almost darker, in fact. But it was not nearly as cramped as she'd thought it would be.

Diam felt Kaileen's hand touch her shoulder as the kalevala peered into the shadows ahead, but again Diam didn't turn to look at her. Instead, Diam kept her focus in front of them – peering into the colorless blanket before her that reminded her of another place, another time, that seemed like ages ago. The inky blackness they were about to submerge themselves into reminded her of the tunnels in the cave by their home…

Home, a place so close and yet so far.

She stared into the gloom-filled shadows and soon began to make out a very small, softly glowing blue light. She reached back and grabbed Kaileen's arm in one hand and Tonia's in the other. The three girls stood motionless as they nervously watched the dimly pulsing light as it wavered in the stale air like a tiny sea-colored candle as it approached.

"Come on, come on, come on!" the bat called out in a harried, impatient voice from somewhere in the colorless obscurity ahead – a single voice lost in an ocean of darkness. It was obvious the small, flying mammal was much farther away than before, yet none of the girls moved to follow him. Instead, they stood frozen in place, watching the dim, single blue aura as it moved up and down, then side to side, in the depths of the cool darkness ahead, an unidentified object heading slowly, yet directly, for them. They watched, mesmerized, as it wavered like a leaf being carried on the breeze. After a few seconds, the miniature beacon suddenly changed course and the single light quickly split into three. Within seconds, it multiplied again until it had changed from a trio of dim lights into a few dozen or more glittering stars. As the girls watched in the odd stillness of the cave, the number of lights continued to increase with each beat of their pounding hearts.

The new arrivals stood in a tight, uneven line, unsure about what they should do next. Should they try to make their way through the glowing blue lights in an attempt to follow the bat? Or should they turn around and go back the way they came? If they didn't follow the bat, would he come back for them? What if something living in the darkness ahead had plucked the bat out of the air, silencing him forever?

These and other questions whipped through each of their minds as the girls gaped at the glowing object, or objects, filling the space of nearly overwhelming blackness between them and the now distant bat. With every passing second, the glowing lights were multiplying with rapid, nerve-wracking swiftness.

Tonia heard Diam take in a nervous breath, then felt her friend's hand fall away from her arm. She didn't need to see what Diam was doing to know what the removal of her hand meant. Without a word, Tonia also placed her hand on her sword, ready for battle.

Were they about to be ambushed?

"Oh, no," Tonia whispered to her friends as her hand wrapped tighter around the handle of her weapon.

With their feet frozen to the floor of the unusual bush, the three friends suddenly realized the glowing blue lights in the darkness before them had begun to grow in size.

Whatever had been mysteriously concealed by the darkness was moving straight toward them!

Thirty-Four

From the cover of large, gray rocks littering the terrain, Zel and Zacharu stood side by side as they waited for the sign from Orob.

Quite a few of the stones surrounding them were covered with thick, winding strands of lime green moss, while an array of dense, sprawling tree branches hovered lazily overhead, moving slightly in the breeze. Behind them, the sun was just beginning to crest above the low, jagged tree line. In the opposite direction, millions of miniature lights twinkled brightly across the top of the lake like a wide, dimpled field covered with miniature, glistening gems.

Zel smiled at the serenity of the scene around him as his eyes examined the lake from one side to the other. This would be a beautiful place to live with his family, he thought as his gaze eventually focused on the area in the center of the lake. Had he heard one of the men in their party mention something earlier about a castle being somewhere out there in the middle of this dark body of water? His weary eyes scanned back and forth in search of something, anything, to indicate there might be such a thing, but after a moment, he came to the conclusion they must have meant some other lake. He couldn't see any sign of a castle out in the middle of the glistening pool of liquid stars.

He tore his gaze away from the rather ordinary body of water, choosing instead to focus on the heavily wooded area at the far edge of the lake as he searched for any sign of the enemy. The cloudless sky above allowed bright, morning sunshine to spill across the trees and bushes on the far end of the lake, bringing a memory to the forefront of his mind of the numerous beautiful sunrises he'd seen back at the village.

He shook his head in an effort to chase away the memory – any memories – of home and other things that he had been missing over the past days, weeks, and months. He forced himself to focus, instead, on the here and now. Once they got past today, he could turn his full attention back to finding his way home.

But not now…

Not yet.

He turned his gaze back to the large body of water and his dark brown, curious eyes wandered across the area surrounding the lake from left to right. He could still see no sign of the enemy. In fact, he could see no other signs of life at all other than his fellow warriors.

Was there really even going to be a battle? Perhaps the messenger misunderstood what he'd heard. Perhaps it was going to happen, but on another day? Or perhaps it was at a different location?

He looked around at the two very different groups of warriors that were intermingling on either side of him. One group consisted of beagons, former minions from the castle. The other group comprised of humans, also former members of the castle, but former prisoners instead of guards. Two entirely different groups of men – well, not all men, but male creatures – working together toward a common cause.

Zel could tell they were all anxious for the battle to begin – the air was thick with anticipation. But what if they were wrong? What if a battle never happened? What would happen to them then? Would they go back to being to completely separate groups again? Would they still get along like brothers?

"Look! There!" Zacharu called out, interrupting Zel's thoughts. It was immediately obvious the former prisoner had forgotten they were supposed to remain unseen as well as unheard until they received the expected sign from Orob. Quite a few of the soldiers threw irritated glances at the only unique member of their group, visually scolding him for his loud exclamation.

Surprised by his friend's outburst, Zel turned to look at Zacharu. The shorter prisoner was standing at the edge of a thick line of bushes, pointing at the northeastern edge of the lake. Zel turned his gaze to follow the direction of Zacharu's finger and within seconds he detected a long, dark shadow slithering erratically across the tops of the trees as it made its way toward a wide, snow capped mountain.

A shadow.

The group of men watched the flying shape in silence for a few seconds – although they couldn't be sure what the airborne creature was, they could tell it was darker and much longer than a bird.

"What is it?" Zel asked quietly.

Before anyone could answer, the former prisoner squinted his eyes and jutted his chin outward in an attempt to get a better look at the shape that threw such a long, dark shadow across the trees on the opposite side of the lake. Zacharu stifled a chuckle as he watched the man, finding humor in the way his friend stuck his chin out – like it would help him better see the creature flying off in the distance! The human ignored his friend, choosing instead to watch the distant shape with caution as well as excitement, unwilling, yet wanting to believe it might actually be what he thought it was.

Zacharu simply shook his head and smiled at the human, keeping his thoughts to himself as he returned his gaze back to the approaching shadow.

"I could be mistaken," Zacharu whispered quietly after a moment, "but I believe that creature over there could very possibly be a dragon."

Zel had been nodding his head absentmindedly when Zacharu spoke but it didn't take long for his head to stop moving as his eyes opened wide with surprise.

"A dragon?" he whispered in disbelief as he slowly turned to look at Zac. "A dragon?" he repeated. It was obvious he'd thought he had misheard his friend.

"Yes," Zacharu said with a curt nod. He looked back at Zel,

who had returned his own focus to the place where he had seen shadowy creature across the lake. "I, for one, will not be the least bit surprised if we see more dragons today…"

"You say true," a deep voice agreed from over their shoulders, causing both Zel and Zacharu to nearly jump out of their skin. They had both been so engrossed in their own conversation that neither had detected the sound of approaching footsteps.

Zel immediately stepped to the side as he turned to look at the owner of the voice.

It was Orob.

"We will likely see quite a few dragons today," Orob said matter-of-factly. He stared off into the distance and watched the shadow curve gracefully from side to side. The large, flying creature had made its way horizontally along the uneven tree line before turning sharply in the opposite direction as if it was looking for something…

Or someone.

Zel's curious glance at the distant shadow suddenly became more focused. For a few seconds, he thought he could make out a different, but also large, dark shadow being carried below the flying creature. Had it just made a kill and was carting its victim back to its nest or family? Just as he was beginning to frown a sudden flash of light around the front of the dragon changed Zel's focal point from the item the beast carried to the upper area of its neck. Was there something glowing in its mouth? The former prisoner shifted slightly and strained his eyes in an attempt to focus on the front most area of the dragon's shadowy profile.

After a few seconds, he nodded with a silent answer to his own question. He could just barely make out a small, dim, white light glinting through tiny, narrow gaps toward the front of the dragon's head. Before he could ask Orob about it, however, the dragon turned abruptly and flew up and over the crest of the mountain, disappearing somewhere on the other side.

"Did you see that?" Zel asked Orob as he turned to glance at the former guard.

"See what?"

Zel's eyes returned to the place where the dragon had disappeared, focusing on the area for a few seconds as he waited

323

to see if it would reappear. When he realized it was not coming back, he shook his head and rubbed his eyes, suddenly doubting he'd really seen the softly glowing light in the dragon's mouth at all.

He turned and looked at Orob with a sheepish expression.

"I thought I saw something glowing near the front end of the dragon – like it was carrying some sort of illuminated item in its mouth."

Orob gazed at the man, frowned slightly then shook his head in denial. After a slight hesitation, he returned his own focus to the place where the dragon had disappeared.

Zel turned a silent, yet questioning, glance at Zacharu, who also shook his head.

"My eyes must be playing tricks on me," Zel mumbled as he turned back and stared at the area on either side of the snow capped mountain. To the east, the sky above the crest of the partially shadowed tree line was beginning to turn a deep orange and pink color. To the west, the greens and browns speckling the landscape looked as though they were being covered with a soft, gray blanket.

"I did not see any light around the beast," Zacharu offered quietly.

"Nor did I," the guard agreed.

Zel struggled to pull his attention away from the place where the dragon had disappeared, choosing instead to focus on the beautiful colors the sunrise was earnestly painting on the eastern skyline.

"With a sunrise as beautiful as this, how bad could the approaching day really be?" the man thought as another question suddenly took precedence in his mind.

"Do you know if it was good or bad?" he asked.

"What do you mean?" Orob answered questioningly as he turned to look at the man.

Zel lowered his eyes for a few seconds as he gathered his thoughts. Why were they scattered all over the place?

Focus...

He raised his dark, curious eyes to Orob's seriously intent ones.

"Was it a good or bad dragon?" Zel asked.

Before answering, Orob's eyes scanned the area around the lake.

"I can't be certain, but I have a feeling it was a good one," Orob answered with a tired sigh. He stared off into the distance as if his mind had suddenly gone to another place.

"Why?" Zel asked, unwilling to give up questioning the guard. He had no idea why he was being so persistent. "Why do you think it was good?"

Orob stared at his former prisoner for a moment, his face filled with controlled annoyance.

Why was the man asking so many questions? Why now? Why not earlier, while they were walking, or back in the dungeon?

Orob quickly stopped this line of thinking and chided himself. The man *had* asked him questions back in the castle, but Orob had not answered. He *couldn't* answer him, really, even though he had wanted to. Within the sacred walls of the castle, one never knew who was watching or listening for traitors.

Zel watched Orob's face as he waited for the guard to answer. Although Orob didn't ask the questions he was obviously thinking, Zel sensed them just the same.

"I'm sorry," Zel apologized as he laid a hand on Orob's forearm. "I have no idea why I feel like I must know the answers to the questions I'm asking you. It's almost as if…"

He paused as his questioning voice drifted into silence for a moment, obviously struggling to gather his thoughts. With a sigh, he held his hands out in front of him, palms up, as if expecting a large object to be handed to him.

"It's almost as if I'm afraid we'll miss something important…"

He shrugged his shoulders and stared at his former guard with a pleading look.

Orob glanced at Zel's outstretched hands before raising his eyes to stare deeply into those of his new friend. Although the man in front of him claimed he had no knowledge of magic, either in himself or in his family, Orob knew better.

He gave Zel a reassuring smile in hopes that the human would see the magic soon. He was afraid if he didn't, it would very likely be too late.

"Well, although Zacharu and I did not see the light glowing at the front end of the dragon like you did," Orob began, but Zel quickly interrupted him.

"I *did* see a glowing light!"

Orob raised his hand to quiet the human.

"I didn't say you *didn't* see the light..."

The guard's tone was defensive as he stared intently at the tall, brusque human, who sighed before lowering his angry glare to his feet.

"I'm sorry," Zel said apologetically. "Please go on."

Orob nodded.

"We are in a very precarious situation here, agreed?" the guard asked.

Both Zel and Zacharu nodded but neither of them spoke.

Orob nodded again.

"The missing amulets belonged to the dragons many moons ago," the guard explained as he peered off into the distance, "and it is well known in this world, and probably in others, that the gems are magical. They've been described as having been awake long, long ago, but for countless years now, they have been asleep."

Orob briefly fell silent before the narrow, horizontal line separating his hairy lips slowly curved into an odd, unexpected smile.

"After being missing and asleep for entirely too long, they have been found and are now awake!"

"Wait a minute," Zacharu interrupted quietly. He must have remembered his earlier scolding – his tone was more of a loud whisper this time. He was just about to continue when Orob again held his hand up. In response, the smaller of the two former prisoners fell into a respectful and obedient silence.

"Can you not see that the amulets and the dragons belong together?" Orob asked quietly.

Zel nodded while Zacharu sat in thoughtful silence.

As if receiving an answer from the hush surrounding them, Orob continued and returned his gaze to his former prisoner.

"The creature we saw flying was – is – a dragon, of that I have no doubt. And although I did not see the glowing light you saw, my friend, I am certain you saw it just the same."

Zel frowned at Orob in confusion, but did not speak.

"I firmly believe the light you saw glowing in the front of the dragon – in its mouth – was an amulet," Orob stated, "and if it was white, it was likely that of the Dragon's Breath."

"Dragon's Breath?" Zel whispered.

"Yes," Orob answered. "There are three amulets in all. The red is Dragon's Blood, the white is Dragon's Breath, and the blue is Dragon's Tear.

"And before you ask another question, let me try to give you the answer I believe you are seeking."

Orob patted each of his former prisoners on the shoulder then turned to gaze at the lake and nearby mountains. For the moment, all was quiet, but the guard was certain the peaceful silence they were now experiencing would not last very long.

"The creature we saw flying was without question a dragon," the guard said, returning his focus back to Zel. "You're certain the glow you saw was coming from the front end of the beast, yes?"

"Yes," Zel answered with an affirmative nod.

"Then that settles it," Orob said quietly.

He glanced around and saw a few of the nearby soldiers listening intently to their conversation. He nodded once to acknowledge them before turning back to his former prisoners again.

"This means the dragon we saw a few minutes ago was not just *any* dragon – it was a Dragon Guard – and in its mouth it carried the Dragon's Breath amulet."

"But what about the other amulets?" Zacharu asked with muffled curiosity. "At some point over the last day or two, I heard a rumor the Dragon's Blood amulet had been found, but you know how rumors get passed around in the castle. We never knew what to believe from day to day."

"Yes," Orob nodded, "I heard the same thing."

"So, that means there's only one more amulet, then?" Zel asked as his eyes twinkled with understanding.

"I have not heard anything about the Dragon's Tear," the guard said as he shook his head and slowly turned to look down at the lake again, "but it appears that the Castle of Tears has disappeared." He pointed to the center of the lake below before continuing. "Unfortunately, I'm not quite sure what that means. I have not been outside the castle walls, especially out here, in quite some time. Things have changed..."

His voice trailed off into silence.

Zel's eyes scanned the horizon for a moment as he pondered Orob's last words. Seeing nothing, he glanced to his left and right, curious as to whether or not their fellow soldiers were still paying attention to their conversation. Although one or two still seemed to be listening, the rest were resting, standing guard, or chatting quietly to each other.

Just as he was about to ask about how things had changed, he suddenly noticed another long, dark shadow moving rapidly northeast along the top of the lake.

Orob caught sight of the dark shadow less than a second after Zel and immediately raised his right hand into the air in front of him. In it he held the dark, black handle of his sword. With his left hand he quickly grabbed the whistle and blew three short, loud puffs.

Prepared for just this sound, the nearby soldiers immediately fell silent and crouched down. They stared through the bushes, focusing their complete attention on the approaching shape as it made its way from one end of the lake to the other.

Over the next few seconds, the ebony shape began to grow in size until its creator came into view. An ominous, dark-colored creature, with a curved, snakelike body, swooped across the large body of water. As it flew, it moved its head from left to right in a repetitive motion, as if in search of some item it had lost earlier in the depths of the cool liquid below. Long, crude horns grew in curved, winding spirals from the top of the dark creature's head.

From this distance, the human was surprised he could see the flying creature's wide, round eyes – they were glowing with a vivid, blood-red aura. Its wings were wide and very short, yet drummed through the air with a deep, muscular rhythm which could be heard like a rumbling, approaching storm across the water. Oddly enough, the stunted wings carried the creature gracefully along a slightly downward angle as it continued its decent toward the lake.

"What is it?" Zel asked in a nervous whisper, but the former guard did not answer. His full attention was focused on the approaching beast.

Just before the flying snake reached the water, it leveled out and flew like a shaded, elongated soldier making its way around a castle. It moved like a bird through intentionally wide, counter-clockwise arcs around the western edge of the lake, quite obviously looking for something. After another few passes, the dark creature suddenly changed its flight course and headed southeast.

Zel stood up and craned his neck as he tried to see where the strange creature was heading, but found himself disappointed when he realized it had disappeared from sight. Just as he was about to question Orob about whether or not the flying oddity was really as bad as it appeared to be, movement near the southeastern shore of the lake caught his eye.

Floating on the water quite a distance away from the nearby beach, he saw what appeared to be two – no, three – dragons. He stared at them intently, surprised he hadn't seen them until now. One was pale colored, almost ghostly, while the other two were smaller, and much darker than the first...

Zel's mouth dropped open and his eyes widened as they locked on the larger of the two dark dragons, almost afraid to ask anyone nearby if he was seeing what he thought he was seeing. After staring for a few more seconds, he no longer doubted what his eyes were seeing.

The white dragon looked much like Zel had always imagined a dragon would look, with a thick, white tail and a long, muscular neck. Its wings were nearly invisible, tucked into its sides, but he was certain they were there due to the bulkiness on either side of the beast. The smaller of the dark dragons looked as though it might be a juvenile, or possibly a different type of dragon, almost like a dwarf dragon of some sort, but this creature wasn't the one that had captured his attention. Instead, it was the larger of the two dark dragons. This was the beast that the man just couldn't take his eyes off of.

The larger of the two darker dragons was smaller than the

white one, but this reason alone is not what filled him with curiosity and caused him to stare. More than the entire dragon itself, it was the head of this darker, ancient creature that had his attention. And more than even that, it was the *two heads* and *two necks* that met the wide, thick, yet obviously smaller body, that had him gawking in complete amazement.

Was what he was seeing even possible? His eyes believed they were seeing a two-headed dragon, but his mind continued to argue with him, screaming, "No! No! It can't be so!"

As he watched the group of dragons make its way slowly eastward, side by side, he heard a muffled grunt of surprise from someone nearby. He turned to look at his fellow soldier, and saw him pointing at something on the western edge of the lake. Zel's gaze quickly moved in that direction and he suddenly realized the shadowy, snakelike creature had returned. This time, however, instead of coming from the place where it had disappeared, the odd, flying reptile had come from the western edge of the lake.

Zel stared at it and wondered if it was even the same creature they had seen just a few moments before. He thought it was possible, but the shadowy flight pattern this time was much different than it had been previously. Instead of circling around the lake, this unidentified figure was flying in a straight, focused line.

Zel continued watching it for a few seconds and his heart began to beat faster. His eyes moved from west to east, from the snake creature to the group of swimming dragons.

With horror, he realized the dark, flying beast was heading right for the group of dragons swimming across the lake!

Thirty-Five

Tonia maintained a tight grip around the handle of her sword as she called into the darkness ahead of them.

"Who are you and what do you want?"

She hated that they couldn't see what was hiding in the shadows. She threw a quick glance behind them, and realized the branches at the entrance into the bush had somehow repositioned themselves, nearly completely blocking the entrance. The unfortunate result? Barely any light around them.

And, of course, because they had been in such a hurry to follow the bat, they hadn't thought to try to light one of their torches.

Great.

The blue lights hovered in the upper area of the pitch blackness somewhere in the passageway ahead. Tonia felt her heart skip a beat when she realized they were getting closer. In fact, they were close enough now that she could hear the repetitive fluttering of air in the darkness ahead. She drew her sword and decided to try one more time to communicate with whatever was approaching.

"Please don't come any closer. We mean no harm and don't want anyone to get hurt."

She heard Diam on her left, also drawing her weapon. A few seconds later, an unfamiliar, feminine voice cut through the darkness ahead.

"We've been waiting for you," the voice said in a quiet, reassuring tone.

As the soft, whispered words faded into silence, a pair of the glowing blue lights suddenly began to brighten as it moved toward the girls. Tonia protectively moved her hand in front of Kaileen, and urged the kalevala behind her like a mother protecting her child.

"I am Teresia," the feminine voice said. The girls stared into the darkness as a soft, luminescent, blue haze began to take shape around a creature that was quite a bit smaller than the kalevala.

"I am a wood nymph," the new arrival said. The approaching creature came to a slow stop and hovered in the middle of the dark tunnel, just a few feet away from the girls. She closed her eyes and bowed a greeting.

"We have been waiting for your arrival."

Tonia nodded nervously, acknowledging the female's greeting. Each of the girls watched as the glowing creature slowly floated downward like a pale, blue snowflake. Once she was standing firmly on the ground, the wood nymph delicately folded her wings behind her back until they were nearly invisible to those before her.

"Are you familiar with something called a Dragon Guard?" Diam asked in a low, skeptical tone.

"Ahh, Ronnoc, yes," the blue-eyed creature agreed. Her still glowing eyes rotated up and down as she nodded her head in answer. "Ronnoc is a friend of ours, but then again, most of the creatures in this world are friends with the rest."

Long locks of straight, light colored hair flowed over the wood nymph's shoulder and covered the top of her torso, the rest of which was hidden by what appeared to be a thin, floor length dress. Tonia caught herself staring at the creature, wondering what color the wood nymph's hair really was, because in the glowing blue light, it appeared to be gray.

"Ronnoc, as well as other dragon guards, are working together to summon up as many of our world's creatures as possible for the upcoming battle. We here are just a small number of those creatures."

Teresia's eyes shifted to look at the blocked entryway behind the girls. They flickered brightly for a few seconds before she turned them back to focus on the girls.

"We really must be going."

Kaileen took a step forward, taking her place in between Diam and Tonia.

"Wow," she whispered, but before either of her friends could ask why she said it, their eyes told them what her lack of words did not.

Behind Teresia, dozens of glowing lights began to emerge. They hovered in the darkness of the tunnel, lighting it with a welcoming, cerulean glow.

"My family," the nymph explained. "Please, follow us. We will take you to a place closer to the lake."

For a few seconds, none of the girls moved. All they could do was stare at the mesmerizing flurry of lights beyond Teresia.

"It's almost like having the rats with us, but with a different color of lighting," Tonia thought. She was about to say this to her friend when she was interrupted by the staccato sound of small, rapid wing beats.

"Come on! Come on! We must go, now!"

The voice of the bat erupted through the tunnel. Although they couldn't see him, they heard him make his way toward them until he flew in a wave directly over their heads for just a few seconds. As quickly as he arrived, he darted back into the tunnel again and disappeared.

"Come on!" his voice echoed in the distance, fading with each word. "We must go now!"

Teresia nodded, smiled reassuringly at the girls, then extended her wings and lifted her small body back into the air.

"Please, follow me," she said as she turned and headed into the darkness.

"Come on," Diam said as she grabbed Kaileen's hand and pulled the kalevala forward, who in turn reached behind her and wrapped one of her own hands around Tonia's arm.

Without a word, Tonia sheathed her sword and followed her friends.

THIRTY-SIX

A fter taking a brief yet much needed detour into his spell
room, Nivri arrived in the west wing of the castle. The first
thing he saw upon his arrival was that a large number of heavily
armored guards were chatting amongst themselves as they
waited for him.

He made his way slowly across the wide, gray marble floor,
his floor length, black cloak wafting through the air behind him.
The hood was pulled over his head, almost completely hiding
his long, gray hair except for a few loose strands on either side
of his head. Beneath the cloak, he wore a plain, black shirt and
black pants. Everything about him was the color of burned flesh,
including a wide, black leather belt that was cinched snugly
around his waist. The only difference in his entire wardrobe
could be found here. Attached to his belt was the single piece of
his attire which was considerably different than the rest of his
dark color scheme…

Just forward of his left hip hung a glittering scabbard, and
jutting from the top end of it was a thick, bone handle, which
undoubtedly belonged to a very long, very sharp sword. As Nivri
made his way through his troops on his way to the now opened
castle doors, flickering light from numerous torches around the
room glistened off the scabbard itself, drawing attention to the
odd-looking sheath that protected the sword. At least two feet

long from top to bottom, the sheath hiding the weapon was covered with an assortment of different sized thick, red scales...

Dragon scales.

Although the sorcerer frequently wore similar attire – a black cloak, shirt and pants – the large group of minions waiting for him had rarely, if ever, seen their master with a weapon. Silence suddenly filled the room as many pairs of curious eyes turned to stare at the shining dragon-scaled sheath hanging at Nivri's side. After a few seconds, the rumble of the whispering voices could be heard in addition to the *clop, clop, clop* of the sorcerer's dark boots striking the gray marble as he strode toward the opened door. When he reached it, he turned and looked back at his troops, his silence commanding their immediate and complete attention. His black eyes squinted and twitched as he scanned the faces in the room, obviously searching for something.

"Has anyone seen Orob?" he asked in a low, yet commanding, tone. His troops shook their heads as they looked around the room, mumbling to themselves.

Nivri waited while he listened to his troops, watching them look amongst themselves for their fellow guard. After a few impatient seconds, he raised his right hand and cleared his throat, demanding silence. He scanned briefly the eager faces staring back at him, silently wondering where Orob had wandered off to, then decided it wasn't important, the guard was probably making battle arrangements that he hadn't thought of himself.

He lowered his hand to his chest and flattened his right palm against his shirt.

"As you all know," he began as his dark eyes surveyed the dozens of focused faces staring back at him, "today is a very important day."

An eruption of murmuring voices echoed in the large room for a few seconds, then fell silent as the group waited for their master to continue.

"Today, we go in search of our amulets, but more importantly, we hunt for those who have stolen them from us!"

A cheer rang out as dozens of fists pummeled the air. Nivri watched as his troops, his minions, and couldn't help but grin with anticipation at their reaction. They were ready for battle, but better than that, they were hungry for blood.

He raised his hand again, commanding silence, subconsciously making sure to keep his left arm well hidden beneath the cloak.

"One of our main priorities is to recover all of the amulets, which I'm certain each and every one of you is aware of. Beyond the gems, however, another one of our priorities is to search for, and find, a handful of menacing children who have brought us to this point – where we are today."

Murmured voices rumbled through the crowd again like ocean waves. After a few seconds, his minions quieted down, sensing there was more to be said.

Nivri's eyes scanned the crowd of soldiers that stared back at him, filled with anticipation. A large number of those standing around the room were various sized beagons, with thick, dark fur and wide, hungry eyes. Although they primarily had the body of a bear, some of the beagons were burdened with elongated snouts which tilted slightly upward at the end, which was more characteristic of a dragon's nose. For all but one of the beagons marked with this odd difference, the elongated jaws also housed wide, sharp teeth. For the one who was different, however, although he had the long snout of a dragon, the area within the snout was empty. This half bear, half dragon creature was aptly named Gummy, for he had no teeth.

Luckily, all of his beagons had been created with dragon wings.

"It would have been better if the wings could actually be used to fly with, but beggars could not be choosers," Nivri thought.

As it stood, the beagons could use the wings to stir up the air, creating dust storms, or they could also use their thick-boned, wide appendages as weapons, if necessary. Granted, some of the smaller beagons might find themselves damaged from broken bones or torn skin on their wings during a battle, but such damages would not kill the beagons.

Besides, damaged appendages were but a small price to pay for the success of a mission, were they not?

"Now, listen carefully, my humble and dedicated troops. I have a bit of an offer for you!" Nivri called to his servants. His right hand swept through the air before him as his dark eyes widened with a spark of mischief.

The rumbling of excited voices flowed through the crowd for a few seconds before silence once again filled the room. Nivri smiled with satisfaction – he could feel the electric anticipation in the air.

Ah, yes, they would happily follow him onto the battle field today.

"In my infinite, magical ways, I have obtained a bit of knowledge that the group of disrespectful, meddling children who have brought us to this day are here in Euqinom. Some of them are down at the lake, or soon will be, which is where we will be heading momentarily."

He paused as his eyes roved across returning stares from one side of the room to the other.

"Although the others are not there yet, I do not think it will be long before these ungrateful thorns in our side will be right where we want them to be," the sorcerer explained. The room was as quiet as a mouse as dozens of eyes stared at him, listening intently to him, hanging on each and every word.

"Yes, when I finally released them to battle, they will be more than ready," Nivri thought.

"So, I have decided to give you, my faithful friends, a very special treat."

Nivri's voice was the only sound echoing through the west wing of the castle. In fact, Nivri was absolutely certain he could have heard a dragon egg cracking in the next room if one had been there. The sorcerer paused to take a breath. He could definitely feel the excitement building in the room.

"I have two things I'd like to discuss briefly with you before we head out – one is an offer and the other is an order.

"First, the offer."

Again, his eyes scanned the crowd as the corners of his mouth turned upward in a mischievous, maniacal grin.

"As a token of my appreciation for your dedication and service, I offer this to anyone who finds these meddling children – if you catch any of them, you may choose what you do with them. If you choose to kill the child with little or no mercy, so be it. If you choose to string them up from a nearby tree by their toenails and tickle them to death, so be it."

Nivri's warm, glowing eyes suddenly blazed with a flash of crimson. He reached up to shift the cloak back along the top of his head, revealing the lower half of his face.

"Or, if you choose to do all of the above, then feast upon your catch in bits and pieces..."

He paused and took a breath, smiling as he did so.

"... so be it."

The crowd of beagons cheered as they smiled and hugged each other. Some were so excited by his words they used the handle of their battle axes and lances to strum a muffled cadence against the tiled floor.

Nivri, pleased with their reaction, lowered his cloak until the shadow from it nearly covered the top half of his mouth. He raised his hand and patiently waited for silence.

"However, you may *not* forget this one small, yet very important, order that goes along with the offer I just described."

The room quickly fell into a quiet, electric silence. His troops were growing more anxious than ever to head out.

"This group of children consists of two boys and two girls, as well as other creatures they've coerced into joining them on their journey.

"I care nothing for the girls or for any variation of creature you may find fighting next to them. Do with them, all of them, as you will."

He briefly acknowledged the nods of approval he saw in the audience, then continued without hesitation.

"Concerning the boys, however, this is where you must take special care."

The guards waited impatiently for Nivri, many of them fidgeting from one foot to the other. Their master's eyes were blazing with excited anticipation.

"The younger of the two boys, he is the one who will be saved for *me*."

More nods and a few whispers filtered their way through the crowd.

"And, as an added bonus," Nivri continued, "whichever one of you brings me the younger boy with the curly brown hair, both alive *and* well, will be given a very special place at my side, as one of the few members of my elite guardsmen."

The room full of heavily armored creatures again nodded, smiled, and looked at each other, a few punching their fellow guards in the arm as a sign of competitive camaraderie. Some moved anxiously from foot to foot, hoping to be the first ones out the door in search of the prize.

Nivri raised his hand one final time, and after a few seconds, the room fell silent.

"Dean, please bring me my dragon," Nivri said to the tall guard near the north side of the room.

"Yes, my lord," Dean said as he turned and made his way into a nearby passageway that led to the dragon room.

"As for the rest of you," Nivri said quietly, "of course we hope to win all battles, but today we must be especially focused and determined to win. Of all the battles we have ever fought or have yet to fight, today I will not accept failure."

Many of the guards closest to the sorcerer leaned back in an attempt to get away from Nivri as his eyes flashed brightly with the color of crimson before fading back to the color of death.

"Is this understood?"

Dozens of voices replied in answer, almost as one.

"Yes, my lord!"

"Very good," Nivri said with a satisfied nod. "Let us go then. The day awaits!"

Receiving the sign they had been waiting for, all of the guards pushed their way forward, past the sorcerer, into the cool, early morning air. Although the sun was not yet up, the eastern edge of the dark blanket above was just beginning to lighten with the dawn of a new day.

Beneath the shelter of his cloak, Nivri's dark eyes began to glow like the warm, forgotten embers of a long burning fire as he watched his troops head off to battle.

THIRTY-SEVEN

After trudging through the eerily dark tunnel for a while, the girls finally stepped through a wide wall of gray, mossy vines. When they made it to the other side of the mossy wall, the first thing they noticed was the drastic change in lighting. Although they were shrouded by a protective, thick covering of short, yet very leafy trees, the surprising brightness of the morning sunshine made each of the girls squint their eyes in protest.

It took them a few seconds to allow their eyes to adjust to the new environment, but once she could see, Tonia immediately began looking for Teresia. Just a few feet ahead, she saw the beautiful wood nymph, waiting patiently for them. Tonia nodded at the winged creature, then quickly scanned the area. There were dozens of creatures like Teresia, some hovering nearby, watching the girls, while others darted this way and that, following the orders of some unspoken mission.

Diam rubbed her eyes and yawned, obviously tired, yet unwilling to complain. As her vision cleared, she found her gaze drawn to what appeared to be a younger and smaller flying nymph. The new arrival rounded a nearby bush, and approached Teresia with a look of concern.

The female wood nymph lowered her head and listened intently as the smaller creature whispered in her ear, then nodded. Without a word, the smaller wood nymph turned and darted back toward the direction it had come from.

"What's going on?" Tonia asked in a worried tone.

"Bayu came to say we missed the beginning of the battle while we were in the tunnel," Teresia explained.

"What happened?" Kaileen asked from beside Diam.

"One of Nivri's minions, a drake, apparently attacked some dragons down on the lake," Teresia explained.

"A drake?" Diam asked. "What's a drake?"

Teresia nodded and gave a halfhearted smile.

"Our lovely sorcerers practice their magic spells on innocent creatures in the same manner as a young child playing with a toy," she said sadly. "Unfortunately, for those creatures whose spell is lacking just the right combination of magic, the disfigured and mutilated remains are often left to their own devices, instead of being changed back to their original form.

"In the case of a drake, which is part dragon and part snake, apparently, the spell again wasn't quite complete. Unfortunately, either Nivri or Lotor, or both, decided to try again and again. The result is perhaps dozens of drakes, which is only a guess, many of whom are more than willing to do the bidding of their masters. They are not seen often, but one was here just a short time ago."

"What happened to it?" Kaileen asked.

"The dragons killed it," the wood nymph answered softly.

While Teresia was talking, Diam had been looking around, and found herself quite surprised when she realized where they were.

"Wow," she said.

"Wow, what?" Kaileen asked.

Diam looked from Kaileen to Tonia, and then finally focused on Teresia.

"Weren't we on the northern end of the lake just a little while ago?" she asked. She clearly remembered seeing the sunrise peeking across the sky to their left while the lake was in front of them. Now, however, the lake was still in front of them, but the sun was rising somewhere behind them.

"Yes," the nymph answered. "We went through an underground tunnel – a shortcut – to get where we are now."

Diam nodded her understanding. After a few seconds, Teresia took a deep breath before changing the subject.

"Very well. Are you ready? It would be wise for us to move quickly and get in position before more drakes show up. They have an uncanny ability to spot movement in the forest."

Tonia glanced at Diam and Kaileen before nodding at the wood nymph.

"Yes, we're ready."

With a nod, the wood nymph turned and began making her way through a narrow path in the woods as the girls quickly followed behind.

Thirty-Eight

"Lemures, I think we should go over to that beach," Nicho said as he pointed at the narrow stretch of shoreline along the eastern edge of the lake.

The older boy's mind was racing as he tried to figure out what they could do for their sick feline friend. Not only had he likely gotten fluid in his lungs, it also looked as though he had been poisoned by one of the mini dragons during the battle the previous night. Nicho shook his head in frustration. He could push on the yarnie's rib cage all day, until he removed every last drop of liquid from Ragoo's lungs, but it would do no good when it came to the poison in his system. For that, it might already be too late.

"Nicho, what are we going to do?" Micah asked his brother as he wiped the back of one hand across his eyes. Water was still dripping out of his hair, but Nicho suspected some of the moisture on his brother's face was caused by more than just lake water.

Nicho turned to look at his brother with a grave expression.

"I don't know, Micah, but I think getting to the beach will be a good place to start."

Lemures, his head lowered in both frustration and sadness, led the small group of dragons through the fairly calm water toward the narrow stretch of sand.

After paddling in silence for a few minutes, the white dragon suddenly lifted his head and listened, staring at the dense area of trees beyond the shore. Micah was busy petting Ragoo, who lay motionless on his side. The cat's breathing had become ragged and eyes remained closed.

As his mind raced in search of a plan, Nicho saw the white dragon's reaction and turned to look at the thick line of trees just north of the beach.

"Lemures, what is it?" the boy asked.

The white dragon continued to paddle toward the shore but kept the wooded area around it in focus.

"We are not alone," the dragon said without looking at the boy. "I sense something beyond the beach, a group of warriors perhaps, both male and female, but I cannot tell anymore than that."

"You can't tell if they are friend or foe?" Nicho asked warily.

"Nay, not really," the dragon answered in a cautious whisper. "I sense they may be friend, but something seems... odd, about the group."

Nicho stared into the distance, but could see nothing but various shades of greens and browns. Tall trees, a thick line of bushes, and a low mountain beyond that. Nothing caught his eye.

"Odd," Nicho repeated, "like how?"

"I know not," Lemures said quietly, "but be on guard."

Nicho threw a worried glance back at Micah.

His brother was bent over at the waist, his smooth face nearly touching the yarnie's furry cheek. He spoke to the cat in a low, pleading voice, begging him to keep breathing, to fight the poison, to stay alive. A fresh track of tears were sliding down the boy's face, pooling at the base of his jaw before disappearing into the gray and white stripes of the cat's fur. Micah was not paying attention to the conversation going on between his brother and the white dragon – his complete focus was on the yarnie cat lying motionless across the dragon's back.

After visually verifying that his brother still had his sword at his side, Nicho turned to look back at the trees beyond the beach. Although he still couldn't see anything or anyone, he definitely knew they were being watched.

Thirty-Nine

The hidden warriors stared into the distance as the dark, snake-like creature attacked the small group of swimming dragons. At first, Zel thought the attacking figure was attacking the dragons themselves, but after a moment, he realized it wasn't the dragons the creature was after – it was something else. This realization totally caught him off guard.

A small group of figures, what appeared to be two boys and another smaller creature that he couldn't quite make out, was riding on the back of the two-headed dragon! As the snake creature zeroed in on them, the boys dove into the water on either side of the dragon, in what appeared to be an attempt to escape from the strange reptilian. On its next attack, however, the snake creature was captured and killed.

"What is that thing?" Zel asked Orob.

The guard hesitated for a moment before answering.

"It appears to be one of Nivri's minions," he said quietly.

They watched as the white dragon carried the dangling, lifeless corpse to the middle of the lake, where it hovered for a few seconds before releasing the body into the cold water below with a quite visible yet inaudible, splash.

"Do you know who those people are down there?" Zel asked. He couldn't help but stare at the odd scene on the surface of the lake. Unless he was horribly mistaken, those were humans interacting, *swimming* even, with dragons! He chuckled quietly to himself as he thought briefly about his children. When he finally made it home and told them this story, they would never believe him in a million moons!

He looked down at his feet, willing the memories of his children out of his head. Now was not the time to get sappy, he admonished himself.

"No," Orob finally answered. "They may be the ones Nivri was looking for, though."

"Who was Nivri looking for?" Zacharu asked curiously. He knew the sorcerer had been trying to pull information from Zel about possible magic in his family, but Zacharu didn't remember hearing anything about the sorcerer looking for humans, especially children.

Orob grunted in reply.

"Something about meddling humans who were ruining his plans for retrieving the amulets."

Without waiting for Zel to ask another question, the guard turned toward his men and whistled a short, quiet note to gain their attention.

"We need to move down closer to the lake," he said as he turned to lead the way down a sharply sloped, narrow trail. "Come, let's move quickly."

At the far end of the line of soldiers, Simcha nodded his approval. As quietly as possible, the guards followed Orob through the underbrush as they made their way closer to ground level.

They were gone roughly ten minutes when, just a few feet away from the place where the men had been standing, one of the thick clumps of moss hanging down the side of the mountain began to move. In seconds Tonia, Diam, and Kaileen emerged into the bright sunlight.

FORTY

Bright, warming sunshine was just beginning to crest over the top of the eastern tree line when a short, yet solidly built, ox-like creature quickly came into view in one of the many dimly lit tunnels beneath Castle Defigo. As the beast shuffled through the maze of pathways, the rest of the castle guards moved quickly behind him in an attempt to keep up.

The bull-like creature was as dark as he was hairy, with wide, black eyes and a large, circular ring through his nose, which dangled unnoticed above his furry upper lip. He walked on his hind feet, clopping through the dirt and rocks lining the floor of the passageway, while his arms swung back and forth at his sides like those of a hairy ape in a deep, forgotten rain forest. Although his body was covered with course, dense hair, the creature wore a thick, sleeveless vest made from stacked layers of dark dragon scales. Across his wide, muscled back lay a long sword, its thick-handled top peeking over his right shoulder.

It was quite obvious to all of the guards that the labyrinth of winding and intersecting tunnels below the castle were home to this shuffling, hairy creature, for he moved through the dark, gloomy passageways without even a hint of hesitation. Many of the castle guards had neither seen nor heard of the tunnels they were now traipsing through, which was quite surprising for those who had lived there for their entire lives. Such was the life of the home of a both feared and respected sorcerer.

There were likely many things the residents of the Castle Defigo didn't know, or didn't want to know, Dean thought as he followed the ox through the darkness.

The small army of beagons had exited the west wing of the castle into the cool night air, only to turn left and follow the castle wall to a mysterious, hidden doorway. This led into an underground passageway which is where they found the ox waiting for them. Without saying a word, the guards followed the fast creature single file through the gloomy tunnels for quite a while. Except for the sound of breathing, and an occasional thump from a rock that was kicked into the stone wall, they followed in complete silence. It was as if they knew, without being told, that if they didn't pay attention and keep up, they would be left behind without even the thought of a look back. One wrong turn and an unfortunate soul would surely be lost forever in these endlessly winding tunnels that smelled of death, itself.

After a while, a pale yellow glow began to fill the dark void at the end of the tunnel, indicating an exit to either the outside world or a room with more adequate lighting. Heads moved from one side to the other as the guards peered curiously around the body in front of him in a vain attempt to see the source of the light. They picked up the pace, each of the guards wondering what waited for them ahead. As they stepped through the arched opening in the thick, rocky wall of the tunnel, they quickly realized they were standing in a wide, somewhat secluded cavern with a low, rocky ceiling. The mouth of the cavern exited onto a light-colored, sandy beach. Glistening sand could be seen through the sparse covering of bushes that partially concealed the entrance to the hidden cavern.

The ox creature stopped abruptly and moved to a shadowy alcove just inside the entryway. It grunted as the rest of the beagons filled the cavern.

"I stay," the ox said gruffly. It leaned against a wall as Dean stepped into the cavern and moved just a few feet away. He turned to look at the ox and discovered there was something strange about the creature's face. Although he looked fairly normal, with a hairy face, a stubby, yet round, and quite moist, black nose, and dark eyes, Dean had to do a double take and look again at the creature's eyes. Very round and as black as coal, Dean suddenly realized the ox's eyes pupils took up the entire orb of each eye, in spite of the fact that they were now standing in a cavern with quite a bit of sunlight.

"You're not going to accompany us outside?" Dean asked the black-eyed creature. He didn't try to hide his doubtful tone as the rest of the castle guards gathered sparsely around them.

The ox grunted and shook his head in answer.

"Sun bad," the ox answered as it shook its wide, hairy head from side to side. "You go to lake. I go back in tunnels."

Dean nodded his silent understanding as the ox creature turned and headed back into the safety of the gloom-filled passageway. He watched the ox fade away into the darkness and found himself struck with something that hadn't occurred to him before – if the creature had only seen the sunless tunnels beneath the castle its whole life, of course it wouldn't want to accompany them into the sunlight.

He turned to peer at the lake through gaps in the bushes. The first thing he noticed were countless sparkling yellow lights dancing across the top of the dark water. The scene was dazzling!

He smiled – there was every indication it was a beautiful day outside the walls of the castle, and judging by what he could see, the sun was well on its way across the sky.

Dean looked around at his fellow guards, who were all watching him, waiting for direction. He stood up and made his way toward the right side of the cavern entrance where he pushed roughly on a black stone in the middle of the rock wall. With a rustle of leaves and branches, the large bush blocking the entrance to the cavern began moving. The gap began by separating at the top, which created a v-shaped gap in between the intertwined, gray branches. Just beyond the opening was a short stretch of shoreline, which disappeared into the cool water of the lake. Beyond that, the snow-capped crest, Mandible Mountain, rose into the sky like a white haired guardian.

Dean smiled as the branches stopped moving, then turned to look back at the room full of serious faces.

"This is it," he said. "If ever you've wanted to do what is right for your master and your castle, today is the day to do it."

The men nodded at him and thumped their weapons on the dirt laden ground once, twice, three times.

"Let's go," Dean said.

Without another word, he led the group of Nivri's minions out into the mid-morning sunshine.

FORTY-ONE

Tonia, Diam, and Kaileen squinted in the glare brought on by the bright, morning sunlight and were all quite surprised with how far the sun had come up since they entered the dark tunnel hidden in the depth of the mysterious bush. Tonia raised her hand to shade her eyes as her gaze swept the surface of the lake, which was much closer now than it had been just a short time ago. She turned and looked toward the north and saw a beautiful, snow-capped mountain top.

"Wow, look at that," she said to her friends as she pointed at the scenic landscape on the far side of the lake. "It's beautiful."

"Ah, yes," Teresia said as she hovered above a nearby tree. "That is where you just came from."

Tonia's mouth dropped open and she gawked at the wood nymph.

"Seriously?" she asked in amazement.

Teresia nodded and smiled.

"Not all magic is used for bad reasons."

"Tonia," Diam interrupted. Her tone was strange and very concerned.

Tonia looked at her friend, surprised by the odd sound of her voice. Diam was usually vibrant and full of energy, but this time, when she called Tonia's name, it almost sounded like the voice of a stranger, someone Tonia didn't know.

The first thing she noticed was Diam's eyes – they were entirely too serious. The second thing she realized was Diam wasn't looking at her – instead, she was staring at something in the distance.

Tonia turned to examine the surface of the water and sure enough, it wasn't long before a sudden movement caught her eye. She stared at the strange activity and quickly identified it as not one, but three, creatures swimming across the lake.

"More dragons," she whispered to her friends.

Teresia stared in the distance before she spoke.

"Ah, yes. That would be Lemures. He is a favored and well-respected dragon."

The wood nymph nodded then squinted her eyes.

"Those other two, though, I'm not sure which creatures they are."

When an unexpected flash of color on one of the dragons caught Tonia's eye, she gasped and raised her hand to her mouth, almost afraid to believe what she was seeing.

"Tonia, what is it?" Kaileen asked in alarm. She held the edge of one of her hands against her forehead in an attempt to shield her own eyes from the sun. "What's wrong?"

Diam had been standing slightly in front of her friends, staring at the activity in the distance. When she heard the concern in Kaileen's voice immediately following Tonia's gasp, she immediately turned to look back at her best friend. Curiosity exploded into concern when she saw two large, round tears rolling down each of Tonia's cheeks.

"Tonia?" she asked as she touched her friend's arm. "Tonia, talk to me! What's wrong?"

The younger girl pointed at the dragons with one hand and kept her other pressed against her mouth. Her eyes were wide and frightened and she looked like she'd just seen a ghost.

"Tonia!" Diam said as her voice trembled with fear. "Tonia, stop it. You're scaring me. What's wrong?"

Tonia's gaze finally broke away from the dragons on the lake and she looked at her friend as fresh tears coursed down her cheeks in slow, winding trails.

She pointed again at the dragons on the lake and tried to get control of her thoughts and emotions. When she finally spoke, although her muffled voice came from behind her hand, she only needed to say two words for her friends to understand exactly why she was so upset.

Diam's gaze followed the direction of her friend's quivering, pointing finger as Tonia finally regained enough composure to say what she'd been trying to say for the last few minutes.

"It's them..."

FORTY-TWO

Lemures and the other dragons swam quickly to the narrow stretch of shoreline along the eastern side of the lake. As soon as he could see through to the bottom of the pale blue, shallower water, Nicho slid off the dragon's back and landed in the cool liquid with a splash. Once he found his footing on the uneven patch of submerged shoreline, he stretched his arms out toward his brother.

"Hand him to me, Micah."

The younger boy sat on the dragon's back, hovering barely an inch above Ragoo's head. He spoke to the motionless yarnie cat in a soft, soothing voice while stroking its wet fur from neck to tail in a graceful, yet firm, repetitive motion. Nicho waited a few seconds, watching his brother continue to stroke the unresponsive cat. After a few more seconds, he decided his Micah was probably so wrapped up in taking care of his feline friend that he hadn't heard him.

"Micah!" Nicho said, louder this time. "Give him to me!"

Micah looked at his brother as recognition flashed in his eyes, then looked quickly from right to left as evident surprise washed across his face.

"Let's get him onto the beach," Nicho said as he gave his brother a nod of encouragement.

Micah returned the nod. He gently scooped up the yarnie

and handed him over to his brother with obvious hesitation and concern. As soon as Nicho had the motionless cat in his arms, he turned and headed for the beach. Without waiting for an invitation, Micah quickly slid off the dragon and landed awkwardly in the water, nearly falling to his knees as he did so. He got up quickly and splashed after his brother, catching up to him before Nicho reached the shore.

As he carried the cat toward the beach, Nicho suddenly shivered. He continued splashing through the water as he thought of a saying his mother had said once – "it felt like a dark shadow walked across my grave". That was exactly how he would describe what he had just felt...

Like a shadow just walked across his grave.

A very dark, very bad shadow.

Caught totally off guard, Nicho stopped so abruptly that Micah nearly walked right into him. The younger boy threw a worried look straight at Ragoo, which changed to relief when he realized Nicho hadn't stopped because of the cat. He looked into Nicho's face for an explanation but his question fell silent on his tongue when he saw his brother's dark, serious eyes scanning the nearby trees and skyline. Micah suddenly felt his skin break out in chickenbird bumps and with some effort, he fought his temptation to look at the yarnie. Instead, he forced his own eyes to scan the area around them. Without warning, his entire body gyrated with a shiver – something was about to happen.

"I feel like we're being watched," the older boy whispered. He glanced back at their dragon friends, who were still a short distance from the shore, wading in the shallow water as they watched the boys. Relieved to see them there, Nicho scanned the nearby trees again. Not seeing anything, yet still unconvinced they were alone, he continued on. Instead of heading for the stretch of sand directly in front of them, however, Nicho grudgingly turned toward a mottled cluster of rocks on the northern edge of the beach.

"Where are you going?" Micah asked as he splashed through the cool water less than a step behind his brother.

Nicho nodded toward the rocks. "I don't feel comfortable laying him down out in the open," he said quietly. "I want to put him over there."

When they reached the rocks, Nicho found an area where a small, unmarred patch of beach sand had been pushed into a small cove. Just a few feet wide by the same length, the sand here was sheltered for the most part on three sides by rocks. He gently laid the yarnie cat down on the round patch of smooth, gray sand, then stood up and looked around.

"Do you feel it?" he asked as he touched Micah on the arm as if consoling him. "Don't make it too obvious by looking around a lot, but I can definitely feel we're being watched."

"Yes," Micah answered as he looked down at Ragoo. He could see the yarnie cat's side rising and falling with slow, shallow breaths, but their feline friend remained almost lifeless and completely unresponsive.

Like Nicho, Micah turned to look back at the dragons. All three of them were floating along the top of the water, waiting patiently just a few feet away from the shore.

"What do we do now?" Micah asked quietly. He turned to look at his brother when a sudden noise behind them caught his attention.

It was Lemures. The ivory-colored dragon had extended his wings and was flapping them in slow motion as he stared into the trees beyond the boys.

"Movement, in the trees," the white dragon said quietly. "On guard!"

The boys withdrew their swords and turned to face the trees just beyond the eastern edge of the beach. At first they saw nothing, but within a few seconds, a line of odd-looking, heavily armored creatures suddenly emerged through parted branches in the bushes. They were marching silently, two by two, as they headed straight toward the boys.

Some of the approaching creatures carried long, glittering swords of various sizes, while others carried primitive looking spears and maces. Although they walked on two legs, the unsmiling figures approaching them appeared to be some form of bear warriors whose hairy bodies were partially covered by thick sheets of protective armor.

The boys stood their ground as their dragon friends splashed their way out of the water behind them. Although he didn't know exactly where the dragons were, Nicho could hear breathing behind them, so he knew they were close. He glanced back quickly and saw that, although Lemures was no longer flapping his wide, white wings, the appendages were extended straight out on either side as if the dragon was ready to wrap the boys up in a giant hug.

Nicho stood upright and face forward, staring at the approaching strangers with nervous trepidation. He kept his sword held out in front of him and took a step towards Micah. The creatures in the beginning of the line stopped just a few feet in front of the boys as the rest of the warriors began to divide themselves on either side of the first two, thus creating a partial circle around their target.

"Who are you?" Nicho asked the gruesome creature who stood staring at him just a few feet away.

With an eerily calm expression, the warrior glared at Micah with an uncomfortable intensity for a long moment before turning his gaze upon Nicho. He looked at the older boy, from his eyes, to his weapon, to his feet, then back to his eyes before turning his attention to the dragons. Lemures and the other dragons had moved to be directly behind the boys, where they now stood protectively glaring at the well-armored group of warriors.

"You will come with us," the hairy creature finally growled in a deep, husky voice while completely ignoring Nicho's question.

"We won't," Nicho said sternly as he raised his sword slightly. "We are here of our own free will and mean no harm. We just need a few more minutes to get our things tog..."

"No," the same creature rudely interrupted as its ominous black eyes narrowed into thin, unwavering slits. "We have orders to find you and bring you back to the castle. Someone of high importance is waiting to talk to you. Forget about your things and come with us – now!"

Lemures immediately moved forward until the lower part of his chest bumped against Nicho's back. Without a sound, the large, white dragon curled his wings slightly forward until they were partially wrapped around either side of each of the boys.

Lemures tossed a glaring look at the lead warrior for a few

seconds and when he spoke, his voice did not waver in the slightest.

"You heard the young man. We mean no harm and are only here for a short time. I would suggest you be on your way to find some other unfortunate creatures to harass."

As Lemures spoke, a large number of the new arrivals shifted their weight as they listened to the conversation.

Micah glanced at Nicho with uncertainty and wasn't surprised with what he saw. He could tell by the way his older brother's eyebrows furrowed into the shape of a dark, flying gull over his steely, dark eyes, that Nicho didn't like the way this was going. Then again, neither did he. They were clearly outnumbered and obviously unprepared for a major battle. As his nervous gaze passed briefly across the odd creatures surrounding them, Micah thought they might have a chance if they retreated into the water. But where would that leave them? Swimming with nowhere to go?

The younger boy's mind raced as he tried to think of a plan, any plan, to get them out of their unfortunate predicament. It was great that he and Nicho had the dragons behind them, but they were still seriously outnumbered. He also had to admit that he wasn't at all sure about what kind of damage, if any, the dragons could inflict. Could they breathe fire? Could they all fly? Of course Lemures could – they'd all seen him – but what about Zig and Zag? And what about Flamen? It sounded as though the youngest dragon had spent quite a long time in the water, so of course he could swim, but could he *fly*?

As Micah thoughts raced through different ideas, he moved his hand and brushed against a cool object jutting out from his side. He looked down and found himself both relieved and surprised to see the belt around his waist. He had completely forgotten about it.

Of course! The stones!

On the heels of that thought, another one followed as his mind continued to search for a hasty resolution to their problems.

Yes, he still had the stones from the cave tucked away in the belt around his waist, but he wasn't impressed with what he had seen so far. Each stone was held securely behind a crisscrossed, mesh type of material, and although they had been full of life and light back in the cave, they now appeared to be lifeless and no longer magical.

Micah looked up and stared at the hard, uncaring eyes of the hairy, odd-looking warriors in front of them, then dropped his gaze back down to the belt. Sure, he still had the magical stones, but he wasn't sure how much good, if any, they would do for him now. Besides, there was one very important thing that was missing...

Well, it wasn't exactly missing – it just wasn't here at the moment.

The amulet.

How much magic would the plain, lifeless stones provide without the mystical powers of the accompanying amulet? In the cave, Micah had needed both the stones and the Dragon's Blood amulet. Once he had all of those items in his hand, all it had taken was holding them together near the small body of water in the cave to create the portal...

Or had it?

"We stopped on the beach to rest for a few moments," Micah said abruptly as he stared at the uneven line of soldiers standing warily around them. "We'll only be here long enough to have a quick snack and catch our breath, then we'll be on our way. Please, don't mind us, and carry on in your travels,"

Micah's gaze remained focused on the apparent leader of the group as he tried to gather his thoughts on something that was lost somewhere in the back of his mind. Some important, yet distant, thought or idea was bugging him like a nest full of mud puppy fleas. He was certain there was something else, something he was trying to remember, something that was missing, something that refused to be dragged to the front of his mind. It was as though whatever 'it' was, it was hiding behind an invisible blanket.

And although he couldn't see it, he could most definitely feel it.

He lowered his eyes to the beach and stared at the sand. Although it appeared that his gaze was moving from shadow to shadow that was being cast across the sand from the rising sun, he wasn't really seeing the different sizes and shapes of the black silhouettes at all. Instead, his thoughts took him back to the cave, and the things they had both found and done there.

The amulet, Dragon's Blood, was used with the glowing stones to make the portal. The stones were magical by themselves, but they somehow became more magical when he held them. But there was something else, something just out of his mental reach that he just couldn't grab onto. This was driving him crazy! He knew it was something special, but what was it about? The magical amulet, the mysterious dark cave, the arrogant reptile that had lived there, or the stones themselves?

He looked up from the sand and saw the lead warrior staring at him with dark, beady eyes that totally lacked emotion. The boy and the odd creature stared at each other for a few tense seconds before some of the nearby soldiers began to laugh lightly.

"Young man," the hairy, bear-like leader said with a short, almost forced chuckle, "I'm afraid I must insist that you come with us."

Micah heard Lemures snort his disapproval from a few inches behind them.

"We will stay here, if you don't mind," the white dragon said as he hissed defensively at the soldiers.

Micah's mind was spinning as he continued to search for a plan. The stones, the amulet, the dragons... the funnels on the lake with the dying fish, the wood nymph, and the yarnie cats. The snake, the cave, and the portal... wasn't there anything that might have happened to them over the past few days that he could use against these strange, hairy, bear-like creatures?

He closed his eyes and imagined seeing his hand in a completely dark room. Only the hand was visible. He saw it reach, fingers outstretched, until finally the last three fingers curled under the hand so that only the thumb and forefinger were extended. And then they were moving, stretching, reaching for something unseen in the darkness. A thought, a memory, something forgotten.

But suddenly, like a ray of sun through a dark storm cloud, the thought hit him, almost causing him to reel back in surprise. He plucked it out of the darkness like a treasure chest. It was remembered!

Bears...

He thought back to the previous day, or had it been the day before that? He and Nicho had left the yarnie village in search of Teresia, but instead they encountered three large and obviously hungry mountain bears. The bears had begun talking to the boys, which in reality had only been a ploy to kill time and allow them to get closer to their prey. The bears would have surely eaten the boys if they hadn't gotten away just in the nick of time.

Micah stared at the group of odd creatures before them who were very similar to those he and Nicho had seen the previous day. He sensed he was running out of time, but pretended to not notice how they scowled at him with what was left of their minimal patience. Although the bears they'd encountered in the forest the day before weren't armored like those in front of them now, they were quite similar in that they walked on their hind legs and had muscular, hairy bodies, and dark, evil eyes. Micah's gaze shifted from the head of one of the nearby soldiers to its shoulder, and he found himself squinting in an attempt to focus on what he first thought was a dark colored bone. After a few seconds, however, he understood that it wasn't a bone – it was a hairy, bony nub that protruded just above the creature's shoulder on the upper part of either side of its wide torso.

Wings...

Feeling like he was racing against time, Micah's mind flew through various options, and within a few seconds, he had an idea he hoped would work. The young boy quickly resheathed his sword and took a step back. The move put him between Nicho and the dragons. Then he hastily knelt down as if to touch the sand.

In the blink of a firebug, he had his hand on the belt around his waist. The first two fingers on his right hand dove into the first mesh pouch he found on the belt. As soon as he found what he wanted, he withdrew his fingers and turned the belt a quarter of a turn before repeating the process. Dig, turn, dig, turn. He did this again and again, hoping the creatures that had them surrounded wouldn't realize what he was doing until it was too late. Within a few seconds, he heard the gruff, unwavering voice of the warrior in front of him speak again.

"I'm afraid you don't have a choice."

As the sound of the voice faded into silence, Micah just had time to remove the last stone from his belt and stand back up. Less than a second later, he heard the familiar sound of a long sword scraping the edges of its case as it was being drawn. A split second after this, he heard Lemures growl ominously behind him.

As he became fully erect, Micah looked up to see the warrior in front of him grinning widely as it took a step toward them. Its mouth was filled with only a partial set of brown, grungy teeth – the rest were missing. As if on cue, the remaining line of warriors also began to step forward, closing the circumference of the circle in preparation of taking the small group of boys and beasts as prisoners.

"No!"

Micah's confident, booming voice startled everyone on the beach, including himself. The sword-wielding bear creature hesitated for just a second, which was long enough for Micah to do the only thing he could think of.

Although he hadn't had time to see what he was hoping to see, he did hear a faint, reassuring humming sound coming from somewhere below his chest. He found himself hoping beyond hope that the sound was coming from the one place he thought it was. If it wasn't, they were going to be in more trouble than he could shake a stick at.

Micah held his tightly closed fist out in front of his body as the bear warriors stopped and waited hesitantly for their leader to give them the word they longed for. Unfortunately for the warriors, Micah opened his hand before the bears had a chance to finish their plan for submission and capture.

As Micah opened his fingers, a rainbow ray of glowing light exploded into the air from the center of his palm – yellow, blue, green, and purple. The stones from the cave, earlier dark and unmagical while being worn in the belt since the previous night, were suddenly glowing with all the magic and brilliance of the sun in the sky. Micah stared at the stones for a few seconds, praying it was enough. When he finally tore his eyes away from them to see how close the warriors had gotten, he was shocked with what he saw.

Every one of the armor-clad warriors had stopped their forward motion. They were completely frozen in time.

Nicho smiled and rested a hand on Micah's arm.

"Great thinking, Micah!"

Micah nodded in both relief and disbelief before he turned to look back at Lemures and the other dragons.

Although their larger friends appeared to be mesmerized by the glowing stones, they weren't frozen like the warriors were.

"I think if we are going to decide to do something else, we'd better do it now," Micah said sarcastically over the soft, almost melodic humming sound that seemed to radiate in the air all around them. "I don't know how long they will stay this way, and I've got a feeling they won't be happy when they become unfrozen."

"Should we kill them before they wake up?" Nicho asked.

Micah turned and looked at his brother in shocked silence.

"Nicho!"

"Well, if they wake up before we're ready, you know as well as I do that we might not make it," Nicho said defensively. "This isn't fun and games, Micah. It's not like we're playing hide and seek or firebug tag in the valley at night. These creatures were serious about taking us wherever they wanted to take us. And they still could! If they do, and we put up a fight, they'll probably kill some of us, or all of us. I'm just trying to think defensively."

"I have an idea," Lemures said from just behind Nicho's shoulder. The white dragon slowly folded his wings inward and tucked them in across his back before he spoke again.

"The stones are keeping the warriors... sleeping, I guess you could say, correct?"

Micah nodded.

"I think so. We encountered forest bears yesterday and when I held the stones out, it seemed to put them into some sort of a temporary daze, too. Unfortunately, as soon as we got out of their sight, they woke up. So if I leave here, or if the stones stop glowing, I'm certain we'll see the same result here... probably a lot quicker than we'd like," the younger brother explained.

"Very good," Lemures said with a nod of his wide, heavy

head.

Micah turned away from Lemures to look at the warriors. They were all standing in the same position, still frozen in place and time. He then turned to look at the stones in his hand, thankful they were still shining brightly and humming their wordless, melodic song.

"Okay, I have a plan," Lemures suggested. "Micah, I'll stay here with you, while Nicho, you get Ragoo and climb back up on Zig and Zag. They can carry you to the other side of the lake, away from these warriors.

"Micah, once they get a decent head start, I'll have you climb up on me and I'll fly you across the lake as well."

Micah looked at Nicho and smiled.

"It sounds like a good plan," he said to his brother, who nodded.

"I'll go get Ragoo," Nicho said. Without waiting for his brother's response, he turned and headed toward the rocky cove where they'd left the yarnie.

Even though the jagged line of warriors still stood motionless on the beach, Nicho gripped the handle of his sword tightly. He tried not to think much about where he was walking as he moved carefully between two of the warriors that were directly between Micah and the cove of rocks where he had laid Ragoo on the sand. Once he had moved safely beyond the warriors, Micah and the dragons watched as Nicho hurried toward Ragoo's resting place. When he reached the cove, he stopped and stared into the rocks. A few feet away from the shoreline, Micah watched his brother as he froze in place.

Why wasn't he getting the yarnie so they could get away from here? What was he waiting for?

"Hurry, Nicho," Micah urged with obvious agitation in his voice. "Now isn't the time to goof off!"

"Oh, no," Nicho said, almost to himself.

"Nicho!" Micah cried, his voice now filled with worry. What was he doing! Why wasn't he scooping up Ragoo to bring him back to the dragons?

Nicho turned and looked back at Micah, then at the dragons. His face was covered with stunned disbelief.

Micah felt his heart skip a beat. Nicho was serious.

"Nicho, what's wrong?"

Micah's first thought was that their friend, the yarnie cat, had died. Maybe his wet and poisoned body had been unable to fight the venom flowing through his feline veins. He could feel his body beginning to shake with emotion, but he fought hard to hold back the tears.

"Nicho?" Micah asked as his voice broke. He began to move towards his brother when Nicho raised his hand and pointed at Micah with his index finger, then held his palm out toward his brother in an obvious stopping gesture.

"Is he dead?" Micah asked as he struggled to control his emotions.

"I don't know," Nicho answered as he turned and looked back at the sandy area where they had left the yarnie cat.

"What do you mean, you don't know?" Micah asked, almost angrily. How hard could it be to see whether or not the cat was breathing?

Nicho looked back at Micah with an air of utter confusion.

"I don't know because he's not here," the older boy said. "Ragoo is gone."

"What?" Micah asked in surprise. "What do you mean, he's gone?"

Nicho turned and began making his way back towards Micah, shaking his head in confusion.

"I mean he's gone," Nicho said with sarcastic anger.

Micah shook his head, unable to believe the yarnie cat had left. Where did he go? Had he miraculously and suddenly become cured from the poison flowing through is veins, and without a word, walked away?

Suddenly, another thought ran through his mind. What if the yarnie cat had somehow found the strength to drag himself into the bushes to die?

Nicho stepped between the two warriors again, and after a few seconds, finally reached Micah's side.

"He's just gone," Nicho said with a frown.

"Did it look like he got up and walked away?" Micah asked.

Nicho shook his head.

"There are no footprints in the sand – there's not even any indication he had been there at all. The sand is as smooth and unmarked as it was before we laid him down on it."

Micah shook his head in disbelief, then looked down at the stones in his hand. They were still glowing, but suddenly began to flicker as if they were running out of energy.

"Oh, no," he whispered. Not wanting to, but feeling helpless not to, the younger boy tore his eyes away from the stones to scan the group of warriors surrounding them. They were still mostly frozen in place, but a few of them were beginning to move ever so slightly.

He gasped for breath as his gaze moved from one warrior to the next, noticing a similarity among them that caused his stomach to lurch in nervous dread.

Each and every pair of warriors' eyes were staring at him. Worse than that, they were glowing with a bright orange light, just like the eyes in the cloud they'd seen on the lake.

Just like Nivri's eyes.

*****

Tonia stared in disbelief at the shapes on the water just a few hundred feet away.

"Diam, is it really them?" she asked, afraid to hope, afraid to believe.

Diam stared through the bushes at the three dragons and two human figures who very much resembled Nicho and Micah and her heart began racing in her chest. The pair of vertical forms were on the back of one of the dragons, hovering over an indistinguishable shape.

"I think it might be," Diam said as her voice rose with excitement, "but I don't think we should call out to them."

"No, we must keep quiet," Teresia cautioned as she wagged an index finger at the girls. "There is much evil nearby, and we don't want to attract attention to ourselves. Come – let's head down to the beach, since that's where they are obviously headed."

It took the girls several minutes to make their way, as soundlessly as possible, through uncooperative clumps of vine

366

covered bushes and thick weeds. When they finally arrived at the northern edge of the small beach, they stopped. Within a few seconds, they heard the sound of a familiar voice.

"Who are you?"

It was Nicho.

Tonia threw a glance at Diam that was filled with hope and longing. Her friend shrugged and touched Tonia gently on the arm then the trio of girls carefully peered through a break in the branches. As her eyes focused on the scene on the other side of the bushes, Tonia had to forcibly stop herself from running out when she finally knew with certainty it was not one, but *both*, of her brothers. They were standing on the other side of the bushes, just a few feet away.

Almost close enough to touch.

As she struggled with her desire to go to them, she heard a gruff, unfamiliar voice speak up from somewhere to the right of Nicho. Her heart skipped a beat, and her entire body froze. For a long moment, she was afraid to even breathe.

"You will come with us," the growling voice ordered.

Once Tonia began to breathe again, she shifted herself just a bit to try to see the owner of the unfamiliar voice. Behind the boys, she could see a glorious, large, white dragon who was obviously a friend of theirs, but the narrowed eyes and stern expression on the dragon's face made it look anything but friendly. Next to the white dragon, she could see a smaller, odd-looking dragon with two heads, and a few seconds later, an even smaller dragon poked its narrow, dark head around the back of the white dragon.

Diam and Kaileen were standing on either side of Tonia, each trying to peer through the bushes without making any noise. Tonia knew they were there, but couldn't pull her eyes away from her brothers to look at her friends. She wished she could let the boys know she was there, but understood it was probably best they didn't because doing so would likely give her hiding place away.

She listened to the conversation as she gingerly moved branches aside in an attempt to see the owner of the unfamiliar voice. Just as she was about to give up, a hairy, armored figure moved into her line of sight. She quickly glanced at her brothers and instantly knew, without a doubt, this creature was the one they were speaking to. Her eyes went back to the hairy creature – she couldn't see its face, but she could see its back. A pair of indescribable, dark appendages appeared to be folded up tightly against the creature's shoulders.

She frowned as she mentally asked herself what kind of hairy creature would be walking on two of its four legs that would also have a pair of wings tucked in tightly to its hairy back?

She shook her head – she had no answer.

As she listened to the conversation between the boys and the hairy creature, her eyes surveyed the back side of the odd creature. It was completely covered with dark brown fur, and there, just below the armor covering the lower end of its back, was a short, stumpy tail.

She looked at Diam and shrugged then quickly looked around to see where Teresia was. The wood nymph was hovering just above the ground on the other side of Diam. As Tonia's eyes met hers, the wood nymph raised a single, feminine index finger to her lips in a gesture of silence. Tonia barely moved her head with an understanding nod before slowly turning to look through the bushes again.

The conversation between the boys and warriors had been going on for a short time, but now there was complete silence on the other side of the shrubs. Even without the conversation, it was obvious from the body language of those on the beach that there was a disagreement between the two groups. Tonia watched as the white dragon moved forward until it was just inches away from her brothers, and she suddenly realized her heart wasn't beating as fast as it had been a few seconds before. The white dragon was obviously protective of Nicho and Micah – what more could a group of renegade, curious kids ask for?

She gently released the branches of the bush until they had moved back to their original position, and then gestured to the others to step back towards her. She moved a few feet away then wrapped her arms around Diam and Kaileen's shoulders, and pulled them into a tight huddle.

"What should we do?" Kaileen whispered quietly as Teresia flitted toward them. She flew between Kaileen and Diam and hovered in the center of the circle, looking up at the girls with a look of concern.

"Those warriors on the beach answer to Nivri," Teresia whispered as her eyes moved from one girl's face to the other. "If the boys go with them and end up within the castle walls, it will be very difficult for us to find them."

Diam nodded.

"Well then, we can't let them go with the warriors, can we?"

Although concern covered Tonia's face again, she couldn't help but smile at Diam's short, sweet point of view. If only it was that easy.

"Listen," Teresia said as a few other wood nymphs hovered just outside of the feminine circle. "If the warriors end up talking the boys into going with them, the other wood nymphs and I will fly out and create a diversion."

Her gaze moved from Kaileen to Diam, and finally rested on Tonia.

"Your brothers have been looking for you," she said to the younger girl. "They were very concerned about your safety – for all of you."

Tonia smiled as her eyes began to pool with tears.

"Stop," Diam said, pulling her friend toward her in a gentle, one-armed hug. "This is *not* the time to get mushy on us!"

Tonia sniffled and nodded. She took a deep breath and turned back to look at Teresia.

"What do we do now?" she asked quietly.

Teresia's lips thinned as her jaw tightened with the severity of the situation.

"Tonia, are you prepared to fight for your brothers?" she asked.

The younger girl's eyes narrowed then flashed with anger.

"Of course!" she hissed. "Why would you ask me that?"

Teresia nodded and ignored her before asking another question that caused Diam to gasp for breath in surprise.

"Are you prepared to die for them?"

Tonia stood up and her arms dropped away from her friends' shoulders. She continued to stare at the wood nymph for a few seconds, then wiped roughly at her moist eyes.

"Of course," she repeated. "I would do anything for my brothers…"

Teresia nodded and smiled.

"Good," the wood nymph said quietly. "That's the kind of loyalty and determination we may need today."

Teresia had been hovering just a few inches above the ground, but suddenly lifted herself into the air until her face was nearly parallel to Tonia's.

"If the boys end up going with the warriors, we will create a diversion," the wood nymph said again. "If that happens, you must quickly join your brothers on the beach. Be prepared to fight for your lives, and understand, without a doubt, that these warriors will show no mercy if it comes to that. Do you understand?"

The hovering creature rotated slowly in the air, moving her gaze from one girl to the next.

"Yes," Tonia answered without hesitation. Diam and Kaileen immediately nodded and whispered their agreement.

Just as they were about to share another quick hug, the girls suddenly heard Micah's voice call out in alarm from the other side of the hedge.

"No!"

Without waiting to see what the other girls would do, Tonia darted back to the narrow opening in the branches. She moved with such swiftness that she didn't take the time to watch where she was stepping, and a loud crack under her foot made her jump as if she'd stepped on a hot coal. She quickly looked down and saw a dry, brittle stick that lay crushed and broken on a wide, thin rock where she'd just stepped. She chided herself, worried the warriors had heard it. If they didn't it, would be a miracle.

She cringed and froze in place but heard nothing to indicate their hiding spot had been jeopardized. When she proceeded to carefully move the bushes aside, she heard Nicho call out to her brother, relief evident in his voice.

"Great thinking, Micah!"

One of the warriors was in the way, so Tonia could only see part of her younger brother. It looked like he was holding something out to the warrior, but the hairy, gruff creature wasn't moving to take it. She watched for several seconds and soon understood that the warrior was frozen in place! Her eyes darted to what she could see of two other hairy creatures, one on either side of the main one, but they, too, were unmoving.

What was going on?

She looked back at Teresia and whispered, "What should we do? Should we go out now?"

Teresia shook her head in denial.

"I'll be right back," she said. Before any of the girls could say anything, the wood nymph darted through the air, disappearing into the trees in the direction they'd come from.

Diam looked at Tonia and shrugged.

"Listen!" Kaileen hissed as she raised a finger and pointed it up at the sky.

The girls peered through the branches as they listened to the conversation between her brothers and the white dragon. After a few seconds, they heard the boys talking about how the warriors were sleeping...

Sleeping warriors? How could they be sleeping when they were just talking about taking the boys to some castle to see someone?

"I'm going out there," Tonia whispered decisively as she gently released the branches. She was just about to stand up when Diam put a cool, firm hand on her arm.

"No, Tonia. Wait for Teresia."

Tonia looked at her friend with confused eyes. She wanted desperately to join her brothers, but not at the expense of becoming a prisoner of these hairy, strange warriors.

But if they were sleeping, they wouldn't be in danger from them, would they?

She was about to move Diam's hand and head towards the narrow opening in the bushes she'd spotted earlier when she suddenly heard Nicho's voice.

"I'll go get Ragoo."

"Tonia," Diam said, but the younger girl shook her head.

"Didn't you hear them?" Tonia whispered without trying to hide her aggravation. "The warriors are sleeping. We can go out there now and join them, get them to come back here and maybe go hide in the tunnel again."

As she listened to Tonia's argument, Diam shook her head in negative silence.

"Diam! They are my brothers, don't you see?" Tonia whispered as a lone tear of frustration wound its way down her dusty cheek. "I can't just wait back here and not do anything."

"I know," Diam said. "Tonia, I know! They're like my brothers, too. You know that!"

Her eyes darted back to the shadowy trees where Teresia had disappeared but there was no sign of the wood nymph. Diam quickly looked around and realized the rest of the wood nymphs were gone as well.

She hated how life didn't always have easy answers!

The trio of girls stood staring at each other, and after a few seconds, realized the boys were talking again. It was hard to miss the worry in their voices.

"What do you mean, he's gone?" Micah asked.

Without removing Diam's hand, Tonia turned to look through the branches. It was no use – she couldn't see her brothers anymore. They had moved.

"He's just gone."

Tonia shook her head, confused about what had her brothers so upset. Who was Ragoo?

She decided enough was enough.

"I'm going," Tonia whispered to Diam. Without waiting for the disagreement she knew was coming, she pulled away from her friend and made her way toward the narrow opening in the bushes a few feet away. "If you want to stay here and keep watch, that's fine, but please understand that I can't just stay here anymore. I've got to try something, anything…"

Surprisingly, Diam didn't disagree this time. Instead, she nodded and watched as Tonia moved hastily toward the gap in the bushes. The younger girl drew her sword then hesitated for a few seconds just before she reached the opening. She turned for one more look at her friends and couldn't help but smile when she realized they were both just a few steps behind her.

"Oh, no."

The smile on her face quickly disappeared. That was Micah's

voice – and it was full of worry.

FORTY-THREE

The younger of the two boys stared at the cluster of bear-like figures surrounding them, realizing they were now facing a serious case of vujadé.

Just like the bears had done in the forest the previous day, these creatures were waking up.

"Nicho," Micah said frantically, "Nicho, I think we should be going now."

Nicho looked back at his brother, and was about to argue that he wasn't going to leave without Ragoo, when a sudden movement near the bushes caught his eye.

Something at the end of the thick line of shrubs had moved – he was sure of it. He stared at the general area where he'd seen the movement, or thought he had seen it, but whatever was there had withdrawn itself. After a few seconds, another movement caught his attention. When he realized what it was, he drew his sword.

The warriors were definitely beginning to move.

He looked at Micah with alarm.

"Micah, what's happening? Why aren't they still sleeping?" he asked in a worried, accusing tone.

"I don't know!" Micah snarled as he glared down at the stones in his hand. Although they were still glowing, the aura coming from them wasn't nearly as bright as it had been. He watched with dismay as, one by one, the stones flickered once, twice, three times, and then lost all signs of life.

"Stand together!" Lemures ordered from behind them. Without any kind of explanation, the large white dragon then turned and jumped into the air. He didn't look back as he headed north.

"Wait!" Micah shouted at the dragon as he closed his hands over the apparently lifeless stones. When nothing about them changed, he quickly lowered his arm to his side.

"Lemures, where are you going?"

Lemures appeared to ignore the boy as he changed direction and headed toward the eastern mountain range.

Trusting the dragon's instructions, Nicho quickly glanced at the place where Ragoo had been. Seeing no signs of the yarnie cat, he hastily moved next to his brother.

"Let me stand between you," the two-headed dragon said. Before it had finished its sentence, the dragon ambled onto the beach and placed himself between the boys. The warriors, eyes still glowing with the color of the earlier sunrise, began moving awkwardly toward the boys, slowly closing the circle surrounding them.

Micah drew his sword.

"I guess this is it," Nicho said without looking at his brother. "We can do this, Micah, I'm sure of it."

"Yes," Micah said, but that was all he could manage.

His throat was dry and he didn't want to spend energy or concentration on talking. He raised his hand, hoping he would see the stones glowing brilliantly again, glowing with the mystical, magical power they held which would freeze the warriors in place and give them enough time to escape to safer locations. As he opened his palm and looked at the stones, his heart sank.

They were still as dull and lifeless as they had been just a few seconds before.

He looked up, his eyes filled with doubt. The warriors were still moving towards them, closing the gap, shrinking the circle.

Zig and Zag began moving their long, muscular necks from side to side and front to back in an effort to stop the advancement of the warriors. They growled and snarled at the approaching creatures, but it did no good. The warriors continued moving forward. Micah felt the dragon suddenly take in a long, deep breath before both heads roared at the approaching figures.

Still they kept coming.

Nicho barely had time to wonder if the two-headed dragon could spew fire at their opponents when an unexpected shadow moving across the beach caught his eye. Just before he had a chance to focus on the movement, he noticed something else that didn't fit.

For some strange reason, the circle of bodies around them was no longer shrinking. Instead, the group of hairy, armor-laden figures were standing at attention just a few feet away.

Confused, Nicho looked up and saw a menacing, black beast circling overhead. When he realized what it was, he leaned toward Zig and Zag and watched the dark dragon weave through the air in a quick, narrow arc before it hovered like a blanket of death over them. Zig and Zag continued moving their necks from side to side as they stared at the beast above, but did so without a sound.

As the dragon hovered overhead, the boys suddenly realized something at the same time that caused their hearts to skip a beat...

A familiar, black bulk straddled the lower end of the beast's neck.

"Nivri!" Micah hissed.

"We meet again," the sorcerer called down in a sarcastic tone. "I see you've met my warriors already."

Although the boys couldn't see the sorcerer's entire face, they could see his wide, triumphant grin below the hood of his cloak. They weren't surprised to see a pair of wide, glowing orange eyes in the seclusion of darkness just above the smile.

"Your magic is useless, young Micah," Nivri hissed as his eyes narrowed into maniacal slits. The carrot-colored orbs focused on the younger brother for a moment, then moved to Nicho. After a few more seconds, they moved to the dragons behind the boys, but quickly lost interest and returned back to Micah.

"I would like to suggest, so no one gets hurt, that you move along and accompany my warriors to my castle. I have adequate accommodations for both of you, and I'm sure you'll soon agree that we have much to discuss."

"I'm afraid you're mistaken," Micah answered with a hint of anger, "we have nothing to discuss with you. There is nothing in your castle of interest to us, unless there happens to be a cell there that we can put you in forever!"

The young boy stood tall as he glared at the sorcerer. Nivri returned the stare, straight-faced and silent, for a few seconds before he erupted with a loud, taunting laugh.

"You really think there is nothing at my castle of interest to you?" he asked as he smiled down at the boys with a hint of sarcasm.

Micah chose not to answer. Instead, a surprising, familiar sound suddenly caught his attention. He struggled to keep any signs of emotion from his face as he glanced down at his closed fist. He shifted his pinkie finger just slightly and was relieved to see a thin ray of green light cascade across the outer part of his palm.

They just might have a chance yet.

Nicho also heard the faint, buzzing noise, and suspected he knew where it was coming from, but he also didn't want to draw attention to his brother. He had to find some way to distract the dark-clothed creature above them.

Nicho looked up at the sorcerer who sat astride the dark, demonic dragon with an air of complete confidence. The beast turned to glare at Nicho and the boy realized it had three eyes, each as white and sightless as a cloud.

"Do you mind if we discuss this for a moment?" Nicho asked the sorcerer. He hoped his voice conveyed the pleasantness he intended.

"There is nothing to discuss," Nivri answered with a sly smile.

"Please," Nicho pleaded. "Just give us thirty seconds to talk about it. I'd like to talk some sense into my brother so he won't get us both killed."

Nivri offered a wry smile and nodded knowingly, pleased to see that at least one of the meddling boys understood the seriousness of their situation. Besides, he really didn't want to kill either of them – there was much information he would like to try to get out of them first…

"Very well," the sorcerer conceded. "You have thirty seconds."

"Thank you," Nicho said. He nodded curtly and turned to look at Micah. He leaned toward him and gestured for his brother to come closer.

"Do you hear what I hear?" Nicho whispered questioningly just a few inches away from Micah's ear.

"Yes," Micah answered as he stared into his brother's knowing eyes.

"I think we might have a chance," the older boy continued. "I also think we may have reinforcements."

"What?" Micah hissed in confusion.

Nicho nodded slightly towards the bushes a few feet away.

"Don't make a scene about it, but I saw movement over there a few minutes ago. If the buzzing was coming from where we think it was, I think we should make a run for it."

"Fifteen seconds!" Nivri said in a playful, sarcastic voice from above them.

"Run for it? Run where?" Micah hissed. "Nicho, we need to finish this once and for all. If we can get him to come down to us, maybe one of us can take him out."

The boys stared at each other as they tried to think of something, anything, to get them out of this situation. Their minds were blank.

"Oh, what a pity – your time is up," the sorcerer called out.

Nicho looked at Micah, who returned his look with a glare of complete desperation.

"My troops will take you into custody now," Nivri said, "and I will see you back at the castle."

The sorcerer's voice drooled with sarcasm and unmasked victory. He waved his right hand to the east and the dragon obediently turned to head off in the suggested direction.

"Wait," Nicho barked urgently. "Can I offer you a small token as a display of peace?"

Without a word from the sorcerer, the dark dragon turned back to the older boy from where it hovered in the air expectantly.

"A token?" Nivri asked. There was no attempt at hiding the curiosity in his voice. "What kind of token?"

Micah turned and eyed Nicho with a blank look of confusion as he wondered what token of peace they could possibly offer the one person in this world they'd come to be cautious of?

"Nicho?" Micah asked nervously as his eyes widened, full of questions. His brother ignored him.

"It's in my bag," Nicho said as he reached his hand over his head and patted the top of the bag slung across his back. "Can I get it for you?"

Nivri's partially visible face appeared to be expressionless for a few seconds, then a small smile curved up one side of his mouth. He loved nothing better than to play games with his prisoners, or prisoners-to-be, and although he looked forward to having both of these boys under his thumb once they got back to the castle, the older of the two boys had shown promise for providing him with many hours of fun. This young man would not give in easily when he finally got around to questioning him, of that Nivri was certain.

His smile widened. He loved a challenge.

"Carry on."

Without giving the sorcerer any time to change his mind, Nicho pulled his bag off his back and held it out to his brother.

"Hold this, Micah," he said harshly as he gave his brother a knowing glance.

"What are you doing?" Micah questioned through his teeth.

"Be ready," Nicho mumbled quietly. He thrust his hands into his bag and dug around one side, then the other.

"It's in here somewhere," he called over his shoulder. "I know I put it… ah, there it is."

Nicho gave Micah a warning look, but said nothing as he removed the item from his bag.

"I'm not sure where this is from, but it looks like something that would be fit for a king," the older boy said as he stroked the item with a loving, tender caress. He held it against his chest for a moment as he struggled with the idea of parting with it. Above him, Nivri's eyes flickered with interest as he motioned for the dragon to lower him down to the ground.

When Micah realized what Nicho had withdrawn from the bag, he made eye contact with his brother as he finally caught onto Nicho's idea.

"No, Nicho, you can't give him that," Micah said as he laid a hand on Nicho's arm. "That's the only piece like it that we have!"

"Hush, Micah," Nicho said as he frowned at his brother. "I'm making a decision for us and I say we hand it over."

"But, Nicho," Micah began, but his brother interrupted him.

"The only way he'll believe that we are offering peace is to give him something of value," the older boy whispered loudly.

The black dragon landed on the beach without a sound. Nivri immediately threw a leg over one side of its black, scaly body, then slid down onto the firm sand. Behind the boys, Zig and Zag growled at the unwelcome dragon, but remained protectively close to the boys.

"Nicho, no... please!" Micah begged. Nivri ignored the pleading boy as his growing curiosity led him toward the unidentified item.

As the sorcerer and his dragon were descending onto the beach, the nearby warriors cleared a path for both Nivri and his dragon. They stood on either side of the sorcerer, watching in curious silence as Nivri approached the boys with confidence that nearly suffocated them. The hooded figure stopped when he was about ten feet away and looked at Nicho expectantly.

The older boy turned and faced the sorcerer as he struggled with every ounce of willpower in his young body, fighting not to give in to his feelings of fear and distrust. With a nod, he knelt down on one knee, then turned the intricately carved spear they'd found in the cave around until the handle was facing the sorcerer. Without any hesitation, Nicho extended his hand and held the spear out to the black clad figure. As he did so, he looked up into Nivri's eyes and wasn't surprised to see the glowing orange orbs flicker with surprise before they dulled to a pale, amber aura.

"Ah," the sorcerer said quietly as he stared at the bone spear the boy held out to him. After all these years, he'd thought it was lost forever. How pleased he was to be wrong!

"The spear of Viviani!" he whispered with satisfied amazement.

Nivri stepped forward to take possession of the spear when Nicho turned and passed a silent look to his brother. Nivri's full

380

attention was on the pale, white spear and he didn't notice the strange buzzing sound coming from somewhere beside the older boy until it was too late.

With a smile filled with hope and confidence, and complete belief in all things magic, Micah took one step backward before holding his hand out, allowing his fingers unfurl like the petals of a flower.

FORTY-FOUR

From a place just beyond the southern edge of the beach, Orob, Zel, and the rest of the soldiers hid in the shadows of the thick trees as they stared at the scene unfolding nearby. They were far enough away that they couldn't make out the faces of the figures they saw, but they were close enough to realize there were definitely two opposing sides.

Zel frowned. The pair of human figures that came to the beach on the back of the dragon were grossly outnumbered, and now it was even worse since the large, white dragon had disappeared somewhere over the eastern mountain range. As he wondered what would happen to the smaller group, he heard the sound of footsteps approaching from behind. He turned and looked up to see Orob slowly making his way over to him. Zel was glad because he had questions for his former guard – it seemed he always had more questions. He saw Orob bend over to speak to one of the nearby soldiers, then nod and pat the soldier on the shoulder before moving on. Since Zel wasn't sure what was going on down on the shore, he decided to see if Orob had any insight in the matter.

Zacharu was also watching the creatures on the beach when he suddenly saw a large, black dragon soar into view.

"Dragon," he whispered.

The small group of nearby soldiers suddenly stopped their

quiet chatter to see what Zacharu was referring to.

"Nivri," one of them whispered back before falling silent.

A few seconds later, Orob joined them.

"My buddy," Zel mumbled quietly.

"Me?" Orob asked inquisitively.

Zel chuckled, but there was little humor in his voice.

"No, that thing dressed in black."

Although Orob nodded toward the human, his eyes stared at the figure atop the flying black dragon.

"I didn't expect to see him out here so soon," the former guard said after a moment. "I fully expected his troops down on the beach to take care of what needed to be taken care of. Then, once that was done, Nivri could have waited for those he was looking for to be brought to him instead of the other way around."

"Is there anything we can do?" Zel asked with a hopeful whisper. "If that small group of dragons and people down there is what he's looking for, I'm all for doing whatever we can to foil his plans. I've got a hankering for as much revenge as we can drum up."

Orob stared through the trees at the scene on the beach with thoughtful intensity.

"I saw movement behind the bushes near the beach," the guard said after a moment. "I have no idea who else is down there, but I have a feeling they may be on our side since they haven't come out to join the other group of warriors yet."

Zel and Zacharu both nodded as they watched the beach scene. They tried to listen to the conversation, but found they couldn't hear much more than the mumbling of voices that floated in their direction across the cool, continual breeze.

"Let's move closer," Orob said, "but before we do, we need to make sure we are prepared for battle."

Without another word, Orob reached down and grabbed the helmet that had been hanging like a bulky heap from his waist. Although the sturdy piece of armor was solid around the back side, the front had been specially designed with enough of an opening to provide space for the wide, staring eyes and accompanying length of animal snout that would protrude from it. Zel watched with curiosity as the guard slipped the strange head piece down over his oddly shaped skull with a grunt. Once he was satisfied the piece of armor was properly in place, Orob glanced at Zel with a smirk.

"Your turn," the guard said as he pointed at the helm dangling at the man's waist.

Zel looked at Zacharu, who was already donning his helmet. Since Zacharu was not human, and there were only two choices for the type of helmet that was available, Simcha had given the smaller, former prisoner a head piece which was an exact replica of the one Orob now wore.

Zacharu slid his helmet down over his head, and after a moment, gently used his opened palm to pat down on the top of the shiny piece of head gear.

"It fits!" he said with a smile.

"You're surprised?" Orob asked quietly.

"Yes, a bit," Zacharu answered with a nod. "I was worried that it would be too tight on the lower part of my head, since my jaw protrudes out a bit more than yours does."

"Be glad you don't have to worry about one of these as well," Orob snickered as he reached up and squeezed the top of his elongated snout.

Zacharu grinned and nodded his agreement before turning to look at Zel. His human friend had finally put on his own silver helmet, which covered most of his face. If Zel's eyes hadn't been so familiar to him, Zacharu decided he would not be able to recognize his friend in a crowd of armored soldiers if he ever had to.

Orob nodded his approval and turned to look at the rest of their group, not in the least surprised to see they had followed his lead. Rounded, shining helmets glinted like giant firebugs in the late morning sunlight. The armor covered nearly every soldier's head, and Orob was happy to see his troops were completely prepared for battle. They stood watching him with their primary weapon held confidently in one hand and their shields, formerly slung across their backs like forgotten bags, strapped securely around their forearms.

After the last of the soldiers secured their armor into place, Orob waved a silently gesture with his hand, then turned and led the troops carefully toward the shore. It wasn't long before the small group found themselves on the far end of a jagged line of bushes. Just behind this line lay a perfect cluster of wide rocks as well as a few tall, gnarled trees. The battle ready soldiers carefully placed themselves around the area, then listened intently to the scene unfolding between Nivri and the small group of renegades just a few feet away.

FORTY-FIVE

Tonia knew by the simple tone of her younger brother's voice that something very bad had either happened or was about to. She stopped as if frozen in time, then turned and looked at Diam with alarm. Before she could say anything, a sudden blur of movement a few feet away caught her attention.

She whirled to face the source of the movement and held her sword out in silent alarm. Teresia, wide-eyed and breathless, stopped just out of reach of Tonia's sword and held her hands out, gesturing wildly to the girls.

"Come here! Come quickly!" the wood nymph whispered.

Teresia flew around the girls in a tight circle before she turned and darted back toward the shelter of the nearby trees. Without waiting for Tonia to respond, Diam grabbed her friend by her free arm and pulled her toward the shelter.

"Wait, Diam," Tonia argued as she tried to pull away.

"No!" Diam said as she followed Kaileen into the shade. "Something is happening and we need to trust her."

Once Teresia reached one of the inner short, wide trees, she stopped and looked back at the girls, waving frantically for them to immediately join her.

"What is it?" Kaileen asked when Diam and Tonia had caught up to her in the cool shade. "What's wrong?"

Teresia raised her index finger to her lips to indicate they

386

should be quiet, and then pointed upward.

The girls suddenly saw a wide, dark shadow move overhead like a flitting, jagged cloud above the trees. As they stared at it, the shadow turned and made its way directly toward the beach.

"What is it?" Kaileen whispered in a low, cautious voice as she hovered close to Diam.

Teresia again held her finger up to her thin, pink lips, and passed a stern look of reproach toward the kalevala. Kaileen glanced at Tonia, then looked back up at the treetops with fear-filled eyes.

"It's Nivri," Teresia answered in a voice barely loud enough to be heard.

They did their best to blend in with the shadows of the trees for a few moments as they listened to the conversation between the boys and the sorcerer. Although Tonia was worried for her brothers, she was also proud of them for standing their ground. She knew if she had been out there with them, she'd be willing to fight in order to maintain their freedom. She smiled as she thought about her brothers, but the smile quickly faded away when she realized, especially after seeing how Teresia reacted to the latest arrival, that it was probably in *everyone's* best interest if she didn't just run out onto the beach to join them.

At least, not yet.

She felt a cool, light breeze blow across the surface of her skin and she shivered. As it faded away to stagnant, warm air, Tonia craned her neck and listened. Somewhere on the beach, or just above it, she thought she heard a different kind of noise. She could just barely hear it below the sound of arguing voices. It was a low, repetitive whooshing sound, but she couldn't identify it. She frowned as she stared off in the direction of the sound, then suddenly felt Teresia touch her arm. As if reading her mind, the wood nymph offered a curt explanation.

"It's the dragon's wings."

Teresia offered an abrupt nod then moved away from Tonia, giving her a small smile as she did so. Tonia stared in the direction of the sound for a few more seconds as she wondered what the dragon looked like. After another moment, although she couldn't see anything on the beach through the thick trees, she could completely picture the creature that had recently arrived hovering in the air somewhere above her brothers.

Tonia turned to look back at Teresia and was surprised to see dozens of wood nymphs hovering in the shadows of the nearby trees and clustered rocks. It was as if their single friend had suddenly multiplied herself over the span of just a few moments.

Diam moved to stand next to Kaileen, and just as Diam was about to comment on the number of hovering, flying, fairy-like creatures in their general vicinity, the girls suddenly realized the pulsing sound from the dragon's wings had stopped. Teresia heard this at the same time as the others, and she quickly darted to Tonia's side.

"The dragon is on the ground," she whispered frantically to the small group of girls. "Go, now, back to the opening in the bushes. Go quickly and stay close to cover, that way, if the dragon becomes airborne again, you will hopefully be close enough to the shrubs that it won't be able to see you!"

Tonia stared at Teresia in surprised silence as the wood nymph gave them their instructions. It was time. She would finally get to see her brothers again, and not just *see* them but *be seen by them*.

"Once you are in place next to the bushes, wait for the signal," Teresia continued. The small wood nymph was nearly out of breath now. Her words were coming almost as fast as her wings were slicing through the air around her small, delicate body. The silky appendages attached to her back were moving so fast they were nearly invisible.

"Wait – what signal?" Kaileen asked with a frown.

"You will know," Teresia said. "Trust me, you will know it when you see it."

And with that, the wood nymph turned and darted through the trees, disappearing from sight. The rest of her kind followed right behind her. In the blink of a firebug, the girls were alone.

On the other side of the bushes, they suddenly heard Nivri's voice. It was deep, it was dark, and it was filled with obvious wonderment.

"The spear of Viviani!"

A knowing look in her eyes accompanied a partial smile on her lips as Tonia gazed at her two best friends. The expression on her face was stone cold serious.

"This is it, girls," she said. "Are you ready?"

Diam glanced over at Kaileen who met her gaze with a smile and a nod. As Tonia was about to turn and lead them to the line of bushes, Kaileen touched her arm to stop her.

"Not so long ago, you saved me," the kalevala said as her russet colored eyes moved from Tonia to Diam. "You made me a part of your small group without question, and gave me a purpose, a reason to live. Without the two of you, I would now have no one."

Tonia and Diam knew their friend was thinking of Ransa, the small snake whose lifeless corpse was left behind on the floor of the cave near the abyss, in another place and time.

"I am ready to do what we need to in order to return the kindness shown to me," Kaileen said quietly. Although she didn't shed any tears, both Diam and Tonia could see the kalevala's wide, oval shaped eyes were more moist than usual.

When she was certain the kalevala was finished, Tonia touched Kaileen's shoulder reassuringly.

"Well said, my friend, but we couldn't have done everything we've done over the past few days without each other. I'm sure I speak for both of us when I say that Diam and I feel the same way."

Diam nodded and glanced toward the beach.

"Okay then, let's go."

With that, Tonia turned and led her friends out into the bright morning sunlight. She didn't have to look back to know that her friends were following less than a step behind her.

FORTY-SIX

W hen Nivri mounted his dragon of death and left Defigo, he headed to the eastern edge of the lake with mixed emotions. He was anxious to take care of those meddling kids, but how much trouble could they be? His soldiers could handle a couple of young, immature non-adults, couldn't they? The more he thought about it, the more he seriously doubted he really needed to even go to the lake!

He grunted to himself as the dragon soared through the air. The cool wind caressing his face and whipping his cloak out behind him felt wonderful. If nothing else, he would enjoy the ride.

Although he hadn't used his magic to check in on the troublesome brats for a while, he had no doubt that the boys, those thieving kids who didn't even *belong* in this world, would still be somewhere around the lake. He also had no doubts at all about whether or not his warriors could capture the brats and bring them back to the castle for some endless games of Torture and Tell. After toying with indecisiveness between going to the lake or remaining in the castle, waiting with likely a very small degree of patience for his warriors to bring the boys to him, he eventually gave in to his incessant urge to see the brats and their dragons. The more he thought about it, the more anxious he became. As he rode his dragon in the direction of the lake, his mind raced with just some of the ways he could give those meddling boys a few good reasons to fear him.

Nivri smiled an evil, angry smile as he anticipated the steps of his revenge. His thoughts drifted back to the boys in the Castle of Tears before they'd stolen the amulet, *his* amulet, and removed it from the castle. Although the gem had somehow found a way to protect itself in the form of a mutilated dragon's body, the boys had gotten past that hurdle and successfully retrieved the gem. Then, when he'd tried to weave his magic and put himself in the castle with them, the magic around the castle had prevented him from doing so. He smirked when he remembered the look in the younger boy's eyes when he realized it was Nivri's eyes that were looking at him through the blade of the sword.

His smirk melted into a sigh of frustration.

When his ploy to scare the boys into leaving the amulet in the castle for him hadn't worked, Nivri had decided his next option would be to approach them through the cloud on the lake. He used his magic to put himself in the cloud, demanding they give him the amulet.

Again they'd refused.

He began to sigh again, but his exhale turned to a moan of agony – his left hand was throbbing! He went to touch it with his right hand, his good hand, but quickly remembered his left hand was gone. It was gone today, it would be gone tomorrow, and unfortunately, it would be gone forever. As the dragon soared through the air, Nivri reached his right hand around in front of his body and pulled his cloak tighter against himself.

Oh, yes, revenge would be sweet.

When he finally arrived at the lake, the boys were no longer riding their dragon on the water. Instead, they stood next to each other on the narrow strip of beach, in between a wide line of thick bushes and the place where curved lines of water lapped at the shore. Nivri was happy to see that, in between the bushes and the boys, his minions had the brats surrounded in a half moon-shaped circle. He squinted as his eyes strained to see into the distance in an attempt to make out the details of the scene on the beach. If he wasn't mistaken, Dean was in the process of extending the unarguable invitation for the boys to accompany the soldiers to the castle.

Nivri slowed his dragon until it hovered just above the eastern tree line while he watched the scene below. A frown washed across his face for a few seconds as he thought about different options.

Unfortunately, since the blue amulet had been recovered from the once tiny, but mighty castle that was now nothing more than a sandbar out in the middle of the lake, his water minions were no longer his. They would have come in quite handy right about now, but that didn't matter much anymore, he supposed. He seriously doubted the meddling, wannabe men on the beach below would resort to heading back into the water, especially after they'd had a fairly decent taste of the evil creatures hidden in the shadows of the lake the night before. Although Nivri knew the spell he'd cast on those creatures to make them serve him had worn off with the loss of the amulet, those thieving kids below him didn't know it...

And that was just the way he liked it.

He smiled and surveyed the area around the lake. Three dragons and two boys – not much of an opposition, was it? He almost laughed out loud at the idea of such a small defense in comparison to his two dozen or so warriors. Was it even worth it for him to give it much thought? He allowed his mind to wander to the larger of the three dragons, Lemures, and realized that the vision in white was nowhere around. Unconcerned about the location of the white dragon, he brushed the thought away like a pesky fly. Besides himself and his dragon, he had a few dozen of his best warriors surrounding the measly boys on the beach. He doubted they would offer resistance when they realized how outnumbered they were, and if they did, well... he still wasn't worried.

The third time is a charm, isn't that how the saying went? Again, he almost laughed – the brats would be foolish to fight him this time.

His eyes glowed softly beneath the shroud of his hood, a pair of amber sunsets floating in a veil of cool darkness. After a few seconds, his smile widened, and his eyes flickered with a star-like brightness as he urged his dragon toward the beach. He was ready now, and very much looking forward to confronting those meddling boys for a few moments. He would be happy to extend his invitation to Defigo with what he hoped was an unexpected, yet inspirational, personal note.

FORTY-SEVEN

The sorcerer dismounted from his large, black dragon fifteen feet away from the boys and landed on the sandy beach with a muffled thud of confidence. As he approached the older of the two boys, his dragon growled a warning toward the youngsters and their two-headed beast, but the sorcerer appeared to not notice. His complete attention was consumed by the single item in Nicho's hand.

For a few seconds Micah leered at the dark, three-eyed beast behind the sorcerer, noting briefly how its eyes glowed with the color of pasty, pale rose petals. He also couldn't help but notice how its gaping, scaly mouth quivered with what he imagined was nervous, yet obvious, expectancy. Thin lines of light green, slimy drool hung from the dragon's lower jaw before dangling in a long, stringy line through the air, eventually landing on the uneven, damp sand below with a fizzle.

Micah's stomach lurched nervously as his mind tried to coerce him into focusing on the dragon – the massively dark shadow waiting patiently behind Nivri. With effort, the younger boy eventually managed to tear his eyes away from the three-eyed creature in order to focus on the black-clothed figure who was approaching them.

Nivri was making his way toward them like a lion stalking its prey by placing one slow foot in front of the other in even, methodical steps. His eyes were glowing again like embers from a campfire on a breezy night, flickering back and forth between orange and black shadows with almost electric anticipation. He stopped for a few seconds and stared at the handle of the weapon Nicho was holding out to him, lost deep in thought. Eventually, he began moving again, taking even smaller steps toward Nicho. Almost mechanically, Nivri's right arm extended with slow precision toward the boy, his hand opened and facing the sky.

"It's beautiful," Nivri whispered. Although he had spoken out loud, he wasn't specifically addressing any of the figures around him. Instead, it was as if the sorcerer saw only his hand and the spear. When Micah took his step backward, Nivri didn't notice at all – his complete attention was on the cream-colored weapon.

Micah was relieved to hear the familiar, low humming sound coming from the lower area of his body. Although he was as nervous as a rabbit being chased by a fox, he smiled slightly as he watched the black-clad shape approach his brother.

Could the sorcerer really have no idea whatsoever about what was in store for him?

Eight steps away…

Did Nivri not hear the low, rhythmic humming sound coming from some unseen place near Micah?

Six steps away…

Did Nivri not see the narrow ray of green light escaping from between Micah's long, thin fingers?

Four steps away…

Did Micah dare believe that his simple, hastily thought out plan might really work?

Three steps away…

All he could do was hope…

And pray.

Two steps away…

When he felt the timing was just right, Micah stretched out his own hand, the one holding the four simple pieces of cool, hardened earth. Relief washed over him when he finally knew without a doubt that the typically unremarkable items were definitely creating what had come to be a familiar, although infrequent, reassuring sound.

Too late, the black beast behind Nivri realized what the younger boy with the outstretched hand was about to do. The sorcerer's minion of death caught a partial glimpse of the colorful light shining along the outer edge of Micah's hand and growled one short, loud snarl before the beast fell strangely silent. Micah glanced beyond the sorcerer to see the dragon staring at his hand. The corner of his mouth twitched with a smile when he saw the beast standing as motionless as a giant lump of coal near the shore.

It was frozen in place.

At first, it seemed that Nivri didn't hear the non-human warning coming from the creature behind him, but a second later, the sorcerer's face suddenly filled with an expression of confusion. Like a ray of sunlight in the middle of a thundercloud, he suddenly understood where the sound had come from and exactly what it meant.

Nivri stopped just a few steps away from Nicho, and turned back to look at his dragon, staring at it in angry disbelief as he realized in the blink of a firebug that something had gone terribly, inexplicably wrong. His blackened heart began to beat more rapidly and he felt his blood begin to boil through his entire body as he struggled to control himself. His eyes, flaming like blood-filled pumpkins and sparked with incredible intensity, glared at the boys.

While Nivri's attention had been on his dragon, Nicho recoiled the hand which held the spear and immediately shifted its position until he was holding the smooth, white handle of the weapon. He gripped it pointed steadily in Nivri's direction, but the sorcerer didn't notice.

Instead, Nivri's complete and undivided attention had changed from the condition of his minion to the two strangers standing directly in front of him – they were in the wrong place, in the wrong time! Why did these meddling kids have to come here, to his world, and cause him so much unexpected, *unwelcomed*, grief and frustration?

From just behind his brother, Micah extended his arm and kept his hand completely opened. In his palm lay four colorful, glowing stones that shone almost as brightly as the sun on a cloudless day; in fact, much like the sun was shining right now as it moved gracefully across the pale, blue blanket above them.

Micah couldn't help but stand mesmerized behind Nicho as he stared at the stones, *his* stones, as they hummed and glowed in the middle of his hand. After a few seconds, he pulled his eyes away from the mystical, magical, glowing orbs and looked up at Nivri. This time his smile twitched more than just the corner of his mouth – his undeniable expression of pride glowed like a raging fire in his eyes.

"What have you done?" the sorcerer whispered at Micah. His voice dripped with a dangerous mixture of anger and hatred as he stared at the grinning, wordlessly bragging boy. Behind him, his pet dragon remained frozen in place by the magic of the stones.

"I'm not quite sure what you are referring to," Micah said. Although he was unable to hide the expression in his eyes, he continued to try to hold back the smile that threatened to burst through his invisible facial veil. His smile of satisfaction was on the verge of pasting itself all over his face, much like a sneeze will tickle a nose before eventually erupting into an explosion.

"Do you mean your dragon, or the stones, or perhaps… the amulets?"

Nivri growled at this arrogant, amateur… *boy*… as his blood sped through his veins like hot, molten lava from a massive, rupturing volcano.

"My amulets," he hissed.

"No, you're wrong," Nicho said. He took a step away from the sorcerer, which put him just a few inches away from his brother.

"The dragons now have the amulets, and the amulets will stay with the dragons."

The boys stared at the black clad creature, watching as his smooth, silky cloak began to tremble. It was easy to see how upset the sorcerer was, and he was becoming angrier with each passing second.

Staring at the boys with his heart thudding in his chest, Nivri decided he'd had enough. As his eyes blazed like a brilliant, orange flame, he growled and began stomping toward Micah.

He wanted the stones and he would get them.

Now.

FORTY-EIGHT

Nivri's thoughts were bouncing around in his head like a jumping pia seed as he slid smoothly from the dragon's back to the ground. Staring at the boys, he thought about his failed attempts at regaining possession of the amulet from these two pale-skinned brats... these two figures who looked like nothing more than average boys on an average beach on an average sunny day.

But they weren't average boys on an average beach on an average sunny day – if only it could be that simple! Instead, they were the meddling brats who had stolen his amulet, and they were on a beach that, although he hadn't been out here in quite a while, was familiar enough to him. Furthermore, today wasn't just an average day – it was the day when he would take control of the situation!

He took a slow, deep breath and tried to maintain control of his emotions and eventually found himself concealing a smile. Once he got the boys back to the castle, he would draw out their torture, but he was certain they would never understand if he tried to explain that doing so would also draw out his own torture. He wanted his answers and he wanted them now! He reminded himself that this was how it felt to be a new apprentice learning new magic spells. The apprentice wants to learn everything – to *know* everything – right now. And as much as he hated to restrict himself like this, he would wait... because all good things come to those who wait, isn't that how the saying goes?

Much like being drawn to a beautiful gem, Nivri turned his attention to the weapon resting innocently in Nicho's hand. He felt his heart skip a beat and his remaining palm began to feel damp with moisture.

It had been many, many moons since he had seen the spear of Viviani, and after a while, he'd convinced himself that he would likely never see it again. But here it was, right here in front of him, and this young, meddling boy was handing it out to him, gesturing for him to take it.

He nearly chuckled with delight. Neither of these two boys had any idea what it was they had gotten themselves into. They had no idea how special, how rare, and incredibly magical, this single, short weapon was.

He hesitated for a few seconds and stared at the cream-colored spear as if in a daze. He knew his eyes were glowing again – they seemed to do that a lot these days – but he ignored the sensation of warmth on his face and behind his cheeks. Instead, he focused on the weapon being held out to him. It had intricate carvings on it and along one edge he could barely make out words that one would think had been engraved in it by someone who had no concept of language...

To those unknowing, it would appear that gibberish had been scribbled on the weapon, but he knew it wasn't just a smattering of letters and symbols inadvertently placed next to each other. The so called "gibberish" was more than that...

And although he would be unable to translate the words written there, it wouldn't take him long to find someone who could do it for him. A little bit of magic, a little bit of torture...

Oh yes, he had ways of finding out information when he really wanted to.

He could almost hear the spear calling out to him...

Come... come to me...

He extended his right arm toward the weapon as a chill of anticipation ran down his spine.

"It's beautiful," he whispered. Without paying attention to either of the boys, he began moving forward again, his palm outstretched before him.

Two steps, then four, then six. As he walked slowly toward the weapon in Nicho's hand, the figure in black heard nothing but his pulse beating in his ears and saw nothing but the spear on the peach colored background.

The spear of Viviani, which would soon be *his* spear...

Once he had it in his possession, he could concentrate on retrieving the stones, and then...

Behind him, a short, loud growl interrupted his concentration, and it took him a second or two to realize what it was. Feeling as though he was waking up from an odd, hazy dream, he stopped and turned as if in slow motion to look back at his dragon.

The beast of death stood motionless behind him, no longer blinking, no longer breathing. It was as if it had changed from a living, breathing beast into nothing more than a dull, unremarkable statue – a simple memory of what it had been just seconds before.

Realization suddenly hit him, and he turned to look back at the boys, his heart thumping in his chest. The place where his left forearm and hand used to be was throbbing and his heart rate jumped. Although he knew it wasn't good to allow himself to get worked up at the situation, he couldn't help it.

They were trying to do it again!

The younger of the two boys stood there, his eyes glowing with pride, the stones glowing in his hand. Four pieces of previously plain land, one yellow, one purple, one blue, and one green. Four simple pieces of solid material that happened to be such a large part of so many things to go wrong these past few days.

Nivri didn't notice that Nicho had withdrawn the spear – now all he could see was the younger of the two boys, taunting him with those stones, those eyes...

"What have you done?" he asked, his voice filled with both anger and hatred.

The boy answered him, but Nivri wasn't really listening now. His head ached, his heart was pounding in his chest, and his arm throbbed. He felt his face flush, then turn hot, and he knew his eyes were blazing.

"My amulets," he heard himself say, but the words sounded

as if they had been whispered by some stranger in the dark from some place far, far away. Pure, overwhelming hatred completely devoured him, and his mind shut down.

As if in a dream, the sorcerer heard an odd sound, and a small part of his mind tried to tell him that Nicho was saying something, but Nivri didn't hear him. Someone's knocking, but there's nobody home, he thought vaguely, as a mental fire spread through his body and blazed deep within his mind.

Nivri's mind and body were completely focused on the boy standing there, just a few feet away. As he stared at Micah, he was suddenly consumed with one thought and one thought only – to take revenge for everything wrong that had happened to him over the past few days...

The amulets were missing, his arm was gone, his warriors were unresponsive, and now his prized dragon was nothing more than a pile of black stone.

Oh, how he hated these boys...

With nothing more than hatred and rage to guide him, Nivri lunged toward the only thing he was able to focus on...

The glowing stones.

FORTY-NINE

The girls carefully peered through the thick line of bushes, focused on the scene that was playing out like a bad dream just a few feet away. Tonia had no idea who this black clad figure was, but it wasn't hard to tell what he represented. Evil – pure, unbridled evil. When Micah held the glowing stones out toward the hooded creature with the disturbing copper colored eyes, she had to force herself to remain where she was, hidden by the thick stand of shrubs, and not call out to her brother and tell him to put the stones away!

"What's he doing?" Diam asked as she leaned toward Tonia. Her voice was barely a whisper. Although Tonia didn't look at her when she asked her question, Diam sensed her friend's anxiety as they stared at the scene unfolding just beyond the shadowy conglomeration of intertwined twigs and leaves.

Tonia heard Diam's question but found herself intently focused on the figure in black. His eyes blazed like the sun, and as she heard him whisper something about the amulets, she felt a lump tumble into the pit of her stomach as a voice whispered in her head.

"Hurry! Hurry! Go! Go now!"

Just as Nivri was about to lunge toward her brother, Tonia jumped up and shot through the narrow space between the bushes, no longer able to contain herself.

"No, Micah! No!"

The sound of her voice shattered the silence as she flew around the corner of the hedge. Mindless of the grainy, damp beach sand beneath her feet, she headed straight for her brothers.

FIFTY

M icah stared at the sorcerer, the big, bad wolf who suddenly appeared to be mesmerized by the glowing stones in his hand. He couldn't believe how well things were going; how bright the stones were shining; how little trouble the sorcerer's soldiers *and* his dragon were giving them.

He was proud of how far they'd come and how much they'd accomplished, he and Nicho. They made a good team, which certainly wasn't how it had always been, but especially over the past few days, they'd found a way to work together almost as though they were twins.

He was proud to have Nicho for a brother, and looked forward to sharing many more years with him.

That thought brought his sister to mind and he wondered where she was and if she was okay. He wasn't worried that she wasn't alive – that was one thought he couldn't bear to think about.

If only she was here now – if only she could see how well things were going, and how easy it was to take control of a situation that everyone else believed would be so bleak.

The younger boy's thoughts drifted. As daydreams of his only sister floated through his mind, he made the unfortunate mistake of not paying attention to what was happening directly in front of him.

He wasn't paying attention to Nivri.

The sorcerer's eyes, earlier glowing with a beautiful orange hue, had changed. Now they were dark and fiery.

The color of crimson.

The color of blood.

Just as Micah was about to pull him mind back to the present, he heard a familiar voice call out from somewhere behind him.

"No, Micah!"

That voice – could it be? Was his daydream so real that he was hearing her voice in his head now?

Micah hesitated only a fraction of a second before he allowed himself to believe it was true. It was Tonia! He'd know that voice anywhere! Without thinking about what he was doing, he turned to look in the direction of the voice. Later, he would be overwhelmed from guilt surrounding that one simple mistake.

If he only knew now what he would know very well then.

As Micah turned, a small, dark shadow suddenly flew through the air between the boys.

"The stones!" it cried. "Watch them! Watch *them!*"

Nicho caught a glimpse of the bat as it flew in front of him before it darted in fast, tight circles around Nivri's cloaked head. The sorcerer didn't notice the shadow. He was on a mission now – a mission for the stones.

As soon as she realized what Tonia was doing, Diam immediately sprang to her feet and followed her friend. With her sword drawn, she ran between the motionless blur of enemy soldiers and headed straight for her brothers.

On the other side of the bushes, Orob blew his whistle. The air had suddenly turned thick with tension.

When Orob and Simcha's troops heard the shrill sound they had all been waiting for, there was no doubt in any of their minds that this time it was for real – the real deal. The hidden cluster of scattered soldiers understood that if they didn't get down to the beach in a hurry, if they didn't make it down to the *children* in a hurry, they might all be doomed.

Events on the eastern edge of the lake were happening fast now.

"Move!" Orob yelled at his small band of warriors. Without

waiting for their reaction, he sprang into action. The former castle guard leaped onto a rock and soared over the line of bushes where they had been hiding. Without any sign of hesitation, he directed his troops straight toward their former master.

"Help them!"

On the beach, Micah caught a partial glimpse of his sister running toward him through the frozen enemy soldiers. Half a second later, he noticed something brush against his hand. At the same time, he felt something else, more than a simple brush against his skin, strike him firmly just below his elbow. The second sensation forced his extended hand upward.

His reaction was too slow. It was as if he was stuck deep within a dream. His fingers wouldn't move...

With a sudden sense of dread, he realized he should have never allowed his attention to be drawn away from the figure in black.

"Watch out!" Tonia cried.

But it was too late.

"No!" Nivri exclaimed as Nicho's left arm arched upward under Micah's. The result of this motion caused the glowing gems in Micah's opened palm to leap into the air like small, colorful frogs. The stones tumbled through the air and scattered in different directions as if they had both a mind and destination of their own.

As soon as the stones lost contact with Micah's hand, it was less than a second before they began flickering like a distressed firebug.

The bat darted around Nivri's head in tight, erratic circles in an attempt to distract the sorcerer, but Nivri's focus was elsewhere. He didn't notice the dark, anxious mammal, and if he had, he wouldn't have paid it the least bit of attention.

While the flickering stones were suspended in the air, Nivri finally reached his destination. The sorcerer didn't realize the younger boy no longer had the luminous stones in his hand even though he did catch a glimpse of movement from the corner of his eye. His large group of guards was beginning to move. The spell which had put them to sleep was wearing off.

Fueled now with both rage and hatred, Nivri wrapped his

arms around Micah and lifted him off the sand. As he did so, the edge of his cloak fell away from his amputated arm, revealing a limb that was not quite human.

A wide, black scorpion claw was melded to the end of the sorcerer's stump. The skin from the end of his disfigured arm had grown like weeds across the smaller, shiny shell of the arachnid's pincer. From there, the strange appendage widened then narrowed as it headed to a single joint, which is where the massive, toothed claw could be seen.

Nivri carried his bulky prize to a nearby tree. The younger of the two boys struggled to free himself, but the sorcerer was too strong. Nivri held Micah against the tree at first with his good hand, then opened his claw-hand wide and threw the boy a malevolent grin. He could almost taste revenge.

Nivri's dark eyes flickered like a firebug as he opened his transformed hand into a wide "v" and his thin, crackled lips curved into a grin of satisfaction. He glared at the boy as his mind flashed through memories of all the trouble the brat had caused him, then he shoved the tips of the pincer into the lower end of the tree trunk. The serrated, inner edges of the claw scraped painfully against both of Micah's sides as the claw was shoved into the bark of the thick, meaty tree.

He was trapped.

When Nicho realized Nivri was heading straight for Micah, he took a step toward his brother but found himself quickly cut off by one of the opposing soldiers that had been standing nearby. Nicho realized the only weapon he had in his hand was the spear, and he held it out in a defensive posture toward his adversary. The hairy faced creature stared at him for a few seconds then barked a low, rumbling laugh, obviously not impressed with the boy's choice of a weapon.

Each of the three girls had drawn the weapons Kennard had given them as they sprang from their hiding places. Focused on helping the boys, they headed toward the guards closest to their exiting point. Tonia's heart sank when she realized how outnumbered they were, but she quickly found new hope when she glanced to her left and spotted a large group of helmeted warriors running toward them. In the middle of this new group was an odd pair of beautiful female creatures, but they were running toward the water instead of into the midst of the battle. The females carried no weapons and obviously weren't prepared for hand-to-hand combat. Although this seemed a bit strange to her, Tonia didn't have time to give it more than a passing thought. The guard running toward her took her mind off just about everything.

Micah watched helplessly as the fight between Nivri's soldiers and the rebels began in earnest. The sound of swords striking shields and men yelling at men shattered the silence surrounding them.

Nivri stood motionless, glaring at the boy with luminescent, satisfied eyes. He turned slightly and glanced over at his dragon, smiled at the beast, then returned his attention back to the young boy.

"Give me the stones."

As he spoke, two curly locks of long, gray hair moved slightly in the cool, morning breeze. Nivri's pumpkin-colored eyes stared into Micah's cerulean ones as he waited for the boy's answer, but instead of telling the sorcerer what he wanted to hear, Micah just smiled.

"I don't have them," the trapped figure said with a smirk. "If you had been paying attention earlier, you would have realized it."

Nivri listened to the boy's words while he struggled to remember the scene from a moment ago.

Had the brat dropped the stones?

"Show me your hand," Nivri ordered with a growl.

Micah's smile widened as he slowly raised his hand and unfurled his fingers. Nivri watched as the boy showed him exactly what he least wanted to see – the hand was empty.

The sorcerer's eyes flashed as he turned back to scan the battle scene on the beach. His troops from the castle were fighting well, as far as he could see, but he wasn't concerned about his troops at the moment – he wanted the stones.

Just as he was about to turn back to the trapped boy he suddenly caught sight of a dark, round object lying in the sand about ten feet away. In less than a second, his eyes flickered with welcomed recognition – it was one of the stones! He held Micah securely in place with his clawed arm and rotated his body slightly until it was facing the stone. His right hand waved in the air as if he was swatting away bugs, and he mumbled a few words that Micah didn't understand.

The boy watched as a narrow funnel of orange light suddenly appeared from Nivri's fingertips and shot through the air toward the stone on the beach. Inches before it reached the colored piece of earth, the light stopped as if running into an invisible, rock wall.

Nivri growled and dropped his hand, then turned to stare at the trapped boy.

"Why won't my magic work?" he hissed as his glowing, carrot-colored eyes stared into those of his young protagonist's. Micah stared back at the sorcerer as the battle raged on just a few feet away.

"I don't know," he answered snidely. "Maybe you should look it up in your spell book!"

Nivri threw the boy a narrowed, hate-filled stare. He could feel his pulse beginning to thud like a liquid drum behind his eyes as his blood raced through his veins.

Micah knew the sorcerer was upset, but movement over Nivri's shoulder suddenly distracted him. He looked beyond the dark cloak and saw the large, black dragon the sorcerer had arrived upon had turned and was moving toward the shoreline.

It was heading straight for Zig and Zag.

The right side of the dragon, Zig's half, realized the black beast was heading towards them and was struggling frantically to head back into the water, back to a place that was safer than being a large target on a small beach. Zag, however, stood tall and confident, glaring at Nivri's pet with a combination of hatred and determination in his eyes.

In the blink of a firebug, Zag drew his long neck back until it was curved just over the base of his wings. Like a rubbery tarza vine, he then launched his head forward and exhaled a wide flume of fire toward the approaching black demon. Nivri's beast stopped and leaned away from the fire, just out of reach of the combusting air. As the orange flame evaporated, the evil reptile

410

began advancing toward the two-headed dragon, yet again, with focused, stalking steps.

"No!" Micah called out to his adversary's beloved steed, but it ignored him, choosing instead to focus completely on its prey.

"Stop! Leave him alone!"

Surprised, Nivri stared at the boy for a few seconds before turning to see what caused the outburst. He smiled when he spotted his pet making its intense approach toward the boy's dragon. He really didn't think the unfolding events between the ancient creatures would provide much entertainment, especially since the two-headed dragon was surely no match for his newly revived pet, but it would be interesting to see how this trapped and helpless, ordinary boy would react to watching his two-headed friend's certain death take place.

He chuckled as he turned back to Micah.

"How does it feel to be helpless? How much does it bother you to know that the intended outcome from one event, or many events, will not happen as you planned and hoped?"

Micah heard the hooded figure's words, but ignored them. Instead, he chose to call out to his friends.

"Zag! Go! Get out of here!"

The upper portion of the dragon's twin necks were drawn far apart but joined at the bottom, with Zig trying to retreat while Zag obviously wanted to fight. On any other day, this type of behavior might have drawn a chuckle out of the boy...

But not today.

Micah pulled his gaze away from the dueling dragons and looked left as his eyes raked across the dozens of figures fighting on the beach. It didn't take long for him to find Nicho and Tonia – they were fighting side by side against a burly, armored beagon near the water. Just beyond them, Diam was jabbing her weapon at another winged beast while Kaileen was clinging to the soldier's back. The kalevala was repeatedly striking her opponent on the side of the head with a large stone.

If it wasn't such a serious situation, the scene would almost be comical.

"I think I'll let you just watch the battle for a moment," Nivri whispered in a taunting tone just inches away from Micah's ear.

411

Without another word, he straightened and waved his right hand towards his left in a small, circular gesture, then mumbled a few words in the same incomprehensible language as before. Micah felt the appendage holding him against the tree tremble briefly before it suddenly fell still.

Before the sorcerer walked away, Micah heard a strange, ripping sound coming from somewhere between them. The black clad figure was moving away but he was still trapped! As confusion covered his young, smooth face, the boy looked down to see what continued to hold him in place.

At the junction where Nivri's arm had just a moment earlier been melded across the top of the wide, black pincer, Micah was surprised to see the sorcerer's stretched, gray skin had pulled away from the appendage. As a result, what should have been a grotesque extension of the sorcerer's arm had inexplicably become its own entity. Before Micah could question what was happening, the black clad figure turned back and threw him a satisfied, knowing sneer. Nivri hesitated for barely a second before he turned and walked away, leaving the unmoving, gripping claw holding Micah in place against the wide, rough bark.

"Excuse me for a moment. I need to go get that stone over there, before it gets lost in the shuffle of too many moving feet."

Nivri's voice was filled with sarcasm as his focus drifted from the boy to the stone.

Micah didn't call out as he struggled in the jagged, unwavering grasp of the detached appendage, but after a few seconds, he realized everything he tried was futile. He began to shake with anger as he watched Nivri saunter toward the stone on the beach like a ghost flitting its way invisibly between the battling figures. Beyond the figure in black, Micah saw Zig and Zag pacing a wide, slow circle near the shoreline with Nivri's ebony beast. It was as if the two monsters were doing some sort of strange dance together.

A short distance away, Micah suddenly noticed something familiar – half a dozen spinning funnels of water began to take shape over the lake, rising out of the water as if being pushed up from some unseen entity beneath the surface. The funnels, wide

412

at the top and narrower toward the bottom, floated upward for a few seconds until they had reached a height of about ten feet.

As he watched the spinning forms above the water, Micah remembered the funnels he and Nicho had seen the day before. These looked similar to those, except the ones he saw spinning furiously above the water now were flipped upside down from the ones they'd seen the previous day. Another difference was, as far as he could tell, these had no fish spinning around and around inside them.

He continued struggling as he watched the funnels for a few seconds, and was surprised when he suddenly detected nearly a dozen shapes beyond the spinning circles of water. Two of the shapes were the two female figures he'd seen running across the beach just a little while ago. All of the figures were standing waist deep in the water, waving their arms this way and that. They held his curiosity for a moment but before he could figure out what they were doing, he suddenly heard a loud buzzing sound coming from somewhere behind him.

He turned and tried to peer around the tree, but the pincer held him snuggly in place. Frustrated, Micah changed his focus and searched among the battling bodies for his brother. It didn't take long for him to find the older boy – he was standing with his weapon extended toward one of Nivri's minions, which stood just a foot or two away from him. Micah watched as the burly beast paused briefly then tottered as if standing on the edge of a narrow cliff. After a little more than a second, Nicho's opponent toppled over and landed on his back on the beach.

Also hearing the now almost deafening buzzing sound, Nicho turned in Micah's direction.

"Micah, are you okay?" Nicho yelled across the beach.

"Yes," Micah shouted back.

A second later, a thick, black cloud of insects flew past his tree and headed toward the battle. Nicho stared at the cloud nervously before he realized the insects were just like those they had seen in the forest.

"Fight on!" Mitna yelled from the cluster of black flying spots as the large group of insects quickly dispersed and began attacking Nivri's soldiers in earnest.

Although the group consisting of the boys, the girls, and the prisoner, had been small compared to Nivri's multitude of soldiers, with the addition of the new arrivals, the battle soon became much more evenly matched. The swarm of buzzing insects aimed themselves at the faces of the opposing army, flying into their ears and noses, buzzing and biting with everything they had.

Nivri, standing in the nucleus of the battle, picked up the single, purple stone and glanced back at the boy pinned against the tree. After reassuring himself that the brat had no chance of escape, he turned and focused his attention on his dragon. The black beast was still circling a section of the beach near the water with its two-headed opponent. The sorcerer then moved his eyes among the rest of the battling bodies, where all he could do was stare at the unfolding scene.

When Nivri arrived on his dragon, he'd had complete and utter confidence that his troops comfortably outnumbered the small mixed group of renegades. It hadn't mattered much to him whether they teamed up to form one large group, or remained as a few, menial, smaller groups. Either way, his minions from the castle outnumbered them…

But he hadn't thought about any of the numerous allies these meddling children may have befriended along the way. As he stared at the battle scene, it now looked as though that single, tiny, overlooked fact might just bite him where the sun doesn't shine – on his big toe.

He stared as he watched one, two, five, ten, then nearly all of his troops as they began swatting frantically at their noses, ears, heads, and mouths like they'd suddenly become possessed by a spell gone horribly wrong. He sneered at the surprising scene for a few seconds, then turned and glared at the boy still trapped against the tree.

The young brat was smiling.

Nivri's heart began to race yet again, and fury wasted no time in overtaking what little part of his rational mind that remained.

This was it. Enough was enough!

"Finish him!" he growled at his dragon. As his eyes blazed and his blood pulsed like a giant wave, Nivri simply stood by and watched the events as they unfolded.

Micah couldn't help but smile as the blinding swarm of insects attacked the opposing force on the beach. Between the miniature flying army and the other group of armor-clad warriors who'd arrived just as the battle began, Micah found he had reason to hope they could actually win this fight.

Now, if only he could figure out how to get himself out of the large piece of scorpion that held him in place!

After getting himself worked up about being trapped, then watching the battle on the beach, Micah's adrenaline was flowing like a river through his body. He didn't realize it until now, but at some point after he became trapped, he had begun to sweat. His skin was slick with the self-made moisture.

Although his earlier attempt at escape had been disappointingly futile, he began squirming again as he tried to free himself from the shiny, black claw. It didn't take long for him to realize he was able to move around a bit more now than previously, but his heart sank when he realized it wasn't enough.

He stared out at the ongoing battle briefly before returning his focus back to the figure in black. He was standing in the middle of the battle, miraculously unharmed, watching his troops.

"Here, take this."

A soft, feminine voice suddenly spoke against his left ear in a quiet whisper.

Micah jumped with surprise, then turned and caught a glimpse of Teresia hovering just behind the tree. She was holding out a large, round rock to him.

"I can't help you with removing the claw, but you should be able to use this as a hammer. Break the claw so you can free yourself! Work quickly – you don't have much time!"

Micah nodded a silent thanks as she disappeared from sight. He waited for a few seconds then began raising the rock into the air and striking down on the upper part of the claw. The raging battle on the beach masked the sound of his attempt to escape, which, at this point, he didn't care if they heard what he was doing. He would take anything, including drawing attention to himself, in exchange for standing helplessly by as his friends and family members fought in a battle that he should also be fighting.

He swung downward with everything he had, making contact between the rock and the confining pincer, over and over again. He focused on what he was doing when suddenly the sound of Nivri's voice caused him to stop yet another strike against the claw mid-swing.

"Finish him!"

For a brief second, Micah thought the sorcerer was giving an order to one of his minions about *him*, telling them to stop him from trying to escape. He looked up and turned his eyes toward the sound of the voice. When he finally understood what was happening, Micah's stomach churned with a combination of relief, then dread, when he realized that the sorcerer wasn't referring to him at all.

Nivri was looking at his dragon, ordering the beast to finish off its opponent. Micah saw the black creature nod at its master before it turned and glared at its two-headed rival.

In an earth-shattering instant, Micah understood what was about to happen. As the black dragon partially extended its wings and reared back in preparation of a strike, the young boy did the only thing that came to his mind.

"No!" he screamed at the top of his lungs, hoping to stop the inevitable. Forgetting about the rock in his hand, Micah struggled against the confining claw with all his might.

It wouldn't budge.

Micah yelled out again at the black dragon, but the beast completely ignored him. He stared as Zag reared his own head back and expelled a mighty stream of flame directly at its opponent. In response, Nivri's beast curled one of its massive, thick wings forward around its neck and face, protecting itself from the approaching flames. Then, before Micah could call out again, the black beast lunged forward towards the two-headed dragon, catching Zag's upper neck in its gaping, sharp-toothed mouth.

Before the black dragon attacked, Zig had been trying frantically to pull them toward the water. His eyes widened, silently screaming with the knowledge that he had to get away from the black mass of opposition that confronted them, wanting nothing more than to get away from the battle itself.

Zag, the stronger of the two heads in more ways than one, somehow managed to keep the bulky, shared body on the shore, knowing full well that the chances of their survival against the large, red-eyed dragon were slim...

If there was ever really any chance at all.

When Nivri's beast sank its razor sharp teeth into Zag's thick neck, Zig felt the pain as if the demon creature had bitten him instead. Both heads of the two-headed dragon cried out in agony before Zig suddenly changed his focus. Instead of trying to pull them away from the shore, the more timid of the two heads suddenly turned toward the black dragon and began spraying it with short bursts of yellow and orange flames.

"No!" Micah cried out when he realized Zag's neck was held firmly in the black dragon's mouth. "Leave them alone!"

Micah began thrashing and twisting in the pincer's grasp, raising and lowering his rock down on the claw at the end of each twist. After countless strikes and infinite struggling, the young boy finally thought he heard an abrupt, muffled cracking sound. Unfortunately, the anguished cries from his dragon friend overshadowed many of the nearby noises.

Breathing heavily, Micah paused briefly and, although he really didn't want to, he turned away from his entrapment to look at Zig and Zag. Zag's eyes were closed and after a few long seconds, his head fell like a limp tarza vine against the side of the black dragon's massive neck. Zig stared wide-eyed at Zag's lifeless head before he turned a pleading stare directly toward Micah.

"Zag!" Micah cried. "No!"

Utter helplessness engulfed him while tears of anger and frustration poured like rivers down his face.

"Nicho, help them!" Micah cried. "Please, help them!"

But Nicho couldn't help – he had his hands full fighting against two of Nivri's minions. Micah turned back to his dragon friend as he struggled not to completely lose himself in a bottomless abyss of anger, frustration and grief.

Zig stared at Micah as understanding filled his wide, scaled face. He turned a glance at Zag, but the other half of their body had slumped down onto the beach, as lifeless as a tree trunk.

"Zig, I'm sorry!" Micah called out with a sob as tears poured like rivers down his agonized, youthful face. Zig simply nodded, then erected his neck so it was nearly perpendicular to the ground. As Micah lowered his head in defeat, the black dragon lunged out and snapped Zig's neck with a crack. As the second of the two heads slumped to the beach, the rest of the body followed, and soon lay in broken, lifeless heap.

FIFTY-ONE

Nivri held out the hand grasping the purple stone and smiled as he watched it twinkle in the brilliant sunlight. He tore his eyes away from the stone to leer at the boy in hopes of taunting him with the fact that he finally had possession of one of his precious stones, but the boy appeared to be deeply absorbed in his problems. Micah was completely focused on the undeniable fact that he was stuck someplace where he didn't want to be, and his special dragon friend was about to die a quick and unexpected death.

Nivri watched as the boy struggled with both his confinement and his emotions. The stone he held flickered a few more times, then glowed like a bright, purple star. At the same time, it also began pulsing in his hand. Within the radius of a few feet around him, small patches of sand began to light up with miniature circles of light – blue, green and yellow.

Nivri continued to hold his hand out as his eyes moved from one colored patch of sand to the next. Within seconds, the rest of the glowing stones erupted like lumpy, colorful crabs from beneath the surface of the beach. After briefly hovering in place, they began floating through the air as if being carried like a leaf on a brisk breeze – directly toward Nivri's extended palm.

This would be the final touch, and everything was going to work out just fine, he thought. He was seconds away from holding the entire group of mystical stones in the palm of his hand, and they were glowing like they had previously done solely for the brat trapped against the tree. His dragon had defeated its rival, which wasn't much of a surprise, and he only had a few more things to do before he could take his troops and return to his castle.

The final devious act he would perpetrate would be to carry the stones and hold them just out of reach of the trapped boy. He wanted to prove one thing to the brat – that whatever menial magic he thought he had possessed wasn't any match at all for the magic Nivri was capable of. He would flaunt this in front of the boy, and he would enjoy every last second of it! Then, once he knew the brat understood what a mistake it had been to come to his world, he would drive his sword through the child's young, meddling and soon-to-be lifeless, heart.

Now that he had the entire set of stones, his next acquisition would be the amulets. Then he could move on to the big fish in the lake…

But that would be another adventure for another day, like tomorrow or next week. Right now, today, he had a job to finish.

He smiled as he wrapped his fingers around the glowing orbs while his heart thumped wildly with anticipation. He mumbled a low, rapid chant then raised the hand holding the stones high into the air.

"Stand down!" he yelled in a booming voice.

His soldiers quickly responded by taking a step away from their opponents then holding their weapons snugly against their chests. Before the children and their fellow allies could react to what at first appeared to be a group-wide act of submission, they fell to the ground, moaning and writhing in pain. Nivri smiled when he saw that even the large swarm of insects had fallen prey to his spell. The tiny black bugs were scattered across the entire battle area, bouncing from place to place like a massive infestation of sand fleas.

Micah, still pinned against the tree, stared at the scene in confusion.

"What's happening? What have you done?" he cried out at the figure in black.

420

About twenty feet away, Nivri grinned at the boy as his eyes flickered with hungry, orange flames.

"I used *your* magical stones in conjunction with *my* spell of torture," he crooned in a sarcastically confident tone. "Your friends can no longer fight, and unfortunately, your dragon is dead."

He threw the boy a maniacal, ear to ear grin.

"That, my friend, leaves just you and me."

Micah's began to shake as and overwhelming, intense hatred for the black clad figure consumed him like an earthquake.

"Let me go, right now, and stop torturing them!" he yelled as he pointed at his friends and allied strangers on the beach.

"Or what?" Nivri asked with a broken, almost growling cackle. "Are you going to use your magic on me? Are you going to have your dragon attack me?"

Without waiting for an answer, the sorcerer turned and glanced at the carcass of the two-headed creature lying motionless on the shore behind him.

"Looks like your friend there won't be doing much more than feeding the hungry crabs later on," he said with an arrogant smile.

Micah felt a flood of anger rise into his cheeks and suddenly just couldn't take it anymore. Without knowing he was going to do it, the young boy roared in frustration and flung the large rock Teresia had given him, aiming for the sorcerer's chest. Nivri saw it coming and moved easily to the side. The round, jagged stone struck the edge of his cloak, where his left arm would have been, before it fell to the ground with a dull thud. Both the boy and the sorcerer watched the rock roll briefly across the sand before it settled into a shallow void not far away from a much larger stone.

Nivri laughed, pleased to see the anger and frustration on the boy's face. He knew his game would have to come to an end sooner or later, but he was certainly enjoying it while it lasted.

He turned to issue one final order to his troops.

"Stand ready!"

The soldiers immediately moved to hover over the still writhing figures on the beach. Although none of them moved to kill their opponents right now, as soon as their master gave them the signal, they would begin their final, fatal attack.

Micah stared at Nivri's minions as they moved themselves into place near his friends and family. Would the soldiers kill them while they were paralyzed with whatever spell the sorcerer had afflicted them with?

"Kill me, but let them go," Micah offered. "You know as well as I do that the stones in your hand were only magical when I held them. If you kill me and release my friends, you won't have that threat anymore. Release them and send them home."

Nivri laughed knowingly but shook his head.

"Why are you laughing?" Micah yelled angrily. "Why is my idea funny?"

"I laugh," Nivri began as he took a single step toward the boy before stopping just a few inches away from him, "because you say I can send them… 'home'."

"Yes," Micah said in a hopeful tone. "Send them home and keep the stones.

Nivri laughed again.

"I would if I could, young Micah, but I can't, so I won't."

"Why not?" the boy yelled.

Micah's mind raced as it searched for ways he could save his friends and family while his body continued to struggle involuntarily against the restraining claw. Even though his mind was focused on the sorcerer's words, his body was obviously still focused on freedom.

"It's simple, really," Nivri said as he waved the glowing stones around in the air before bringing them down close to Micah's glaring, blue eyes. Although Nivri's own eyes were emitting a soft amber color, the colorful stones painted his face with a pale, multicolored sheen. Micah thought he could see a very wrinkled, very scary face beneath the cloak, but before he could be sure, Nivri lowered the stones again and his face melted back to the safety of shadow.

"You no longer have a *home*, that's why. Isn't that a good reason?"

Micah's eyes widened as he stared at the dark figure. Nivri shrugged and glared at him with pride.

"What do you mean?" the boy asked in a shocked whisper.

"I mean exactly that," Nivri cooed. "I mean you no longer have a home. Your village, and everyone in it, has been destroyed."

"No!" Micah yelled as he shook his head in denial. "Don't play games with me, sorcerer! You're just trying to get me all worked up and it's not going to work!"

His eyes flashed as he continued shaking his head.

"If you're such a man, why don't you release me and fight me one on one? I have a sword, and I'm sure you can find one if you don't already have one. Let's duel it out! If I win, my friends, family, and I go free. If you win, well, you win the stones, the magic, and no more opposition from either my friends or family."

"That's a splendid idea, young Micah!"

Nivri hesitated for effect before continuing.

"But unfortunately, I already have other plans for you. I will quell my magic on your friends and family at the same time that I release you from the tree."

Micah held his breath when Nivri said he would release him, but he knew it was too good to be true when he heard the sorcerer's next words.

"Then, you will all die together."

With that, Nivri tossed another knowing, evil smirk at the boy before he paused and stared back at the battlefield. He took a deep breath then extended his arms out on either side of his body and began to recite another one of his spells. The young boy watched helplessly as the orange orbs beneath the cloak became more and more narrow until they released just a hair's width of reddish light. The eyes drifted closed as the sorcerer mumbled some quite indistinguishable spell, and within a few seconds, a large, gray shadow appeared on the sand partially behind and beneath the sorcerer's body.

In an instant, Micah suddenly understood what the sorcerer was doing. Although he couldn't see any appendages growing out of the cloaked figure's back, the young boy was certain it would just be a matter of time before Nivri cast a spell where he would turn himself into some sort of dreadful beast. And from what he knew of the sorcerer so far, he doubted it would be a plain, ordinary beast – it would be one that would probably kill them all.

FIFTY-TWO

Nivri was elated at the reaction he was getting from the young, meddling brat who stood so helplessly in front of him. The boy had first lost possession of his precious stones, then he had witnessed the death of his friend – the bumbling two-headed dragon. Once Nivri cast his final spell, the boy would watch both his friends, as well as his family members, die a violent death just before he said goodbye to his own young, miserable life.

Nivri had it all planned out.

He would approach the boy with the glowing stones still held out in his hand, which, in combination with the spell he had recanted, continued to keep this young man's cohorts helplessly rolling around on the beach in agony. When he tucked the stones into the inside pocket of his cloak, the spell would wear off. Next, his remaining castle guards would finish off the recovering group of the boy's allies. Then, and only then, he would finish off the boy… personally!

Ah, yes, he would release the boy from the claw that held him against the tree, only to put him back there like a piece of chickenbird on a skewer shortly thereafter. It wouldn't be long before the boy found himself pinned to the tree with Nivri's sword guided perfectly through his lungs. The boy wouldn't die right away, though… of this Nivri was certain. One thing he *was* sure of, however, was the boy would be in incredible pain, he would be livid with anger, and he would want nothing more than complete and utter revenge!

Unfortunately, the brat would not be able to do anything about his situation, which was really the beauty of the whole thing!

He could visualize the final scene in the boy's miserable life as he stared into the trees...

The boy would watch as Nivri walked away, mounted his dragon, and headed toward the Castle of Death. The brat would then have no choice but to watch his allies fall at the hands of the mighty guards of Defigo, and eventually, he would die still pinned against the tree. He would then find himself helpless, in pain, without magic, and utterly alone as his life slipped away into eternal darkness.

The sorcerer smiled beneath the veil of his cloak. His plan was perfect! He raised his arms and chanted the spell of death, the spell that would be the beginning of his newfound journey with the magical cluster of stones. Once he located each of the amulets as well, he, and he alone, would rule Euqinom.

The world, and everything in it, would be his!

He saw a mixture of fear and understanding fill the boy's eyes just before he closed his own, but he was too caught up in his spell, his magic, and his quest for authority, to care.

This is why he didn't see the large shadow fall across his smaller one, swallowing it on the sand around his feet.

FIFTY-THREE

Micah briefly raised his eyes up toward the shining sun, and silently prayed to anyone who would hear him to help him in his infinitely dismal situation. Nivri's black beast stood as still as stone over Zig and Zag's lifeless body as the sorcerer mumbled his spell, and when Micah dropped his gaze back to the scene in front of him, he assumed the dragon's reaction had to do with pride at the accomplishment of its orders. It didn't take long for the boy to understand that the dark creature wasn't standing still with pride… it was frozen in surprise.

At the same instant he realized the black dragon was staring at something above him, Micah heard a booming voice cry out from somewhere over his head.

"Micah, catch!"

Startled into movement, the boy looked up and thought he caught sight of a flash of white hovering overhead, but it quickly disappeared over the trees. Just in the nick of time, he spotted three colorful objects falling toward him like a narrow shower of rain from the sky. Without realizing he was even doing so, he reached his hands out to catch them.

One…

Two…

Three…

As the somewhat familiar, solid items fell into his outstretched hands, the boy finally recognized what they were. He hesitated for only an instant, fighting an overwhelming desire to stare at the items in confusion and total disbelief. Wasn't the whole point of their being in this world to recover them and give them back to the dragons? If so, why did the dragon just give them back to him?

Interrupted before he could finish his spell, the cloaked figure began to growl, emitting sounds similar to an incessantly rumbling, unfed tummy. Micah looked up to see Nivri's blazing orange eyes glaring at him. In the sorcerer's hands, the four, colorful stones began to flicker like a muscle spasm, then quickly fell dark again. In a matter seconds, they changed from a cluster of magical stones to nothing more than a few plain, colored rocks.

"No!" Nivri cried as he began to shake with fury. "You can NOT do this to me again!"

He raised his glowering eyes toward the sky and caught sight of Lemures circling over them as he turned and headed for the far end of the lake.

"Get him!" Nivri yelled at his dragon. "Kill him now, kill him quickly, or you will remain here as crab food!"

The black beast offered a curt nod of acknowledgment and lunged into the air like a giant frog. As the black dragon began chasing after the ivory-colored beast, Micah stared at the trio of items in his hands.

One red…

One blue…

One white…

All three amulets! The magical gems that belonged to the dragons were there, right there, in his hands…

And they were just as dull as the stones in Nivri's hand.

The formerly writhing bodies across the beach were slowly getting to their feet now that the spell of pain had worn off, but Nivri's minions simply stood nearby, waiting for their master's order to finish the opposing army. Their master, however, was almost at the breaking point, overcome with rage and disbelief because his magical stones were no longer showing any signs of magic.

"What have you done?" Nivri growled at the boy. Micah

427

looked up at the black clad figure, but didn't answer. From everything he'd seen up until that very moment, the stones *and* the amulets had only offered magical powers when they were glowing…

And right now, every single one of them was dull and lifeless a forgotten corpse.

Across the beach, Tonia stood up and rubbed her stomach. The incredible pains she'd felt there just a few minutes before were finally gone, but a dull ache still lingered which stretched from one side of her abdomen to the other. She looked up and scanned the figures on the shore until she finally found what she was looking for.

"Micah!" she called out.

Without looking for Diam or Kaileen, Tonia turned and began running towards her trapped brother.

Just past Tonia, Dean saw what the young girl was doing and turned to chase after her. He knew that Nivri planned on killing all of the renegades once he had recovered his stones, but Dean thought perhaps he could find a way to sneak the girl to safety, possibly beyond the thick line of bushes nearby. Although it appeared to be too late to save the younger boy, perhaps he could save the girl and her other brother.

After many years in the castle, Dean finally decided he'd had enough. Seeing Orob fighting alongside the former prisoners had shown Dean that he *could* turn his life around – he *could* do the right thing, if he really set his mind to it.

And his mind was made up.

Micah heard his sister call out to him in the distance. When he turned and caught sight of her running towards him across the sandy beach with one of Nivri's minions hot on her tail, he was suddenly overcome with the need to protect her.

"Tonia, watch out!" he called.

Although he thought he had been loud enough, it looked as though she didn't hear him. She continued to run toward him without any indication that she knew she was being chased.

Micah's heart began to race again, and he ignored the cloaked creature growling at him as he focused on trying to save his sister.

"No!" he yelled again.

As his scream of protest fell silent on his lips, the amulets in Micah's hand suddenly flickered to life.

Tonia still didn't hear him, and the beagon behind her was closing the distance all too quickly. The trapped boy began writhing against the tree, moving from side to side within the grasp of his secure, serrated prison. He didn't notice the amulets were glowing brightly in his hand because his fingers had closed over the stones, but he did hear something else...

The claw was cracking!

"Tonia!" he called out as he pushed his body into the tree, then launched himself forward into the claw. He repeated this motion over and over, completely ignoring the pain he felt along both of his sides. When he least expected it, the claw suddenly split into two large pieces with a loud, splintering crack, and the young boy stumbled forward. He quickly regained his footing and focused on Tonia. She was still running toward him, but it was obvious the beast chasing her would catch her before she reached him. Micah took a deep breath and did the only thing he could do. He extended his hands toward Tonia and yelled at the lumbering, hairy beast just a few steps behind her.

"No!"

As Tonia continued running toward her brother, a strange transformation began to take place. A purple, shapeless cloud of smoke surrounded the young boy, much like a cocoon, but it quickly took on the shape of a small, yet clearly defined dragon. As Micah yelled at the figure chasing Tonia, the cloud dragon diminished in size as it melded into the boy like an oversized but rapidly shrinking costume. He called out again to his sister and as his voice echoed across the beach, something very strange happened.

The younger boy reared his head back as if his neck was long and slender, then threw the upper part of his body forward. Wide, iridescent, purple wings appeared out of nowhere and rapidly extended out from either side of him where they froze in place as if he was in mid-flight. The boy yelled again and a bright, purple ray of electric light spewed from his mouth like lightening. The beaming line of electricity extended straight across the beach like a long, lilac-colored tongue, darting between friend and foe until it finally found its target.

One second Dean was chasing the girl, and the next, he exploded into hundreds of thousands of tiny, dark ashes. The fiery remains of the beagon quickly arced through the air and floated downward, littering both the beach as well as the shallow area of the nearby lake.

Dean was nothing but a memory.

FIFTY-FOUR

Nivri stood about twenty feet away, staring at the boy as his eyes began to see nothing but the color of blood. A thick layer of red covered everything in his sight – the beach, the boy, the bushes, the trees. He lowered his eyes and looked at the stones in his hand. They, too, were covered with a rose-colored film, and although he was disappointed by the sight, he was not surprised to find they were still nothing more than simple stones.

The boy was struggling frantically in the grasp of the claw, his trio of gems just as dull. Nivri glanced back at the scene unfolding behind him, but didn't care about his soldier who was chasing the girl – right now, he was thoroughly consumed with one thought…

To end this miserable boy's life.

He tucked the stones into the pocket of his cloak and drew his sword, then began moving slowly toward his prey. It was time to end the game.

Now.

FIFTY-FIVE

As the ray of purple light shot past Tonia, she stopped abruptly and stared at the place where Micah had been just a moment before.

Was that her brother up there near the tree? It didn't look like him! The figure she saw there was surrounded by a bright, purple cloud that looked strangely like...

A dragon.

She looked around and noticed that every one of Nivri's minions appeared to be startled by the purple cloud in the distance. She muttered a brief sound of thanks that they weren't trying to stop her and was about to continue forward when an unexpected male voice over her shoulder made her jump with surprise.

"Are you okay?"

She swung her sword back defensively before she realized the voice was a friend, not a foe.

And it was familiar.

"Nicho!"

Her heart skipped a beat and she lunged at him for a quick hug when movement out of the corner of her eye drew her attention. In the distance, the white and black dragons were dueling in the cloudless sky, taking turns shooting flames at each other as the defensive dragon ducked out of the way.

"No!"

She jumped in surprise again when she heard Nicho's yell and turned to see what caused it. He wasn't standing next to her anymore. Now he was running across the beach, straight towards Micah. Sensing something bad was about to happen, Tonia instantly ran and tried to catch up to him but he was too fast. She hadn't been sure why Nicho took off like that, but her heart sank when she finally realized the reason.

The cloaked figure closest to Micah had drawn his sword and was heading straight for the younger of the two boys. A soldier stood on either side of Micah, each of them holding one of his arms firmly in place. Micah stood motionless, staring at the approaching sorcerer with calm brevity. Although Tonia couldn't hear the words, she could imagine how Nivri's soldiers might be whispering in his ear, describing how they would rip his body apart as he was dying. One of the soldiers suddenly reached around behind Micah's head and covered the boy's mouth with a thick, hairy hand. They were so focused on filling Micah's mind with fear that they didn't see what was coming toward them until it was too late.

Nivri saw his minion to the left raise his head with a startled look of surprise, then heard the sound of hasty footsteps landing rhythmically on the sand somewhere behind him. He held his sword out before him as he turned in the direction of the sound. A split second later, Nicho stepped on a wide, smooth rock and launched himself through the air. The spear of Viviani was held firmly in front of him.

"Nicho, no!" Tonia screamed.

As if in slow motion, the young girl saw the tip of Nicho's spear touch the front of Nivri's cloak. Since her older brother was facing away from her, however, she did *not* see the tip of Nivri's sword pierce the center of a ringlet on the front of her brother's shirt.

The eerie sound of silence that followed was quickly shattered by a piercing, blood curdling scream that quickly echoed all the way around the lake.

Fifty-Six

Zel had been fighting alongside Zacharu for a short time when he suddenly realized one of the younger figures a hundred yards away looked vaguely familiar. He didn't dare take the time to look more closely at her while he was in the midst of battle, but once his adversary fell to the ground with a mortal knife wound to the chest, he allowed himself a few seconds to stare at the girl fighting her own battle.

He swore she looked strangely like one of his daughter's best friends!

Although he'd lost track of time after endless days and nights cooped up in Nivri's castle, he knew it had been close to, if not more than, a year since he'd seen Diam. As he stole glances at the young female figure fighting a few hundred feet away, his heart raced with hope that it might really be her. He stole glances in her direction every chance he got, and when he finally allowed himself to believe it was indeed his daughter's friend, he began looking earnestly for Tonia.

As the battle raged on, his eyes scoured across the battling figures until he finally spotted another female. She was tall and thin, with long brown hair that was tied back with a rope of what looked like tarza vine. He stared at her and after a long moment, he knew.

It was her, his daughter, fighting near the shoreline against a

434

tall, thin soldier. She was darting around her opponent much like he and Andar had taught her when she was younger. Although back then much of the training they had done was in the form of a game of one sort or another, it appeared as though those games had paid off. In spite of the fact that he was in the middle of his own fight against one of the larger, burlier castle guards, he couldn't help but smile with fatherly pride.

Every opportunity he got, Zel inched closer and closer to the brown-haired girl. Just when he thought he could almost reach out and let her know who was hiding behind the shiny, metal mask, he and his fellow soldiers all dropped to the ground in sheer pain. The battle, the beach, his daughter – all forgotten. Excruciating pain erupted in his midsection, and after what felt like an eternity of relentless agony, the throbbing ache finally subsided and he slowly crawled to his knees. After a moment he looked up and saw Nivri's minions scattered all around he and the rest of his fellow warriors. Oddly, none of the opposition was recovering from the strange pains he had just suffered, but then again, they weren't attacking either.

He pulled himself to his feet and realized all of Nivri's soldiers were focused on something happening along the northeastern edge of the beach. He easily picked out the black-clad sorcerer, but he couldn't quite make out the shape in front of Nivri. As the ache in the middle of his body slowly ebbed away, he realized the dark-haired form in front of the sorcerer was being held in place by two of Nivri's minions.

When he heard Tonia call out her brother's name and saw her sprinting in that direction, Zel suddenly recognized the figure being held against his will.

"Help me!" he called out to Zacharu. Without waiting for his friend to respond, he rushed after the young slender girl as she ran toward her brother.

FIFTY-SEVEN

For the lucky ones, death arrives in the blink of a firebug and life is removed from an object so it can be taken somewhere else, some place where one hopes there is more love and less pain. For others, however, the act of dying may take days, even weeks. These are the unlucky ones.

For many of those congregating on the shore of the place that used to be home to the Castle of Tears, luck was with some, but not all.

When Nicho spotted Nivri heading toward his brother, he reacted without allowing himself to think about what he was doing. His brother, Micah – son to Zel and Jeane, brother to Tonia, and friend to many – needed his help.

Nicho's anger flared when he realized Micah was being held against his will by two of Nivri's guards. As he spoke to his sister, asking her if she was okay, he suddenly saw the sorcerer sway his hips to the left and knew the result of this motion would free the long, crimson colored sheath from the protection of the black, satiny shroud that was his cloak. As if in a dream, Nicho stood frozen in place as he watched the sorcerer's hand move toward the handle of his hidden weapon, then remove it from its protective covering.

When he saw this, Nicho understood with undeniable clarity that if he didn't do something right now, his brother would die on the end of that sword.

Without further hesitation, he turned away from Tonia and raced toward the figure in black. The cool sand along the shore slowed him down slightly, but Nicho had always been known to be pretty light on his feet. He ran like he was being chased by a rabid mud puppy and smiled when he saw the wide, smooth rock right in the middle of his path…

It was just a few feet away from his final destination.

Nicho lunged forward and stepped on the solid, gray rock, then flew through the air toward the figure in black. At the last second, just before he landed on the rock, he knew perfectly well what he was doing.

He also understood exactly what it would mean.

This was his brother, his blood, his best friend. He would do whatever he had to in order to protect him like a brother, a relative, and a friend, was supposed to.

Nicho's brown eyes made contact with Micah's azure stare for less than a millisecond, but that was long enough. Silence surrounded them as the older boy refocused his gaze on the sorcerer. Nivri heard his approach and was turning toward him at the last second. Nicho saw the sorcerer's eyes widen with surprise, then he felt a slight bump of resistance before he plowed into the cloaked mass with a thud. He felt the sorcerer crumble beneath him as the handle of his spear pushed through the black material. As they both landed on the sand, Nicho suddenly felt a warm, sticky liquid flowing across the top of his hand.

He tried to get up right away, but discovered he was having a hard time breathing. He smiled with pride, thinking he must have hit the sorcerer with such an impact that he knocked the wind out of his lungs! When he realized the figure in black was lying on his back, gasping for air, his smile widened. He would take full credit for the wind being knocked out of both of them!

Nicho rolled to his right and found it odd that the sorcerer wasn't reaching up to remove the foreign object from his chest. The long, slender spear jutted from the center of the black shirt like an arrow piercing a large apple. With effort, Nicho rolled away from Nivri, not realizing he moved on and over the sorcerer's missing hand. When he was finally on his back again, the boy wondered why his lungs burned as if they were on fire.

Getting the wind knocked out of you wasn't supposed to burn this much, was it?

In the distance, he heard a faint scream of horror, but he didn't put much thought into why. Other things were a priority to him right now. He was still struggling to breathe and needed to find a way to get air in his lungs. He'd climbed his fair share of trees, and fallen enough times from them, too, but he'd never had the wind knocked out of him as much as he had this time. He had to take a breath!

He closed his eyes and balled his bloody hand into a fist, then quickly struck himself in the chest. It didn't help.

He opened his alarm filled eyes and vaguely noticed Micah struggling to get away from the soldiers. He could just imagine how they must have been so frightened to see their master fall at the hands of a talented warrior! If they didn't release his brother in about two seconds, he would get up and teach them a lesson, too!

Just as soon as he caught his breath…

Micah lunged forward and fell to his knees at his brother's side. Nicho saw Micah's lips moving, but he couldn't hear any words. He figured Micah was playing with him, and he would knuckle punch him just as soon as he caught his breath. As he struggled to breathe, he remembered he had been trying to punch himself in the chest, so he balled up his fist, about to inflict another strike, when he suddenly felt a pair of warm hands grab his arm.

He looked back to see who had grabbed him and Tonia was suddenly on his other side. It took him a second to realize she had wide rivers of tears running through patches of dirt and grime on her face. He saw her looking from him to something next to him, which he assumed was the dead or dying sorcerer, but when he turned his head to the side, he was shocked to see something that brought him to the realization of what was really happening.

The sorcerer lay on his back, gasping for breath of his own. His hood had fallen away from his face, revealing long, thick strands of gray hair shrouding an ancient, extremely wrinkled face. His eyes had lost their orange glow, and now looked like two lumps of coal embedded in a pool of gray, rough skin.

Seeing the sorcerer's face wasn't what brought Nicho to understand the seriousness of the situation he was in. Instead, it was the item the sorcerer held in a firm, unrelenting grip at his side.

A long sword jutted into the air, it's bloody, red blade quivering in the afternoon sun.

Nicho stared at the sorcerer for a few seconds, then stared at the weapon being held perpendicular to the ground. It was covered in clumps of beach sand and a red, sticky liquid...

Blood.

Nicho struggled to focus on the hand that had been holding the spear of Viviani – the hand attached to the arm that Tonia was still clinging to. It was covered with streaks of black blood as well as patches of sand. He raised his head and looked at the spear – it was embedded deep in the sorcerer's chest, but the handle of the spear, once white and beautiful, was also covered in thick, ebony goo.

He raised his other hand and touched his own chest, then lifted it into his line of sight so he could look at it. All he could do was stare at the warm, red substance covering his fingers.

As reality set in, Nicho finally admitted to himself that he was dying.

FIFTY-EIGHT

Tonia screamed when she finally understood what Nicho was about to do, but it made no difference. After running at full sprint toward the black-clad figure, her older brother didn't even flinch as he crashed into the sorcerer.

When she finally reached him, she prayed the sword she'd seen Nivri holding had totally missed him, but when she saw his fist hitting his chest and heard his struggles for air, she knew right away that the sorcerer's weapon had done some kind of serious damage. She knelt down beside Nicho's head and cradled it in her lap as she offered words of reassurance, all the while knowing deep down in her heart that every last word was a lie. She saw streams of sticky red blood spurting out of her brother's chest, and heard the undeniable rasping of internal bubbles as he struggled for each breath. She wasn't surprised when she soon saw a thin trickle of blood oozing from the corner of his mouth.

Although she knew he couldn't do anything, she turned her pleading brown eyes toward her younger brother. He was hovering over Nivri's trembling body and didn't notice when she looked at him. The sorcerer glared at the young boy with a look of pure hatred mixed with a gasping admission of defeat.

"You… will… pay," the gray haired figure whispered.

He reached toward the younger boy with the stump of his partial arm, then coughed and dropped his arm to the ground.

As tears streaked down his face, Micah raised his sword and was just about to plunge it into the sorcerer, more than willing to help the demon find his way into death, when Nivri closed his eyes. For a few seconds, the partially cloaked body shook with jerking tremors, then lay motionless and he said no more.

Tonia stroked Nicho's damp, brown hair as he struggled for every breath, and stared at the black-clad figure just a few feet away, her brown eyes filled with hatred. If her brother hadn't needed her so much right now, she would have jumped at the chance to do to the sorcerer what she'd done to the ice dragon the previous day. She would have ripped his heart out, chamber by chamber, with complete, revengeful pleasure, instead of fear. Unfortunately, she understood it was too late for revenge – his blood-covered lifeless body lay motionless on the sand...

Food for the crabs.

In seconds, she and Micah were surrounded by a group of unfamiliar, armored warriors, as well as Diam and Kaileen. As Tonia's friends joined her at her brother's side, one of the warriors just a few feet away cried out Nicho's name and pulled his metal helm off with the urgency of one being burned when cooking.

"Nicho!"

Zel pushed his way through the crowd of soldiers and knelt down on the sand next to his oldest son.

"Father?" Nicho whispered in a strangled gasp as his bloody hand reached for the vision of the man just a few inches away.

"Yes, son, I'm here," Zel said as his eyes filled with tears. Tonia stared at her father with astonishment, but refused to move from where she was. Instead, she reached out and touched her father's arm to acknowledge his presence, then resumed running her fingers gently through Nicho's short, brown hair.

Micah made his way slowly over to his father and rested his hand on Zel's shoulder.

They remained this way for a long moment when suddenly, Nicho began struggling. He reached up and tried to grab Micah's arm, but the younger boy was too far away.

"Mic..." Nicho gasped as his bloody hand opened and closed, reaching for his brother.

In an instant, Micah knelt down on the other side of his father and leaned over until he was hovering just above Nicho's face.

"Yes, brother?"

As he waited for Nicho to answer, Micah feared he would begin screaming with rage, anger, hatred, and dozens of other emotions causing an overwhelming turmoil in his heart.

He had to control his emotions!

"Are you... okay?" Nicho rasped as he reached up and tenderly touched Micah's cheek.

"Yes, Nicho, I'm fine. You saved me."

Nicho nodded and smiled as more blood oozed from the corners of his mouth. Although he had grown too weak to get up, he still managed to mumble a final, single worded question.

"Nivri?"

"Dead," Micah answered quietly as a single, lonely tear ran down his cheek.

Nicho nodded with a small smile then said, "Micah?"

"Yes, Nicho?"

Nicho closed his eyes as he muttered, "Save the dragons."

"Yes, but first, we'll take some time for you to get better, then we'll continue on our way."

Tonia glanced up at Micah, recognizing the lies of reassurance. She nodded without saying anything.

Just as she thought he might try to reply, Nicho shuddered for a few seconds as if he was cold, and then lay still.

"Nicho?" she whispered as she continued stroking his hair. There was no response.

"Nicho?" she repeated, louder this time, but again there was no response. She didn't notice when her father stood up and nodded at Micah. He pointed at Nicho's head and Micah moved closer to Tonia.

"Let me help," Micah said softly to his sister as Zel positioned himself behind her.

"Nicho?"

Tonia's cries for her brother reached a frenzied pitch as she began struggling in her father's arms. As Zel pulled her to her feet, Nicho's head fell into Micah's waiting hands. He held it briefly, closing his eyes as he did so. Tonia began beating her father in the chest as she squirmed to get away, her squeaking voice reaching higher and higher pitches as she cried her brother's name over and over. Her voice finally broke and she resorted to lurching, grieving sobs as she collapsed in her father's arms.

With tears streaming down her face, Diam joined Zel, and the two of them smothered Tonia in a hug of support. In seconds, Kaileen was also part of the hug. Micah opened his eyes, laid Nicho's head on the sand with extreme tenderness, and stood up to join the cluster.

Time stood still for the family and friends of the young boy who lay lifeless on the beach. They stood this way for what seemed like forever, offering support and love as they hugged and cried together. Although they forgot about the other figures around them, it wasn't long before they were interrupted by the distant, angry shouts of some of Nivri's scattered minions.

"They killed the master!" one of the castle guards called out accusingly.

"The master is dead!" another growled.

"Get them!" a third shouted.

As Zel, his fellow warriors, and his children stood huddled around the lifeless body of his oldest son, the remaining castle guards began to head toward them like an angry village mob.

FIFTY-NINE

J ust before Nivri's remaining troops reached their opponents, an odd flash of white above them caught Micah's attention. He had completely forgotten about Lemures and was both relieved and surprised to see their dragon friend, especially when he saw that the large, white shape was now flying alone. The black dragon was nowhere to be seen.

Micah broke away from the group hug and drew his sword then turned to face the approaching soldiers. He was happy to see they were no longer outnumbered, but he didn't want them to suffer any more casualties. He wished there was some way he could convince their opponents to just turn around and go back to the castle, but he couldn't think of any reason why the minions would want to. They came here with a job to finish, and it was quite obvious that, with or without their master, they were going to do the job they'd set out to do.

Movement from the corner of his eye made Micah turn and look toward the water, but before he could identify what it was that had snagged his attention, he felt an unexpected spray of cool droplets splash across his skin. Littered across the lake, he spotted a group of figures launching funnels of water at the approaching soldiers. Some of the funnels hit the soldiers with such force that it knocked them down onto the sand, and Micah soon realized the spray of water he'd felt seconds before had been

444

the after effects of one of the funnels striking its intended target just a few feet away.

He glanced behind him and saw the rest of his group spread out across the sand, ready to fight to the death if that's what it took. The approaching soldiers stopped the forward motion of their own line and stared at Micah and the rest of the armored group standing behind him. Overhead, Lemures came out of nowhere and roared at the soldiers approaching his friends, emitting such force that Micah felt the ground beneath his feet tremble in response. Some of Nivri's minions cursed angrily when they were hit with more funnels of water, and just when Micah thought the second round of battling was about to begin, their opponents experienced an unexpected change of heart. On the heels of a barrage of angry, rebellious shouts, Nivri's soldiers turned and fled the beach.

When they realized they had won the battle, Orob and the rest of the cluster of soldiers began to sing the chant of winners. They hooted and hollered and raised their swords into the air, calling out thanks for the lives that were spared and asking for blessings on the ones who weren't. The narrow stretch of sand was littered with dead and broken bodies from both sides of the battle, but thankfully, quite a few from Orob's group, as well as the humans, remained standing.

Those remaining understood the price of war – none needed to be told that they had been very lucky.

Tonia first noticed her father as she knelt next to Nicho, and when she finally settled down, she leaned against him for strength. His strong left arm was wrapped around her, pulling her gently towards him with silent reassurance. Nicho's death would be hard on all of them, of that Zel had no doubt. Although he wasn't happy to see the girls in this world, or in this situation, he was glad Tonia had both himself and her remaining friends to lean on.

After a moment, Orob weaved his way through the crowd and rested a large, hairy hand on Zel's shoulder.

"I'm sorry about your son," the former guard said quietly.

Zel looked at his hairy friend, nodded, and closed his eyes. "Thank you."

When Zel opened his eyes, he looked for his other son. At the same time, Tonia moved away from him to go talk to her friends. After a few seconds, he spotted Micah looking around a section of rocks at the northern edge of the beach. As he watched his daughter join the other girls, he was relieved to see Diam wrap an arm around Tonia's shoulder. Diam and Kaileen held her as Tonia leaned into them, her shoulders quivering up and down with silent cries of heartbreak.

As hard as it was to fight the urge to protect her, Zel decided to give them space. The damage had already been done. Although he was certain there would be many more tears to come, Tonia and Micah would have to figure out how to deal with the loss of their brother in their own way. He knew it would be difficult, but he had confidence that Tonia, as well as the rest of them, would get through their immense grief. They had to if they were to carry on.

He glanced at Orob and offered him a slight nod, then turned and made his way over to Micah.

"What are you doing, son?" he asked quietly. "Are you looking for something?"

Micah shook his head.

"Not some*thing*, some*one*."

The boy tried to disguise a sniffle with a sputtered cough.

Zel looked left and right but didn't see anyone.

"Who?" he asked in a puzzled tone.

"Ragoo," Micah answered. "One of our... my... friends."

His blue eyes darted back to Nicho's body, and lingered there for a few seconds, before he turned and continued searching the area around the rocks.

"Does your friend have a name?" Zel asked.

He wondered why the boy was looking in places where a body the size of a person's wouldn't fit very well. Was the stress of losing his brother taking a mental toll on his other son?

"His name is Ragoo," Micah answered. "He's a cat that we met in the yarnie village."

"I see," Zel answered. "What does he look like?"

Micah briefly explained his journey through the yarnie village, how he and Nicho had found each other there, how Ragoo had volunteered to join them, and eventually how their battle the previous night had ended with surprising success – with the exception of their feline friend's bite wound.

With the threat of battle behind them, the trio of girls wandered over to Zel and Micah. They found seats on a cluster of smooth, flat rocks, and listened to the conversation between the man and his son. In the distance, Orob and the rest of the soldiers began making their way through the bodies on the beach, looking for injured comrades as well as assisting the fallen enemy with their passage into death.

"Ragoo was sick, and Nicho carried him over here so he would be out of the way," Micah explained as he glanced nervously back at his brother's body again. "We were going to see if we could find some help, but Nicho felt like we were being watched. That's when the soldiers came out of nowhere."

"And then what?" Zel asked.

"I don't know," Micah whispered as he shook his head. "After they surrounded us, they said we needed to follow them. We probably would have had to, but somehow I was able to freeze them with the stones."

Zel nodded while Tonia and the others listened in silence. Although Tonia's eyes were red and puffy, she was no longer crying...

For now.

"Once the soldiers fell under the spell of the stones, Nicho went to get Ragoo so we could take him to the other side of the lake."

The boy paused as his eyes scoured the nearby rocks before he continued.

"But he was gone."

"Hmm," Diam said with a scowl of concentration. "Did you see any footprints in the sand?" Before he could answer, she stood up and began climbing over the rocks as she started her own search for the missing cat.

"Nicho looked, but there were none," the boy answered. "Ragoo just disappeared."

"Why don't we all search the area?" Kaileen suggested as she watched Diam.

Before they could follow the kalevala's suggestion, Teresia flitted around a nearby bush and headed straight for the group sitting on the rocks. She suddenly stopped in mid-flight when she caught sight of the pair of lifeless bodies lying on the warm, welcoming sand just a few feet away. She changed direction and hovered in midair for a moment, then slowly drifted over to the older boy. The group watched as she lowered herself down until she was floating just above Nicho's face. She lingered there for a few seconds before reaching out with one of her small, trembling hands to caress the dead boy's cheek, then she rose and flew toward the group. Her focus was on Micah.

"I'm so sorry," she said gently. She reached down and took hold of his hand before gently kissing the back of it. She immediately flew to Tonia next, then Zel, then Diam, and finally Kaileen, repeating the affectionate ritual with each of them.

"Thank you," Tonia whispered as a lone tear refreshed a narrow, partially dry path down her cheek. She had promised herself she would not to lose control again, but at times like this, she wasn't sure if she would be able to keep her promise.

As Teresia moved down the line of surviving family members, the rest of their fellow soldiers made their way over to the rocks, and scattered themselves around the area. Although some stood guard in case Nivri's troops returned, they were all close enough now so they could hear anything being said.

"I overheard part of your conversation as I was approaching," Teresia said finally. She paused to briskly wipe moisture away from her own eyes. "And I know what happened to your friend."

Micah looked past the wood nymph again, his focus lingering on his brother's body.

"Not him," Teresia said with a curt shake of her head. "Your other friend."

"Ragoo?" Micah asked with surprise.

"The fork-tailed one," she replied with a nod. "That is his name?"

"Yes," Micah nodded as he took a step toward her. "Where is he?"

Teresia lowered her head as if she was trying to decide how to word what she wanted to say. After a brief hesitation, she looked

448

up at the younger boy with a grim expression.

"He is very sick," she said quietly. "He has bad blood now."

"Bad blood..." Micah repeated. He stared across the lake as a thoughtful expression fell like a shadow across his face.

While he stared at a cluster of wide, scattered ripples caressing the top of the lake, Micah thought about how rough the water had been the previous night. He remembered how difficult it had been for he, Nicho, and Ragoo to defend themselves against the attacking mini dragons while struggling to maintain their balance on the narrow, wooden raft.

He had never been so scared in his life.

He closed his eyes as memories assaulted him, one after the other. The events of the previous night played through his mind as if they were happening right now, all over again.

Dozens of flying miniature demons swarmed around them, some getting sliced in half with the swing of their swords. He couldn't help but remember how, immediately afterward, he had caught the scent of an awful, almost unbearable stench, hanging in the thick air all around them. He hadn't said anything at the time because he'd thought it had just been his senses working overtime after the battle, even though he had planned on mentioning it to Nicho later on. At the time, he hadn't quite gotten around to it, then later, he'd completely forgotten.

Now he would never have the opportunity.

As his mind held him close to the events from the night before, he could almost hear the sound of hissing in the nearby fog when some of the defeated, dying creatures landed in the water with a splash. At the time, he'd thought the sound was being caused by the little minions hissing at him as they splashed to their deaths. Now, however, he wondered if the strange noise he'd heard had actually been something else – something more sinister?

He frowned as he silently questioned what kind of sound unhealthy, poisonous blood might make when it hit the water. It *could* sound similar to pouring a pia seed filled with water on a flaming camp fire, couldn't it? He shook his head in disappointment and denial as what happened to his feline friend became very clear to him in the blink of a firebug.

Ragoo had been bitten by one of those little winged demons.

As a result, he was now poisoned and probably suffering somewhere nearby…

If he was still alive.

Micah's shoulders slumped with worry and exhaustion as butterflies of fear darted in crazy, spinning patterns throughout the inside of his stomach. He heard the wood nymph take a slow, deep breath, and when she finally spoke, her words caught him completely by surprise.

"I can sense him."

The group around them fell silent as she closed her eyes for a moment, deep in concentration. She held out one of her hands as if trying to feel something unseen in front of her, and after a few seconds, she lowered her hand back to her side.

"I cannot tell where he is, but I can sense his presence."

"So he's alive?" Micah asked as his voice trembled with hope.

"Yes, for now," she murmured, "but I am unable to discern anything else."

"Do you have any idea where he might have gone? What direction?" Micah asked, unwilling to give up. "Did he leave this place on his own?"

Teresia opened her eyes and stared at him for a long moment, then shook her head.

"I cannot see how he left, and I cannot tell if he will be okay. I can only see that he is somewhere in that general direction."

As her words faded into silence, she raised a hand again and pointed toward the northeast.

Micah stared into the distance as he thought about what the wood nymph had said. With a silent nod and a frown of worry, he turned and weaved his way through the cluster of friends and family surrounding him. Sensing his need for privacy, they watched him go as he made his way toward the remains of his two-headed friend.

Kaileen's heart ached for Tonia and she gently stroked her arm – she was worried about her. As she tried to think of what she could do for her friend, Kaileen didn't notice the short, dark shape slowly inching its way toward them through the crowd. Tonia turned to look at Kaileen in hopes of giving the kalevala a partial smile to let her know she was okay when she suddenly froze.

At first, Kaileen thought Tonia was staring at her with a focused stare, so she returned the stare as she wondered what Tonia found so intriguing about her. It took her a few seconds to realize her young friend wasn't looking *at* her – she was looking *beyond* her.

"What's wrong?" the kalevala asked in a nervous, low voice. Before Tonia could answer, Kaileen hastily turned to look over her shoulder. Worried that the evil, black-clad corpse on the beach might be coming back to life, she placed her hand on the handle of her sword as she turned to face whatever was behind her.

"No!" Tonia called out as she gently laid a hand on Kaileen's arm to stay her weapon.

"There's nothing wrong, Kaileen. I was just... surprised, that's all."

Before the kalevala could ask why, her eyes caught sight of the reason. Standing less than five feet away was something, some*one*, she thought she would never see again.

Zacharu had removed his helmet and was standing a few steps away from Zel when he caught sight of the smallest figure in the trio of girls. It didn't take him long to recognize the dark skin, the protruding jaw, and the short, familiar profile.

Kaileen stood frozen in place like a nervous valley rabbit as she stared at the male form creeping toward her through the crowd. He inched forward a few small steps then paused, his eyes filled with uncertainty. A mixture of doubt and surprise covered his face like an ash-colored blanket. He took a visible breath, inched forward, then stopped again, obviously afraid his eyes were misleading him. It was as though he was afraid she would disappear if he approached too quickly.

When Kaileen recognized the dark, brown eyes staring at her through the crowd of armored soldiers, she hesitated for a long moment as she watched him. When she finally allowed her mind to believe what her eyes already knew, she squealed, dropped her forgotten weapon onto the sand, and launched herself through the air toward Zacharu.

"Zacharu!" she called out with a cry of happiness. In a flurry of motion, she landed in his arms and knocked him abruptly into one of his fellow soldiers. Zacharu staggered on his feet and smiled with relief. It was obvious that the female kalevala did not at all notice she had nearly knocked over some of the surrounding bodies like a line of armored dominoes. Instead, she did the only thing she could do once she was actually touching this important fragment from her past. She wrapped her arms tightly around him and began to cry with happiness.

"Whoa, there!"

The soldier who took the brunt of the kalevala's impact chuckled as he steadied the stumbling creatures, but neither Zacharu nor Kaileen appeared to hear him. They were in their own little world that neither thought they would ever see or be a part of again...

It was a world that belonged to the kalevalas.

"Wow," Diam whispered to Tonia as she smiled. "I haven't seen her get that worked up or move that fast since we met her!"

"I know!" Tonia replied with a giggle. "They do look alike, don't they?"

Diam nodded as she glanced around them. Her eyes lingered on Micah, still hovering near Zig's head, gently stroking the dragon's mangled neck. A smaller, dark-colored dragon was partially submerged just a few feet away from the shore, its head lowered in a respectful pose. After a few seconds, a large, white dragon approached from the west and lowered itself down in the water not far from the young boy. The two surviving dragons touched noses briefly before the larger one moved toward the grieving boy. When the ivory-colored creature was just a few inches away from the brown-haired human, it lowered its head and appeared to be talking to him.

Diam gave them a few moments together alone before she moved across the sand to join their small group. When she reached them, she gently stroked Micah's back then rested her head on his shoulder as a gesture of comfort. She felt him lean into her, and for a few seconds, she thought he might begin to cry, but he suddenly stiffened as he straightened. She lifted her head in surprise just in time to see him turn toward the white dragon.

His blue eyes were dark, blazing and full of anger.

"Where did you go, Lemures?" Micah asked the dragon in a harsh, accusing tone. "Why did you leave us when we needed you the most?"

The white dragon's focus moved from the carcass of his fellow beast to the boy for a moment, then he slowly closed his eyes and nodded with solemn understanding. He had expected he would have to provide an explanation, but he didn't think it would be under these circumstances.

"I know you are angry," Lemures tried to explain. He was interrupted before he could finish and quickly realized Micah wasn't done yet.

The young boy's eyes began filling with unrestrained tears as his angry voice echoed across the beach and into the nearby trees.

"You left us before the battle even began! If you'd have stayed, Zig and Zag would probably be alive! The bodies lying on the beach belonging to those who fought with us might still be alive..."

His voice trailed off as he turned to look back at his brother's lifeless body in the distance.

"And although any loss of life is a tragedy, for Tonia and I, this was particularly personal! Not only did you abandon everyone standing here now, you also abandoned us, my sister and I... our friends... and our brother!"

A strangled sob caught in his throat as he struggled to release one more sentence that was full of all the emotion he was feeling, yet it came out as little more than a choked whisper.

"Nicho would still be *alive*."

Without warning, Micah began pummeling the large, white dragon with his fists. His arms flailed up and down, up and down, as he finally let the anger, fear, frustration, and grief explode from within him like a long dormant volcano erupting tons of lava from somewhere deep within.

Lemures understood the boy's anger, and stood without moving as the sobbing, grieving boy continued to pound on his thick, white skin. After a moment, Micah's anger finally subsided and his arms dropped to his sides like limp tarza vines. The boy lowered his head as if in thought, then threw his arms around the dragon's thick, cream-colored neck, and held him as long, gut-wrenching sobs consumed his young body. He held the dragon tightly, and didn't seem to notice that Tonia, Diam, and Kaileen had gathered together behind him. As tears coursed down each of their young faces, they silently wrapped themselves around the boy like a cocoon against the ivory-colored beast. They stood like this for several seconds before the sounds of small cries and whimpers were heard coming from somewhere within their circle of grief.

"You have my most sincere apologies and condolences," Lemures whispered after a few moments. Those closest to the dragon looked up at him with grief-stricken eyes as he spoke. No one seemed to notice the way the entire group of those who had joined the fighting children in battle had moved in to share their support. They were now supporting the grieving children in sorrow.

"It's true, I wasn't here when you needed me, but I thought I was doing the right thing by leaving," the dragon continued.

Micah lifted his head up and slowly pulled himself away from the Lemures. He leaned back against the girls as stared up at the dragon.

"How was it the right thing to abandon us, Lemures? I don't understand. While you left us to go who knows where, we were trapped here! We had no choice but to fight against Nivri and his army of minions! Because you left, my only brother is now dead!"

Anger dripped from his voice like rain from the sky in a thunderstorm. Micah held his hands out with both palms up in a questioning gesture.

"Why, Lemures? Why? Why did you leave us?"

The large, white dragon nodded as he acknowledged Micah's question as well as his anger. He stared at the boy and took a deep breath before continuing.

"I left because I had to."

"But why?" Micah insisted.

Questioning whispers moved like hungry waves through the surrounding soldiers as they all waited for an answer. Lemures glanced around at the listening crowd, then turned back to the

454

inquisitive boy.

"All three amulets have been recovered and returned to the dragons, and we are well on our way to reclaiming our world. Unfortunately, we now have a small problem."

A hush fell over the crowd as they waited for Lemures to continue.

"The trio of amulets you have recovered are the main parts of a larger, very special amulet that was broken long ago. As I think you already know, this gem used to belong to the dragons. When it had the misfortune of being broken, we knew it would not be a problem to put it back together when it was eventually found."

Lemures stared off into the distance for a few seconds, deep in thought, before turning back toward the group to continue his story.

"You know the story of Little Draco?" he asked.

Zacharu was standing near Zel now, and they both nodded in answer to Lemures' question. Many members of the crowd also nodded, but a few shook their heads in denial.

"Little Draco's parents were Margaris and Anthonon, some of the oldest dragons in our land. They, and they alone, knew the special spell that would need to be recanted over the broken amulets when they were found. Once the final amulet was brought to the Castle of the Dragons, to the North, I knew it wouldn't take long for the two ancient ones to cast the necessary magic on the amulets."

Lemures paused and lowered his head.

"I left here to go get the amulet, which could then be used along with Micah's stones in the Spear of Viviani. Once the stones and amulet have been placed correctly within the spear, we would have the single thing we *must* have in order to defeat Lotor.

"Unfortunately, when I arrived at the Castle of the Dragons, I was told some very disconcerting news."

Lemures paused for a few seconds, then shook his head, took a deep breath, and continued.

"Little Draco is still missing, which is something else we must deal with. More importantly, Anthonon is also now missing."

"What about Margaris?" Zacharu asked.

As he waited for an answer, the male kalevala knew just by the look in the dragon's eyes that the answer he was about to receive was not the one any of them would want to hear.

"She's dead," Lemures whispered as the entire group fell into a shocked silence. Those who had heard of the mated pair of ancient dragons knew the death of Margaris was a horrible loss for their world, while those who were not from this place understood the loss of Little Draco's mother to be a tragedy for other reasons... first, because she was the mother of a very special dragon, and second, because she was one of two dragons who knew the spell to repair the damaged amulet.

"Do you have any idea where Anthonon could be?" Zel asked as he rested one of his hands on Micah's shoulder. The boy had finally calmed down enough to listen to the dragon's story, but he was still tense with emotion.

"I don't know," Lemures answered, "but I suspect, if he is still alive, he is likely being held captive by Lotor."

"Why would Lotor want him?" Diam asked as she shook her head in a slow, side to side motion.

"If we have the amulets and he has the dragon, he knows we will likely come to rescue the dragon," Tonia offered.

"And once he has the amulets along with the dragon, maybe he can find some way to magically force the dragon to incant the spell to fix the amulet," Kaileen added.

Diam nodded her head as everything began to make sense. Again, muffled whispers traveled through the crowd like a set of waves on the ocean.

"Micah."

The young boy looked up at Lemures with red-rimmed eyes. He was finally in control of his emotions – if only for a little while.

"Do you understand that I left here with the intention of retrieving the single, repaired amulet so I could then bring it back and help us win the battle?"

Micah stared at him without answering as he considered the dragon's words.

"If I had any idea that things were going to turn out like this," Lemures continued, "I would have stayed in an instant! You and your family are the ones we have been waiting for! I would give my life for you, without hesitation, if it meant you could continue on and save our world. I'm sure many others who live here feel the same way."

Lemures paused as Zel moved to stand between his surviving children. Once there, he moved an arm around each of their shoulders and drew them close.

After patting his father's hand, Micah nodded his answer to the white dragon then turned to examine the devastation that stretched across the shore. Lifeless bodies were lying on the beach, their spilled blood staining the sand around them. There were also a few injured soldiers that were being tended to by the female figures that had created the funnels.

"Who are they?" Micah asked as he pointed at the females.

"That is Aseret, Ilamet, and other members of their family," Orob explained. "They are naiads."

"Naiads?" Tonia asked.

Orob thought for a moment as he tried to decide the best way to explain to the outsiders what a naiad was.

"They are creatures who are very comfortable in water who also have special healing abilities."

As Micah thought about this, his eyes suddenly lit up with hope, and he looked back at the familiar, inanimate body lying on the sand in the distance.

"No," Orob said harshly. He shook his head as he read the young boy's mind. "It is too late for them to help your brother."

Micah nodded with disappointed understanding and turned his focus back to the naiads. The two Orob called Ilamet and Aseret were now assisting a soldier with a leg injury. After a moment, the young boy spoke again.

"So, what do we do now?"

"Why don't we gather up the stones?" Diam suggested. "We don't want to forget about them in the sand when we leave."

"Good idea," Kaileen said with a nod.

Without another word, the girls and a handful of soldiers made their way over to the area around the pair of lifeless heaps and began searching for the missing stones. Luckily, the small earthen orbs were not difficult to find. Although they were no longer glowing, their color stood out enough in the trodden sand so it only took a few minutes to find them all.

"What will happen to those who did not survive the battle?" Zel asked as his gaze lingered on the body of his oldest son. His heart filled with turmoil and nearly overwhelming sadness as he struggled to come to terms with the thought of a life without one of his three children.

He shook his head as he thought about how drastically life could change over the course of just a few days. One day he woke up as a prisoner in the dungeon of an unfamiliar castle, a stranger in a strange land. After the sun rolled into a new day, everything suddenly changed when he discovered he was free of the castle as well as its evil owner. To top it all off, he then found out his children were all in this same odd, unfamiliar place, not far away.

His mind raced with too many questions and too few answers. How had his children gotten here? The more he thought about it, the more it seemed like a dream, even though he was certain it wasn't. Once they got back home, what in the world would he tell his wife?

He struggled to brush these and other questions out of his mind, deciding he would worry about trying to figure it all out once they got out of this place. Somehow they had to find their way home!

He heard voices in the distance and looked up to see Orob and Simcha talking to their troops. After a moment, they began gathering up the bodies of the deceased, both human and beast.

"Let's pile them up here," Simcha said as he pointed at an area a few feet away from the water line. Although it wasn't spoken, it was expected that once night fell again, the lake crabs would likely claim anything left of the fallen.

They worked together in silence, carrying the lifeless hulks to the edge of the shore near the bushes where they assembled them into a disorganized pile. Soon, only two bodies remained that had not yet been moved.

As a group of soldiers headed toward the lifeless, cloaked figure lying on the sand, Micah suddenly caught a glimpse of something glittering around Nivri's neck area.

"Wait!"

He quickly made his way over to the figure responsible for

his brother's death. Without a word, Micah stepped between the soldiers, and crouched down near Nivri's stony, gray face. Tonia followed him, worried that her brother might take some of his anger and grief out on the corpse, much like he had done to the white dragon not so long ago, but after a few seconds, she realized she had nothing to worry about. Instead of hitting the corpse, Micah extended a hand and reached for some unseen item on the side of the sorcerer's neck. He wrapped his fingers around the object and yanked his hand back, causing Nivri's head to jerk an inch or two off the sand before falling back down again. Tonia hid her mouth behind her hand when she had a sudden, absurd thought that the lifeless hulk might have the beginning of a case of hiccups. She struggled to keep a poorly timed chuckle from escaping her lips when she realized that Nivri didn't have hiccups at all – Micah had removed something from around the sorcerer's neck.

"Okay," Micah said as he stood up and moved away from the body.

"I think we should take this, too," Diam said.

She leaned in toward the corpse and, after a moment of struggling with the item, withdrew the spear from Nivri's chest. She used the tail end of his cloak to wipe the coagulated, dark substance from the end of the weapon, then removed her bag from her back and dropped the spear inside.

Micah watched what Diam was doing before moving toward Tonia. When he reached her, he extended his hand to show his sister what he had retrieved from the body.

A thin, silver necklace lay in his opened palm and wound around his fingers like a cluster of long, narrow snakes. Blue-green, spherical objects were scattered an inch or so apart from each other throughout the links of the chain, glinting beautifully in the afternoon sunlight. Directly opposite the clasp, which was now broken, was a halfmoon-shaped pendant. At first, Tonia thought it might be a bone, but she soon realized she was wrong.

It was a tooth.

"Ew," she said as she leaned away from the odd piece of jewelry. "What are you going to do with that?"

Micah shrugged.

"I'm not sure yet, but I have a feeling about it, so I think I'll hold onto it for now."

"A feeling, eh?" Diam said with a small snicker. "Yeah, save it for later. Maybe you can use it to pick slivers of chickenbird meat from your *own* teeth..."

Micah groaned at her teasing comment, but said nothing. Instead, he watched as the soldiers hefted Nivri's body and carried it over to the pile. He tucked the necklace into his pocket as the sorcerer's shell was tossed on top of the pile of corpses. A few seconds later, his stomach did a flip flop of protest as he realized the group of body-carrying soldiers was returning from the pile. They were heading towards the single, remaining corpse.

"Leave him," Lemures called out toward the soldiers as he nodded toward his fallen friend. "The dragon guard will return for him soon."

"Return for him to take him where?" Tonia asked in a worried, possessive whisper.

Lemures nodded, both hearing and understanding the concern in the young girl's voice.

"We cannot leave him here," the white dragon explained. "He will be transported to the Castle of the Dragons, where he will be kept safe and... intact... until you fulfill your quest."

"I'm not sure if that's a good idea," Tonia said as she shook her head in protest.

"Tonia, what are we going to do? Take him with us?" Diam asked as she struggled to control the sarcasm in her voice. She moved and leaned her face towards Tonia until their foreheads were touching, then they both stared down at the sand around their feet. She didn't want to upset her friend, but she knew she would need to be firm with her, now more than ever.

"Tonia," Diam whispered. "You can tell, as much as I can, how much Micah and Nicho trusted these dragons, in spite of how upset Micah got a little while ago. Let them take his body to their castle and keep him safe while we go do what needs to be done. Once we finish that, we can figure out how to get home – all of us."

SIXTY

Tonia looked up at Diam with sad, moist eyes, before turning her gaze toward her deceased brother. They could all see the battle between trust and indecision raging across the smooth skin of her face, but they gave her the time she needed to think about her decision. She stood between Diam and her father, with Micah just a few steps away, and turned her gaze down at the sand. After a moment, Zel wrapped a gentle arm around her as a gesture of support. They stood like this in silence until she finally turned her attention back to the white dragon. Although her eyes were still filled with sadness, her expression was resolute.

"Do you promise he'll be safe?"

Lemures nodded.

"You have my solemn word."

Tonia took a long, deep breath before looking back at the pile of bodies.

"What about them?" she asked. "Shouldn't they go to the castle, too? Or back to their families?"

"No," Lemures answered as his focus followed hers.

"It is standard practice to burn the remains of soldiers who die in battle – all soldiers, including those belonging to Nivri. That is the way of this world."

Tonia nodded silently as she watched a figure move towards them from the group of surviving soldiers. She recognized the odd-looking creature as one similar to the soldiers who came with the dead sorcerer, but this one was definitely not on Nivri's side.

"We are ready for you," Orob said to the great, white beast as he stopped close to Zacharu.

"Very well," Lemures answered. The dragon nodded and turned before making his way towards the pile of bodies. When he was just a few feet away from the corpses, he addressed those standing nearby.

"Please step back."

The small cluster of survivors near those of the deceased did as they were asked. Once he was certain they were at a safe distance, Lemures closed his eyes and took a long, deep breath. He raised his chin slightly as his head and neck arched into the shape of a half moon. They watched as he held his breath for a split second, then launched his head forward. A wide line of fire exploded from his mouth, igniting the pile of corpses into a brilliant burst of flames. Clothing, fur, and hair immediately caught fire as a wide tower of orange tongues reached skyward. A thick cloud of black smoke rode the fiery waves. The cloud billowed into the air, eventually thinning out as it hugged the tree branches overhead.

Those standing on the beach watched in respectful silence for a while as the bodies burned. Thankfully, a slight breeze blowing across the lake carried both the smoke and the stench into the trees, away from the crowd of onlookers.

Lemures turned to look back at the small group of familiar faces.

"If you would like to say anything to your brother and friend, I would suggest you do it soon. The dragon guard will likely be here very shortly."

Tonia looked at Diam, then Micah and Kaileen.

"You go first," Micah suggested to his sister.

Tonia nodded as she looked over at Nicho.

"Are you okay?" Diam asked quietly as she placed a hand on Tonia's arm. "I can go with you."

Tonia looked at Diam and gave her a small, sad smile.

"No."

Without giving herself a chance to change her mind, Tonia slowly moved toward Nicho as if she was the only person left in the world. When she reached him, she paused for a moment then floated down onto her knees, her upper body collapsing like an accordion beetle until she was seated on her legs. Her friends and family watched as she extended one trembling hand toward her brother, then stopped.

Worried about her friend, Diam moved to take a step toward Tonia, but Zel stopped her when he touched her arm. The older girl nodded and held her place as fresh tears threatened to spill from her eyes. She hated seeing, *feeling*, her best friend's pain.

Tonia's hand wavered in the air for a moment, then she lowered it and gently brushed Nicho's tussled hair away from his face. Thankfully, one of the soldiers had cleaned the smeared blood from his upper body and covered him with their shirt a short time before. Tonia hadn't known who the soldier was, and wasn't even sure which one it was, but she didn't care. She was just glad that he looked more like the Nicho she knew and loved…

Would always love.

"I love you, Nicho."

She spoke quietly to him for a moment, then bent over and kissed his cool forehead. She hesitated there briefly before she got to her feet and glanced back at her friends. Although she knew her face was smeared with an unladylike combination of tears and grime, she felt as though she was fairly in control of her emotions. Without waiting for anyone to say anything, she walked away to sit alone on a rock on the northern end of the beach.

Once Micah was sure his sister wasn't going to fall apart again, he took slow, nervous steps across the sand toward his only brother. When he reached him, Micah knelt down on one knee at Nicho's right side, and gently laid a hand on Nicho's cool, right arm. He stayed in this position for a moment as he stared wordlessly at his brother's corpse.

"I love you."

His choked words floated across a cool breeze to the group. Seconds later, he stood up, wiped at his eyes, then walked away with a downward gaze and slumped shoulders. Instead of moving toward the rocks where Tonia sat alone, looking down at the sand, Micah walked towards the lake and began meandering slowly along the waterline.

Zel turned to look at Diam.

"Go ahead," he said with a nod. "I'll go when you're done."

Diam nodded and held her hand out to Kaileen. Without hesitation, the female kalevala took Diam's hand, and together they made their way to their friend to say goodbye. Zel watched as the pair of female figures knelt down to speak to the shell of their friend. After a few moments, they stood up and moved to sit near Tonia on the rocks.

Zacharu patted Zel on the shoulder as the former prisoner made his way to say goodbye to his son. He knelt down and laid his hand on the top of Nicho's head as emotions threatened to wash over him like a raging river. He couldn't imagine life without Nicho, and he couldn't imagine having to tell his wife about their loss. Those two thoughts left him on the edge of a bottomless ravine filled with both anger and grief. As he stared down into his eldest son's innocent, lifeless face, a sudden thought worse than the previous two erupted into his mind, nearly overwhelming him. If they ever found a way to return to their own world, there was no way he could leave Nicho in this unfamiliar place.

"If there is a way for us to get home, I will bring you," he vowed as he leaned down and kissed Nicho's cool, dry forehead.

He gently patted Nicho's arm one more time, then stood up and made his way towards his other son. When he reached Micah, he enveloped him in a secure, loving hug. The man and his son stood silently holding each other as gentle waves lapped at the shoreline just inches away from their toes. After several minutes, they turned and made their way over to the girls, where they huddled together and let their tears flow freely yet again.

A brief melody of sniffles broke out through the remaining group soldiers as they watched the despairing family, but no one moved to intrude on their moment of grief. Although the entire situation did not allow much privacy for those who mourned, the nearby soldiers gave them as much space and silent support

464

as they could.

While Nicho's friends and family were saying goodbye, Orob and Simcha stood near the bushes, discussing their options. After a few minutes, they began mingling among the rest of the soldiers to identify the extent of their injuries. Once it was determined that there were only two who needed to return to the village, Simcha arranged for one of the uninjured soldiers to escort them.

While the grieving family spent time together, Simcha looked at the placement of the sun in order to see how much daylight they still had. The formerly yellow ball in the sky was beginning to change to bright orange and was well beyond the point of noon. His focus then turned to the burning bodies. At the rate things were going, the bodies would be very close to being burned down by sunset, which was good because he didn't want to attract attention to their location at night.

"Can we please gather around?" Simcha called out as his eyes canvassed those on the beach. He extended his arms and waved his hands toward himself, gesturing for everyone to come to him.

He waited a moment for the group to form a loose cluster around him, then held up a hand to get their attention.

"Goodbyes have been said, yes?" he asked as his eyes moved from the girls, to Micah, and finally rested on Zel.

"Yes," the former prisoner answered quietly.

"Very good," Simcha said with a nod. "I'm very sorry for your loss, as are my warriors. Please trust in the dragons, for they will certainly take care of him."

Zel nodded, but said nothing.

"Very good," Simcha repeated. "Goodbyes are done, and the bodies of the fallen have been dealt with. Next, we will wait for the dragon guard's arrival. Once the young man has been taken away, we will camp in the shelter of the trees for the night. Tomorrow morning, I will take my troops back to our village, and we will see about rounding up more soldiers."

"We don't have time for that," Orob said with a frown. "We must head east and defeat Lotor – now – before he can organize his own soldiers. I'm certain it won't take long for him to realize we have defeated his rival and will move on to our final target."

"I understand your feeling of urgency," Simcha nodded at

465

Orob, "but I also do not believe we should go into another battle before we have enough strength behind us."

"We can recruit others of this world," a familiar feminine voice called out from one of the nearby trees. In a burst of color, a large group of wood nymphs suddenly flew out of the woods toward the group on the beach.

"Other naiads are on their way," Ilamet said from somewhere near the back of the circle of winged bodies.

"And I'm sure I can find more dragons," Lemures offered.

Simcha nodded as he quietly considered the suggestions that were being thrown at him like a horde of insects. After a few moments, he raised his hand into the air, commanding silence.

"Let me consider this through the night and I will make my decision at sunrise."

Murmuring voices rolled through the group as Zel's former guard raised his own hand into the air.

"There is one thing we must do before we continue on to Lotor's castle," Orob called out in a booming, authoritative voice. Surprised silence fell across the group as dozens of questioning eyes turned to look at him.

Simcha's were among them.

"We must return to Defigo," Orob said as he turned his focus to his former prisoner.

"Why?" Simcha asked. "Defigo is in the wrong direction. We must head east, towards Immolo."

Orob shook his head.

"Not yet, Simcha," the guard argued. "We must return to Defigo to release one more prisoner."

His eyes found Zel in the crowd and held his stare for a few seconds. That was how long it took before realization dawned on Zel's face.

One more prisoner?

Of course! The creature that had been held captive in the cell next to his! The one he could hear moving around, but had never been able to see. He thought he'd seen the shadow of a dragon on the wall at one point, but what if it hadn't been a dragon at all? What if the prisoner in the cell next to his was not a some*thing*, but a some*one*? What if it was someone he knew, someone from

466

his world? What if it was the only person from his immediately family who he had not been reunited with yet?

What if it was Jeane?

"Orob?" he asked quietly as his voice shook with dread. "Who is it?"

"It is not who you think it is," Orob answered as he shook his head.

"Who is it?" Zel repeated as he stared at his former guard.

Orob glanced at Simcha before allowing his gaze to pass from soldier to soldier for a few seconds before finally answering.

"Now that Nivri is dead, we should have no problem returning to the castle," Orob explained as his eyes settled on Zel. He knew the man was about to ask him for a third time who the prisoner was, but Orob raised his hand again to stop him.

"The prisoner we must rescue is Little Draco."

SIXTY-ONE

A small cluster of dark, unidentifiable figures stands quietly in a crooked line a few feet away from a shadowy form, where it lies motionless on a narrow, desolate beach just before the arrival of twilight. The heights of the shapes vary, ranging in staggered sizes. Not far away, a larger group of odd-looking creatures stands like statues slightly behind the group of human shapes in respectful silence.

As the sun continues to set in the west, the unidentifiable group of friends stands in a mournful, wordless huddle around the horizontal object lying on the firmly packed sand. It remains where it fell, cold and motionless on the grainy expanse of earth not far from the place where the water meets the land. The shape is that of a once vibrant yet now lifeless corpse.

A colorful blanket of darkening clouds litters the sky above them as a soft, cool breeze caresses their bodies after a long, life-altering day. The rippling edge of the nearby lake licks the shore in a rhythmic, gentle cadence as it whispers liquid condolences to those who grieve.

Other than those surrounding the corpse and the repetitive back and forth motion of the waves brushing the shoreline, the rest of the beach is deserted. The eerie growls heard the previous night have fallen silent and the fog that covered the lake earlier that morning has since transitioned upwards with the rising of the sun, evaporating into the sky above them like a ghost. Even the previous day's spinning, fish-spewing funnels are nowhere to be seen across the horizon of what had been a dark, menacing body of water the night before.

The mourners watch in quiet disbelief as the surrounding shoreline suddenly comes to life, giving birth to dozens of sand crabs as they erupt from their hiding places like lava from sleeping volcanoes. The emerging hard-shelled creatures of varying shapes and sizes have oddly-shaped, spine-covered, spindly legs, and pay no attention to those huddled near the body where it waits like a stone. The well-armored platoon of crustaceans works quickly, as if driven by a single mind, each taking a place next to an empty location alongside a sling brought by a newcomer. After working in unison to spread the sling out like a flattened alia leaf, the crabs turn and make their way toward unmarked, yet unquestionable, locations next to the last body from the battle.

The group of mourners watches the scene in silence, somehow knowing what was happening – what MUST happen – to their former comrade, each of them struggling with their own flood of emotions – stifling cries that begged to be released...

Each one understanding that grief is both a powerful emotion and demon that everyone must face...

Each one hoping the demon from this particular day is one that can be overcome with vigilance, time, and a little bit of luck.

The only sounds heard as the sand crabs take their invisible stations alongside the corpse are the gentle lapping of the waves against the shore, restrained liquid cries for the loss of one so special, one so young, and the *click, click, clicking* of the sand creatures as they speak to each other in their foreign tongue.

Perhaps the crabs are sharing tales of other senseless deaths? Perhaps they are asking each other why something so unfortunate, so *wasteful*, had to happen to this particular human on this particular day? Perhaps they are offering sympathies in a strange language that, no matter how hard the humans try to understand, will remain forever misunderstood?

Once the sand creatures have completely surrounded the fallen hero, many of them move in harmony to raise his body off the sand. As they work together, countless other crustaceans rush

469

beneath the body to help support the weight. Then, inch by slow inch, they move together, carrying it toward the laid out material like a group of peasants bringing offerings to a king. The clicking sounds intensify as the sand creatures transport the body to the sling, where they finally set it down on the thickly woven fabric with indescribable grace and gentleness.

The two largest of the non-human creatures watches the proceedings in silence.

Once the body has been moved, the crabs shuffle into a scattered, broken line at the border of the lake, just shy of the water's edge. As the tide rhythmically pulls away then returns, small waves lap at their armor-covered legs. Although the water is cool, the sand creatures seem to not notice.

The sound of a sniffle breaks the silence as a trail of tears cascades down one of the mourner's pale, thin cheeks.

Today they have lost a friend.

$ixty-Two

All at once, the armored crustaceans turn and look at Ronnoc expectantly, waiting quietly for their next unspoken order. The large, green dragon supervises the sand creatures with narrow, squinted eyes where yellow orbs glow as if they have small candles burning deep within. The scaled creature's mouth is closed and its lips are drawn into a tight, thin line covering a razor-sharp arc of stained, pointed teeth.

Satisfied with the work of the crabs, the dragon turns toward the group still huddled together on the beach. No words are spoken between any of the creatures, but then again, none are necessary. He nods once at the group of onlookers, then moves to stand beside the sling that holds the shell of the boy who was. As soon as the dragon stops, the line of crabs quickly moves back into action, surrounding the sling once more.

Large, circular eyelets have been woven into the tapestry of the sling in preparation for such an event. First, the crabs work together to gently drag one edge of the sling across the corpse to the other side, essentially folding it in half. Then they begin working together with the long line of rope, weaving it through one eyelet at a time, moving methodically from one end of the sling to the other. The crustaceans then tie each end of the rope to a section four eyelets away from each end, forming two crude handles.

The dragon positions himself next to the sling, and turns to look at his miniature assistants.

"It is time," he says.

Taking their cue from the dragon, the crabs immediately work as a single unit to lift each of the newly created rope handles off the beach, then wait patiently for the dragon to join them.

"Until we meet again," Ronnoc mumbles to the group of humans, beagons, and fellow dragons. Then, with a final nod at the crabs, he extends his thick, green wings, flapping them up and down, picking up speed as he slowly ascends into the air. As soon as he is no longer touching the sand, Ronnoc positions himself directly over the top of the sling. The crabs stand together like frozen sentries as they hold the rope handles over their spiny heads, and with the grace of a gull, Ronnoc's wide, heavily-scaled talons grasp each of the handles. Ever so slowly, he begins to raise both himself and the sling into the air. After waiting a few wing beats to be sure the body has settled within its woven cocoon, the dragon nods a final time at the group of mourners below, then turns and flies eastward.

"No!"

The sound of a human voice cries out in overwhelming anguish. From somewhere within the shadowy group, a thin, pale arm shoots into the air as if in hopes of catching the sling and returning the body to the beach.

But both the dragon and the life that used to fill the body are well beyond reach.

"No!" the gut-wrenching cry comes again before the shape who had been reaching for the sky just seconds ago suddenly crumbles into a defeated, devastated heap on the sand. As the group of humans and friends huddle to share the overwhelming grief, the remaining non-humans turn toward the heavens in search of Ronnoc.

The dragon and his cargo are nowhere to be seen.

SIXTY-THREE

Diam knelt down next to Tonia and wrapped her arms around her sobbing friend like a protective mother consoling a child. Tonia was like a sister to her, and Nicho was, had been, like a brother. It pained her to the bone to know her best friend and extended family were experiencing a tragedy unlike anything any of them had ever known, and she absolutely hated that she was helpless to do anything about it.

After a moment, Kaileen moved to stand close to Diam, and both of them waited patiently for Tonia to get control of her emotions. They helped their friend to her feet, then guided her to a cluster of nearby trees. Zel, Micah, and Zacharu, along with a handful of soldiers, followed a few steps behind.

They walked beneath the veil of thick branches, dozens of heavy, tired feet crunching the leaves scattered on the ground. It wasn't long before they came to an area where one small group of soldiers was working to clear places for sleeping, while another group was clearing a scattered group of separate areas for small campfires.

Micah, who had been following them in slow, shocked silence, suddenly came to life.

"What about Zig and Zag?" he asked with alarm as he turned to walk back to the beach.

"It's okay," his father reassured him as he wrapped one of

473

his large hands around Micah's upper arm, stopping him. "Stay here, son."

"But we can't leave them there? What will happen to them?"

Micah's eyes were wide with evidence of a long, heart breaking day. He tried pulling away from his father, but Zel held him in place.

"No, Micah."

"The night creatures will take care of them," Simcha said from next to a nearby tree. "It is as it should be. They suffer no more."

"But what about the burning bodies?" Micah asked, "and Lemures, and Flamen?"

"They will be fine," Simcha nodded reassuringly at the boy. "The bodies are nearly gone, and the dragons – well, they can take care of themselves like they always have."

As darkness descended upon them, the group of survivors converged around a cluster of three small camp fires. They passed around food to share as well as fresh water, sharing stories and telling tales. After a while, Diam decided to try to get Micah talking, so she asked him about his feline friend who had gone missing. When Micah thought about Ragoo, his eyes lit up in spite of his worry.

"I met him in a field when I was looking for you guys," he said quietly. After a moment of silence, he went on to describe the yarnie village, the other cats, including Katielda and her strange, magical home, and finally his reunion with Nicho.

Tonia leaned against him with her eyes closed, listening to him talk. He told them about the effect the stones had on the hungry bears, their meeting with Teresia, and their ride across the dark, growling lake the previous night. He explained their journey to the Castle of Tears, then how they eventually retrieved the Dragon's Tear amulet.

Tonia suddenly sat upright when Micah described the mutilated dragon he'd had to destroy to gain possession of the amulet.

"Really?" she asked in surprise.

Micah turned sideways and threw her a quizzical expression. "Yeah, really. Why?"

Tonia looked at Diam and Kaileen with bright eyes as she

shook her head in disbelief.

"The Dragon's Tear amulet was in the place where the dragon's heart would have been?" she asked.

Micah sighed.

"Yes... what's the big deal?" he asked.

Tonia stared into the fire as she remembered the cavern at the top of the mountain.

"Because we had to retrieve the Dragon's Breath amulet the same way," she answered as her female friends nodded.

It was Micah's turn to look surprised as Tonia explained their story. When she finally finished, Micah was the one shaking his head in wonder.

"A frog who swore he was a dragon, and a couple of spider riders!" he chuckled as Tonia punched him lightly in the arm.

"I bet you never thought you'd ever, EVER, get that close to a spider, did you?"

"You should have seen her," Diam jumped in with a smile. "She was pretty scared at first, but eventually she conquered her fear."

She patted Tonia on the back.

"Did the frog have a name?" Micah asked. "And what happened to him?"

Diam looked from Tonia to Kaileen for a few seconds before answering.

"His name was Kennard. He died after we made it through the mountain."

They paused for a moment before chatting about random things, when Diam suddenly yawned.

"I agree," Zel said. "Let's get some rest. I'm sure we will have another busy day tomorrow."

While some of the soldiers found places to rest on the outside perimeter of the group, the girls, Zacharu, and Zel lay in a close cluster, happy to be together.

"Good night, Nicho," Tonia whispered quietly. A lone tear slid sideways down her cheek as she settled in. Exhaustion quickly overpowered her grief, and after a few minutes, she drifted off into a much needed, dreamless sleep.

Sixty-Four

The next morning, the group in the woods woke to the sound of a breeze blowing through the trees and a multitude of birds singing in chorus all around them. It didn't take long for each of the once sleeping bodies to wake up, stretch, and eventually find their way into the morning sunshine.

Diam was one of the last ones to rise. She took her time waking up, lying on her back as she watched the birds chasing each other from tree to tree. After a few minutes, she stretched, yawned, and got to her feet. She looked around, but only saw a few unnamed soldiers a few trees away discussing some item hidden in one of their bags. She grabbed her own bag and walked alone through the trees as she headed toward the beach, twisting her head from side to side in search of her friends.

She found Tonia and Micah sitting on the rocks near the place where Ragoo had last been seen. In the distance, Kaileen and Zacharu walked slowly, side by side in shallow water, arms linked together.

Diam took a seat next to Tonia and rubbed sleep from her eyes.

"Who is he to Kaileen… do you know?" Micah asked as he pointed to the odd-looking, strolling figures.

Tonia shook her head.

"She hasn't said, but he's definitely someone from her past."

476

Diam nodded.

"How are you today, Micah?" she asked as she rubbed his arm with gentle affection.

He sighed.

"As good as can be expected, I guess."

Again Diam nodded.

The children looked at the place where the pile of bodies had been burning the previous afternoon. Surprisingly, the only sign of the fiery event was black ash scattered within a radius of about ten feet above the waterline. Between the tide and the night creatures, any remains of the corpses had completely disappeared.

Even more of a surprise, the two-headed dragon was also gone. No one mentioned anything about the missing beast, but the girls knew Micah was thinking about it. He kept glancing back to the place where the creature's bulky corpse had been the day before as if he expected it to reappear at any moment.

Tonia turned her attention back to Kaileen and Zacharu. They had turned around and were heading back toward the rocks. After a few minutes, Simcha and Orob also moved toward the larger part of the group and called for their attention.

"I have made my decision," Simcha said in a loud tone. "My troops and I will head back to the village. Orob will take his troops and return to the castle to release Little Draco. Just before sundown on the evening of the fifth day, we will meet near the Cave of the Afanc. From there, we will head toward the Castle Immolo."

The group ate a quick breakfast together, then Simcha rounded up his soldiers. With pats on the back and the promise to meet up again in less than a week, the small group of armored men turned and headed back through the forest.

Not long after they were gone, the remaining group of men, children, and creatures, worked together to gather their things.

"Let's have a few minutes of quiet time together before we leave," Zel suggested.

Orob nodded his approval and everyone gathered into a wide, loose circle. They stood an arm's length apart, each in silent thought with their heads down, remembering the events from the day before as well as pondering what lay ahead. The only noise that could be heard was the relaxing sound of the waves kissing the shore a few feet away.

"Thank you," Zel said as he turned and picked up his bag. The metal helm he wore the day before swung at his side like a large, tarnished pia seed. He looked at Micah and Tonia and smiled, suddenly remembering a chant they'd often said around the village camp fire at night before settling in for yet another fantastical tale from one of the old ones.

Tonia looked up and caught her father gazing at her with a mischievous expression on his face.

"What?" she asked.

He didn't answer her in words. Instead, he began snapping his fingers together in rhythm to a beat that only he could hear.

Snap, snap, snap, snap!

"Wagon, wagon, save a dragon!" he called out in a sing song voice. "Wagon, wagon, save a dragon!"

Snap, snap, snap, snap!

For a few seconds, Tonia thought her father might have lost his mind, but then she began to giggle as she joined in.

Snap, snap, snap, snap!

"Wagon, wagon, save a dragon!"

Pretty soon, the kids, the kalevalas, even some of the remaining warriors, had all joined in. They were dancing around on the beach, chanting and singing the silly, made up song.

Tonia smiled at Diam, glad to finally have something, even something as silly as a spur of the moment song about a wagon and a dragon, to provide some relief to the tidal wave of emotions they'd all had to endure over the past few days.

They carried on this way for a little while longer before Zel gathered Micah, Tonia, Kaileen, and Diam into a big bear hug.

"Are you ready to go save a dragon?" he asked them in a loud, boisterous voice. When they didn't answer him like he was hoping, he repeated his question, this time much louder and with an exorbitant amount of enthusiasm.

"Are you ready to go save a dragon?"

As the group gathered their things and got ready to head out, a sudden, unexpected noise in the distance caused Zel to freeze in place and wonder if he had fallen into a strange dream – one he'd had more times than he cared to count. He turned toward the direction the sound had come from, straining his eyes to focus on the creator, afraid to trust his ears since they hadn't heard anything like it in more than a year.

It was a woman's voice from long ago – a beautiful sound that had become nothing more than a memory. Not long ago, he'd finally convinced himself that he may never hear her voice again.

But now it was calling his name. Did he dare to believe his ears?

Did he dare believe his heart?

He stared, unable to move, when he suddenly spotted two human figures running towards them.

One was a tall, gruff-looking, hairy man. The other was a woman. He didn't need to see her face to know she was a female, and he definitely didn't need to see her face to recognize her shape or her gait.

It was Jeane.

Sixty-Five

Jeane and Andar had been walking through thick stands of trees and over sharp, unmerciful rocks for two days that felt more like two years. Their drinking water was almost gone, they'd gotten very little sleep, and her feet were absolutely screaming for relief. She wanted nothing more than to stop for a break, just for a few minutes. She thought she'd finally convinced Andar that resting for more than twenty minutes might be a good idea when the sound of voices in the distance suddenly caused them to stop as if they were inches away from the edge of a mountaintop.

Were they dreaming? Although she couldn't be sure, it almost sounded like multiple voices were singing some silly song about a dragon.

Could it be that she was so dehydrated and exhausted that her mind was playing tricks on her? She'd heard of things like that happening, but had never experienced anything like it herself. Perhaps she was just being paranoid?

She looked at Andar and he shrugged. After a few seconds, she was about to start walking again, but quickly stopped and turned to frown at her cousin.

There it was again! Those strange voices were singing and laughing! This seemed extremely odd to her since they hadn't seen a single living person after going through the portal. After searching for her children to the point of exhaustion, how could

480

it be that the first signs of life were mixed voices singing a silly song?

She must be losing her mind, she thought.

"Are you ready to save a dragon?"

When she heard the bellowing male voice this time, she froze, unable to move. It echoed around them like a memory, and sounded like it was coming from somewhere just beyond the trees. She and Andar both stopped and stared ahead, then looked at each other. Before Andar could say anything, Jeane took off, running as fast as her sore, aching feet would carry her.

Just after they exited the thick stand of trees, Jeane and Andar found themselves on a welcome area of cool, smooth sand. They stopped side by side, and stared into the distance at a group of a dozen and a half people.

"Oh, Andar, it's him," she whispered. "He's alive!"

Without any further hesitation, she called out to the tall form on the other end of the beach.

"Zel!"

She began to run toward her husband, her eyes filling with tears of disbelief and happiness. He was alive! He was here!

"Zel!"

She didn't recognize all of the figures standing near her husband, but she didn't care. As her eyes glanced from one person to the next, recognition flooded into her face and she suddenly stopped.

She couldn't breathe.

She couldn't *believe*.

Tonia was standing a short distance away from her father. Next to her was Diam, and about ten feet behind the girls was Micah. For a moment, all she could do was stare at the group standing in the sun. How was it possible that she could see this many familiar faces in such an unfamiliar place? What were they all doing here?

Her eyes cut back to Zel, and she finally found the ability to move forward again, slowly at first, but within a few paces she began to jog, and then run. She sensed Andar running beside her without seeing him, and all she could do was focus on her family in front of her.

"Mom!" Tonia screamed. Her voice was a mixture of surprise and joy. She turned to run towards the pair of approaching figures when she was scooped up by her father.

"Wait!" he called out as he set her roughly on the beach. She began struggling to get away when her father gripped her chin in his hand.

"Tonia, stop! Look!"

A large, black shape suddenly appeared over the tops of the trees where Jeane and Andar had just exited. Although there were roughly two dozen people standing in the sun, easy targets, the flying figure's red, blazing eyes were focused completely on the running pair.

"Look out!" Zel called out, but neither Jeane nor Andar heard him. They were too lost in their thoughts, too focused on their goal. They ran as fast as they could toward Zel and the rest of the group, but as Zel and his remaining children watched in helpless disbelief, they realized it wasn't fast enough. It took only a few blinks of a firebug for the large, ebony dragon to descend upon the running figures.

"Mom, look out!" Micah screamed, but it was too late. He saw the look of curiosity in Jeane's eyes as she ran towards them, but she was too overcome with emotion at seeing her family to stop and listen to his words.

In a split second, Micah grabbed his bow and pulled an arrow from the quiver he'd just slung across his back a moment before. He fired off one quick shot at the dragon... it missed. He grabbed another arrow and was just about to let it fly when he realized it was too risky.

Micah heard his mother scream in both surprise and pain as the dragon clamped one wide, sharply-clawed talon around her shoulder and lifted her off the ground. Before he realized what was happening, the other talon clamped around Andar's shoulder in similar fashion. In seconds, the black beast had both adults dangling above the beach as it turned and headed across the lake.

"Jeane!" Zel cried as he ran after them. "Bring them back!"

The dragon ignored him.

In an attempt to follow them, Zel ran into the shallow water.

He didn't feel the cool liquid splashing up everywhere around him. After a few steps, he realized it would be no use. He called out for his wife again as her cries of anger and surprise faded away on the cool, morning breeze.

One of the unnamed guards stood in shock as he watched the dragon carry the man and woman through the air. He held out a hand as if trying to reach for the figures and called out for the one he suddenly recognized.

"Scurio!"

ABOUT THE AUTHOR

MJ Allaire grew up in South Florida and after graduating high school, she joined the Navy and ended up in Pearl Harbor, Hawaii. Three children and ten years later, she moved to Connecticut. In her late 30's, she stumbled into her dream – not just writing and creating a world for both young and old, but visiting schools where she promotes both reading and writing. She is currently working on book five in the Denicalis Dragon Chronicles series. MJ is also working on designing multiple websites, two of which are for authors who love visiting schools as well as for young adults who love to write.

For more information, please visit any or all of her websites below:

www.mjallaire.com
www.denicalisdragonchronicles.com
www.grizlegirlproductions.com
www.getkidstoread.org
www.booksbyteenauthors.com

Other books in this series are:

Dragon's Blood:
Denicalis Dragon Chronicles – Book One

The Prisoner:
Denicalis Dragon Chronicles – Book Two

Dragon's Tear:
Denicalis Dragon Chronicles – Book Three

Please visit us at:
www.denicalisdragonchronicles.com
www.mjallaire.com

Book 5 in the Denicalis Dragon Chronicles should be available in late 2011. Check the website for more information.